THE PICKERING MASTERS

COLLECTED NOVELS AND WORKS OF
WILLIAM GODWIN

Volume 8. *Deloraine*

COLLECTED NOVELS AND MEMOIRS OF
WILLIAM GODWIN

GENERAL EDITOR: MARK PHILP

VOLUME
8

EDITED BY
MAURICE HINDLE

DELORAINE

Routledge
Taylor & Francis Group

LONDON AND NEW YORK

First published 1992 by Pickering & Chatto (Publishers) Limited

2 Park Square, Milton Park, Abingdon, Oxon OX14 4RN
711 Third Avenue, New York, NY 10017, USA

Routledge is an imprint of the Taylor & Francis Group,
an informa business

First issued in paperback 2017

British Library Cataloguing in Publication Data

Godwin, William, *1756–1836*

The collected novels and memoirs of William Godwin

I. Title   II. Philp, Mark   III. Clemit, Pamela

IV. Hindle, Maurice, *1944–*

823.6 [F]

ISBN-13: 978-1-85196-007-1 (Sct)
ISBN-13: 978-1-1387-5823-0 (hbk)
ISBN-13: 978-1-138-11130-1 (pbk)

INTRODUCTORY NOTE

Deloraine was first published in three volumes by London bookseller Richard Bentley on 12 February, 1833. Through the efforts of Mary Shelley's admirer and Godwin's friend the American writer John Howard Payne, a two-volume edition was issued by Carey, Lea and Blanchard, Philadelphia, the same year. No other edition was published. The present text is based on the 1833·London edition. A guide to the principles of textual treatment will be found in volume 1.

Critical response to the novel was generally good, with most commentators agreeably surprised to see a new novel from the elderly writer. *The Court Journal*[1] expressed wonder that someone of Godwin's advanced years – he was now 76 – could write with such youthful vigour. The critic in *The Atlas*[2] thought that only Goethe had been able to produce work of comparable energy at such an age, and ranked the rich drama of volume three with Harriet Lee's *Kruitzner* (1797). The *New Monthly Magazine*,[3] *The Age*[4] and *The Atlas* all noted the power which Godwin was still able to wield in portraying and analysing dark human passions. Interestingly, though the *Metropolitan Magazine*[5] judged *Deloraine* to be a failure compared with Godwin's previous fictions, it still found the efforts of this 'tottering king' compared favourably with the best novels of the day. *The Examiner*[6] was virtually alone in finding the plot disagreeable, the main character barbarous and the shooting of William improbable.

In fact, Deloraine's shooting of William probably points to a major source for the story, the famous eighteenth century case of Eugene Aram. Aram, a self-taught scholar and teacher of great learning and exemplary habits, had impulsively murdered his friend Daniel Clark in 1745, believing him to have committed adultery with his wife. Continuing his life of teaching and studying, it was fourteen years before the crime was discovered, after which he was brought to trial and hanged. Godwin had alluded to the celebrated case in *Caleb Williams* forty years earlier, but about 1829 or 1830, with his interest in it probably revived by the publication of Thomas Hood's poem *The Dream of Eugene Aram* (1829), he projected a novel arguing for an Act of Parliament that would absolve a man of a crime such as Aram's if, after a lapse of ten years, he had been found to have 'spent that period blamelessly, and in labours conducive to the welfare of mankind.'[7] The book was never written, but it seems likely that the young author Edward Bulwer, an admirer of Godwin who became his friend in 1830, and whose work in turn drew praise from the older man,[8] was inspired to write his own *Eugene Aram* (1832) as a result of their discussions. Godwin read Bulwer's novel immediately it was published in December, 1832, at a time when he was drawing to the close of volume two of his own work.

There are some, but not many, literary sources for *Deloraine*. The names for the eponymous hero, William, Margaret, and Travers all evidently derive from Scott's *The Lay of the Last Minstrel* (1805), a copy of which was in Godwin's library. Sir William of Deloraine, 'good at need'[9] and Lady Margaret, both figure prominently in the poem, and the name Fitztraver, which Godwin adapted to Travers, also appears. The more than passing resemblance the plot of *Deloraine* bears to *Othello*, one of Godwin's favourite Shakespeare plays, suggests an obvious source for the name of Deloraine's first wife Emilia.

Yet more important perhaps than literary sources for much of the affective substance of the novel are its biographical sources. Quite apart from the use Godwin may have been making of the poet Shelley's death in plotting the supposed drowning of William, both Mary Wollstonecraft and Mary Shelley are heavily deployed in developing the characters of Deloraine's first wife Emilia and his daughter Catherine. Mary Shelley's relationship to the novel is important, both in terms of Godwin's attitude to her as the only surviving daughter of Mary Wollstonecraft, and as a major source of inspiration when Godwin had serious problems completing volume three.

By the late 1820s, at a time when, as a survey of his diary shows, many of Godwin's close friends were dying off, Mary Shelley had become a major support for Godwin, both emotionally and professionally. During the period 20 March, 1831 to 11 November, 1832, when Godwin was writing *Deloraine*, the diary shows Mary visiting him frequently with her son Percy. The closeness he felt for her in his nostalgic old age emerges clearly when after Emilia's tragic death in the novel, Deloraine comes to regard their baby daughter as 'her living representative. I desired to heap all sorts of benefits on its head. I sought its society, not always, but often ...' (p. 36). Shortly after writing this, Godwin read Mary Shelley's novella *Mathilda*, the MS of which had been in his possession since 1819, when he refused to help her publish a work whose theme he regarded as repulsive – that of the incestuous love a father feels for his motherless daughter.[10]

Catherine's decision to aid her father in his Continental exile clearly reveals Godwin using his close bond to Mary Shelley as a source. But it is evident she also provided him with inspiration as a literary professional at one crucial point in the writing of *Deloraine*. Godwin wrote to her on April 13, 1832 complaining he was 'at a loss for materials to make up my third volume'.[11] He asks her to 'give it one serious thought' for his mind was like 'a train of gunpowder, and a single spark, now happily communicated, might set the whole in motion and activity'. Mary Shelley supplied the appropriate 'spark' and Godwin finished the first draft of the book within three months. Yet it is a telling fact that the

source for this rapid completion of Godwin's last novel referred back to a time
of trying difficulties for him and his household. When forced to flee Belgium
and the pursuit of Travers, Deloraine and Catherine take the same route along
the Rhine river that Mary and Percy Shelley had done when they eloped in
1814, and which they had turned to literary account in their *History of a Six
Weeks' Tour* (1817).

NOTES

1. *The Court Journal*, 202 (March 1833), 163.
2. *The Atlas*, (March 17, 1833), 163.
3. *New Monthly Magazine*, 37 (April 1833), 503–4 (504).
4. *The Age*, 9 (March 1833), 74.
5. *Metropolitan Magazine*, 6 (January 1833), 114.
6. *The Examiner*, (March 17, 1833), 164.
7. See Charles Kegan Paul, *William Godwin: His Friends and Contemporaries*, (2 vols,
1876), II pp. 304–5.
8. Their exchange of letters is printed in Paul, op. cit II pp. 305–9.
9. Walter Scott, *The Lay of the Last Minstrel*, (1805), I xxii. 23.
10. See *Introduction*, vol. 1, pp. 66–7.
11. The letter appears in Florence A. Marshall, *Life and Letters of Mary Wollstonecraft
Shelley*, (2 vols, 1889), II pp. 241–2.

Deloraine

Epigraph: Alexander Pope, 'Elegy to the Memory of an Unfortunate Lady' (1717), ll. 3–4.

D E L O R A I N E.

BY

WILLIAM GODWIN,

AUTHOR OF "CALEB WILLIAMS," "St. LEON," &c.

Why that bosom gored?
Why dimly gleams the visionary sword?

Pope.

IN THREE VOLUMES

VOL. I.

LONDON:

RICHARD BENTLEY, NEW BURLINGTON STREET:
SUCCESSOR TO HENRY COLBURN.
1833.

PREFACE

The plan of the following story in its rude outline was first committed to paper on the seventeenth of January 1830. I had just concluded the composition of Cloudesley. The Great Unknown, as he had for years been denominated, had sufficiently shewn that it was not absolutely necessary for the mind of an author to lie fallow for years, between the conclusion of one work of fiction and the commencement of another.[a] And, old as I was, and / little as it might become me in other respects to put forward a comparison between myself and the writer now recently deceased, I felt an ambition to shew that I upon occasion could be no less unintermitted in the invention of a narrative.[b] The circumstances that compelled me to lay aside the undertaking for a time, are such as it would be impertinent in me to intrude upon my readers.[c] Suffice it to say that, after an interval of many months, I was induced, with no mixture of irresoluteness, and, as I would hope, with no flagging wing, to resume my task.

December, 1832. /

---

[a] Sir Walter Scott (1771–1832), Scottish novelist and poet, who wrote with great rapidity, sometimes producing several novels in a year. cf. Godwin's comment on Scott in his 1831 Advertisement to *St Leon, Collected Novels and Memoirs of William Godwin*, vol. 4, p. 7.

[b] Godwin was 73 in January, 1830; Scott died on 21 September, 1832.

[c] Godwin was writing his collection of essays *Thoughts on Man* (1831) from 3 February, 1830 to 14 February, 1831.

CHAPTER I

My father was an English gentleman with an estate of three thousand pounds a year. I was his only son. I was brought up with every imaginable indulgence. My wishes were anticipated. Every gratification was procured for me, that by any chance might make my days pass in cheerfulness and joy. Yet I was not utterly spoiled. I had a tutor, the most amiable and exemplary of men. His plan was to teach me, by making the things it was / intended I should learn interesting to me. He was an excellent mathematician. He had a most discriminating taste in poetry, history, and fine writing of every kind. Add to this, that he was penetrated with the deepest enthusiasm. He had a voice, musical and silver-toned: he had an eye that varied to every sentiment that passed within him, and that impressed all these sentiments in succession upon the bottom of my heart. I learned, because I desired to learn. The beauties of Virgil and Horace and Homer were unfolded before me by the skill and susceptibility of my tutor.[a] I did not learn the construction and the language first, and afterwards come to discern the merits of the author I read. My instructor, when he opened the first page of the book I perused, taught me to feel its excellence. His enthusiasm became mine: and all which is trying, harsh and repulsive in the common modes of education, was in my / case turned into delight. It scarcely ever happened that the summons which announced the hour of study sounded harshly in my ear: on the contrary I obeyed it with the same alacrity, with which other boys listen to the summons that calls them to scenes of sport and recreation.

In the midst of gratifications and peace like this I passed the early years of my life. I am now the most forlorn and odious of men. All the pleasures of life have at length deserted me; and every calamity and misery is heaped on my head. I have no friend; or only one, whom the ties of nature and her own excellent dispositions have rendered mine by bonds never to be dissolved. Like Cain, I have a mark trenched in my forehead, that all men should shrink from me.[b] I sit alone; for no one will come near me, no one will endure me. Seldom do I go out from my apartment; seldom does the fresh air of heaven breathe upon me; and / that only in the darkest night, when even all the stars are wrapt in impenetrable

---

[a] Publius Vergilius Maro (70–19 BC) and Quintus Horatius Flaccus (65–8 BC), celebrated Roman poets; Homer (1050–850 BC), Greek epic poet.
[b] Gen. 4: 15.

gloom. Oh, how deep is my remorse! how unvaried and endless are the days and nights that succeed each other in my desperate existence! But I am wrong to say, unvaried. The variety is endless; but the change is only of misery. My life is spent in eternal alarms. I cannot call an hour my own; for the next hour may render me up to the vengeance that my crimes have so amply deserved.

But all that I am here stating is disjointed and abrupt. The feeling of what I am, confounds and overwhelms the recollection of what I had to say. I must conquer myself. I must beat down and trample under foot this devil that for ever rises before me, and will let me see nought but himself. I have sat down with a determination to record the fortunes of my life; and the task shall be performed.

I have said that I passed in all right dispositions / and all happiness the period of my boyhood. But I did much more. I lived from the day of my birth to the day in which I completed the fortieth year of my age – it were ludicrous to say – in a state of enjoyment that kings might have envied. Kings cannot know felicity like mine. They have the cares of empire. They are placed in an unnatural situation. They are seated on an eminence, that the shafts of ill fortune may strike them the more surely. A king has neither brother, nor genuine associate. The 'favourite' of high fortune 'has no friend'.[a] He knows no sympathy: he stands alone in the world.

But I was placed in all seeming security. My situation in life was like that of the obscure and sequestered valley. A thousand storms might brew in the skies above; contending tempests and hurricanes might sweep from point to point among the mountains: but from my sheltered nook I looked up, and / smiled at the impotent tumult and fury of the elemental war.

Every day that I live, I think of the quiet and beautiful stream of my former years. More than half the period ordinarily assigned for the longest term of human existence I passed in blameless tranquillity. Why, before the scene thus became changed upon me, did not I cease to exist! Many of the most illustrious characters recorded on the page of history died without having reached the age I have mentioned. Alexander the Great deceased in the thirty-second year of his age.[b] The author of our holy religion dwelt in this vale of tears for about the same interval.[c]

What a thing is character, honour, or virtue! I passed through all the ordinary relations of human life unblamed. I have been a good son, a good husband, and a good father. My friendships were warm and sincere; my enmities temperate and placable. My tongue / was ever at the service of the honest and the generous cause; my purse was ever open to the claims of the

---

[a] Thomas Gray, *Ode on the Death of a Favourite Cat* (1748), 1. 36.
[b] Alexander (356–323 BC), King of Macedonia from 336 BC.
[c] i.e. Jesus Christ.

distressed. How many tears of earnest sorrow have I shed over the calamities of the deserving! How sincerely have I pitied and allowed for the faults, even the crimes, of those who were strongly tempted into the paths of error! If I had died then, those who loved me might have turned over the most copious collection of epitaphs, have selected the one that was most panegyrical, and with unblushing front have inscribed it upon my tomb.

I have often compared my case with that of the emperor Tiberius.[a] He did not arrive at the empire, till he was far descending from the vigour and flower of human existence. He was an able statesman, and an accomplished warrior. He was courteous in his demeanour, and considerate in his conduct. The very steadiness and moderation of his temper won for him universal / confidence and applause. It might be said of him, as the Roman historian has said of another emperor, that, if he had never mounted the throne, all men would have judged he deserved it.[b] What he was, when he became possessed of absolute power, is emblazoned in the imperishable records of history.

I have described the period of my boyhood. When I said, that I was brought up with every imaginable indulgence, that every gratification was anxiously procured for me, and that I had a tutor the most amiable and exemplary of men, in making this enumeration I have recorded the character of my father. He discharged every duty towards me that arises out of the important relation in which we stood to each other; and he regarded me with the fondest partiality. It is no foolish pampering of my vanity and selfishness, when I say, covered as I now am with wretchedness and disgrace, that I deserved his love, that he saw in me / every thing that could most gratify his parental anxiety. My understanding was of no common order; my taste was pure, vivid and refined; my application and learning worthy of the education I had received; and my dispositions noble and generous, full of affection, and formed for the reception and cultivation of friendship.

When I had reached a suitable age, I was introduced into parliament, an honour which had been commanded by my father before me, but from which he had afterwards retired. Previously to this occurrence, I had not been without such a circle of connections and friends, as might best contribute to my enjoyment and advantage. I had visited several of the courts of Europe, and endeavoured to store my mind with such observations and experience, as might best qualify me for the offices of a senator.

But it was not till I set up an establishment in London, and was regularly engaged in my / parliamentary functions, that I in the strictest sense became a member of the fashionable world. I was two-and-twenty years of age. My figure

---

[a] Tiberius Claudius Nero Caesar Augustus (42 BC–37 AD), Roman emperor.
[b] Said by Tacitus of the Emperor Galba in *Histories*, I. 49. 20: *capax imperii nisi imperasset* ('capable of ruling – had he never ruled').

was prepossessing; my countenance procured me general favour and acceptance; and my speech was musical and impressive. I possessed in full measure
the ordinary accomplishments of a gentleman. My address was happy; and I
rarely wanted the presence of mind, or the flow of words, to do justice to my
conceptions. My intellect was stored with copious information; I had read, I
had seen, I had reflected on all that could best enable me to do justice to myself
in whatever concurrence of circumstances I might be placed. My judgement, so
far as it had yet been tried, was sound; my penetration considerable; and I had
those powers of imagination, that could best make the future present to my
thoughts, enable me to enter into the condition and feelings of others, and
qualify me to adorn my / own remarks, or my share in general conversation,
with such animated pictures, and such happiness of illustration, as might send
away those whose circles I frequented with pleasing recollections, and
embalmed my name with an agreeable odour. – I have no gratification in
putting down these reminiscences. I am composing the record of one who, in
every valuable sense of the word, is already deceased.

It was in the circles of fashionable life that I first met with the beautiful
Emilia Fitzcharles, by whose appearance I was immediately captivated, and
whom in no long time I made my wife. It is to say little, to affirm that she was
superlatively handsome; though the soft brilliancy of her eye, the fairness of her
brow, and the fresh morning roses that glowed in her cheek, were such as I
never saw equalled in any other of her sex. There was something in the simplest
of her attitudes, that expressed a being just descended from the celestial
spheres, / new lighted on the earth. The charm lay principally in that very
simplicity, the total absence of all design, and even of consciousness. Her soul
shone through her corporeal frame, composed her limbs, and gave them an air
and a grace, which, if you saw it, you would easily apprehend, but which no
imagination, no power of the inventive faculties, could parallel. She was all a
miracle. When she looked at you, her eyes were fraught with intelligence,
combined with a benignity that was more than human. You could scarcely have
the audacity to accost her – not that there was any thing in what you saw, that
was proud, imposing, forbidding, – she was the gentlest of her sex, – it was her
perfection, her faultlessness, that awed you. It was, so to express myself, her
attraction, her frankness, her unreserve, that kept you at a distance. It was like
what I have remarked at one point, of the waters of the Tweed:[a] you have but
to step over a brook, / and you are at once in a new country, and under the rule
of another government. The thought itself must give you pause. The step is
decisive, and may be incapable of being revoked. It is thus that it is related of
Mary queen of Scots, when she had already urged her horse into the stream that

---

[a] River in SE Scotland and NE England, flowing east and forming part of the border between the
two countries.

she might seek the protection of Elizabeth, that one of her faithful counsellors followed her, seized the bridle of the steed, and endeavoured at the latest moment to convince her of the portentous results that might attend her proceeding.[a]

My first acquaintance with Emilia was made in London, and in the brilliant circles of fashion. But this introduction was speedily succeeded by an opportunity to see her under a different aspect, and to observe her qualities, and the inestimable treasures of her head and her heart, more fully than I could otherwise have done, in a rural retreat. As the summer advanced, a friend of mine, a brother member of the house / of commons, invited me to spend some days at a country-seat he possessed in the neighbourhood of that of the father of Emilia. I was secretly charmed with so fortunate a coincidence. I had often been delighted with the society of this friend; our views of life and literature for the most part coincided; and there was a liveliness in his wit, and an originality in his remarks, that gave a nameless grace to his conversation. But this was not the principal cause why upon this occasion I accepted his invitation with so much eagerness. His residence was at only seven miles distance from that of Fitzcharles.

The first morning after our arrival, we rode over to pay our respects to the amiable old man and his interesting daughter. The road lay partly through the park of a nobleman, the wealthiest land-proprietor in the county, the surface of which was beautifully variegated with hill and valley, with forest-trees and underwood / which a fresh and limpid river divided into two unequal parts, over which we passed by a bridge: and, when we quitted the park, the rest of our way lay for the most part through an avenue of lofty trees, whose branches nearly united, and formed a continuous canopy over our heads, now and then broken by an unexpected vista to the neighbouring country.

Our ride was delightful; and the thought of the point in which it was to terminate, rendered it doubly interesting to me. The old man and his daughter were at home and alone; and he insisted on our staying to dine. We accordingly dismissed one of our servants, to announce to my friend's household that we should not return till late in the evening. Another neighbour of Fitzcharles dropped in soon after and joined us. We strolled about the grounds; and occasionally reposed ourselves in the alcoves with which the gardens were interspersed. Whether by accident or / otherwise, the three gentlemen who were in a manner at home in the scene, kept together, and canvassed their rural politics, the agricultural and other improvements they contemplated, and the little anecdotes of the neighbourhood, while Emilia and I were left to amuse each other as we could.

Here, amidst the calm and serene scenery of nature, she appeared to me a

---

[a] Mary Stuart (1542–87), Queen of Scotland from 1542; Elizabeth Tudor (1533–1603), Queen of England from 1558.

new creature. In the ball and the drawing-room she outshone all her com-
petitors; she sparkled with diamonds; and the taste and elegance of her attire
pointedly distinguished her, at least in my eye, from the crowd of females of
fashion and beauty that surrounded her. Her motions were more graceful, her
voice of a more happy and heartfelt intonation, and her remarks infinitely more
striking and agreeable than any thing I could observe in the ladies that were
then most in vogue.

But it was a totally different, and a much / more enchanting scene, to behold
her with all the wealth, and yet all the sobriety of nature, so to speak, for a
back-ground. She adorned the most exalted and the noblest circles. By the
resistless character of her charms she extinguished all the lesser stars that
sought to contend with her. But amidst the woods and the groves the whole
was infinitely more gratifying. Here there was no contention. It was all harmony, and the parts of the picture seemed to belong to each other. Nature
united with Emilia; and Emilia united with all that was most ravishing or most
tender in the objects of nature. In the ball-room all was rivalry; a struggle,
however ineffectual in the rest, for superiority; and the spectator could not
avoid the having, as it were, copied into his soul, the uneasy sensations, the
heart-burnings and the envy, that prevailed around him. But with Emilia,
among parterres[a] of flowers and majestic trees, while the light and / fleecy
clouds floated along in a thousand fantastic, yet graceful forms and in all their
stainless freshness over our heads, I felt that every thing within and around me
emanated from one sacred and ineffable source, 'whose body Nature is, and
God the soul'.[b]

The day appeared too short; and I started with surprise when my friend told
me it was time for us to take our departure. A few days after, my host set out for
a meeting of country-gentlemen upon some affair of local interest. We called in
our way at the house of Fitzcharles; and, as I had no concern with the meeting
that was to take place, I contrived to remain with Emilia, while the two
gentlemen proceeded to their place of appointment. Emilia had now a female
cousin with her on a visit, a kind, good creature, whose presence gave decorum
to our colloquy,[c] and who, like Celia in As You Like It, being herself character-
ized by the absence of egotism and pretensions, / suffered no pain from my
almost exclusive attention to her charming relative.

Fitzcharles remarked the partiality that was taking root between me and his
daughter, and was not unwilling to favour it. He invited me, when the term of
my visit to my present host was completed, to come and favour him for an
equal period with a residence under his roof. I loved his frankness; we understood each other without further explanation. There was no contract or precise

---

[a] Formally patterned flower garden.
[b] Alexander Pope, *An Essay on Man* (1733–4), I. 1. 268.
[c] Formal conversation.

anticipation between us. Each party was free; and, on that account, the silken cords of ingenuous passion sat a thousand times more lightly upon me; and I was only the more happy, because there was no possibility that, in hours of gloom, and in the necessarily variable weather of human life, I could ever have occasion to look back to a liberty I had too suddenly parted with, or too hastily compromised. I might repent, if I pleased; I might withdraw, without / slur to the nicety of my reputation, and without giving to any one a right to complain; and that very circumstance effectually barred the door against so much as the thought to repent.

The eligibleness of the match, and the integrity of my character, freed us from even the forms of restraint. We wandered wherever we pleased. We found ourselves sometimes in the most impervious thickets and recesses, which we had plunged into without the slightest premeditation. The scene had to me the recommendation of entire novelty. I had never before been in unreserved communication with an accomplished female of my own age. All the topics of conversation, all the thoughts that pass through the mind, are in that case entirely different from those which occur with a friend of our own sex. With a male friend each party has his own pretensions, is careful to maintain his ground, and feels a rivalship / even in the midst of the most entire apparent reciprocity. There is a jealousy; each party lays down the law, the law of his own mind, takes care that there is a clear stage, and summons his faculties to enable him to render the justice due to his case; even when he listens to his friend, when he attends with deference, and is grateful for the light he receives, still he thinks of himself, is anxious that he should not be found in the act of betraying the clearness and independence of his understanding, and in the warmest paroxysms of amity remembers that he and the partner of his heart are distinct beings.

In the graver and more sentimental communications of man and man the head still bears the superior sway; in the unreserved intimacies of man and woman the heart is ever uppermost. Feeling is the main thing; and judgment passes for little. We go immediately to the point, not whether this thing / or that thing is true, but how do you like this thing or that, what pulse of approbation or disapprobation, of delight, of emotion, or sympathy, does it rouse in your bosom? If I and my male friend agree in a certain opinion, it is well; I feel so much the more kindly towards him, so much more gratification in our acquaintance. Still however we are two. But, with a female, and that female the object of my growing partiality and preference, every new agreement of sentiment and approbation brings us nearer to each other, removes one more brick from the wall which originally separated us, dissolves our several identities, and, as it were, melts us, like different chemical substances, in one crucible, and mingles us in heart and spirit, with a feeling that we can never thereafter be divided.

Between man and woman in matters of affection, there is no rivalry, no

13

competition. We are two different species of being; or at / least the distinction
of sex divides us no less effectually. I should not more think of a contention of
this sort with the woman of my heart, than with a being of the animal creation
below me, or with my guardian angel above me. With my male friend I still
stand upon my defence; I reserve a corner in my heart, that is sacredly and
exclusively my own. But with the female I love it is otherwise; I throw open the
gates of the citadel, and lay the keys of the fortress at her feet. I never have the
imagination that we can have separate interests; and I invite her to enter into
my soul, and to possess the 'crown and hearted throne of my love'.[a] We are
truly united; she is 'bone of my bone, and flesh of my flesh'; and for this
obvious cause 'shall a man leave father and mother', comparatively estrange
him from all other living things, 'and cleave to his wife'.[b]

We married; and, if ever man was happy / in the wedded state, I was so. But
all the pleasures I afterwards experienced, never had the power to obliterate my
vivid remembrance of the days of courtship. Hope is in some respects a thing
more brilliant, more vivifying, than fruition. What we have looked forward to
with eager and earnest aspiration, is never in all respects equal to the picture we
had formed of it. The very uncertainty enhances the enjoyment. Rest is not the
natural, the most elevated state of man. As virtue, so happiness, consists in
action, in a perpetual progress towards that which we have not. Love acquires
an additional principle of gratification from the uncertainty of its climate, its
smiles, its frowns, *inimicitiæ, induciæ, bellum, pax rursum,* 'its little quarrels, its
subsequent capitulation, its brief hostilities, and their never-failing attendant
and follower, peace'. We are not satisfied with a climate of unvaried sunshine.
When the zephyr[c] plays, and the branches / are moved, and light summer-
clouds flit along the sky, we experience a more entire, an ever-renewing
gratification. The very uncertainty, the thought, 'Here it may all break off, and
be at an end', imparts a tingling delight, a life that shoots through all my veins.
It is like the flickering of a lamp that guides us in an untried path; it seems
dying, but to revive again; and, when hope most appears to have deserted us,
lo, it suddenly bursts forth with a brightness that we think will never more
subside and be extinguished.

The imperfection of the state of courtship is its perfection. We have always
something to look forward to. However extatic may be my present state of
enjoyment, there is still better behind. The prospect, the comparison of the
present and the future, 'when we shall hunger and thirst no more', gives to the
soul a peace that no words can describe.[d]

Courtship is a holy state. In the midst of / temptation we are chaste. We put

---

[a] *Othello*, III. iii. 447 (adapted).
[b] Gen. 2: 23–4.
[c] Soft or gentle breeze.
[d] Revelation 7: 16 (adapted).

a bridle into the mouth of passion, and no incorrect motion or gesture, no word but of entire purity and delicacy, escapes the lover. We feel this sanctity, and are fully aware of the robe of honour with which it invests us. As our words, so also we turn our thoughts and the topics on which we discourse, to refined and elevated themes. We feel how widely we are removed from the 'beasts that perish',[a] and how we approach to the sublimity of an angelic essence.

Yet all this would have been nothing but in such a courtship as mine. Not for one moment did I doubt of the rectitude of mind, the generosity of spirit, of my Emilia. I knew that all was right in the ultimate result. Had the case been that of a waywardness of purpose, a capriciousness of determination, a thought that loved to tyrannise, and delighted in the anxiety and affliction of her lover, our position would have been different. But, no. Her course / was like that of the orb by which the world is enlightened. Though the clouds might gather, and the heaven be obscured for a moment, yet I knew that the cherisher of my soul was in essence unaltered, and that its beneficence would presently shew itself with only the more advantage for this transitory interruption. The sensitiveness of a lover indeed from time to time taught me to be afraid; but, when I had leisure to recollect all the kindness and loveliness of her nature, my tranquillity once more was restored, and I became full of reliance.

We married; and, if ever man was happy in the wedded state, I was so. As we knew more of each other, we had fewer topics and occasions of difference. We were united by the most sacred ties; and the cultivation of a mutual harmony was a sort of religion to both. In courtship nothing is to be considered as concluded; / we play with a knot, the plications[b] of which are shaped out, but the bows are not yet drawn into the form in which they are destined to remain in perpetuity. Courtship is a sort of sport:

> My Phyllis me with pelted apples plies:
> Then, tripping to the woods, the coy one hies,
> And wishes to be seen before she flies.[c]

Courtship is an experiment; it is the month which the stripling spends 'upon liking'[d] previously to his indentures. He is yet free, and may be disposed of elsewhere. And the liberty of which he feels he is the possessor, unavoidably gives birth to a thousand freaks and sallies, and unbridled imaginations. 'Why should I not', says the lover, of the fair one he addresses, 'use my freedom, for the short time that it remains to me? The use of it may be the means of mortal offence. But I will take my chance. If I give in, the moment the thing / becomes serious, I trust that all will be well. Even though the mischief should not be

---

[a] Psalm 49: 20.
[b] Folds
[c] cf. John Dryden, 'The Third Pastoral, or, Palaemon' (1697), ll. 97–9, the original reading 'wanton' for Godwin's 'coy one'.
[d] Quotation unidentified.

15

instantaneously healed, I can humble myself, and exhibit the tokens of a sincere penitence; and that must be enough'. /

CHAPTER II

No society is comparable to that of an accomplished wife: at least such I found it in the engagement into which I thus entered in my early period of man's estate. Our topics of conversation were inexhaustible; for we were wholly without reserve, and conversed with each other, even as a man might be supposed to commune with his own heart. We told all that we knew; for neither of us had any thing that we desired to possess exclusively. Every portion of information of which either came into possession, we were forward to impart. Every subtle distinction of sentiment, every nice[a] division of meaning, every use of the words / and phrases of our native tongue that would enable us to give appropriate language and luminous expression to what before existed in the mind undeveloped and only in the ruder elements of thought, we were eager to add to the common stock, and make a property for both.

Nothing is more beautiful than the relation of tutor and pupil, where love adds its zest to the intercourse. The true delight which the instructor feels in developing what else might be obscure, the pleasure which he reaps in finding his meaning thoroughly apprehended, and in the docility of the novice, and the ingenuous enquiries that are addressed to him in return, are all and each of them sensations in the highest degree gratifying.

We talked together in the usual apartment of our house, which overlooked the lawn, and the slopes, and the gay parterres of a thousand flowers: or we walked in sequestered and solitary lanes, on the margins of the running stream, or on the uplands where a delicious / prospect unfolded itself to our view. The freshness of the air, the singing of birds, the fragrance of the morning, the whispering of the breeze, or the gorgeous colours of the departing luminary of day, gave a healthful tone to all our communications, and to the effusion of our souls. We were not without neighbours, and the interchange of agreeable society. But our own society unbroken in upon, pleased us most, when our guests had withdrawn, or when we felt secure that no third person by his appearance would diversify the scene, and by enlarging, give a comparative restraint to our unstudied and spontaneous interchanges of sentiment. Other

---

[a] Exact.

men, better informed on certain points than myself, might visit our retreat; but Emilia preferred learning whatever she was not yet fully acquainted with, from my lips, who,

> she knew, would intermix
> Grateful digressions, and solve high dispute
> With conjugal caresses.[a] /

Occasionally we separated. Business relating to the affairs of the neighbourhood, to the administration of my landed property, to the wants and desires of my tenants, would call me from home. In the conduct of every domestic establishment the departments of the husband and the wife are different; her affairs are partly those of housewifery, while the male superintendant of their common interests does not fully discharge his duties, unless he is in some sense his own steward, and refuses to delegate all his authority to another. But these separations only gave to our subsequent meetings a further charm, and imparted to what might otherwise have had a cloying monotony, a provoking and spirit-stirring novelty. After every separation our meeting again was like that of friends whom lands and seas had divided from each other: we came together with impatience, and felt as creatures that had escaped from an odious banishment, and returned / once more to the enjoyment of all that they had loved best in the world.

I was never alone, but when I wished to be alone. Solitude gave new charms to society, and society to solitude. I was secure not to be exposed to a satiety of either. There are occupations that can be most satisfactorily and most effectually pursued in solitude. In the every-varying landscape of human life solitude has sometimes its charms that nothing else can countervail. Hers is the province of deep meditation, of profound self-examination, of looking steadily into the 'seeds of things',[b] and weighing the universe in a balance, of winnowing the abstruse questions which present themselves concerning good and evil, the respective advantages of enthusiasm and apathy, and the respective probabilities that attend on 'happiness or final misery'.[c] Hers is the realm of criticism. And, to conclude, hers is emphatically the consecrated ground of the / sublime, the silent, the abstract, the concentrated religion. But my periods of solitude were a thousandfold the more satisfactory, inasmuch as I could, whenever it so pleased me, open the door of my retreat, and immediately engage myself in the society and converse that I loved best. In the next apartment, or at the end of an adjoining gallery, I found waiting for me the most perfect specimen of female excellence that ever existed, welcoming me, smiling upon me with her beautiful eyes, anxiously enquiring for my health and my peace, imparting to

---

[a] John Milton, *Paradise Lost*, VIII. 54–6.
[b] John Dryden, *Lucretius* (1685), III. l. 35.
[c] *Paradise Lost*, II. l. 563.

17

me tranquillity and cheerfulness when my thoughts had been too grave, suggesting amusements when I had grown weary from severe application, and, by some ingenious sally, or happily recollected anecdote or tale, bringing me back to myself, and rendering me as fresh and ready for any purpose that might be started, as if I had just awaked from the most balmy slumbers. /

Solitude is one of the highest enjoyments of which our nature is susceptible. Solitude is also, when too long continued, capable of being made the most severe, indescribable, unendurable source of anguish. But I was in no danger of ever having too much of it, or that the Goddess would ever approach me, clad in her Gorgon terrors, and circled with the wild, formless, terrific, maddening images she is capable of conjuring up in the soul.[a] The intellectual climate in which I dwelt was not for ever perhaps serene; but I could call up a cerulean[b] canopy and horizon, whenever I pleased; I had a sun that rose upon me at any moment, at which I wished for the newness and freshness of a delightful morning. It is much at all times to have access to society, but more to have within call the best society that the great Creator in his bounty ever assigned to the lot of a human being.

If at any time I was, as it were, ready to / sink and give way under the anxieties, the obscurity, the never-ending weariness of my progress 'through the valley of the shadow of death',[c] I had, to adopt the language of the most sacred of records, 'an angel from heaven appearing to me, strengthening me'.[d] I imbibed new vigour from the beams of her affectionate countenance, and new animation from the accents of her melodious speech. If I fainted by reason of infirmity or over-earnest application, the balm of her sympathy and love was at hand to restore me. Her soul was purity; her suggestions infallible. I had a petitioner, through the medium of whose voice and eyes, all charity was wakened up in my bosom; and I became worthy and revered in the censure of all around me, because she made me so.

If we read, or if we spoke together of the creations of genius, as they are to be found in its richest treasuries, if we summoned one / another's attention to its most tender or spirit-stirring effusions, the specimens that occurred gained I know not what of life and beauty by our thus enjoying them together. Each passage, each image, each burst and pouring out of the soul in our authors, was ever after valued by either of us, from the recollection that it was first recommended to observation by the other. In the female bosom in particular, there is a quickness, a truth, an intuition of feeling and taste, by which I was specially the gainer, and with which no individual of the sterner sex may ever hope to compete.

---

[a] In Greek mythology, any of three winged monstrous sisters, Stheno, Euryale, and Medusa, who had live snakes for hair, huge teeth, and brazen claws.

[b] Deep blue, or azure.

[c] Psalms 23: 4.

[d] Luke 22: 43 (adapted).

Our communications were characterised by the most perfect unreserve. Of consequence we had an advantage in studying the inmost recesses of human character, which perhaps no other human creatures ever possessed in an equal degree. 'The eye sees not itself, but by reflection from some other thing.'[a] The study of the heart of man is only perfected by our / looking into ourselves. But this insight is of a precarious nature. A man 'beholds his natural face in a glass, and goeth his way, and straightway forgetteth what manner of man he is'.[b] We cannot hold the glass steady for our own inspection. When we are conscious that we are aiming at that subtlest of all exercises, the knowledge of ourselves, the very consciousness new-models every feature, and we never see ourselves as we should appear to the eye of the impartial spectator. The recollection that we are engaged in the act of introspection cramps our muscles and our limbs, gives a new pulsation to the heart, and annihilates that free play of every articulation, which is necessary to our arriving at a genuine verdict. But no human creature is so deeply sensitive to the inspection of another, as to his own. We can on such an occasion the more easily steady our joints, and preserve ourselves on our centre. To this we may add, that the / examined may not be at all times sensible to the process that is going on. He may be subjected to the process of the analyser, when he is himself least aware of it. – Thus we became in a singular degree adepts in the science of the human heart; and I can answer for at least myself in this investigation, that the more I knew the chosen partner of my life, the more I found to commend. We had no reserve with each other, for we had nothing which either our inclinations or our interests prompted us to conceal.

A prominent characteristic of our intercourse was, that it was never my practice, as is elsewhere almost universally the mode in human society, to examine my thoughts in silence, and recite inwardly what I was going to say, for the purpose of discovering what there might be in it, that would produce upon my hearer a different effect from that which I had in contemplation. Every thing was listened / to by us on either side in a spirit of mutual deference. In ordinary society even the most intimate, there is apt to be a sort of concealed warfare going on, that prompts either party to receive with jealousy the suggestions of the other. The husband or the wife says tacitly, 'I have known your judgment to be so often at fault; you are so hasty, or so much under the control of a superfluous caution, so easily duped, or so unreasonably sceptical, so much guided by your general associates, or so wedded to the doctrines of a sect to which you adhere, or of particular authors whose works you are accustomed to admire, your views of morals, of religion, of the exceeding importance, or the comparative valuelessness, of affairs that are going on upon the stage of nations, are so different from mine, that your espousing and advocating a

---

[a] *Julius Caesar*, I. ii. 52–3 (adapted).
[b] James 1: 23–4.

19

certain sentiment is itself a reason why I should look upon it with suspicion'. The husband or the / wife therefore speaks mistrustfully, anticipates objection and hostility, and preserves unsaid many things that are in themselves as it were part and parcel of his inmost soul.

But between Emilia and myself there were no reserves; as there was no fear of misconstruction. We talked to each other even as a man talks to his own heart. There was no prejudice that lurked in the hearer, no alienation: on the contrary every thing that was suggested, was listened to with a disposition to be convinced, and to adopt what was offered. Our creeds were the same, and our tastes; we were predisposed to the same occupations and the same preferences. Our pulses beat responsively to each other. The excursion and the amusement that one liked, was an object of choice to the other. It was as if one soul ruled in two bodies; that, 'each heart being set' upon the same generous purpose, the same common result, our intercourse, could / in no wise be made 'a stage to feed contention',[a] but was a cooperation of two equal and consenting powers to produce one effect.

Between two persons intimately connected with each other, and who are continually in each other's society, intervals of silence will frequently occur. This may happen when all their modes of thinking and feeling are already known to each other, and their topics are exhausted. But it will oftenest happen between persons of opposite sexes, whom the Power that made us has cast in so dissimilar moulds, and whose ways of arriving at their conclusions, and shaping their sentiments, are so unlike, – it will happen, I say, because a thousand topics, a thousand deeply cherished feelings, and most valued trains of thinking are shut out of the pale of disquisition, as being points in which the parties are already aware they shall not coincide, and by starting which they will only produce the effect of stirring up / unfriendly feelings, and discord, either latent or avowed. It is surprising how numerous, when once the list has been begun to be formed, these topics will become. The very circumstance, that we refrain from giving them utterance, makes them occur more frequently to our silent reflections. We would give the world that the partner of our days and our board agreed with us in these things; but we believe that the attempt to bring about this agreement would have no other result than to set us further asunder.

It is thus that private comes to resemble general society. In general society there are a multitude of topics upon which I am not tempted to open my mouth. I anticipate, that what I should feel prompted to say, would not be received in the same spirit in which it would be delivered. It would rouse a whole host of prejudices against it. Each of the hearers would abound in his own sense, and would be little / disposed to weigh, or, in any just interpretation of the term, even to hear, what was alleged in behalf of a different doctrine.

---

[a] *Henry IV, Part II*, I. i. 155–6.

Why should I give myself the trouble to utter what will not be listened to, or to support a proposition by arguments when I know it will make no converts? The cause of truth will not be benefited; and I shall myself gain no credit, either for the singleness of my intentions, or the ingenuity of my reasonings. – In reality indeed it is not so: seed sown in stony ground will not be totally without a crop; an argument that meets with nothing but apparent discouragement at first, may not be wholly lost; and the good that we have attempted to do, will sometimes return to us, and shew the solidity and depth of its effects, at a time when we were most inclined to despair. But the impatience of the human mind urges us to desist; and, if we do not effect every thing in its most conspicuous form, and in the shortest / imaginable period, we persuade ourselves that we do nothing.

Between Emilia and me the case was altogether different. We were in no instance parties working in opposite directions, and who, the more active they are, the more they impede each other's progress, but were like labourers, both employed in breaking up the soil of one field, or enlarging and levelling the same road. Our united force was directed to one object; and, as if we had been the component parts of one mighty machine, we removed mountains, and conquered obstacles, which seemed to bid defiance to human power. The variety of our faculties insured but the more success to our efforts; and the masculine firmness of the one, and the feminine delicacy of the other, enabled us but the more securely to lay open the inmost recesses of truth, and disclose her mysteries, yielding as she did to the joint energies of both. /

If at any time we differed in judgment, we searched with sincerity into the cause of our difference, and endeavoured to find out on which side the truth really lay. A sentiment delivered by either, that might at first sight appear to the other startling and strange, was saluted with a love, and welcomed with an encouraging smile, which shewed the hearer to be more than half converted already, by his confidence in and deference for the speaker.

This was checked however on the other side with an honest caution, that seemed to say, 'Come now, no treachery; you must be a friend, and not a flatterer; if you do not weigh my suggestion with soberness and impartiality, you will too surely mislead me, and, when I relied on you for sound direction, will unwarily urge me forward in a path which leads to delusion and folly'.

The frankness we exercised was perfect. We talked to each other, as a man talks to his own / soul. We did not utter all our thoughts: for thought is endless; its process is such as no words can follow; but we uttered every thing worthy to be recited, and to which a precise or intelligible form could be given. The sound of our own voices encouraged us; our mutual answers, replies and rejoinders gave an indescribable animation to our dialogue. We led each other on; we gave breath to each unfinished conception. There was no fear on either side that an uncandid advantage would be taken of trips and mistakes that might be incurred. We rather resembled what has been affirmed of certain animals, who are said by their parental assiduity and care to complete the

21

conformation of their half-unfinished progeny. Our policy was like that of Jupiter, who, when the mother of Bacchus perished untimely before the birth of her offspring, by a miracle supplied the place of the dam; or, as in the case of Triptolemus, whom Ceres covered with / glowing embers, till his energies expanded, and his limbs became endued with a suitable firmness.[a]

The habit of entire and unhesitating explicitness which we cultivated towards each other, removed us as it were into another class of beings from the human creatures with which we were surrounded. We had no distrust. Our hearts were ever on our lips. We considered the faculty of speech as given us to express our thoughts. We had no idea of those ambages[b] and prevarications by which the majority of our species are ever seeking to defeat the curiosity, the one of the other, by which they are taught continually to look at their phrases before they are uttered, lest by any accident they might tell that which it was intended should remain unknown. The difference was this: social man is essentially a coward; we were fearless. Social man regards all those by whom he is surrounded as enemies, / or beings who may become such. He is ever on his guard, lest his plain speaking should be wilfully perverted, or should assume a meaning he never thought of, through the animosity or prejudice of the individual that hears him. The duration of the married state of Emilia and myself was brief: but, as long as it lasted, the whole world wore a different hue to me, from that which it has exhibited since her decease. Then I had the sunshine of the soul; and the light I carried within, came back to me by reflection from every thing I saw. The whole world was beautiful; and all that dwelt upon its surface were friendly. Love was uppermost in my bosom; and the love that I bore to Emilia was in some degree shared among every thing that lived. My forehead was without wrinkles; my eye was steady and serene; my lips were curved with the curve of philanthropy; the purple light of complacence for ever showed itself on my cheeks. I spoke / to every one with confidence; for I was a stranger to fear. And, as my heart beat with kindliness to all, so I believed every one felt a responsive kindliness for me.

It is not my purpose to relate the events of my married life: otherwise I could write volumes on this single theme. I could rehearse whole conversations, some of which were all mind, others all soul. I could describe tones that thrilled my soul. When I call them to mind, they come to me sometimes with such vivid emotion, that I no longer appear to recollect them, but actually to hear them. I turn round, and expect to see Emilia, present to the sense of sight, as well as of hearing. It is not in words to express what my disappointment then makes me feel. I worked myself up to such a pitch, that obstacles were no longer

---

[a] Jupiter, supreme god of Roman mythology; Bacchus, Roman god of wine, the Dionysus of the Greeks, whose mother was Semele; Triptolemus, Greek hero and demi-god who was taught the arts of agriculture by Ceres, Roman name for Demeter, protectress of Mother Earth.
[b] Tortuous paths.

feel. I worked myself up to such a pitch, that obstacles were no longer remembered. Seas and mountains were removed. Time, that creature of the imagination, which is, and is not, no longer / interposed between me and the consummation of my longings. The grave gave up its dead. But why do I say that? There was no grave. The body no longer mouldered in the tomb. It was as we read in the Evangelist, when 'the bodies of saints which slept, came out of their sepulchres, and went into the holy city, and were seen of many'.[a] My state had been that of a trance; and, when I awoke, words cannot speak my anguish and my agony.

The attitudes of Emilia are not less present to me. Her walk was not like that of any other human being: it had such dignity and ease: it ravished the soul, at the same time that it had no design or consciousness. I remember that quick motion of her hand, which expressed a sweet, an affectionate, yet somewhat impatient rejection of an idea that was named. I remember her smile of scorn, her disdain, so noble, yet so truly feminine. I remember her smile of tenderness, in which, / while a sudden flush mantled in the cheek, and the eyes seemed to emit sparks of fire, the heart melted, and the whole soul dissolved in affection.

She was without a fault: at least I can remember none. Her emotions were sudden; and sometimes before I was aware of it, I looked up, and saw a cloud gathering on her brow. Then she would for a moment be silent, and proudly shut up within her a discontent that would not stoop to complain. But ten words of ingenuous expostulation on my part would disarm her anger, and remove the preparations of hostility that seemed collected to defend the fortress of her independence. An angelic smile would follow; so that the wrath (if such it may be termed) was like a thin curtain or cloud, that temporarily obscured the refulgence of her goodness, which removed, the luminary would shine forth more brightly than ever. And the inexpressible grace with / which she would confess her error the instant she was aware of it, imparted a delight such as the world can never know; and in transport I would swear that sinless perfection was inconceivable folly; while thus to err, and thus to avow it, was a triumph unapproachable by the condition of angelic natures. /

[a] Matt. 27: 52-3.

CHAPTER III

The first fruit of our union was a daughter, that individual whom I have named in the outset of my narrative, as being, when guilt with all its terrors at length overtook me, my only friend, 'a friend, whom the ties of nature and her own excellent dispositions have rendered mine by bonds never to be dissolved'.[a]

When our child was about a year old, a vehement desire seized me to visit the continent. I felt as if my present period of life was peculiarly adapted to sustain change of place, moderate fatigue, the climbing of mountains, the descending into the depths of the earth, and all those exertions which an inquisitive / spirit suggests, and those difficulties which the grand and magnificent style of natural objects presents to the traveller. I became desirous to see pictures, and survey buildings, to contemplate art in the climates where she had especially flourished, to hear the languages and accents of many-visaged man, to remark his habits, his disposition, and his aims, as they are variously modified by the temperature of the elements, and the forms of government under which he subsists; in a word, like Ulysses,[b] to understand the minds of my species, and see the clusters of their habitations.

All this was not to be accomplished but in a leisurely progress. And I could not endure the idea of being so long separated from the light of my life, the presence of that creature who seemed to me to be as much required, as corporeal nourishment, for the recreation of my mortal powers, the incomparable Emilia. She consented to be my companion. My choice / became her choice. The object that attracted me, appeared to have peculiar charms for her.

But what was to become of her child, the being she seemed to love scarcely less than her husband? She had never yet endured an absence from it that exceeded the period of a few hours. Was it possible that she should suffer herself to be deprived of the sight of this creature, so fascinating in her eyes, for the entire period of twelve months, to which length of time it was not improbable our travels might be drawn out? Who would take such charge of it as the anxieties of a mother demanded, would supply its wants and anticipate its wishes, defend it from all accidents and evil, watch its early indications of temper and understanding, mould the one and direct the other, and forward,

---

[a] Quotation unidentified.
[b] Or Odysseus, hero of Homer's *Odyssey*.

with incessant but wholesome progress, the improvement that was required for so precious a treasure?

We had a remedy for all this. Emilia had / a friend, Catherine Fanshaw. They had been bred together from their earliest fancy. They, like

> two artificial gods,
> Had with their needles shaped a single flower,
> Both on one sampler, sitting on one cushion,
> Both warbling of one song, –
> As if their hands and sides, voices and minds,
> Had been incorporate.[a]

Emilia and Catherine had been married in one day – first made distinct in this, that Catherine had no child. Their affection for each other was unparalleled; never did sisters, twin-sisters, entertain such mutual love as they did. My daughter was named Catherine in memorial of this friendship.

When we left England for the continent, Mrs Fanshaw had been two years a wife; but she was neither a mother, nor appeared to be in the way to become so. This circumstance seemed to render the temporary adoption which Emilia's friend proposed to my wife, particularly suitable. /

Never was attention so exemplary as this friend paid to her little namesake. She felt perhaps more than she would have done, if the child had been her own. She loved her not less than her own flesh and blood: and in addition to this, she regarded her as the representative and pledge of her absent sister. She never spoke to the child, but she thought of the mother. She lavished on it a thousand caresses, the manifestations of her long-fixed attachment. She exerted herself to trace in its expanding limbs and unfolding features every thing that might bring before her the playmate and companion of her youth. And, in every thing she did for the child, she not only obeyed the impulses of her generous spirit, and aimed at the approbation of her own judgment; she also remembered for ever that she had another umpire, that must be satisfied, and that would come at no distant time to examine her performance, and see how she had employed her / talent; an umpire of the clearest discernment, the soundest understanding, and the acutest feelings, who would detect any mistake, if even a rose-leaf almost had lost its smoothness and become wrinkled.

Mrs Fanshaw particularly applied to the contriving expedients, by means of which the absence of the mother might least affect the child, and least produce the results of estrangement. Among others she bethought herself of this. She had a portrait of Emilia, painted by an incomparable artist, and which had all the vivid colours of life. The painter had seized one of the happiest expressions of the exile, an expression which bespoke condescension and tenderness, and seemed to have the power of exciting correspondent tenderness in the

---

[a] *A Midsummer Night's Dream*, III. ii. 203–8 (adapted).

beholder. This portrait she regarded as capable of being made the instrument to produce in the child the sentiments she desired.

She did not suffer the picture to be always / in the presence of the little Catherine. It was placed in a select and retired apartment, to which the child was only led, for the most part once a day, at well chosen periods. These periods were such at which the child was in the best frame of mind to receive impressions of complacency, and at which her preceptress (if such a term may be admitted in speaking of a pupil at so immature an age) was most delighted and in good humour with her. To see the picture was treated as a regale[a] and a reward. Further than this, the picture was so placed that it could not be viewed but at a certain distance. Emilia's friend told the child that that was its mother; and, when the child was able to speak, the first articulate sound she uttered, as she saw the picture, or thought of the picture, was, Mamma! Her guardian knew that that which is immoveably in one position a child soon learns to separate from the idea of life, and passes by with carelessness / and indifference. Mrs Fanshaw devised a remedy for this. A curtain was spread before the recess in which the portrait was placed; and this curtain was drawn back with a certain degree of ceremony. Means were contrived that the portrait should be viewed through an optical delusion, sometimes through a magnifying medium, and sometimes looking as if it were a miniature. The picture grew into a sort of amusement; and the child and her protector went to play at mamma. But each exhibition concluded with a kind of epilogue, judiciously adapted to the capacity of the spectator, of which Love and a sort of worship formed, if I may so express myself, the concluding notes. In quitting the scene, the child was taught to kneel, and join its little hands as in the attitude of supplication. The curtain that had been drawn back, was then spread again, and the child resorted to her ordinary scenes and amusements, but with a kind of chastised and / gratified feeling, as if she had been engaged in a ceremonial of a religious sort. Mrs Fanshaw told her pupil, that her real mother, of whom this was the representation, was far, far away, travelling in a coach and in a ship, but that in time she would come back, and, if her daughter conducted herself rightly, and Mrs Fanshaw felt authorised to make a good report of her, would stay with her, and remove no more.

All this made a deep impression upon the little Catherine. She was ever eager at the appointed time to visit the dear mother, that smiled upon her so kindly, though she could not speak.

One day, by some accident, the door of this apartment was left not quite closed; and the child had found means unobserved to steal into the sanctuary. The curtain was half drawn back. The picture, as I have mentioned, was placed in a recess, so that it could / be viewed at a distance, but not touched, or

---

[a] Feast.

approached. The child had been taught to kneel; she kneeled now unbid. She stretched out her little hands, and said in a soft voice, as if persuading, Come, mamma, come; I want you! Mrs Fanshaw appeared at this moment, caught her in her arms, motioned her with a wave of her hand to take leave of the object before her, drew the curtain, and overwhelmed the child with a thousand kisses and embraces. This happened when the infant was nearly two years old.

What I have related may seem too precocious, and improbable. But every thing, in an effect to be produced on the human mind, depends upon the manner in which a thing is done. That which, repeated by an unskilful imitator, would awaken no single emotion, and even scarcely have the power to arrest the infant thoughts in their wanderings, may yet, if done in another manner, be found to still the / soul, to stop the youthful blood as it courses 'up and down the veins', to suspend even the breath, and make the child lift up its eyes in innocent wonder, expecting, yet eager to know, what will come next.[a] All depends on the clearness of feeling, the singleness of heart, and precision of spirit brought into action by the instructor; and these endowments were possessed by Mrs Fanshaw in the most extraordinary degree.

We returned from our excursion to the continent in about twelve months from the time that we left England; and the reunion of Emilia and her friend, and of Emilia and her child, were fruitful of no common delight. The little Catherine was puzzled at first between the mamma of the recess, whom she had been accustomed to visit every day, but who, however intreated, never moved or spoke, and the living mamma, who now held her in / her embraces, addressed to her words of love, and sung to her with her soft voice,

Uttering such dulcet and harmonious breath,[b]

that would now soothe her into 'a sacred and home-felt delight',[c] and now cause a tear, unconscious and unbidden, to stray down her cheek. The child insisted upon leading the truant and new-come mamma to the mamma that was always to be found, whenever sought, would compare the two with intent and interchanging gazing, and conclude with burying her face in her mother's bosom. /

---

[a] *King John*, III. iii. 44.
[b] *A Midsummer Night's Dream*, II. i. 151.
[c] John Milton, *A Masque Presented at Ludlow Castle, 1634 [Comus]* (1637), 262.

CHAPTER IV

We parted no more, till that blow came, which parted us for ever, and extinguished the only perfect happiness of which I could form even the idea. Short indeed was the period in which such enviable society was continued to me. We had been home only about a year, and the little Catherine was but three years old, when we took an excursion upon a lake, which was but at a small distance from my habitation. The day was specially serene, without being oppressively hot; a pleasant western breeze played upon our cheeks, and refreshed our spirits. It occasioned however only a quiet and lazy ripple of the surface, and no wise interfered / with the plan of our course. Never had I experienced a more complete felicity. We began to lay the plans of future years. Sportively it occurred to us to anticipate that decline of life, which, if the thread of our existence is not suddenly cut off, must to all mortals arrive at last. We both of us agreed that that would occasion no diminution to our content, that even wrinkles would turn into motives of endearment, and that the longer we were accustomed to each other's society, the more impossible we should each of us feel it was to live without it. The rash impulses of headstrong youth would be gone; we should have tried the scenes of many-coloured life, without arriving at the repining and unsatisfied inferences of the wise man, should talk over the old times, and read together once again the favourite authors of our youth. We should smile at the different aspects with which things would appear to us with a few decads[a] of years / between, the same, yet not the same, with such variation as the objects of nature display in the ascending and the setting sun. In books, in tales, in characters, the thing we looked at would be unaltered; but it would have a frequent novelty of appearance, that arose not from itself, but from the change which had insensibly taken place in the mind of the observer.

From one species of idleness and luxury we proceeded to another. Our little girl had fallen asleep in my arms. We spread some clothes that we had with us, in the middle of the boat, and drew a slight covering over her, that she might remain undisturbed. As I laid her upon this species of couch, I bestowed on her a gentle kiss, taking care not to rouse her. She is a sweet child, said I: what can we wish her to be, that we do not find in her? – But you know the burthen of my song, Emilia: I desire a son. /

---

[a] Decades.

Man is the substantive thing in the terrestrial creation: woman is but the adjective, that cannot stand by itself. A sweet thing she is; I grant it: no one has a greater right to say this than I have. But she is a frail flower; she wants a shelter, a protector, a pioneer. She is all that omniscience, that principle of divine meditation (so far as we can understand it), could produce, for the best consolation, the entire repose and good of the stronger sex; and, in forming his happiness, she forms her own. She has beauty of form and exterior, and gentleness of soul. She has understanding, so as to form the suitable helpmate of her husband, the partner of his counsels, the controller of his excesses, the mitigator of his stoutness, the inspirer of all true gentleness and refinement, and of the tenderest and most extatic effusions of the soul. She has understanding such as he may not despise; she has the good and desirable qualities which he has / not, or has not in an equal degree. Sometimes she is in intellect the rival of her father, her husband, or her brother; sometimes, but rarely, she outstrips him – to remind us, if I may so express it, what the Creator could have done, if that had been reconcileable to the great plan of the whole.

I have always thought that one of the most beautiful pictures of the angelic control that woman may exercise over the sternness of man, is that which is given by Froissard in his account of the surrender of Calais.[a] Edward the Third had besiged the town nearly twelve months; and it was now reduced to the extremity of famine, and was left without hope of relief. In this condition the citizens offered to surrender on terms. But Edward determined that they had held out longer than the rules of war authorised them to do; had they submit- ted earlier, it would have been different; but they had subjected him and the besieging / army to much hardship and calamity, and arrested the career of his victories from sheer obstinacy, when there was no longer any hope of a favourable result; and he was resolved to inflict a severe retaliation. It would have an ill effect upon the inhabitants of other places similarly circumstanced, if he did not shew inflexibly in this instance, that the time of the invader was not to be trifled with, through hopeless stubbornness and contumacy. At length he relaxed from his severity, and said that, if six of the most considerable citizens attended him, barefooted and bareheaded, with ropes about their necks, bearing the keys of the city, and to be disposed of as he thought proper, he would spare the lives of the rest.

This stern decree was heard by the besieged with consternation; and they saw no means to comply with the demand of the conqueror. At length six citizens were found who voluntarily came forward, and offered themselves as an / expiation for the rest. They entered the camp of the English monarch in the costume of malefactors, and were ordered for execution. Such was the

---

[a] Jean Froissard (1338–?1410), French chronicler and raconteur, historian of his own times, whose account of the siege of Calais 1346–7 is in his *Chronicles* (1498).

decision of a barbarous age: so broad was the line of distinction that was then drawn between gentlemen, men of generous strain and descent, and ignoble citizens!

It happened that Philippa, consort to Edward the Third, had just arrived in the camp, having fought a decisive battle against David, king of Scots, who at the instigation of the French had entered Northumberland with fifty thousand men, and carried his ravages to the gates of Durham. Philippa with a very inferior force defeated the enemy, and made their king her prisoner. Crowned with this success, she crossed the sea, and presented herself to her husband in the midst of his triumph. She witnessed the demeanour of the heroic burgesses, and, struck to the very soul with the order she heard awarded against / them, threw herself on her knees, and with resistless tears and intreaties prevailed that their generous self-sacrifice should not be thus recompensed, but that they should be dismissed with the commendation and honour due to their virtue. Here was the characteristic exhibition of female prowess, interposing with grace, with beauty, and all the melting softness of the sex, powerful, nay irresistible, in its weakness. (I did not tell this story in detail in our conversation; the whole was familiar to Emilia; it was enough that I alluded to it.)

I was well disposed to do the amplest justice to the perfections of a sex, the consummate exemplar of which was the life of my life: but – I wished for a son. 'All ages and nations have recognised the practical inferiority of the female sex. They are not admitted among our legislators: in representative governments they have not even a direct voice in the choice of / our representatives. Every path of society is open to the male; an infinite majority is shut upon the female. We know for her scarcely any independent choice of life; her proper station is the condition of marriage. Of an equal prospect in the ample plain of existence she is deprived; the single woman feels her disadvantages and her weakness, and she is exposed to temptations and dangers which, once yielded to, render her the outcast of the earth. Of this condition of the frailer sex we must make the best that we can, and exert ourselves that it may have a prosperous issue in the case of our child. I am contented to have a daughter; but I desire to have a son.'

So luxuriant and unconfined was our talk; happy, beyond the powers of words to declare, almost of thought to conceive. When suddenly the face of the heavens above us began to alter: the sky was no longer in every part un-obscured; a cloud appeared to gather in the / horizon. It became larger and blacker; the wind whistled with a wintery cold. The air, which had hitherto been balmy and cherishing, opening all the pores of the body, and giving exaltation to the spirits, suddenly turned chilly and somewhat piercing. Unprepared as we were for the change, it produced an uncomfortable sensation, a shiver. Presently the whole hemisphere darkened above us; and first rain, and then hail, and then rain again, beat upon us with impetuosity. The thunder rolled; and the lightning flashed. Emilia endeavoured to smile, for she knew there was no danger. She pulled her cloak close about her, and nestled her little girl in her bosom.

We had been for more than two hours exposed to all the inclemency of the weather, before we reached the shelter of our own roof. I insisted on it that Emilia should immediately retire to bed: she appeared to me seriously indisposed. She was in a state of pregnancy, / perhaps in progress to give birth to the son, upon the thought of which my mind so inordinately doted. But, alas, no such blessing was in store for me. Of mother, and of all hope of future progeny by her, I was at once bereft. The accident seemed a slight one: but, as the poet testifies,

> We dally idly with the darts of Death:
> Wet, dry, cold, hot, at the appointed hour,
> All act subservient to the tyrant's power;
> And, when obedient Nature knows his will,
> A fly, a grapestone, or a hair can kill.[a]

Emilia retired to bed seriously indisposed. In the morning she had all the symptoms of a violent fever. The period was critical. She was attacked with repeated shivering fits. She became delirious. On the evening of this day she had a miscarriage. On the third day, in defiance of all the aids of medicine, she died. She had brief intervals in which she appeared somewhat collected and composed; and in these she earnestly recommended to me the care of her child. /

CHAPTER V

It is impossible to represent in words the total revolution this event made in my existence. It was as if in a single moment 'sun and moon were in the flat sea sunk'.[b] Nature that had been so beautiful, so resplendent, so fascinating, lost at once the soul to which it was indebted for all its charms. The rainbow tints of the globe in which I dwelt, the soft and tender hues, the delicate blendings, the undulating lights, varying for ever, and chasing one another beneath the cope of heaven were gone; and, in place of them, every thing was stained with one

---

[a] cf. Matthew Prior (1664–1721), 'Ode to the Memory of Colonel Villiers' (1704), l. 42: 'which play'd so idly with the darts of Death'; and ll. 51–4, which are quoted accurately.
[b] Milton, *Masque*, 373.

31

melancholy colour, one deadly and unwholesome brown. / The air appeared to me murky and thick, an atmosphere that bore pestilence on its wings. I looked around me; the outline of things, though obscure and dim, was the same: but where was now the grace that so lately animated them, the ornament that had tingled in all my veins, and shot through my soul?

The whole world comprised to me but two species of things; the things that were associated with the recollections of Emilia, and the things that were not so related. Upon the former of these I dwelt endlessly. The sensations I drew from them were bitter and sweet. They told me, Emilia was no more! Watch for her as earnestly as you please; you shall never see her, never hear her. Watch the opening of her chamber-door; it shall never open; or, if it does, it shall be opened by another, never by her upon whom your heart and all your thoughts are fixed. At one time / and another I heard footsteps; my thought was of Emilia; but, ah, how different! Never that step so light, so airy, that even talked to me as it approached, that was full of promise, that was all health, and spirit, and love. Her chair was vacant; her place at the table unsupplied; and at times, when accidentally I turned my eye to the spot in which I had been accustomed to find her, it almost threw me into convulsions; it made every fibre of my frame tremble again.

This indeed was bitter. But in the midst of bitterness, I found something fascinating, that said to me, Go on; steep your soul to the very lips in these melancholy recollections. I never willingly shut the book of grief, never sought to withdraw my thoughts from what saddened me. Grief was all my joy. All other things were disgusting, shrivelled and withered up my heart: this opened the sluices of my / affections; and I experienced a nameless satisfaction, when I felt that it was exhausting and destroying in me the principle of life.

The things that had no connection with Emilia, that did not talk to me of her who was the object of all my preferences, were insupportable. They occupied my time, but excited in me no interest. They called upon me for attention, which, when given, ran counter to every thing that I desired, and, when withheld, left me in deadly vacancy, disturbing the Lethe[a] of my spirit with its nothings, and importuning me with a consciousness of that existence which I would have given worlds to forget.

I busied myself among all those things, which told me that Emilia once had lived, and once had been mine. I turned over a thousand times the articles of her attire, and what had been the ornaments of her person. I doted on the desk at which she had been accustomed / to write, and the inkstand which had afforded her a medium for recording her thoughts. Her miniature, set round with brilliants,[b] and the back of which was ornamented with a lock of her

---

[a] In Greek mythology, a river in Hades that caused forgetfulness in those who drank its waters.
[b] Diamonds of the finest cut and brilliancy.

beautiful hair, was a companion of which I never tired. Her handwriting to my eyes was the masterpiece of the creation. The lines which her pen had traced were of unrivalled elegance and grace; and the words, which imaged on paper her sentiments and thoughts, were inimitable. Her style was the style in which angels would have desired to talk. I kept all the letters I had received from her in a casket; they were often on subjects that fastidious men would have sneered at, of the lightest and most evanescent nature, the pen dipped in the tints of the rainbow; but they were all precious to me; they contained some fragment of the soul of this 'divine perfection of a woman'.[a] I numbered them; I read them a thousand times; / and the last time they appeared to me as fresh as the first.

The late incomparable companion of my days had a truly original mind. She was naturally learned; she studied not the world through 'the spectacles of books',[b] or the teachings of her instructors; there was to her no medium, no 'seeing as through a glass darkly';[c] she communicated immediately with external nature, or with the living habits and tempers of her fellow-creatures. She was in this respect as if there had been no such thing as literature; by an intuitive discernment she read the book of nature, and all her conclusions were her own.

This circumstance had at all times given a peculiar charm to her talk. It was not a lesson, 'learned and conned by rote; set in a note-book'.[d] You were sure to hear from her something new; new in the substance of what she reported, or new in the manner in / which she saw the things she described. She viewed every thing in a way characteristic of herself; the temper, the wholesome frame of her mind, was as an aerial perspective, giving a fresh and enchanting hue of its own to every thing she observed. You gained an insight not only of the object itself; you received in addition that frame of an angelic spirit, which made her see the world in a manner in which perhaps no other person saw it, more harmonised, the colours blended, every part belonging to and altogether constituting a whole.

There was no preparation in any thing she delivered, no tint of affectation, no wrinkle produced by any retrospect to herself, her own glory, and the expectation to be admired for what she said, or what she did. When I sat, or when I walked with her, I saw the thoughts of her mind exactly as they rose. It was all simple, and at the same time all wise. Every thing was sound, every thing fresh and / sensible; and, if it had been written in a book, it would have shewn itself with the liveliness of Montaigne,[e] and the depth of thought we are

---

[a] *Richard III*, I. ii. 75.
[b] John Dryden, *Essay of Dramatic Poesy* (1668).
[c] 1 Cor., 13: 12 (adapted).
[d] *Julius Caesar*, IV. iii. 97 (adapted).
[e] Michel Eyquem de Montaigne (1533–92), French writer whose *Essays* established the essay as a literary genre.

accustomed to ascribe to Zoroaster.[a] It was prompt eloquence, a rapid and unimpeded stream. 'more tuneable than needed lute or harp to add more sweetness'.[b] It was a stream that enlivened its banks, while 'with fresh flowerets field and valley smiled',[c] and the heart of the hearer leaped with delight, and all his circulations became cheerful and gay. It was wisdom in its newest gloss, unblown upon, unfaded. She was indeed and in truth, 'fancy's child', while to your astonished sense she 'warbled her native woodnotes wild'.[d]

When I lost her, I at first loathed my existence. Wearisome nights were appointed to me. When I laid down, I said, When shall I arise, and the night be gone? I was full of tossings to and fro unto the dawning of the day. The light was importunate; food / was distasteful. The visits of my friends were past endurance; and solitude was intolerable. I longed to close my eyes, and shut out daylight for ever, to be gathered to my fathers, and be at rest.

There is something in man however, that will not let him be long at quiet. The first thing is the cravings of nature. The constitution of our existence is truly pourtrayed in the well-known story of the Ephesian matron.[e] However she gave herself up at first to the excess of her grief for her husband's death, and resolved to be shut up with him in his tomb, not many days had passed, before she felt the empire of human infirmity, and was glad of any thing that would deliver her from the monotony of her own meditations, and the eternal wearisomeness of days, 'that cream and mantle like a standing pool'.[f]

There is an indescribable something that ties us to life. For this purpose it is not necessary / that we should be happy. Though our life be almost without enjoyment, we do not consent to part with it. Without going to the extreme of Mæcenas,[g] who said, 'Though my hand, my foot, my hip should refuse their functions, though I have a mountain on my back, and my teeth be loosened in their sockets, nay, nail me, if you will, upon a cross, still I desire to live': without this, there is nevertheless a sentiment that stirs within us, that produces an undefinable aversion to the thought of ceasing to be, to 'lie in cold oblivion and to rot'.[h]

It was this that inspired Robinson Crusoe, or whoever was his actual

---

[a] Zoroaster, or Zarathustra (?628–?551 BC), Persian prophet, founder of the dualistic Zoroastrian religion.

[b] *Paradise Lost*, V. 151–2.

[c] *Paradise Lost*, VI. 784 (adapted).

[d] Milton *L'Allegro* (1632), 133–4.

[e] The Ephesian matron was so overcome by her husband's death that she spent whole days and nights mourning him in the tomb, refusing to eat. When a soldier discovered her plight he urged her to desist from useless grief and to share his wine and food. She refused at first, but eventually succumbed not only to the lure of the food but also to the soldier's advances, after which they spent three nights of secret love together (Petronius, *Satyricon*, Chs. CXI–CXII).

[f] *Merchant of Venice*, I. i. 89 (adapted).

[g] Gaius Maecenas (?70–8 BC), Roman statesman, adviser to Augustus, patron of Horace and Virgil.

[h] *Measure for Measure*, III. i. 117. The original reads 'obstruction', not 'oblivion'.

prototype, and has inspired every shipwrecked mariner, when he has found himself thrown upon a coast without human inhabitants.[a] It is a dreary thing to be cut off from the society of our fellows and the accommodations of civilised life. We should almost expect an individual so circumstanced, / as soon as he had had time to survey his forlorn situation, to climb a neighbouring promontory, and cast himself back into the element from which he had been rescued. But it is not so. He looks round, and begins to collect the fragments and broken planks of the vessel in which he had been embarked. He is like the wretch who watches a dying flame. He gathers together every combustible material that offers itself to his view, that he may detain the celestial visitor. He casts about and considers how he may supply himself with nourishment and shelter. He meditates perseveringly, and counts up all his resources. He shrinks from no labour. He is appalled by no privations. Life, life, is the inexplicable thing we cling to; and, however we may pretend to hold it cheap and to brave death when at a distance, we all of us, with very few exceptions, and those arising from a preternatural / tension, verify the apophthegm of the scripture, 'Skin for skin, yea all that a man hath, will he give for his life.'[b]

The mind of man bends itself after a short struggle to the yoke of necessity. 'Things without all remedy', are found to be 'without regard'.[c] We shut ourselves up within the compass of possibilities, and become reconciled to what cannot be avoided. There are indulgencies without which a man thinks he cannot live; there are benefits that seem to constitute the core and soul of our existence; but, when these can no longer be had, we make the best of what is still within our reach.

I considered, that I was young, that I had but recently come into the possession of all my faculties of body and mind. According to what is called the course of nature, I might live many years. Should I, out of the consideration of what I had lost, throw away what was left? Or, should I still, notwithstanding / the fearful wreck I had experienced, draw in my expectations and my desires, clip the wings of my aspirations, and suit my mind to the narrowness of my possessions? I was an exile, driven out for ever from the pleasant land where I had been so much delighted to dwell. I was condemned to abide under inclement skies, with dreary and unvarying prospects, and on a barren soil. Yet surely it was more worthy of the inherent energies of man, of the powers with which God had endowed me, to make the best even of this. I could exercise my mind in reading and contemplation. I possessed the property which had descended to me from my ancestors. With this, dispensed with judgment and a beneficent spirit, I could do much good: and he that does good to others, will

---

[a] The castaway of Daniel Defoe's novel *Robinson Crusoe* (1719) was modelled on Alexander Selkirk, marooned for four years on the island of Juan Fernandez in the South Pacific.
[b] Job 2: 4.
[c] *Macbeth* III. ii. 11–2.

infallibly catch the advantage on the rebound to himself. The world, in its revolutions and changes, is for ever new: I could observe this, and gather, unless by my own / fault, much instruction and excitement from what I saw.

I remembered the last injunctions of the adored partner of my life. She had adjured me to watch anxiously for the welfare of our only child. She had said to me, 'Now that our Catherine is about to be deprived of her mother, it is your office to take care that you discharge to her the duties of both, and be to her a father and a mother.' Now that I could no longer see my Emilia, no longer contribute to her pleasure, and be rewarded by her smiles, it was by so much the more incumbent upon me to build up a monument to her memory, and to regard her last suggestions as inviolable. Starting from this thought, I gradually came to regard her child as her living representative. I desired to heap all sorts of benefits on its head. I sought its society, not always, but often, and at stated returns. I found a thousand things in the child that reminded me / of Emilia, certain tones of her voice, certain movements of her limbs, now serious, and now playful. When these things occurred, they would sometimes shoot through me with the force of electricity, and at others all at once fill my eyes with an unexpected gush of tears. By degrees they grew less agonising, and changed into sources of melancholy pleasure.

Before I had been thus unhappily installed the sole guardian of my child, she had already attained in a certain measure the faculty of articulate speech, and by the condescension and judicious care of her mother had come to exercise it in a sounder style and with more reflection, than is usual in so early a period of life. But the constancy with which the child exercised the talent of reflection, and appeared to unrol and consult the volume of her thoughts, had by no means the effect to render her phlegmatic and slow. The consultation had the air of being instantaneous; the light / from heaven, so to express myself, that attended her, seemed mechanically to fall on the right passage, the very canon[a] that was wanted. It was like the difference I have seen in boys at school: while one boy of duller intellect pores down the page of his dictionary, and by dint of mere industry comes at last to the word and explanation required, another catches it in a moment; the rest of the page is as it were annihilated, and the thing that was sought presents itself alone to him. This felicity in my little Catherine converted what might have been meditation into inspiration, and gave to her otherwise original vein of thinking, the air of a spontaneous production. – The description I have here given may seem to be incompatible with the fewness of her years. But let it be considered that I studied her, made her a theme for my reflections, and marked the present state of her faculties with something of the same diligence, that an anatomist takes up / his dissecting knife, or a chemist resolves a complex substance into its simple elements. I

---

[a] A principle or accepted criterion applied in a branch of learning or art.

frolicked with her; I asked her questions, in a manner the furthest in the world from suggesting the gravity of my purpose. I appeared to be playing the fool with her the most egregiously, when I was most perseveringly engaged in experiments of the highest philosophy.

When I concentred my attention the most deeply in reading or writing, when I folded my arms, and sought to develop in my own mind the perplexed mazes of thinking, when I shut my eyes, and conjured up the image of Emilia, held conversations with the dear departed, and lived over the scenes of our recent intercourse as if they had been present, the little Catherine would often be seated in one corner of the apartment, and would sometimes race from end to end with her lapdog, uttering shouts of laughter, and making noises that might almost have awaked the dead. I was not interrupted; / I did not hear it. My mind was abstracted; my attention held on its course: such is the power of habit.

I would then suddenly thrust my table on one side, and say, Come, Kate, now play with me. Or she would occasionally insist on a similar pliancy on my part. At one time and another perhaps I did not attend to her infant importunities. In that case she would pluck my sleeve, or embrace my knee. This was always effectual. I instantly descended from my altitudes. Plato and Euclid were put to rout in a moment.[a] The only instances in which she failed, were when I was engaged in devotional intercourse with the fancied image or the intellectual representation of her mother. I would sometimes in that case snatch up my hat, and withdraw into the gloomiest recesses of my garden, while the child, impressed with awe, would follow me with its eye, and wonder what could be the matter with papa. /

Mrs Fanshaw would often desire that the child might be left for a while under her care; and Catherine spent almost as much of her time with this maternal friend, as at her own home. Mrs Fanshaw lived only twelve miles from my residence, and had no child of her own. She loved the little Catherine, I had almost said with more than a mother's affection. Between mother and child there is often no third party; and the elder of the two is, as we say, accountable only to God and her conscience. But Mrs Fanshaw was but the deputy of the real mother of my Catherine. She had a report to give in, and no principal to receive it. When an officer of state and his auditor pass their accounts together, the auditor writes his name at the bottom of the page, and this operates as a quietus. The officer is encouraged; the sanction of approbation is visible; and the officer proceeds with new courage to discharge the duties of the following quarter. But Mrs Fanshaw / could receive no such sanction: the image of Emilia was for ever before the eyes of her mind; but the

---

[a] Plato (427–347), Greek philosopher; Eucleides (fl. c. 300 BC), Greek mathematician whose geometry has become synonymous with his name.

divinity to whose approbation she aspired, preserved for ever the same passion-less placidity of features, and did not so much as once nod the head in token of honourable acquittal. This mute intercourse that subsisted between the living and the dead, gave to the former by so much the more tenderness and delicacy of conscience. For want of the final and solemn adjudication she would have sought, the surviving friend was compelled to be the auditor of her own accounts, and she revised them with unceasing diligence, in the fear that self-flattery might induce her to pronounce the sentence of peace, when there was no peace.

The time of the little Catherine was divided between two places of abode. She would have been puzzled to decide which she was to consider as her home; but that the servants of an / establishment always kindly exert themselves to remove this perplexity. The child was early instructed by her female attendant to consider herself as an heiress, and was assured that fortunate would be the youth, who should obtain such a beauty, with the estates of Deloraine, for his bride. Catherine loved me much; but she scarcely entertained less affection for the matron to whom her visits abroad were longest and most frequent, and who, to judge from her vivacity, the facility with which she entered into all her juvenile feelings and fancies, and the undiminished lustre of her cheeks and her eyes, might almost be taken for her sister. Mrs Fanshaw had infinitely the advantage of me as an instructor in one respect, inasmuch as she ever stood before Catherine as a model of female delicacy. This inestimable friend was a glass in which the child might look, and learn every quality, I might say every motion, that would most become her; / at the same time that the clearness of understanding, and the faultless truth of feeling, with which this lady explained every thing, and inculcated whatever was most worthy to be recollected in the progress through life, were such as I was never tired of admiring, but was never vain enough to imagine I could rival.

Mrs Fanshaw outlived the friend she so inexpressibly valued ten years. Each time that my daughter returned to me from the gracious and soul-improving visits she paid to this her second mother, I did not fail to remark her added proficiency. Her absences on the score of these visits gave me a fresh happiness in her society. The frailty of our nature is such, that that which presents itself to us each day as surely as the rising of the sun, never fails to be rated by us below its value, and to be regarded with a degree of negligence and apathy. For myself, I certainly cannot boast of a competition / with the gifted female in the story-book, who could hear the grass grow.[a] If my child had been with me uninterruptedly, I could not so well have marked her advancement. I do not doubt that with every day of her life she in various ways improved; but I should not have seen it. But now, that she came home to me it may be after five or six

---

[a] cf. Wordsworth, 'The Idiot Boy', ll. 282–6 (285), in *Lyrical Ballads* (1798).

weeks' absence, I immediately observed that she was another, yet the same. There was more breadth in her gestures, and new intelligence in her eye. Each happy day, that I understood, as it advanced, would bless me with the return of my Catherine, was a day of jubilee to me. When the carriage rolled up the avenue, when I hastened over the broad staircase to receive her, and she flew with light and elastic swiftness to my embrace, this little scene, which words can scarcely express, was like a new opening in the clouds, a new light spread over the horizon.

Before the death of Mrs Fanshaw, my child / had completed her thirteenth year. In females an air of consciousness and maturity comes earlier than in my own sex. With what new wonder and exultation did I now regard my daughter! She had been my plaything; she was now my friend. I had been accustomed to talk to her in a baby style, coming down from the marvellous elevation of a masculine understanding to the level of the battledore[a] and the bilbo-catch.[b] But now I could reason with her; and often I derived new lights from her unassuming and random suggestions. Now she could feel my feelings, sympathise with my joys and my sorrows, and be in the noblest sense my companion.

My life had not all been spent during this period in the mansion of Deloraine. I had migrated at something like the ordinary seasons to the metropolis. I had mixed in the fashionable and the political world. In one instance I had accepted a public mission to one of the / courts in the North of Europe, and had discharged the office intrusted to me to the satisfaction of the government that employed me. But my country-seat was the favourite place of my residence. Each time I returned to it with a new zest. My turn of mind led me to the secluded and domestic scene; and in this sense I was 'never less alone than when alone'.[c] I loved my books; I loved my pen; I loved my solitary rambles through the woods, and the endless train of my visions and meditations. /

---

[a] Small racket used in the ancient racket game of battledore and shuttlecock.
[b] Also known as bibler-catch or bilboquet, a game of cup and ball originally found in Norfolk and Sussex.
[c] Samuel Rogers, *Human Life* (1819), l. 763.

CHAPTER VI

When Mrs Fanshaw died, she had a sister who lived abroad with her husband
and a family of daughters, sometimes in the South of France, and sometimes in
different parts of Italy. Believing that my daughter would be in a somewhat
forlorn situation upon the death of her female protector, this lady invited the
young Catherine to come and spend a few months with her young people. The
first emotion I felt on the receipt of this invitation was chagrin. Catherine was
more than ever necessary to me; and I had imagined that, when Mrs Fanshaw
died, I should scarcely have had cause to part with her again. /

But upon second thoughts I condemned the selfishness of the hope and wish
I had entertained. My child must not be for ever shut up with her father. I did
not indeed live entirely out of the world. But I was not the most eligible
protector of her growing years; and it is almost universally admitted, that a
residence in different cities on the continent, an observation of the manners
and national characters of the kingdoms of the earth, and a familiarity with
their languages and modes of thinking acquired on the spot, have the happiest
effect in finishing the education of youth of either the male or female sex. It
happened that a family with which I had been on terms of cordial acquaintance
for years, was on the point of setting out for the very city where the sister of Mrs
Fanshaw resided; and I gladly accepted the opportunity which their overture
presented, for transporting my favourite in safety, and under the most eligible /
circumstances, to the place of her destination.

I received letters from my daughter from Paris, from Lyons, from Turin, and
the different cities she visited on her route. The pleasure these letters conveyed
to me was more than can easily be conceived. I loved her handwriting, which
was regular and delicate in an uncommon degree. I loved even her way of
folding a letter. I kissed the impression of an allegorical seal, suspended to a
watch which had once been her mother's, and was now hers. The tender
recollection of Emilia and her Catherine went to my heart as I viewed it. I never
beheld it, without feeling my eyes suffused with a tear of affection.

It is surprising in how many and in what unexpected ways the dear girl
expressed her regard for me as she wrote. But love was not the only subject of
her epistles. She set before my eyes by a few picturesque touches the provinces
/ she passed through, the busy scenes of Parisian life, the rich plains of
Languedoc, and the sublime and terrific precipices of the Alps. She spoke of
the societies into which she was introduced. There was nothing, or there

appeared to me to be nothing, of empty and common-place in her remarks. She saw every thing with eyes of the truest taste and the most impressive sensibility. Whoever was allowed the perusal of her letters would immediately observe in them, that she seized by a sort of divine intuition the clue which gave to every thing its just explanation and its becoming arrangement. Whatever she spoke of seemed under her observation to exhibit a delicacy, a vividness, a sweetness, for which it was indebted to the disposition of her that wrote concerning it. When she breathed upon roses, they assumed an added fragrancy. The places she visited I had also seen; I recollected the main outline; but in her description / it was as if the pencil of Claude or of Gaspar Poussin had passed over the landscape, and brought forth at one point and another hidden beauties, which but for their inspiration would never have been revealed.[a] As I read her communications, I became reconciled to the temporary loss of her society. I saw what infinite advantage she was gaining from this admirable unfolding of her faculties. I felt that it would have been foul sacrilege to have deprived her of opportunities which afforded her so rich and golden a harvest. She remained abroad with this family nearly six years.

It was during the absence of my daughter on the continent, that I was attacked with a fever of the most dangerous nature. It was a species of typhus. It was accompanied with great depression of spirits, a want of power to interest myself in any object of pursuit, a disinclination to engage in amusement and to all kinds of exertion, and a total want of appetite. / Life seemed incapable of yielding excitement, and existence was a burthen to me. My nights were without sleep and restless; a low fever appeared to be undermining my vital functions. My flesh gradually wasted away; the colour of my skin became dark and inky; death seemed advancing upon me by sure and unremitting strides; and, though consciousness, or more properly the power of receiving impressions remained, my outward appearance in many respects scarcely differed from that of a corpse.

After a course of several weeks the fever subsided; but it left me in a state of such extreme debility, that it was judged more than probable that death would be the result. I did not however die. But it was long, very long, before I recovered any degree of strength, or was strictly speaking out of danger. My appearance was that of a walking ghost: and all who shrunk from the alarm of a *memento / mori*,[b] shunned to encounter me. I seemed like a person dug up from a grave; and it was a long time before I could walk across my room without help. By degrees I was got down stairs, and into my garden, where it was a great refreshment to sit on the benches, to inhale the balmy air, and to

---

[a] Claude Lorrain, pseudonym of Claude Gelée (1600–82), French painter noted for his subtle depiction of light in idealised landscapes; Gaspard Poussin (1615–75), French landscape painter.
[b] (Latin) 'remember you must die' used to describe an object, often a skull, intended to remind people of the inevitability of death.

enjoy the pleasing warmth of the sun. An easy chair proceeding gently upon the lawns of my garden, or the slopes of the park, was the next step in my recovery.

I was anxious that my daughter should not be made acquainted with the danger of my condition. She was eligibly situated with young ladies of her own age. Her mind was opening and expanding among the new countries and scenery that she visited. Of what use could she be to me, if she were at home? She was too young for a nurse; and I felt happy that she was spared the gloomy and depressing scene of a sick chamber, and, as it / might be, of a death-bed. Near as I had been to the gates of the grave, I was led to reflect on the situation in which she would be left, if deprived of her sole surviving parent, and to revise the provisions I had already made for the years of her minority, in case that event should occur.

My recovery once ascertained, I proceeded with sure, but lingering steps in the reestablishment of my health. I travelled by very short stages from one place to another, thus procuring to myself moderate excitement without fatigue. I staid sometimes two or three days in a place, or went forward without interval, as fancy or convenience suggested. During my route I passed the country-seats of several persons with whom I was more or less upon familiar terms, but I visited none. I could not have borne the disquiet which such scenes would have produced, or submitted to the observance and attention to others which / they would have imposed upon me. I was accompanied by a young person, the son of an early friend, who was the most accommodating companion in the world. He was all gentleness, all vigilance, of the sweetest temper imaginable. When I was disposed to retire into myself, he took care not to disturb me. When I shewed indications of a frame inclined to communication and amusement, he had a particular adroitness in adapting himself to my humour. He could talk of poetry, of history, of scenery, of arts, and the world. His remarks were not deep, but sensible, utterly free from pretence and affectation, unintrusive, and with that sort of agreeable animation, which frequently attends the morning of life. His society did me a world of good, and I never tired of it. – This person will come again on the stage at a later period of my story. /

CHAPTER VII

My journey was brought to a close for the present at the village of Harrowgate in Yorkshire, a spot frequented in certain seasons of the year for the imputed virtues of its spa, and of which the air is incontestibly salubrious and invigorating. A residence in this place I was assured would be considerably beneficial to me; and the society was easy; every one without remark mixing in it as much or as little as he pleased.

The scene on the whole was highly agreeable to me. The health of the human frame may be considered as a negative attribute, of which we have in a manner no feeling at those / times when we most unequivocally possess it. It is only by comparison that we are enabled to apprehend its value. For myself, I had been so long in a state of deadness and languor, that the simplest enjoyments came to me like the dawn of a new life. The flowers never smelled so sweet, the skies never looked with so celestial a blue; the song of the birds, and the murmur of the waters supplied to me a ravishing gratification. The joy was however short; I soon became exhausted; and then sunk into no unpleasing listlessness. I often fell asleep in the shade, the breezes of heaven playing on my cheek; and my dreams were then all of soft and unexhausted pleasure; the cup no longer overflowing, but the savour and the sense remaining. The very frame and articulations of my body were like a new possession to me; I was agreeably surprised to find my limbs move easily and without pain, and that I once more engrossed in no contemptible / proportion the attributes of a human being.

Among the persons I encountered at Harrowgate there was one that particularly engaged my attention. This was a young lady of the name of Margaret Borradale. She was of a slight figure, but exquisitely delicate and beautiful. When I met her, she was about three-and-twenty years of age. I was already forty-two. I was told that she had been of a fine complexion, in which the roses and the lilies vied with each other. But the roses were now all faded. Her skin was as fair and as smooth as marble. There was a melancholy in her countenance, the most interesting that can be imagined. Her eyes had entirely lost the light of youth; and she seemed scarcely to notice the things around her.

She was at Harrowgate accompanied by her parents. She went into society, because they desired it; but her thoughts were not in the / places where she was corporeally present. Her air was disconsolate and neglected. She spoke occasionally; she sung; she danced. The melody of her tones was inconceivably touching; her dancing was characterised with a pathetic languor. Those who had been acquainted with her before, described her as the ghost only of the resplendent being they had formerly known; but the ghost presented to you, though in a faint and half-obliterated outline, the image of something inexpressibly engaging. Fancy unavoidably went on to fill out the picture; and the spectator perhaps admired it the more, because it was in some measure his own creation, melting into thin air when the enthusiasm with which you contemplated it was turned away and gone. She was a being not of this world; she was a monumental statue personating the thing that had been; she was like those creatures we read of in the fairy tales, touched by the wand of a malignant enchanter, / condemned never again to mix in the realities of life, but still retaining a portion, however incomplete, of vitality and sense, still mournful and sad, and destined never to rise again into interest and energy and hope.

Her story was a sad one. She had been crossed in love. Her father had been a younger brother. He had married imprudently; and he had brought up his daughter in great retirement, and in a way little calculated to stir up in her ambitious thoughts. They lived on an income of a few hundreds a year. Their residence was among villagers; and the first hints of youthful affection were awakened in her bosom towards a stripling of her own age, who resided at a short distance from her father's dwelling, named William. He was the only son of his mother. He had been some years absent under the care of an uncle; but, upon the death of his father, a simple farmer, in the occupation of two hundred acres of land, / he was recalled to the parental roof, that he might be the stay, the comforter and assistant of her who bore him. He was eighteen, a blooming youth, with active limbs, dark-brown, curling hair, and a heart, the softest and gentlest that ever dwelt in a human bosom. His uncle had been the member of a college, and William had gained a larger range of ideas, and much intellectual improvement, while he lived under the guidance of this relative.

Had he been uninterruptedly the neighbour of Margaret, they would neither of them perhaps have been so much struck with the other. But, as it was, their feelings were those of ancient neighbourhood, combined with the novelty that is peculiar to love at first sight. They had been playfellows; and they felt the confidence and familiarity which that relation, when connected with agreeable qualities and accordant dispositions, seldom fails to produce. And yet, meeting, as they now did, after / years of separation, neither of them could think the other the same being as at the period at which they parted. Their former familiarity had been that of children, without apprehension, without consciousness, the mere exuberance of youthful spirits, void of all feeling of sex, except as the party more robust of muscle and limb is instinctively delicate in his treatment of the frailer flower, and as the female, with an obscure and undefined anticipation of the scenes of after-life, occasionally practises a few coquetries, or imposes a task on her more athletic associate, or ridicules his awkwardnesses, or laughs him out of some fit of unseasonable gravity.

But now, in the renewed acquaintance of the two, they each felt that they were entering upon a more important scene of existence. They did not suppose, as is frequently the case in the buoyant and idler hours of youth, that each day was a duration by itself, cut off from / all that had preceded or might follow, and that what was done in each successive period involved no consequences, and imparted no colour of its own to what was to come. They felt that life was a serious affair, that whatever they did had a responsibility attached to it, and might mark for good or for evil the character or fortune of the party that acted, or the party that was the object of what was done. They looked into it therefore with a keener eye and a more awakened mind. Their apprehension was alive. Sometimes they blushed; sometimes their speech faltered and was broken; and sometimes, even when they smiled, or laughed outright with unrestrained gaiety, there was more passed on one side or the other, than any external indications gave expression to.

William and Margaret were the same as they had been in the early years of their acquaintance. They were the same; and yet / how different! The comparison was as between the rosebud, and the flower still young, fresh and untarnished, but arrayed with all the glory that nature out of her inexhausted storehouse is accustomed to bestow. It was in the manner of the metamorphoses of the ancient mythology. If narrowly examined, you detected the identity; the elements were what they had previously been. But, oh, how resplendent was the form which now presented itself! There was the same sweetness of disposition, ever accommodating officious and complying, the same frankness, the same generosity, the same warmth of spirit and congeniality of soul; but how expanded, how assured, how full of tender heart and pregnant meaning!

As they dwelt near each other, they encountered every day, perhaps several times in a day. The unrestrained intercourse in which they lived, had however, one singular effect. / That which might be done at any time, still remained undone. They in fact scarcely adverted to the situation in which they were mutually placed. They were lost a thousand fathoms deep in love, before they knew that they loved. They were happy in each other's presence; they were uneasy and restless in absence. They dwelt on each other's voice; they repeated each other's words; their dreams had but one subject; the principal person in those wild plots which make the story of our sleeping hours, was still the same. If they read, they each imagined the other to be at hand, and did not so much consider how the reflections and paintings of the author affected themselves, as how they would be received by the other. Their union of hearts was like a deep, pellucid stream, which, flowing over an even bed, and meeting with no interruption, passed on unnoticed; while the same stream, if opposed, or on uneven ground, leaping from / rock to rock, would shew that it was omnipotent, and that no power on earth had strength to arrest its progress. They talked of every thing out of themselves; the beauties of nature, the beauties of literature, the irregularities of climate, the change of the seasons, the flowers, the crops, the animals. They were both botanists; both delighted to observe the various habits

45

and instincts of the animal creation. They were both fond of music. They sometimes sang in concert, and at other times called in the aid of the instrumental to give variety and copiousness to the natural music of the voice. William became the instructor of Margaret, a little in language, more in science and matters of literary taste; and it is well known how critical the relation of tutor and pupil often becomes between persons of opposite sexes, when both are just advanced on the threshold of life.

It is indeed specially characteristic of the / passion of love, that it has the faculty of giving a perpetual flow to the interchange of sentiments and reflections in conversation. The parties feel no reserve with each other; they are eager to communicate every thing that is new; no remark seems insignificant; and every thing that is said is sure to experience a favourable reception. They learn more and more to think alike; and it is scarcely in human nature that we should feel weariness or disgust in hearing our own sentiments articulated by the lips of our companion. This is a genuine and natural echo, that will be listened to for ever. Between lovers the modulations of the voice are always delightful in the one who speaks to the one who hears; and the expressive varieties of the countenance, the gesticulations of sentiment, of gaiety, of tenderness, of disapprobation, of light-heartedness and frolic mirth, afford endless occasions of observation and interest. /

CHAPTER VIII

In this manner the days of these lovers, for such they were, glided on in an Elysian[a] tranquillity, till a mere accident had the effect of producing a striking change in their situation. The mother of William had been absent for several weeks, on a visit to a friend who dwelt at a distance of one hundred and fifty miles. William, as I have already said, was the stay, the comforter and assistant of her who bore him, and had been recalled to her side by the decease of his father. He amply supplied to her the place of the protector she had lost. He had always been remarked for his duty as a child; and now, that his mother had no other / domestic friend, he had greatly increased in his assiduity and affection towards her. They were all the world to each other, with no considerable exception, unless the embryo and unexplained passion he entertained for

---

[a] Of or relating to Elysium, or Elysian fields, in Greek mythology the dwelling place of the blessed after death.

Margaret. The time was come when he expected his mother to return; the day of her arrival was fixed; and William was to proceed some miles upon the road, to meet her and escort her home. The hour of meeting drew nigh; and the youth had already gone to the stable, and was about to harness his horse to the simple vehicle, in which he was accustomed to accompany his mother in her little recreations, when a messenger arrived with a letter, informing him that an unexpected circumstance had occurred, which would oblige her to defer her return from the Wednesday to the Saturday following.

In the little *ménage*[a] of the widow's house, the absence of the mistress was of course / strongly felt: she and her son had been accustomed to sit down with no other companion to their simple board. He had felt his late solitary state as a privation; he had counted upon the return of his mother as upon one of the bright days in his calendar. He had taken care to have the house 'swept and garnished' in the way that he knew would please her best.[b] He had the garden put in the exactest order, and a few vases containing those productions of Flora which were her special favourites, ranged in the window. He had begun to watch the weather, and to count the hours. He called over the little events of the house and the homestead, which he was sure it would gratify her to hear, and eagerly anticipated the pleasure it would give him to encounter her well-known and much-loved features, and to light up the smile of maternal approbation in her venerated countenance. It therefore struck a damp upon him, to have this near approaching / delight deferred even for three days. He murmured. He felt that all the mighty store of his affection and attachment had been waked up, and brought into unusual activity, to be now repressed with blank disappointment.

He had no sooner perused the billet of his mother, than he shut the stable-door, went to the house to announce the altered arrangement to their female domestic, and sauntered into the fields. Mechanically he turned his steps to a knoll, which had been a favourite haunt of himself and Margaret. The young person who was the object of his secret partiality, knew the way in which his morning was destined to be employed, and proposed to herself the pleasure, unseen and alone, of remarking the little features of the scene, all of which were in so many ways associated with her William. She expected no interruption, and was fully disposed to give way to her feelings after that mode, which we only employ / when we imagine ourselves secure against the being witnessed by human eye or ear. Solitude has its special prerogatives; and we talk to ourselves, where solitude reigns, in a franker, I had almost said a tenderer style, than we indulge in to the brother of our soul, or to the mistress of our most secret affections.

---

[a] (French) household.
[b] Matt. 12: 44.

47

As Margaret felt certain that William was at a distance, so William, per-suaded that at this time he could not be expected near the accustomed brow, had not the slightest anticipation of meeting her. He had been pondering upon his mother. He had been calling up all the little circumstances and thoughts with which he had purposed to gratify her at meeting. From thence his mind had wandered to the recollection of his infant days, and so forward even to the hour of his present review. So far as his mother was concerned, it was all delightful. He remembered her anxieties, the vigilance with which she had ever provided for / his welfare and comfort, how she had smoothed for him the pillow of sickness, the tears she had shed over his disappointments, the sweet smiles which had illumined her countenance when she saw him entering with full relish into such pleasures as she provided, or as occurred in the simple scheme of their life. His heart was entirely open. His thoughts were unclad even with that simple armour of which we are almost never divested in any of the intercourses of society. His bosom was laid bare, and seemed to court the gentle, yet enlivening and health-giving breeze, with which the year in its most genial moments visits the breast of mortals.

He had proceeded for some time with his arms folded, or with his left hand on his chin, in that attitude into which we inadvertently fall, when we are in the act of recollecting something which had almost escaped us. Anon he spread his hands abroad in the fulness of his / emotion. His step was irregular, and would occasionally grow rapid as if he trod on air. He stopped again. His eyes would then be cast upwards, with the kind of devotion we feel, without being aware of it, in the remembrance of that for which we might well be thankful to the mysterious power, which 'careth for us' in things in which we are least able to care for ourselves.[a] His cheeks glowed with pleasure. His eyes were moist with that soft suffusion which comes over mortals, when most impressed with the joys of affectionate sentiment. Margaret perceived him; her first emotion was that of surprise at seeing him there, which was succeeded by an impulse to observe him, that made her for some time careful neither by sound nor gesture to break in upon the current of his thoughts. She was very near him, still without being remarked.

Suddenly, by the mere effect of accident, he / turned his eye, and saw the beloved of his soul. There was a stile between them. With the rapidity of agile youth he vaulted over it. 'With love's light wings did he o'er perch' this trivial obstacle, and in a moment was by her side.[b] His soul was already harmonised to every thing that was tender, and frank, and ingenuous. This was an instant in which all reserve was out of the question. He could not but speak all he felt. He had a window in his bosom, less for the use of the bystander than for his own in

---

[a] 1 Peter 5: 7 (adapted).
[b] *Romeo and Juliet*, II. ii. 66 (adapted).

which he could read all secret things, thoughts which even to his own spirit had been hitherto unknown. It is of the nature of the human mind, that one emotion flows into another of a similar species; and small is the interval between the love of a son for his mother, and the love of a swain for the mistress of his affections. His soul was worked up to the highest pitch by the musings that had occupied his mind; the spirit of Margaret / had been elated, as she stood mutely contemplating the emotions and the loveliness of her friend. The sentiments of the one flowed into the channel and swelled the stream of the sentiments of the other. It was like the meeting of rivers, the marriage of the Thames and the Medway,[a] as commemorated by the poet,

> Whose blended waters are no more distinguished,
> But roll unto the sea one common flood.[b]

My Margaret! exclaimed William, are you here? Oh, what can make me happier than this encounter? I did not know before, how much I loved you. – Yes, loved you!

> Dearer than eyesight, space and liberty,
> Beyond what can be valued rich or rare.[c]

Till now, I knew only the pleasure I enjoyed when we were together. I attended only to what you said, the sweetness of your tones, the ineffable beauty of your looks. But now I think of you, of the spring from which these / transcendent excellencies arise. I think of you as that without which I cannot live. I must have you perpetually near me, familiar as the air I breathe, indefeasible as the vital heat which gives me existence, and is my existence. The glances of your eye, the smiles of your countenance, the tones of your voice, constitute my nourishment; all else is vegetation; but this is happiness. This only gives me power to think, to act, and to enjoy. I cannot bear to be without your presence; or, whenever I am so, the time must be short; only as long as the frame of mind you have given me can continue unimpaired. You must be every thing to me; I must be the thing you love best. Till now I never made love to you. I thought only of you as the most inestimable of friends. I was restrained by ideas of decorum. I was afraid lest, if I overstepped a certain bound, your delicacy might take the alarm. But now I can be silent no longer. I understand / my own sentiments; the veil that hid me from my observation is removed. – You must not be offended with me; you will not be offended; for, if I continued silent, I should die. /

---

[a] The River Medway flows through Kent, emptying into the estuary of the River Thames off the Isle of Sheppey.
[b] Quotation unidentified.
[c] *King Lear*, I. i. 56–7.

CHAPTER IX

It was not long after this that a circumstance occurred, in which William had the good fortune of apparently saving the life of Margaret. She had been engaged in a casual visit to a young female of her own age, who lived little more than a mile from the abode of her parents. On her return the girl had accompanied her part of the way home. Soon after they separated, Margaret had occasion to enter and pass through a field into which thirty or forty oxen had been turned to graze. Unfortunately she had a little dog with her, that was the ordinary companion of her perambulations. The animals that fed in the field were not indeed so / formidable and ferocious as bulls; but, like bulls, they felt the effect of the season of the year, and at certain periods were more gamesome and ungovernable than was their ordinary wont. Margaret had not been without adverting to the hazard which might attend her passing through this field. She caught up the dog in her arms, which was indeed no other than a lap-dog, and with this precaution concluded that she should proceed without accident. But the dog felt something of the same sort of stimulus to which the cattle were subject. There is a sympathy in these creatures, by which they understand each other's minds in a way that we cannot explain. The dog became restless, and with a sudden spring escaped from his mistress's arms, and was in the midst of his enemies in a moment. With his yelping and barking, and flying in this direction and that, he compelled their attention and annoyed them. The tables then speedily became turned. / The aggressor was filled with terror; and the pursued were now the pursuers. The cattle, excited first by the irritation and impertinence of their assailant, and next stimulated by society and imitation and the common impulse which pervaded the whole herd, entered into a confederate rally against the foe. As the cause that moved them had more in it of disturbance than terror, they played a thousand antics, and ramped about the field, still however from moment to moment forming a closer line of advance.

It happened that the field was circumscribed on one side by the course of the river Severn, and that its verge in that quarter was a cliff descending towards the water, and of surface almost perpendicular. The cattle were on the other side of the field. The dog, when he found that he had roused a whole host of enemies, ran to his mistress for protection. The animals pursued. Margaret immediately became aware / of her danger. What would be the issue she knew not. The oxen continued to direct their attention and vengeance against the dog. Whether they would ultimately come to regard her and the dog as leagued in a common cause, and alike meriting their hostility, was uncertain. Their horns, if they sought to wreak their injury on her, were weapons not to be set light by. The least evil that could happen was that she would be thrown down, and trampled on successively by the feet of the whole herd. But she had no time for reflection; she retreated as they advanced; they pressed upon her closer and closer; they drove her to the edge of the precipice; the ground gave way under her feet; and she fell from a height of sixty or seventy feet.

William was in a boat on the river, at no great distance from the shore, for the purpose of fishing. He saw the scene that was going on, though very imperfectly. He saw the / cattle in the field in an extraordinary state of commotion and violence. He saw the figure of a female who seemed as it were in the midst of the herd; there was an indefinable something in her appearance, which suggested to him the idea of his Margaret. What it could be that introduced such a thought into his mind, it is difficult to conceive. The whole was so foreshortened and contracted by distance, that the cattle were scarcely bigger than kittens new yeaned,[a] and the rooks and crows, that seemed to be disturbed by the scene, and were taking their flight over the river, shewed like so many insects. But the truth of the suggestion that thus arose in his mind, was not required to rouse him to exertion, and to advance towards the spot. He could scarcely doubt that what he saw was a young female in imminent distress and peril.

In a moment he forced his boat on the beach, and leaped ashore. Swifter than thought he / began to climb the opposed ascent. Accustomed to scenes of rural exertion, his limbs had an almost unparalleled nimbleness and agility. He was ready to accomplish what the poet speaks of, and 'run up a hill perpendicular'.[b] He had climbed but a small part of the ascent, and was endeavouring, by means of catching at a stunted and gnarled shrub that had struck its roots into a fissure of the rock, to give himself breath and strength for a further start, when he saw the unhappy girl tumbling with frightful velocity over the precipice, and threatening to fall almost upon his head.

It is one of the marvellous properties of the human mind, that, while on ordinary occasions the march of our ideas seems to go on at a certain steady and prescribed pace, we are no sooner placed in a situation of peculiar and unprecedented excitement, than our souls, so to speak, break away at once from the routine to which they are accustomed, and think a million / of thoughts in a moment, not in a wild, incoherent and hurried train, but with all their incidents and reasonings. The very inebriation, as it were, of our spirits, steadies and sobers us. The man who would escape from a house on fire, bursts

---

[a] Newborn.
[b] *Henry IV, Part I*, II. iv. 343–4 (adapted).

through bars and bolts which on any other occasion he would have judged proof against ten times his power, and, like Samson in the Bible, ropes twisted a hundred fold, are in his hands 'as flax that had been burned'.[a] His whole energy and resolve becomes as one concentrated effort; and he possesses at once the penetration of a sage, and the strength of a giant.

The female, as she fell from the summit of the rock, would have descended directly on the head of William; but he steadied his body, by the hold, as was already said, of the shrub which was rooted on its surface, and fixed his eye with intent gaze on the falling figure. As it approached, he swayed himself head and / shoulders to one side, and then, stretching out the hand that was free on the other, succeeded in catching hold of some of the girl's garments. This action arrested the progress of her fall for an instant; but in the next the momentum and impulse which was thus given to the young man, proved too strong for the slender support the shrub afforded, and William and Margaret were hurried together down to the path below. What remained however of the descent was comparatively small; the frightful velocity with which Margaret had been falling was effectually checked, and the force with which she would otherwise have reached the plain, was no longer fatal. She received some bruises in the fall, but they were inconsiderable. By some mischance which it is impossible accurately to explain, William was found to have dislocated his shoulder. Several workmen were near the spot below, where the accident terminated; and the female and her deliverer were speedily conveyed / to a place of safety. After the reduction[b] of the dislocated limb, William wore his arm for some time in a sling; and the sensibilities of both parties towards each other experienced a considerable addition from the adventure of that day. Margaret felt that she was indebted for her life to the gallantry, the discretion and firmness which William had put forth at the moment: the scarf that he wore was to her a permanent memorial and an affecting trophy of his exploit. That they had thus been united on an occasion of so extraordinary peril, mutually endeared them to each other. The scene occurred to them again and again on both sides in their dreams. The deliverer and the delivered fondly dwelt on each other's excellencies and virtues in their waking contemplations: they were all the world to each other. To two persons who had passed through so terrible a trial together, the idea of their ever hereafter being separated and becoming indifferent / to each other, was little less than blasphemy. The pulses of their hearts beat in entire harmony; they were like the twins I have some-where read of, who on whatever kingdom or shore of the earth they were cast, however separated by mountains, deserts, and tracts of the unbounded sea, felt each other's sensations, were subjected to the same infirmities, sickened with

---

[a] Judg. 15: 14.
[b] After being restored to its normal position.

the same disease, and at one indivisible instant expired, the spirit which animated them returning at once to its place. /

CHAPTER X

I have already mentioned that the father of Margaret, though living at present in the most unaffected rural simplicity, still retained the notion that he belonged to another class, and was of a higher order of beings, than the inglorious neighbourhood by which he was surrounded. Since he had been discarded by his more opulent relatives, he had indeed sought to make a virtue of necessity, and had pretended, even perhaps to his own heart, to 'scorn delights, and live laborious days', to be fully reconciled to his lot, and to think of himself no better than the village hinds in the midst of whom he dwelt.[a] But the spark of ambition, / though smothered in him, was not extinct; favourable circumstances might yet fan it into a flame.

Such circumstances occurred. Lord Borradale, the head of his house, had heard of the beauty of Margaret. He resided at a distance in the North of England; and, when his kinsman, the father of Margaret, had been discarded by his family, pride, or shame, or some similar feeling, had impelled *him* to retire into the West. Lord Borradale was a man of the most cultivated taste; but of a singularly cold and unimpassioned heart. In early life he had been a great traveller; he had visited France and Italy, and had even passed into Greece and the East in search of the remains of ancient architecture and art. He had been careful to take with him draughtsmen and designers, who should enable him to bring away an exact representation of the most approved models. He shipped off for his native seat a large collection / of fragments, however imperfect, of statues, that were supposed to be the works of Phidias and Praxiteles.[b]

When at length he ceased from his wanderings, and resolved henceforth to take up his principal residence on the lands of his ancestors, the first thing upon which he resolved was to rase to the ground the mansion which had been built by them in the reign of Henry the Third,[c] and which from age to age they had

---

[a] Milton, *Lycidas* (1637), 72.

[b] Phidias (5th century BC), Greek sculptor, famed for his sculptures of the Parthenon and the colossal statue of Zeus at Olympia; Praxiteles (4th century BC), Greek sculptor, whose work included the statue of Hermes at Olympia.

[c] Henry III (1207–72), King of England from 1216.

piously preserved and beautified. He then set himself to fix on a spot about half a mile removed from the site of the old house, that appeared to him better to correspond with the suggestions of Italian taste. He studied indefatigably the delineations and rules of Vitruvius and Palladio.ª And, when at length he had built himself a house to his mind, he began to adorn it with such furniture, statues and pictures, as he thought would redound most to the credit of his taste. In particular he had / constructed a spacious gallery, which by its sinuosities might conduct the wandering spectator to the inspection of still new and inexhaustible beauties.

Lord Borradale had one son, an only child. His lordship knew that he should not himself live for ever; and therefore he directed some of his principal anxieties to this son. If he died without issue, the estate would fall into the hands of a distant branch; and they might pay no respect to the improvements he had achieved, and the wonders he had collected. From his son, bred under his eye, he expected a better taste, and hoped for a more filial regard. And he was anxious in future generations still to hand down the monuments, which owed their existence or their locality to his exertions.

While he was thus employed, and such were the subjects of his contemplations, it happened by some accident that a miniature of Margaret / fell into his hands. He regarded it as of exquisite beauty; the features appeared to him to be moulded upon the purest Grecian examples. The thought struck him that nothing was wanting to complete his columns and porticoes, and the succession and variety of his statues, but the placing the person from whom this miniature was drawn at the head of his circle. He therefore delayed not a moment to open a negotiation with her father. He commissioned an artist of high character to proceed to the neighbourhood of her residence, to furnish him with a whole-length portrait of the maiden with whose features he had been so powerfully struck. And, presently following in person, he brought about an interview with her father, to whom he communicated the project he had conceived. This poor, but rootedly ambitious man, was but too easily seduced to listen to the proposition. The idea of being placed at his ease in point of expenditure, / of being associated with persons of rank, and seeing his daughter united to the heir of the elder branch of his house, had charms in his eyes which he felt himself unable to resist. His wife, a woman of good dispositions, but who had never been accustomed to contradict the will of her husband, was with little difficulty prevailed upon to enter into his views: and a consultation was speedily held, how most effectually to put an end to what they were now willing to call the unworthy amour in which their daughter had been engaged.

ª Marcus Vitruvius Pollio (1st century BC), Roman architect, noted for his treatise *De architectura*, the only surviving Roman work on architectural theory and a major influence on Renaissance architects, such as Andreas Palladio (1508–80), whose symmetrical neo-Roman designs for villas and palaces profoundly influenced 18th century domestic architecture in England and North America.

The plan fixed on for this purpose was to lose no time to accomplish the removal of Margaret and her family from the western province, where she had been born, and had spent her earlier years to the present moment, to a cottage which was tendered to their acceptance upon the estate of lord Borradale. The motive for this removal was for some time / kept a secret. Margaret regretted the distance which would thus be interposed between her and the polestar of her affections; but she was totally unsuspicious of the design which prompted this revolution. The lovers bade each other adieu with a mournful feeling; a sad anticipation beset them, as the carriage approached which was to convey Margaret to a distant home. Scarcely a day had passed for the preceding twelve months without some personal communication; now it was uncertain when they should meet again. They promised each other however a perpetual commerce of letters; they promised that at a certain hour of every day they would not fail, however circumstanced, to retire that they might think of each other. The consolation on both sides would be inexpressibly great, that was afforded by the consciousness, 'Now my William – now my Margaret is employed in the contemplation of our mutual loves: we cannot see / each other's features, we cannot hear each other's voice with the gross organs of sense; but we can with the organs of the mind. He speaks, I answer; he replies, I rejoin: shall not this mitigate to us the sorrows of absence?'

They mutually vowed to each other, that their separation should not endure: the following spring should put an end to it, and unite them for ever. The father saw with astonishment and alarm the strength of their attachment. He had not the courage, he did not think it the wisest way, to oppose the tide of affection in its full career. He judged that new scenes and new connections would do the business more effectually. Amidst the splendours of Borradale Castle Margaret would speedily forget the low and inglorious pleasures she had once prized on the banks of the Severn. It could not be, that the noble blood that flowed in her veins should not, in the / favourable position in which she was about to be placed, assert its origin. All, the old man assured himself, would go well; and the triumph he aspired to would only be the better secured, by his pursuing it in caution and silence. His praise would be like that of Fabius in the Roman story, who by deferring the contest and avoiding a battle, accomplished the overthrow of Hannibal.[a]

They accordingly proceeded on their journey, and finally reached in safety the *cottage ornée*[b] that was provided for them. They had scarcely unpacked their moveables, and admired the elegant accommodations of the residence which had been prepared for them, when lord Borradale and his son appeared,

---

[a] Quintus Fabius Maximus Verrucosus (d. 203 BC), Roman general and statesman called Cunctator (the delayer) for this tactics as commander of the Roman army during the second Punic War 218–202 BC against the Carthaginian general Hannibal (247–182 BC).

[b] Picturesque and well-appointed cottage.

to welcome their arrival, and to conduct them on a visit to the seat of their ancestors. Margaret could not but admire to a certain degree the magnificence of what she saw. It was all in a manner new to her; and much of it had an / elegance, a beauty and a taste, that forcibly appealed to the soundness and purity of her power of perception.

But such was by no means the case with the youth who offered himself to her approbation. He was coxcombical, empty and conceited. He had in a certain degree the faculty to learn and to imitate. But he had not the soil of the mind: all that he learned lay like manure upon a hungry and impenetrable surface. It never mixed with the stratum beneath, and only deformed what under kindlier circumstances it might have enriched, and have rendered both ornamental and useful. He was incapable of sympathy and generous feeling. He was not indeed ill-natured; but he was pedantic, and formal, and thought only of himself. He would have appeared to more advantage, if he had taken less pains. If he had given nature her way, he would at least not have been offensive. But he was perpetually studying / how he should present himself, and how to make the most advantageous impression. With all this he was very slenderly endowed with the gifts of the mind. But his phrases were studied; his gestures full of affectation; he could not laugh or smile but by rule. He was essentially a dull person. He could never learn the things his father desired to have him learn; he was incapable of any thing liberal or noble; but he was apt and adroit in imitating the weaknesses and follies of those among whom he lived. The figure he presented therefore was all in shadow; there were no striking lights that fell upon it; nothing was firm or great; it was all obscure, misty and opake. Yet he never intended any harm; he was incapable of malignity. His only fault was that of an exuberant self-sufficiency. He was insipid, but pert. At the same time he was unboundedly pliant to whatever his father dictated to him. Lord Borradale told him / that it was proper and suitable that he should marry his cousin; and he was prepared to go through the forms, and make her his bride.

It may easily be conceived what a contrast he presented in the eyes of Margaret to the youth she had left in the West. William was all fire and soul. Every thing he said was pregnant with sense, and still more abounded with feeling. He was impetuous; and he was natural. He never considered twice of what he should say, or what he should do. His first thoughts were full of understanding, and still more of grace. Margaret and he understood each other intuitively, and almost without the aid of words. The heir apparent of the barony of Borradale for ever pumped up his thoughts, turned them on every side, and admired them, before they found their way to his lips. With William the days of Margaret flew like hours, and hours like minutes. But between these new companions the conversation on the part / of the admirer was all effort, and on the part of Margaret every thing passed in insupportable languor and fatigue.

There was that in the character of William which resembled witchcraft. He was, so to speak, enshrined in an atmosphere of precious odours, which it was almost impossible for any one to enter, without feeling his senses lulled in pleasing imaginations, and his spirit robbed of tranquil self-possession. But, if this were the case with him in his indifferent and accidental connections, what must it be supposed to have been in relation to Margaret, whose soul had been united to his from infancy, and who, since the terrible adventure of the rock, had felt that she did not so truly belong to herself as to him? She had been on the brink, or more properly in the jaws, of destruction; one moment only was interposed between her and the most frightful catastrophe; he had shewn himself like an intervenient[a] angel, or / rather like a special and miraculous act of Providence, that she might come forth whole and unhurt, and that no injury might assail her. He had risked every thing to accomplish her deliverance, and had sustained much pain and inconvenience that she might be placed in a condition of safety. If Jephthah had vowed to sacrifice his daughter in case God delivered the armies of Ammon into his hands, was she less bound to conse-crate her life as a remuneration for the existence, the continuation of which this gallant youth had procured to her?[b] /

CHAPTER XI

Gradually the father of Margaret disclosed to her the scheme, which had furnished the cause of their removal from the banks of the Severn to the vicinity of the Mersey.[c] He represented to her in the most lively colours the degradation and dishonour, for such he esteemed it, in which he had so long vegetated, from even before the birth of his daughter to the present hour. He said that the noble representative of his race, for (it may be) little better than a whim, had now proposed to take off this dishonour, and restore him to his proper station. He adjured Margaret, by all the love she bore him, by the care he had exerted for / her from her earliest infancy, by the indulgences he had never withheld from her slightest wishes, not on the present occasion to make herself the obstacle to the fortune that seemed to smile upon him. He intreated her, that she would assist him to spend the remainder of his days in sunshine and content. What was good fortune to him, would also be good fortune to her. She

---

[a] Intervening.
[b] The story is told in Judg. 11.
[c] River Mersey, in Lancashire, N.W. England.

would be placed in the station which she was so eminently qualified to adorn. She would be the boast and the ornament of her sex; and it was impossible that that which won for her the homage and commendation of all the world, should not also be a source of gratification to her own bosom. Lord Borradale was essentially a cold-hearted man; and, as he had taken them up for a purpose that pleased his own imagination, so he would cast them off without remorse, if he found himself thwarted of that purpose.

The habits of Margaret's life from childhood / to the present hour had been those of filial obedience. There was a gentleness in her nature, that would not suffer her to engage in inflexible controversy against her father. She pleaded with him. She said, You have known of the attachment of myself and William from infancy; you loved him; you brought him to me; you encouraged our attachment. You have observed all the steps by which our earliest and instinctive kindness to each other has been turned into love. You saw it with complacency; you bade me entertain him as my future husband. Now all the preliminaries of this final engagement have passed between us; now we have poured our hearts into each other's bosom; now he has saved my life, and in return I have given him my soul. The happiness of all our future existence depends upon this engagement's not being retracted; I may obey you, but if I do, both I and he shall be made your victims. We shall be two withered plants, / which, while they were tended and fostered and nourished, grew up in strength and beauty, their branches full of sap, their foliage bright and healthful and vigorous, but which shall hereafter be rivelled,[a] and unblest, left on the plain two monuments of wretchedness and blast.

The expostulations of Margaret were ineffective to change the purposes of her selfish father. He told her, that this was all the idle romance so characteristic of that early season of life, and that the passions of a boy and girl on the threshold of puberty, as they were impetuous and unsubmissive to reason and restraint, so they were sure to be short-lived and evanescent. He intreated, he adjured her to have compassion upon him. All his early days had been spent in misery, the fruit of a precocious error. The heyday of his life was passed. The evening of his existence was coming on, and demanded its indulgences and its comforts. / She had herself never known any thing but a plain and homely mode of life; but it was different with him; his early years had been passed in the midst of elegance and splendour and luxury. She had only to conquer a fleeting fancy, a mere girlish impulse; and they should all reap the reward. Surely this was a moderate return for all the care he had spent upon her, the love he had borne her, and the anxieties she had cost him from the hour when she began to exist.

These were but feeble arguments, and might with force and advantage have been retorted upon him who urged them. But Margaret was ill qualified for

---

[a] Shrivelled or wrinkled.

such a contention. She had ever felt the duty she owed her parents as a branch of her religion. Her father had not much passed the meridian of life; but in her eye he was a patriarch. While she was yet an infant, she had viewed him in the full maturity of manhood. As she had advanced in dexterity / and accomplishments, as her mind had opened to the beauties of nature, the magnificence of the universe, and the qualities of the beings around her, as she had shot up in stature, and her form had developed itself, the system of things most assuredly had not stood still with him; and he had passed into another class of mortals, even as she had passed. Deference and honour therefore she believed was his due; she was bound to treat him with the utmost tenderness, and in all things to consult his pleasure. Nor was the present affair a question of imaginary benefit and accommodation; however slightly she might value the mere ornaments and trappings of life, it was not so with her father. In a word, her temper was all gentleness; and the bare thought of entering into warfare with the author of her existence, and by dint of inflexible constancy extorting his slow and unwilling consent, was intolerable to her. If the proposition had been started in / their homely and rustic dwelling on the banks of the Severn, the matter would have been somewhat different. But their removal had already been effected, ere she was aware of its purpose. And that she by her wilfulness and her selfishness, should occasion her father to forfeit the protection and smiles of lord Borradale, and drive him back upon the humble life he detested, was a fault she could never have forgiven herself.

Yet she was not without those feelings, that shrinking back and revulsion, which are inseparable from the passion of love, when the question is of sacrificing its most cherished visions and the object it adores. The image of her William was perpetually before her; she saw him in her dreams, sometimes emphatically and earnestly claiming the performance of that which she had given him cause to expect, and sometimes with a melancholy and wintery countenance, reproaching her for her inconstancy, / and assuring her that he could not survive the shock that was given him. She counted up his virtues, his manly and generous qualities; she recollected the boundless debt of gratitude she owed him. She could not therefore wholly avoid the shewing her father by her demeanour, or in the expression of her eye and her attitude, how bitterly she would feel the privation, if she should ultimately yield to his wishes.

On the other hand her father was not without his compunctions and his tenderness. Had it been otherwise, she could not have loved him as she indeed loved him. Seeing therefore how much it cost her, he determined, whatever were the consequence, that she should follow the bent of her inclinations. The choice of the partner of her existence was properly her affair, and not his; she would probably long survive him, and therefore her choice of life merited to be preferred. All this he expressed / not by words, but actions. He pressed her no longer; he wore a look of grief and resignation. He ceased to frequent the house of lord Borradale. He ceased to take pleasure in any thing. He wandered about the house and the adjoining fields, 'hollow as a ghost',

As dim and meagre as an ague-fit.[a]

He yielded to his fate, and resolved that his passions and desires, however vehement, should not have the effect to subvert his daughter's happiness.

But this was an issue she could not endure to think of. The less her father pressed her with expostulation and the weight of words, the more she felt herself impelled to yield to the course his wishes pointed out to her. Had it been for herself only, she felt persuaded that she could without a struggle sacrifice her own preferences on the altar of filial duty. But she dreaded the mischief which the disappointment would inflict on William. She had no right to / trifle with his peace; and, in return for all his love and all he had done for her, to entail upon him the miseries of perpetual grief. With the ingenuousness that so eminently distinguished her, she resolved to write to him on the subject, and to set before him without reserve the perplexities that assailed her. She addressed him as follows:

My friend,

Allow me to invoke you by that appellation, for any other would be foreign to the purpose of this letter. I loved you; I love you. All the visions of happiness I ever formed, included you, and the joys that I believed would be my lot if we were united to each other. But we are not born for ourselves alone. I had a duty to the author of my existence, older in its date, even than the hour when first I had the happiness to know you. It has been the ambition of my heart to pass through life irreproachably. If my faculties were so confined as to enable / me to do little good, I might at least hope to avoid the actual perpetration of evil. I feel that I could never endure the miseries of self-reproach. If I were to see my father suffering the mischiefs of disappointment and a broken heart by any wilfulness of mine, my existence would from that moment become insupportable to me. I could never be an instrument of pleasure and contentment to another, for the worm of undying remorse would prey upon me for ever.

I write to you at the present moment with a certain degree of confidence, to intreat you to second my virtuous resolutions. You are perhaps the only being I know on the face of the earth, from whom I could expect such disinterestedness and magnanimity. Release me, I intreat you, from the unspeakable obligations you have conferred on me, from the promises I have made you, from the prospects of future felicity which your partial thoughts may have / created to you out of the idle and visionary talk, castles in the air, in which we have mutually participated. Whatever I have promised you, has had, if not for its expressed, at least for its implied condition, the consent of my father. Our attachment grew up under his auspices. It proceeded with his knowledge, and

---

[a] *King John*, III. iv. 84–5.

could boast his entire and hearty concurrence. This concurrence he has withdrawn. I do not enter into the question whether this change in his views is founded in wisdom. I am not my father's director; and have no right to arraign the sentiments he forms, and the wishes he entertains, at the tribunal of my judgment. It is enough that there they are, there they will remain, and it is not in my power to reverse them.

Is it not better for us to do what is right, than to yield to what we inordinately desire? I do not apply this rule to my father: for he has, as well as all other human beings, and, to / my apprehension, and as far as I am concerned, more than any other human being, a right to be the judge of the conduct he shall pursue. But I do apply it to myself. I am sure I shall have more internal peace, and more unalloyed and entire resignation, in obeying my conscience, than in pursuing the promptings of my will. I think, William, that you are formed like me. It is this thought that lies at the foundation of the unreserved attachment I have entertained for you, and the perpetual satisfaction I anticipated (if Providence had favoured our views) in being united to you. You love therefore what is right, even as I love it; and, when I call on you to concur with me in this most important crisis of my life, I therefore do you no violence.

I require however, my dear William, your agreement in this great act of filial duty. I have entered into such engagements to you, not only in the secret recesses of my own / mind, but in speech, in countenance, and in the accord of all the powers of my frame, that you and you only can release me from the engagements I have formed. I am like to one who, 'on double business bound, stands in pause' in which direction he shall proceed, and how he shall comport himself, and can perform no essential duty on the theatre of life.[a] Release me, I conjure you. Snap the chain which, as long as it subsists, renders me incapable of any thing decisive, any thing that I should look back upon with satisfaction and complacency. Assist me in the sacrifice I feel myself called upon to make. Let us together approach this altar, consecrated to fortitude and disinterested virtue, and offer up our own dearest wishes to a principle, without an obedience to which I feel that I can never escape the bitterest self-accusation and remorse. /

---

[a] *Hamlet*, III. iii. 41–2 (adapted).

CHAPTER XII

When Margaret had finished, and had dispatched this letter, she felt herself more at her ease. She had put a violence on herself, and achieved a conquest, of the practicability of which in her case nothing could have assured her, short of the actual experiment. This, when the experiment was completed, was her first feeling. But, the next day, and the day after, her satisfaction abated. Having discharged to the full her duty to her father, and prepared for the event against which her very soul revolted, she began to think principally, almost exclusively, of her lover. She set herself to calculate the time at which her letter / would reach him, and at which she might receive his answer. She thought of his surprise, the distresses he would suffer, the fatal blow he would sustain, and the upbraidings with which he would overwhelm her.

The result however was more trying to him than anything that she had anticipated. When the letter of Margaret came to his hands, it found him attending the death-bed of his mother. Only a few weeks had elapsed from the period when they had taken leave of the Borradales. In a retreat so thinly scattered with inhabitants as was that where William and his mother resided, the removal of one family to which they had been bound in the ties of sympathetic and intimate intercourse was an epoch. The good woman had contemplated the growing affection of her son and their fair neighbour with exceeding delight. She had anticipated that herself and the young couple in the event of their union, would reside under the same / roof, either in the cottage where she now dwelt, or in some other that might perhaps afford them a fuller accommodation. She loved Margaret scarcely less than she did her son. She therefore watched with peculiar anxiety the effect which this change would produce upon him. And, though he was most careful to conceal from his mother the disturbance he felt, and though in reality, encouraged by the unequivocal tokens of attachment he received from his mistress, he believed that their separation would be of short continuance, yet she could not but see that he was unusually pensive, and that the interest he took in his ordinary occupations was no longer such as it had been. It was at this time that she was seized with an inflammatory fever. The disease was of a dangerous character. But its symptoms were undoubtedly aggravated by the unsettled state of her thoughts. She became delirious; and in the wanderings of her mind she talked / continually of William and Margaret. She intreated that the young woman might be asked to visit her, might administer her medicines, and support her

62

aching head. When she was silent, her eye still roved in search of something; and she complained that the nurse and the girl who attended her, most unkindly hid from her what she was most desirous to see. William received the letter of Margaret precisely in this situation. He refused to open it. He felt an undefined anticipation of some evil tidings that it would communicate. Superstitiously he deemed it unlucky to open a letter from one he loved, by the side of the bed of a person dangerously ill. He would have judged himself criminal, if he had deliberately sought to withdraw his attention for a moment, from the heart-breaking scene before him, to a consideration of his own desires in any other quarter, his inclination and pleasures.

The good woman died. William felt all the / tenderness and agonies of a son. He had no one to console him. The far-distant abode of the friends, who had so long dwelt at but two fields from his own residence, and whom he so entirely loved, struck him now with tenfold bitterness. The preparations of the funeral went on. He was assisted in them by the wife and two daughters of a neighbouring farmer, who were impressed with the sincerest esteem for William and his mother, but whose 'coarse complexions and cheeks of sorry grain'[a] with aptness expressed the texture of their minds.

For two days William was stunned by the unforeseen disaster that had fallen upon him, and totally absorbed in grief. He resorted many times in an hour, to gaze, with feelings that no words can express, upon the body of her who bore him, and who, tenderly as she had ever watched for his advantage and pleasure, could now shew to him no tokens of recognition, could neither hear his voice, nor answer / to any of his passionate apostrophes and laments. The only things that diverted him from the depth of his depression, were those cares and attentions, which nature and the customs of society require towards the remains of the friend we have lost.

At length, in the morning of the second day from the death of his mother, the letter he had already received caught his eye, and he no longer refrained from examining its contents. 'No doubt', said he, 'it comes to tell me that at least I have one friend left: and God knows I am in want of one!' At first, overwhelmed as he was with the calamity the evidences of which were still before his eyes, he could not understand the letter. Its tenor was not such as he had expected. But he had that confidence in Margaret, he considered that they were bound to each other by ties of so ancient a standing, and of so indissoluble a character, and he believed her to be so single-minded and / affectionate, that, 'though one rose from the dead to persuade' him, he would not believe that she was capable of inconstancy or change.[b] – At length he satisfied himself of the reality of the paper before him.

It is well, said he. I was once – a very short time ago I was – happy. I had two

---

[a] Milton, *Masque*, ll. 749–50.
[b] Luke 16: 31.

friends – such friends – they were indeed that which my heart required. How perfect was my delight, when I found myself supplying to my mother the place of the protector she had lost, drying her tears, and reconciling her again to life! There is nothing which makes a being of a pure heart so happy, as to feel his importance to those he loves, and to be able at the close of each succeeding day to say, I have proved myself 'a good and faithful'[a] assistant, I have not thought of my own gratifications, but have given myself honestly and unreservedly to the interests and the comfort of one, whom above all the earth I was bound to cherish. And I / had my reward. If with my full heart I gave myself to the service of my mother, there was still an approving angel that stood by, and that counted my good qualities a thousand times beyond their intrinsic merit. These two, the being to whom I devoted my services, and the being who was ever at hand to reward them, are taken from me at once. I am indeed alone. What have I to do with the world? There is no part nor place for me in any of its mansions. I look round me on every side, and find nothing to support me, no one to encourage my efforts, or to lend me a helping hand amidst the complexities and difficulties that every way beset me.

William brooded over his sorrows and his desolate condition incessantly for several following days. He attended the funeral of his parent, and saw her body deposited in the silent grave. As he returned to his forlorn home, he found there waiting for him a young / man of some family and consequence, whom he had repeatedly seen during the season that he had spent under the care and superintendence of his uncle, the clergyman formerly mentioned. This young man, to whom his uncle had at no remote period been a tutor, had many times paid a visit to the person under whose instructions the powers of his mind had been unfolded, and on each occasion had paid considerable attention, and shewn much partiality to William, who was only by four years younger than himself. Young Bouverie, that was his name, was of an open and generous disposition, and had afforded to William the first specimen of a friend, whose studies had been similar, whose sentiments in a striking degree coincided with his own, and who, from the advantages of birth and fortune, might be of some use to him, if such assistance were needed, in pushing him forward in the road to fortune. /

Bouverie had learned by accident of the death of William's mother. He well knew with what exemplary duty the young man had determined to consecrate all his efforts to console the widow in her destitute situation, and to superintend the interests of her little concern. Bouverie would have been the last man, to endeavour to divert the stripling from so noble a devotion of his activity and his time. But now, that that obligation was discharged, and obscurity could no longer be a duty, he felt extremely desirous to engage the nephew of his tutor in

---

[a] Matt. 25: 21.

a closer connection with him. He had himself just obtained a considerable appointment under general Murray, governor of Canada;[a] and he came to propose that William should join him in his expedition. He apologised to the young man for the abruptness of his overture, but added that he was so circumstanced, that there was no time to lose. He should himself be obliged to embark in a few weeks. /

Bouverie found his friend in a state of the most pitiable dejection. This was the more remarkable, as William was constitutionally of a very sanguine temperament. The excellence of his disposition led him to regard all the world with kindness; and the nature of the human mind is found to be such, that the world around serves in the effect of a mirror to what passes within us. The philanthropist sees on every side of him the impulses of love, while the malevolent man observes in all his fellow-beings the indications of spite, hostility and ill will. But the events which now befel William were too much for his fortitude to sustain. On returning to his own habitation the frame of his mind had become gloomy and morose. But he no sooner saw Bouverie than he burst into a flood of tears.

His tender-hearted friend at first endeavoured to soothe him by all the common topics of consolation. He told him of the unavailingness / of grief, and reminded him that he had still duties to perform. He spoke of the friendly feelings and the interest in his welfare that were felt by his uncle and himself. You must change the scene, he said.

And wherefore should I change the scene? There is no one that loves me. There is no one for whom I should desire to live. My uncle and you feel compassion for me; and I thank you. But this is not the thing my nature requires, the nourishment of my soul. It is woman only that is truly susceptible, that can fill the cravings of my spirit. I found this consolation and support in my mother. Our interchanges of kindness were of the most tranquillising nature. We were fitted for each other; we understood each other. In the course of nature it is true I must expect that one day my mother would die, and I should survive her. I had hoped indeed that she would live long, and would finally pay the debt of nature, full / of days, and having exhausted the strength that heaven allots to mortals. I must indeed lose her; but I had provided for that. I had a friend, that had sworn to be my comforter, a friend that was young, even as I am young, and who, being in the same period of life, would not have failed to understand my wants and wishes, and to act in unison with me. We had sworn to live together, to feel each other's wishes, to have partaken in each other's joys and sorrows, to have smiled when either smiled, and to have mingled our tears in the moment of disappointment and trial. I have lost my mother and my friend at once. The adored of my heart has abjured all her vows and discarded

---

[a] Sir George Murray (1772–1846), Provisional Lieutenant-Governor of Upper Canada, April–July, 1815.

me. I received her letter of rejection in the room where my mother lay dying; I opened it by the side of her corpse.

The recollections of William, which accompanied these words, were agonising. He felt that he could not refuse what Margaret demanded / from him. He felt that he could not utterly deny that her decision was just: at least it did high credit to the purity and singleness of her mind. But he was not the less impressed with the conviction that the sun of his existence was for ever set, that the rest of his days was condemned to 'disastrous twilight and dim eclipse', and that no hope and no prospect of happiness remained to him.[a] Why should he exert himself? What motive could he have to engage in any new occupation?

By dint however of much kindness, unequivocal sympathy, and the most unwearied patience, Bouverie at length succeeded in convincing him, that the thing which his case most urgently demanded was change of place. He could not recal his mother from the grave. The inexorable law of mortality was equal to all. He did not expect that he could reverse the triumph of filial piety in Margaret. He / had not so studied the laws of religion, he had not so learned the lessons of humanity, as to believe that the effect of the two grievous calamities that had fallen upon him at once, was to be a discharge in full to a young man from all the duties which his being born into society imposed upon him. He was young; he had powers which would not be without their use in the great community; he especially owed to others an example, whether that should operate to a greater or less extent, of patience and resignation, 'None of us liveth to himself; and no man dieth to himself'.[b]

There is something magical in the operations of sympathy. William could not altogether resist the assiduities of his friend. He had said that he was left alone in the world; but he found that he was not. The arrival of Bouverie was like the descent of an angel to his relief. Bouverie had patience with all his inflexibility and perverseness; the tones of his / voice, the affectionateness of his looks, penetrated to the soul of the disconsolate youth. He was ultimately victorious. William thanked him in the most gratifying tones, the more gratifying because despair had scarcely yet quitted its throne in the heart of the mourner, for all his kindness. Bouverie had indeed convinced him, that he was not utterly alone, that there was one that cared even for so very a wretch as he was. He suffered himself to be led, passively, and without resistance, even as a young child might lead a lamb.

The preparations for the voyage were short. Bouverie directed his own steward to take the affairs of William under his superintendence, and to dispose of his property to the best advantage. Before they departed, William addressed a letter to Margaret, yielding all she demanded, acquainting her with the death of his mother, the interposition of his friend, and the voyage and new

---

[a] *Paradise Lost*, I. 597 (adapted).
[b] Rom. 14: 7.

scheme of life to which he / had dedicated himself. The letter was couched in terms of the most rigid simplicity. There were no interjections, and none of the innumerable subterfuges of self-pity and reproach. He did not complain of his fate, assure her that he was heart-broken, or attempt to record the struggles and the tortures he felt within. He wrote with the plainness of an Evangelist, setting down facts only, unaccompanied with a comment. But Margaret understood her lover. There was not one feeling, one contention that took place in his bosom, one mastery that he obtained over himself, which her imagination did not pourtray with the utmost minuteness.

The answer of William was substantially such as Margaret had expected. She knew, that he would not have the hardness of heart and the illiberality to wish to bind her in ties which she asked him to dispense her from. He was doubtless aware that no true happiness could grow out of such an union. He was / much too generous of soul to consent to accept from her any thing that was not a voluntary offering. But she did not the less believe that the sacrifice she required of him was such, as would wrench his nature from its strongest holding. And she was shocked beyond the power of words to express, when she found at what a season of distress and agony her ungracious letter had reached him. She had taken for granted, that his mother would be the very person to soothe his griefs, to read to him the lessons of wisdom and virtue, and to supply to him in the most perfect and gratifying manner all that he would have judged himself to have lost in the dissolution of their promised union. /

CHAPTER XIII

Margaret had made the most uncalculable sacrifice on the altar of filial duty. But, when that sacrifice was complete, her heart recoiled upon itself. She saw the son of lord Borradale; but that sight was not the appropriate medicine for the disease of her mind. She saw him; but the doing so had the effect of contrast: she could not prevent the image of William, the beloved, the exiled, from recurring to her thoughts.

Margaret however was not of a temper to do things by halves. She had chosen her part; and her virtue and her honour required that she should complete what she had begun. The / pang upon William had been inflicted; he was exiled; she had surrendered herself without reserve into the hands of her father; she had been presented to lord Borradale; she had encouraged his son. It was necessary that she should dress her countenance in smiles, that she should personate the exactest courtesy, that she should carefully close up every avenue through which the agony of her mind might discover itself. She had decided that this was the part that justice and duty imposed on her. It was necessary to be firm. The power that an energetic and elevated mind exercises over itself is of vast extent. She commanded her features; and they obeyed. She regulated her gestures; and they conformed themselves to her will. She called up certain tones and inflexions of the voice; and the organs of speech became accommodated to the authority of the master – mind. She resolved to banish from her thoughts so much as the recollection of her / late-favoured lover; and to a great degree she succeeded in this. The recollection sometimes did not recur to her for hours together. She sang; she danced. She recited in her mind the duties of an ingenuous female to an accepted lover; she accustomed herself to the recapitulation of whatever would justly be required and looked for in the conduct of an exemplary wife. All this she did, that she might not prove herself inferior in resignation to what has been told of the daughter of the general of the Jews.[a] She looked at her father, and was satisfied. He would succeed to the full extent of his wishes. He would live in the midst of magnificence and splendour. He would contemplate with all the pride which was congenial to his nature his noble son-in-law and his right honourable daughter. Whatever became of herself, she would have the satisfaction of performing without a blemish all that could be demanded of her towards the / author of her existence. Nay, she did not despair of herself. If the punctual discharge of the first of all duties could make her happy, had she not a right to look for happiness? She had often heard that the soul's true sunshine was derived from an approving conscience;[b] and she believed it.

Nothing could be more admirable than the intentions of Margaret; nothing more strenuous than her efforts. Many persons in her place probably would have succeeded; but she failed. The attempt was too mighty for her. The feebleness of her nature sank under the giganticness of the undertaking. The whole of her days was passed in unremitted exertion; never did she suffer her attention or her resolution to subside for an instant. But the night came. As long as she was in society, it was well. But the very winding up of the strings to a too great degree of tenseness, conduced to destroy the instrument. Perhaps she played / her part in too exemplary a style. When she was alone, when she was no longer called upon to exert herself, the very springs of life within her appeared to give way. She was scarcely able to support herself. Tears, of which she was unaware till she felt the moisture on her face, rolled down her cheeks in an abundant stream. She sighed, as if her heart would break. She sobbed; she became hysterical. And this in its beginning, not from any thoughts that rushed over her mind, but merely because she had continued to tax herself too rigorously.

---

[a] Judg. ii. 30–40.
[b] Probably alluding to Pope's *Essay on Man* (1733), Epistle IV, l. 168.

Thus the reaction began, probably from the mere animal relaxation of the fibres. But this was but the beginning of evils. Her nights were almost altogether without sleep. Her limbs were restless, and she tossed from side to side, even, if I might borrow a simile from Homer, as a steak cut from an ox agitates itself on the burning embers.[a] And, when she slept, / or, more properly speaking, for a few moments forgot her individuality and the material substances that encompassed her, her dreams were even more distressful and unrefreshing than the wild and incoherent thoughts that beset her when she was neither wholly awake nor asleep. In dreams the reins of the soul are no longer under the guidance of reflection or reason. The power, whatever it is, that presides over that state of existence, hurries us wherever it will. The rudder of the mind is powerless; our sense of morality is reduced to almost nothing. We witness crimes, and we commit them, undogged by that moral sense, of which the disciplined spirit can at no time time divest itself, while the sun is in the heavens, or the sun of truth penetrates the inner man with its beams. She saw her lover sometimes in a mood of bitter upbraidings, and at other times the wasted, wan and colourless shadow of desolation and despair. She saw her favoured / suitor assault him, now that the gallant youth seemed deprived by melancholy and sorrow of his wonted energies of defence, and pierce his manly limbs with a thousand wounds, and scatter his remains to all the winds of heaven. In this situation her imaged William would utter the most piercing screams, and implore her to interfere to save him, while lord Borradale and her father held her back with inexorable effort from making the smallest advance to his rescue. The recollection of his voyage to Canada would then occur to her; she saw him standing in the gallery of the ship; a sudden tempest would assault the vessel; he was washed overboard; he was devoured by a shark; and in the countenance of the shark she all at once discovered the lineaments of her destined husband. Repeatedly did she start out of her sleep with the terror of what she had appeared to behold; and it was often a very long time before she could thoroughly / convince herself, that what had so exceedingly terrified her was unbased in reality.

It was thus that the bodily strength of the self-devoted victim gave way, unable to keep pace with the energies of her mind. A female of a different character would probably have been more successful in going through with the part she had determined to sustain. The virtue of Margaret destroyed her. There was too much tenacity and consistence in the frame of her soul. Another female, having resolved to dismiss her earliest attachment, would have fixed her thoughts on the splendours of rank, and have felt her mind led away from its original simplicity, even as her father had been led away. But these splendours had no charm of power to divert the temper of Margaret from its first bias.

---

[a] cf. Homer, *Odyssey*, XX. 25–7: 'as a man with a paunch pudding,that has been filled with blood and fat [i.e. a sausage], tosses it back and forth over a blazing fire ...'

Other females would have called to their aid the volatility that is so often found characteristic of their sex. They are like butterflies that wander from flower to flower / through the whole inclosure of an earthly paradise; and this levity sufficiently secures them against the chance of falling victims to any single disappointment. But Margaret's mind was of a different constitution: where it fixed, there it rested. There was in it no infusion of perverseness. She desired the happiness of all; and especially of those to whom she was bound by the most familiar and the oldest ties. Selfishness seemed not to enter in the smallest degree into her character; she appeared to regard it as the proper business of her life, to study the happiness of others. But her disposition was firm and unvarying. She was in the most striking degree gentle. She was tranquil of spirit, and clear of soul. Her mind had the smoothness of a lake, the surface of which was unvexed by so much as a single breath, and at the same time the steadiness of an edifice the materials of which were of marble. /

But, however unalterable was the substance of her mind, and however delicate the mould in which it was cast, she had not the smallest inclination to depart from the scheme of conduct she had elected. She gave no quarter to that species of impulse, which in so many cases whispers to the timid spirit, You have done enough; you have shewn how willing you were to conquer your weakness; human nature cannot bear more than you have borne, or resist more than you have resisted; it is fit that you should now give way; your efforts to obey, well entitle you to call on your elders at length to cease from their requisition, and to acknowledge that what they require is unfit to be executed.

Margaret on the contrary was fully resolved not to play booty, nor stop half-way in the course of duty she prescribed to herself. The union therefore between the elder and the younger branch of the house of Borradale, day / after day drew nearer to its consummation. The preparations were advancing; the wedding garments purchased; the jewels and other presents which the intended bride is accustomed to receive on such occasions, were in complete readiness. The day was named for the ceremony; four days were suffered to elapse between the period when it was fixed on, and that on which it was to arrive.

The father of the lovely victim had the whole powers of his soul fastened on one point. The very energies with which he desired to see it accomplished, made him regard all delay, all uncertainty, with an impatience almost amounting to frenzy. He could not but see that his daughter, who, as long as they dwelt on the banks of the Severn, had been the very personification of the Goddess of Health, was incessantly growing more and more thin and delicate in her appearance. The roses in her cheek were completely faded; the lustre, the laughing / serenity, that lately flashed from her eyes, was no more. If colour was at any time to be found in her complexion, it was unwholesome and hectic;[a] if

---

[a] With cheeks flushed, a symptom associated with consumptive or other wasting diseases.

fire was in her eyes, it was the indication of disease. Her father would occasionally question her respecting her health with a certain alarm. But so surely as
the question was proposed, Margaret would rouse herself. She called up a
languid smile to grace the beauty of her lips; she composed her voice to an even
and a cheerful key. She assured her father that she was perfectly well. The old
man, fixed to his purpose, and willing to deceive himself, was easily satisfied.
He kissed her parched and burning lips, and almost believed that what he
found there was the genial glow of health; he felt the cold, clamminess of her
palm, and thought the skin was elastic and dry. He said to himself. She must
know the state of her health better than I do; and she assures me she is well. /

Thursday was the day appointed for the wedding. As it drew nearer and
more near, Margaret felt an insupportable load on her spirits, weighing her
down to earth. With all the power of her will she resolutely sent the vital
principle through every joint and articulation in her frame. She roused herself.
She said to her own soul, It is little now that remains to be done. The bitterness
of death is past. Two days more, and all will be over. And I have no doubt, that
when that shall be the case, I shall feel relieved. 'Things without all remedy, will
be without regard'.[a] I shall no longer then have these strange shrinkings and
contractions of the soul. I shall have discharged a great duty; and the sense of this
will bring with it congratulation. The recollection of my childish partialities will
then become a crime. I shall no longer dare so much as to dream of William.

But with the best intentions in the world, / and with all the resolution of
which her nature was capable, she grew worse from hour to hour. Her mother,
as has already been mentioned, was a weak woman, and accustomed to yield
without resistance to the will of her husband. But she had the affections of a
mother. She had at all times regarded the decisions of her husband as so many
oracles. He was a person of rank; she was by birth a peasant's daughter. He had
forfeited the favour of his family by marrying her; and the least she could do in
return, was to take care, so far as depended on her, that he should not have
further reason to repent his rashness.

But the mother of Margaret, with all possible submission to the will of her
husband, could not in every case see things in the same light in which he saw
them. Her mind was formed on a different principle. Her actions were regulated by another code. She had not the smallest tincture of ambition in her
composition. / She was therefore much more clear-sighted as to the external
face of things, and the deterioration of her daughter's health than he was.
Margaret never complained. She was infinitely above the pitiful art, the low
trick, of endeavouring to make her mother a party against the will of her father,
to which she herself professed to submit. Such as she was to one of her parents,
she was to the other. She never thought of sacrificing herself by halves. She

---

[a] *Macbeth*, III. ii. 11–12.

would not for the world have introduced discord under her parental roof. Her whole soul was simplicity. Her whole conduct was of a piece. She never told her regrets; she never whispered them to the vacant air; her scheme was entire self-conquest, without reserving one corner in her heart for weakness or folly. /

CHAPTER XIV

Early on the morning of the second day before the marriage, the mother came to the bedside of her daughter. She had previously been much alarmed. She stooped over her pillow, that she might make her own observations, and draw a surer prognostic and a more impartial report from the evidence of inspection, than she would have a chance of deriving from the answers of the patient sufferer. Margaret was still asleep. She had passed a feverish and restless night, till at length nature was worn out, and the young woman had fallen into a short oblivion. Though asleep, her eyes were not closed. There was an uneasy twitching / of the muscles of several parts of the body. Her lips moved, and uttered several indistinct sounds, though the mother could not make out the meaning. She gently recalled her to the perception of things around her.

She first asked how she had passed the night, and received from Margaret the same answer she would have returned to her father; an answer, the purpose of which was to suffer things to go on in the train in which they had lately proceeded.

The soul of the good woman was stirred within her by the position in which they stood. She was like one inspired. Her features enlarged. Her attitude was marked with a striking solemnity.

My child, said she, you never knew me any thing but passive: and that which a human creature has been for a series of years, is seldom likely to be altered. Your father took me, and made me the thing he would; he has at all / times found me an obedient wife. But you, my only child, are about to leave me, to be placed under another jurisdiction, and to dwell under a stranger roof. I know that this is the law of our existence in society, and I could have submitted. I could have borne it, if the change had promised to be a happy one for you. But, oh, Margaret! –

Think you, because I have been a silent, that I have been an inattentive, observer of you and your goings on? You look to my eye, like a victim that is to be sacrificed, like an innocent creature, who had fallen under the gripe of the law, and who, having been pronounced guilty, has the days of his short remaining existence numbered on the calendar. If I saw the matter otherwise, my feeling would have been different. If I thought only of a marriage the scheme of which had been selected by your father, I would have stood by and said nothing. He has made his choice; / and this is according to the practice of those who live with us, and those that lived before us. You have subscribed to his choice; and I should have subscribed too. I should have been contented that you formed other and nearer ties than those which have hitherto subsisted between you and me; and, impressed with the thought of the comparative narrowness of my understanding, I should not have conceived myself entitled to look minutely into the affair, and to have weighed its merits in my private scale.

But I do not view the matter in that light. Not having the prejudices your father has, not being swallowed up, as he is, in the vision of something that he prizes beyond the power of words to describe, I suppose I see more clearly the things that are before me. I see the dimness of your eye; I see the deadly paleness of your cheek. I have attentively remarked the cold damp that bedews your forehead, and the / unhealthy pink that from time to time marks your countenance. You will not live, my Margaret! Your heart is broken, my Margaret! I could follow you to the altar; but I cannot follow you thither, when at a short distance beyond I see the tomb.

Tell me, my child, if this is not so! Do not refuse your confidence to me, your mother! If you can assure me that you shall be happy, that peace will dwell within your bosom, that you accept with your whole soul the husband that your father has chosen for you, that health will attend the scene of your married life, and that you feel yourself capable of cheerfully discharging its duties, it is enough; I shall be satisfied; I will believe a child, that never from the hour that she was capable of distinguishing good from evil, told her mother an untruth.

Margaret was overwhelmed by the solemn appeal made to her by her mother. She adjured / her to stop. She said, You should not have done this, mother! But the good woman, as has already been said, was elevated above herself. She had worked herself up to meet the occasion, and would not be interrupted. She was wholly unlike what she had been found at any other season. She, who had all her life been passive and neutral, was at once swelled into independence. It was for a life, the life of the creature that she loved most deeply on the face of the earth.

As the appeal proceeded, Margaret was drowned in a flood of tears. She sobbed; her bosom heaved; it seemed almost as if her heart would burst the boundary that inclosed it.

The mother finished. She ended with the adjuration that Margaret would pour her whole heart into the bosom of her that bore her. Silence ensued; a silence that was unbroken on either part for some minutes. The mother would have followed with caresses the words / she had uttered. But there was something in Margaret's manner that forbade it; a solemnity as of one prepar-ing for the consummation of what she meditated. Yet Margaret was the gentlest

73

creature that lived. There was strangely mixed with the loftiness of her resignation, an imploring gesture, that asked for forbearance and pity, the most
childlike that it is possible to imagine.

She composed her features into an expression of exemplary resignation. It
was nevertheless sufficiently perceptible to an observing eye that she was
playing a part.

From my heart, mother, I thank you. Yes, I always knew your love, and
knew, however, like the lamp of Vesta, it burned for ever, that it would display
its greatest power on the greatest occasion.[a] I ought to have expected from you
what I have now witnessed. But it is to no purpose. I have chosen my part.
Here is my hand (said she, stretching it from / the bed): see, if I am not firm.
Put your fingers upon my pulse: you will find that it beats with entire steadiness
and regularity. This is the greatest trial to which I can ever be called. Permit me
to rise. I will but put on my morning dress. I will go to my father.

The mother carefully watched all her motions. The mind of Margaret was
fixed; but her frame was unequal to the exertion. She trembled, and was
compelled instantly to seat herself.

Never mind! never mind, dear mother! I shall go through with it yet. I will
not hurry myself. I was to blame to be in a hurry. Let the girl come to me. Let
me have some breakfast. I have not been well. I have had some bad dreams. I
will go about it, as fits the duty of a daughter. I will go through it, and my father
shall be satisfied. Never fear me, mother: you shall find that you had no need. /

The good woman shook her head with a mournful air. But she did, as she
was desired. She left the room; and the girl presently made her appearance.

The mother instantly proceeded from the apartment of Margaret to the
garden, where she found her husband, as she expected. He was sitting on a
bench.

Well, my love, said he, have you seen our daughter this morning? How is
she? I expect her spark and my lord to be with me within the hour.

I have seen Margaret. She is very ill. She wanted to come to you; but she
could not. She has been obliged to remain where she was.

Yes, yes, I know she has been unwell. She is a simple girl, and likes the banks
of the Severn, where she was born and bred, better than she does the North.
But she is a dutiful child; and she will find her virtue and her duty crowned
with an ample reward. /

Indeed, my love, she will not. Her lot is cast. Her reward and her crown will
be in heaven, and not here.

Maurice, I have hardly ever had the courage to speak to you, to contradict
you. We have lived upon these terms now for almost twenty years; and I

---

[a] Vesta, in Roman mythology, goddess of the hearth and its fire whose temple contained a
perpetual flame tended by the vestal virgins.

thought to have gone on so to the end. I do not matter for myself. I do not live for myself, but for you. It has been my purpose, that every attention I could give, should be for your accommodation. I have but one other tie to the world.

Forgive me, if I love Margaret nearly as well as I love you. We have but this one. I know that you are a slave to the pride of birth, and the trappings of nobility. The longer you have been condemned to be without them, you love them the more. Old man, old man, what will you do without your daughter? You have been accustomed to see her every day: when / you do not see her, you think of her. What will you do with your nobility, if you have none to inherit it after you? Will you give your daughter in exchange for it? You may indeed place a coronet on her coffin. You may bury her in the sepulchre of the Borradales. Will that be a sufficient equivalent, and satisfy you for cutting off the thread of her life?

The old man was greatly startled with this address. The view of things that was thus forced upon his attention, was new to him. He was not without his superstition. He was a believer, if I may so far force the word from its ordinary acceptation, in second sight. He believed that mortals, upon extraordinary occasions, have a secret sympathy with the invisible and the future. He had never seen his wife in the least like what he now saw her. She was as one inspired. Her organs seemed as if they were usurped and taken possession / of by a power above herself, as if her unconscious tongue was made a vehicle to declare the secrets of the world unknown.

He made little answer, and requested to be left alone. He said, I expect lord Borradale and his son anon. The mother had the discernment to see, that the salutary wound she purposed to inflict, had taken effect. She believed it was better to leave the thing as it was, than to irritate her husband by further contradiction.

Lord Borradale and his son arrived, as they were expected to do. They found the old man unusually thoughtful and sad. They had uttered little more than the customary compliments and enquiries, when Margaret joined them. She was leaning on the arm of her mother. The young man, who had been bred in the knowledge of all the courtesies of life, flew towards her, and with a gallant air took her by the hand.

Lord Borradale had been absent several / weeks. He fixed his eye on the intended bride. He had chosen her originally as he would have chosen a statue from the hands of Phidias or Lysippus to place in his gallery.[a] His choice had been founded first upon a miniature that had accidentally fallen in his way, and then upon a portrait of the size of life. He had subsequently visited her in person. She had passed victoriously through these successive examinations.

---

[a] Lysippus, (4th century), Greek sculptor known for introducing naturalism into sculpture.

Lord Borradale was, in his quality of a virtuoso, *elegans spectator formarum*, 'a discerning observer of the pretensions of the human figure and countenance'. Margaret now stood before him with all her original graces of person, and all that exquisite beauty of feature, by which he had been struck from the first. But there was much that he could no longer perceive. Where was the celestial rosy red in her cheek, that so beautifully contrasted with the alabaster fairness of her forehead? Where was that / glow of health, and that enchanting smile of content, which had once formed the crown of her appearance? Where was the shew of firm, plump, elastic substance, which had taught the spectator to believe that paradise was to be found in her embraces?

She would still have served perhaps to the statuary, as a model for a Niobe mourning for her desolate and childless condition, or rather for an Iphigenia in Aulis, as she was delivered over by her father to the priest, that she might be sacrificed on the altar of Diana.[a] She seemed as if the thread of her life were already cut, as if she had already received the mortal wound, the trace of which was indeed unseen, but which had full surely marked her for the grave.

This was not the thing that lord Borradale had contemplated. He wanted, as I have said, a beautiful and graceful bride, to preside at his table, and do the honours to his visitors. He wanted an object for envy, not for pity. He / wanted a health-breathing and fruitful mother to his posterity, that, of the nobility of Borradale, *Genus immortale maneret, multosque per annos Staret fortuna domus, et avi numerarentur avorum.*[*]

He started at the sight of her. He said, My dear, you seem very ill. He turned to the father, exclaiming, Here is something wrong. Have you called in proper advice? I must by all means request that the marriage may be deferred. Thursday must no longer stand, as we had purposed.

The eyes of the father were opened. He had been previously struck with the expostulation of the mother. She had appeared to him like a prophetess, delivering the oracles of heaven. The warning she had pronounced to him, was impressively inforced by the scene / before him, the meek submission of his daughter, trembling and deadly pale, and the effect that had obviously been produced upon lord Borradale.

No, my lord, exclaimed he, neither Thursday, nor any future time. Pardon me; I have been dazzled with your lordship's noble and generous propositions. My daughter had a lover, her equal as our circumstances then stood, who once saved her life, and between whom and herself there subsisted a thousand

---

[*] 'The race might be immortal, the fortune of the house perpetuated for myriads of years, and the succession continued through countless generations.'

---

[a] Niobe, in Greek mythology a daughter of Tantalus, whose children were slain after she boasted of them, but despite being turned into stone she continued to weep; Iphigenia, the daughter of Agamemnon, taken by him to be sacrificed to Artemis (sometimes identified with Diana), but who finally saved her life.

endearments. But she so generously consented to sacrifice herself to my foolish and contemptible ambition, that I was deceived. I thought that, where there was a heroical resolution, every thing else would follow. I accepted her surrender. I admired her filial resignation, and believed that with so much virtue, she could not fail to be happy. I have played the tyrant. My bowels yearned for her: but I have said every day, 'A little more perseverance, and all will / be right. I have gone far; I have extorted her consent; I have been the means of banishing the lord of her affections to the other side of the globe; it would be foolish to give in now'.

But no; I will not be the death of my Margaret. She is of ten thousand times greater value than I am. She is worth all the world. What shall I ever hereafter think of myself, if I were to be the means of the miscarriage of so glorious a creature? The unmurmuring sacrifice that she has consented to make of her most bosom preference and her dearest affections, gives her an omnipotent title to my tenderness and indulgence. Shall I take this willing victim, and lead her like a lamb to the slaughter?

No; Margaret, beloved of my soul, call back your health, call back the roses to your cheeks, and serenity to your soul! Never more shall you be thwarted by me. I will not break your heart. Heal, I intreat you, carefully heal the / wounds that my obduracy has inflicted on you!

My lord, I intreat you to allow me to resign into your hands this pleasant retreat, sheltered as it is under the wing of your magnificent mansion. I desire nothing better, than to return to the little shepherd's hut, that for so many years formed my retreat on the banks of the Severn. I bid farewell to the illusions and enticements of ambition. Margaret, my beloved Margaret, henceforth I will love nothing but you. I have been in danger of losing you, and I shut my eyes on the danger. Cheer up, my child! No longer 'with your vailed lids seek for your chosen lover in the dust!'[a] Henceforth I will be your indentured servant, having no will but yours, seeking for nothing so much as your gratification and content.

We will immediately send to William from the other side of the globe. Be assured, he will come, and that suddenly. He loves nothing / but you. He knows no happiness, but in your endearments and your smiles. Henceforth the sun of no day shall shine but upon the advancement and completion of your wishes.

Margaret heard the words of her father with uncontroled amazement and transport. She leaned upon her mother; she tottered to a seat; the mother drew a chair near her; the poor girl hid her face in her mother's neck; she wept abundantly; her frame was convulsed with her sobs; she was unable to utter a word.

The whole scene was to her a scene of enchantment and miracle. The dutiful

---

[a] *Hamlet*, I. ii. 70–1 (adapted).

girl had prepared herself to do whatever her father required. She had bid all the aspirations of her soul be still; she had determined to be nothing, if not dutiful. If she had sunk, and must ultimately have expired under the greatness of the trial, it would at least not have been for want of the firmest resolution, and the sharpest and most unflinching struggles. And now, / that all this should suddenly be terminated by her father's giving up his cherished projects, coming over to favour and encourage the dearest secret of her thoughts, and telling her that nothing would make him so happy as her union with the object of her earliest affections, this was more than her most ardent hopes could have aspired to, and went beyond the bounds of her wildest credulity.

Lord Borradale was struck with the scene before him. He was of a cold and unimpassioned nature; but the coldest natures are sometimes liable to be excited upon extraordinary occasions; and then it not seldom happens, that the flame, so difficult to light, catches with a pertinacity, and burns with a steadiness, though not a fervour, that might do honour to a nobler class of characters. He was edified and impressed, as who would not have been? with the dutiful self-abandonment of this noble creature. He resolved not to be outdone in / generosity. He told the father of the girl, that he forgave him all his engagements, and approved of his present decision. He added, that he could not express his admiration of the gallantry of Margaret's conduct, and was determined, as far as he could contrive it, that they should not be losers by the present alteration. He approved of the proposition of their returning back to their residence in Somersetshire, and engaged to settle an income of two hundred a year on the father, and to give the daughter a thousand pounds as a marriage portion.

The young gentleman conducted himself with the most edifying philosophy on this critical occasion. He had been ready to marry his cousin, because his father recommended it. He believed her to be as good, or nearly so, as a Grecian statue. But he did not doubt, though he was so acutely disappointed in the present instance, that his merits would procure him a / suitable establishment and a beautiful bride, who might hereafter be presented with himself at court to the admiration of a crowded and a brilliant drawing-room. /

CHAPTER XV

The sudden change which took place in the feelings and prospects of Margaret was of the most memorable nature. It was like a reprieve to the unfortunate wretch who has already mounted the scaffold. It was like the unexpected announcement of favourable symptoms to the sick man who has received his last absolution, and passed through the sacrament of the extreme unction. This person has in supposition entered the mournful portal through which all mortals must pass; he has shaken hands with hope; he is satisfied that help is vain; he has dismissed the illusions of the world; the grave has opened its jaws to receive / him. The muscles of his countenance are fallen; upon his eye-balls rest the sadness of a compelled resignation. If then unexpected tidings of gladness reach his ear, what music is there in the sound! It has the long-drawn, delicious melody of the Lydian lyre.[a] He believes that he shall once again behold the blue heavens and the green earth, breathe the breath of health, and scent the fragrance of the morning air. He apprehended that he had done with all things sublunary. and persuaded himself that they had no longer any beauty to his spirit. But how is every thing changed in a moment! A new life has descended upon him. It is the birth not of an unconscious infant, but the regeneration of a matured humanity, of a creature who knows, and knows the more perfectly because he believed the whole at an end, the joys of sensation, of thought, of reflection, of a conscious being, admitted to mix once / more in the activity, and hopes, and busy scene of things below.

Margaret and her parents were not long in removing from their new habitation, and returning to the scene of her former joys. As they entered the neighbourhood, and caught sight of the village spire, how did her heart leap within her! She could no longer contain herself. She begged to be allowed to leave the carriage, and walk the remainder of the distance. She was in no hurry. She was rather desirous to savour the sweets of this her genuine home at her leisure. Her mind would then change. Alternately she leaped like a young roe on the mountains, or advanced with such slow and measured steps, as if she wished that the tell-tale air might not syllable the report of what she did. Her father supported her, and led her on. He opened the little wicket that admitted them to the garden. A / servant already appeared at the door, and invited them

---

[a] Ancient stringed instrument.

to enter. Margaret fell down on the earth, and kissed the threshold, and bathed it with her tears. Never, never again had she hoped to enjoy this unspeakable happiness. It was a full and a rich reward for all that she had lately suffered.

And now came the question of the return of William, and the meeting, the image of which she dwelt on for ever. She did not doubt that he would come back on the wings of sympathy, the first moment it would be practicable to do so, after having received her father's letter.

She allowed her father to be the communicator of good tidings. She believed that that was the best form in which they could be conveyed. The old man wrote in the frankness of his new-found liberty, intreating to be forgiven for his injustice, describing the fidelity of Margaret, stating in explicit terms how her invincible affections, invincible even to her own / most strenuous efforts, had conquered his worldly-mindedness, inviting William to return with the least possible delay, and assuring him that the life of his beloved hung suspended upon the promptness of his compliance. To this epistle Margaret subjoined a postscript, written with the simplicity which so eminently distinguished her, and couched in terms of the most fervent and unbounded regard.

William had been already some months in Canada, before this letter came to his hands. The struggle of Margaret had been of considerable duration; she had placed herself entirely at the disposal of her father; it was by slow degrees that the work of destruction manifested itself in her frame; and it was nothing less than the full conviction of every bystander that her life would be the sacrifice, which brought about so memorable and unlooked-for a revolution.

William welcomed the letter with unimaginable / transport. It was in desperation only that he had yielded to the remonstrances of Bouverie, and consented to live. He had never for one moment lifted his head in cheerfulness. He had moved about on the deck of the vessel, and in the colony after he arrived, rather like a meagre, gliding, unlaid ghost, than a living member of the community of man. He had no spirit in him. He was like a man that had almost forgot to speak, or at least who spoke with reluctance, and to whom the most ordinary communications of human society were attended with effort and pain. There was no sullenness; the original gentleness of his frame of mind remained undiminished; but the main spring that maintained the operations of the machine was worn out, and seemed as if it were every moment in danger to perish altogether. He wept, as though he wept not; he used whatever presented itself to his hands, as one possessing nothing; he walked, as a man that / walks in his sleep, whose eyes are open, but the sense that should accompany them is shut. 'Even such a man, so dull, so dead in look, so woe-begone', was William, who not many months before had been the life of every circle, the envy of all his companions, the happiest of the happy.[a]

---

[a] *Henry IV, Part 2*, I. i. 70–1 (adapted).

When he received the letter of the father of his beloved, he could not believe his eyes. He recognised the handwriting in a moment: every thing that had relation to Margaret made an impression upon him never to be obliterated. He said, For what purpose is this letter addressed to me? There is nothing left to be demanded of me. I have surrendered every thing. I have abandoned the casket where every thing that was dear to me was enshrined. I have evacuated the fortress which could alone have preserved me from every ill. – Yet, whatever the letter might contain, it was welcome to him. It must bring him news of his Margaret, / of one for ever lost, but who could not fail to be dear to him, as the light of his eyes, and must always be remembered by him, as that being who alone of all mortal existences had made his heart beat with the deepest interest, and the most perfect rapture.

William read the letter three times, before he could properly be said to comprehend one word of its meaning. It was a light from heaven that shone all round him, and extinguished in him for a time the faculty of seeing. It could not be true. The words must have a meaning different from that which was obvious and direct. It was like as if the letter had been written in an alphabet that was familiar to him, at the same time that it presented words he had never seen before, or had never seen in such a combination. That the father of Margaret should have written to invite his return, and to sue to him to accept the hand of / his daughter, that father, who had proved himself the veriest slave of glitter and ostentation, who was in his mind a most merciless tyrant, who had not hesitated to break the most perfect of all ties, a harmony and consent of souls which nothing could parallel. It was impossible!

He believed, and disbelieved. But the most agreeable state of mind gradually became the predominant. He trod in air. He could not well tell where he was, or in what part of the world. For a short interval, every door that opened he expected would set Margaret before him, every new direction of the garden-walk he pursued, every carriage that advanced from the other end of the street. He flew to Bouverie, and put the letter in his hands. It was well for him that he did so. The sympathetic looks of his friend, the kind tones of his voice, modulated by feelings of earnest affection, brought William back from the incoherent and / the unreal, and excited in him the ideas of time and place, of plans to be considered, and schemes to be digested.

Bouverie at once perceived that it was unavoidable but that he must concur with William, and assist him to return with all practicable speed to his native country. No prospect of improving his fortune could enter into competition with the imperious necessity he felt to throw himself at the feet of his beloved, and yield to the master-passion that ate up all the springs of his being. Even if hereafter he should conform to the suggestions of prudence, and determine to take advantage of the patronage he might reasonably hope for in the colony, yet the marriage that was proposed to him must at all events be his first step, and then he might, if it appeared eligible, recross the Atlantic with his bride, and make one of the speculators, who, in this province newly acquired to Great Britain, saw a thousand advantages leading on to / prosperity, and were enchanted with the idea of the amusements of a Canadian winter, and the rich exuberance which distinguished its summer.

Some small delay was still necessary. Bouverie, and the young men of the colony who could yet discern in William the gallant youth he had been, and anticipate in fancy the period when he would break through the cloud which had hitherto overwhelmed him, would not permit him to leave them like one who fled. A vessel was about to quit the harbour for England on the third day from that on which he received the welcome epistle; and by that vessel he dispatched an answer, announcing that he should revisit the shores of Britain in one month from the period when that letter should reach the hands of those to whom it was directed. It happened that he was able to name the vessel, the Roebuck, merchantman, of Plymouth, in which he should take his passage; and, as a / passenger with his family would be landed at that port, while the ship with its freight proceeded to London, William would take advantage of the opportunity to quit the vessel, and proceed by land to the place where his mother had lately lived, and where his beloved had newly taken up her residence.

From the time that Margaret's father dispatched his letter to Canada, the love-sick girl had on the whole enjoyed a sweet serenity. She anticipated the most enviable happiness. She had but to count a few short months, and her William would join her again, never more to be separated. She felt assured of his truth. She felt assured of his forgiveness. What an incredible reverse of fortune had thus befallen her! The future she had lately looked forward to, consisted in her being destined to what was construed as the most intimate union within the pale of our social institutions, with a youth who could excite in her neither respect nor / attachment, and who was himself incapable of these emotions. She could rely upon herself for the most exemplary conduct. She did not believe that the young man would use her ill; and she expected to pass her married life in a calm, like that she had read of in the Dead Sea. She did not expect to die; she resolved punctiliously to discharge all her duties. She determined in no way to desert the station in which the order of events seemed to place her. She believed that, when every uncertainty was at an end, she should recover her health and strength, and go on to the end in the dull, hopeless, vegetative life, in the journey over the wild, desolate, sandy, unproductive desert, that lay before her. She would, in recompense for this immeasurable sacrifice, have the satisfaction to reflect that she had done all this in unreserved obedience to the author of her being. But then she felt with agony that she was not sacrificing herself alone. She believed, that / the person round whom her affections were inextricably twined, would be no more happy than she was, that he, like herself, would be consigned to perpetual blast. And, in proportion to the degree in which she admired and adored him, was her anguish in anticpating the gradual sinking and destruction of the noblest creature the earth had to boast. It was these thoughts that had so lately brought her down to the brink of the grave.

But now that every prohibition to their union was removed, Margaret indeed possessed her soul in peace. She, who had shewn what command she could exercise over herself in the greatest of possible trials, without difficulty subdued her spirit, and regarded as nothing the interval that was placed between her and the consummation of her hopes. The mountains were removed, the vallies were exalted, and the rough places made plain. All seemed smooth before her. She thanked her father / every morning, who appeared to her the author of her present felicity. In the sweetest accents she lamented over the disappointment of his prospects, and chid herself that any infirmity of hers should have occasioned that disappointment. Why did he give way to her weakness? It would have been her greatest glory to be the sacrifice to the accomplishment of the thing he aimed at. At the same time she thanked him in most heart-felt tones for her William. In thus generously surrendering the edifice of ideal greatness he had built for himself, she considered him as the author of all her happiness. He was a second time, and in a question above all others most interesting to her, her father. He gave her life, not in blindness and ignorance, but because he loved her with distinguishing preference. Every day of that blessed life she was assured she should pass with her William, she should recollect the relentings and condescension of her father, and / consider herself as indebted for all to his unparalleled kindness.

In this harmonious frame of spirit it is no wonder that the health of Margaret perpetually improved. The unfavourable symptoms which so alarmingly threatened her life, one by one disappeared, and left no vestige behind. Her cheeks became smooth, and resumed the rosy hue that was the unavoidable result of functions restored. Her eyes became once more bright and lustrous, and the smile of cordiality and enjoyment sat on her lips. The muscles of her frame grew plumper and more elastic. She wandered in the paths that William loved; she revisited with conscious recollections the scene, where the declaration of his love had first broke through the control of diffidence and the fear of offence, and burst in a stream of eloquence from his trembling lips. She did not forget the field in which she had been hunted by the infuriated cattle, or the tremendous / precipice down which she had fallen, and where William had so miraculously saved her life.

Meanwhile she did not fail to calculate the days and the hours that must elapse, before she could hope to see him again. First came the dispatch of her father's letter of recal. Weeks must elapse between the time when she printed on the address her farewel kiss, and winged its speed with her prayers, and the time when he would receive it. Then she saw her William in fancy when the letter was delivered to him, and pictured to herself his emotions. Yes, she did not doubt that he would hail it with joy unspeakable, and regard its contents as bringing to him a restoration from death to life. But how many things might happen to protract his return! Going out, as he did, under the patronage of a person of greater opulence and worldly importance than himself, he could not be altogether his / own master. She revolved the various struggles that might occur between the impetuosity of passion, and the demands of the situation in which her father's letter might find him. William was the truest lover, the most pure and single-hearted youth that ever existed: but he had also the most exquisite moral feelings, and would leave no relative duty unpaid. /

CHAPTER XVI

At length his answer arrived, in which he promised that, in one month from its receipt, he would make his appearance before her in person. He named the ship in which he was to come, and the port, Plymouth, where he was to land. Oh, how she doated on this letter! She had preserved many preceding billets that she had received from him. But she had locked them in a cabinet, and placed them in a remote corner, where she would be least likely to fall upon them by accident. She scorned the idea of preserving them as fuel for her ill-fated and discarded passion. What she did, she resolved in the integrity of her heart, and / in the most entire good-faith, to accomplish. But she could not prevail upon herself to consign them to the devouring element. She could not consent to the violent and profane destruction of what was his, and might still be considered as representing him. It was enough, she thought, if she never opened the casket that contained these letters, never pampered her sight with a line that composed them, never voluntarily even looked upon the case in which they were enshrined.

But how little, a short time ago, had she expected to add another letter to the heap! When she removed from the North to the banks of the Severn, she took care that this cabinet should accompany her; and she no longer imposed on herself the severe restraint that it should never be opened. On the contrary she regarded it as a day of jubilee, when, fearlessly and without remorse, she threw back the lid; and, every day since, she had made it / one of her foremost indulgences, to gaze on the lines which William had traced, to admire the beautiful phraseology and the words of fire in which he recorded his love, and to trace every variation and gentle transition from sentiment to sentiment, which his clear and transparent language conveyed. But his last letter was dearer than the rest. It assured her of the continuance of his affection, which no rejection, no change of climate, and no new connections and prospects could destroy or diminish.

As the time appointed for his arrival drew near, a certain restlessness and impatience became visible in the deportment of Margaret. Her hopes were sanguine; she did not doubt she should once again embrace the lover whom her father generously restored to her. But she recollected every thing she had heard of the treacherous element to whose mercy he was now committed, the rocks, the shelves and / the quicksands, that often lurked beneath its smiling surface, and lured many a tall bark to its ruin. She thought of the violence of the raging winds, and of the broad, turmoiling waves, that rose 'Olympus high, and ducked again as low, as hell is from heaven'.[a] She pictured to herself the broad Atlantic, from the midst of which the keenest eye from the tallest mast could discern no shore, and then the approach of shore, which was often fraught with more danger than could arise from the most gigantic billows in the widest ocean.

Her father at length took pity upon her exceeding uneasiness, and kindly proposed that they should remove to Plymouth about the time of the Roebuck's expected arrival, and surprise the way-worn traveller with the pleasure of an early encounter. They hired a lodging within view of the sea; and Margaret several times in the day paced the sands, and looked out with an anxious eye and a beating / heart, whenever a white sail appeared in the distance. Sometimes she climbed to the top of Mount Edgecumbe,[b] that she might give to her prospect a more extensive range.

The state of the weather changed a few days after the removal of the family of Margaret to the coast of the English Channel. The summer had been genial and serene; and every thing appeared prosperous for the navigation of William. But, as the days shortened, the winds grew loud and hollow and blusterous. This state of things continued, and even increased day and day. The oldest inhabitant of Plymouth never remembered so tempestuous a season. The father of Margaret began to repent of his precipitate step, in bringing his darling child so near to the scene of danger. Yet what could distance have done? If she had remained at her remoter home, she would have heard the contention and roaring of the winds, and her soul would have been shaken / with a thousand terrors. Suspense is often a great aggravation of the most fearful calamity. Here at least with the earliest means she would know the worst.

Every day brought the word of vessels foundered, or driven on shore; and the sea-coast was strewed with wrecks. At length intelligence was received of the Roebuck being seen, in the greatest distress, her masts over-board, her rudder gone; and the most vehement apprehension was entertained for her safety. Finally she drifted near the shore; her condition was plainly to be discerned;

---

[a] *Othello*, II. 188–9 (adapted).
[b] Mount Edgecumbe, headland lying across The Sound from Plymouth.

she fired minute guns; but no boat could venture off to relieve her. You could almost see the countenances of the crew; at least you could observe their attitudes and their despair. The long boat pushed off with as many passengers as it could safely receive, and was at no great distance from the ship, when, from the force / of a new sea, she made a violent plunge and went to the bottom.

Margaret was within sight of this fearful catastrophe. She looked with agonizing alarm at the boat, as at one time it rose to an intolerable height on the giddy wave, and then suddenly vanished out of sight, as if it had been swallowed up by the billows. It drew nearer and nearer, but with an irregular motion. No material accident however interfered with its career. She pushed close under the lee, and the passengers leaped out. They were to the amount of nearly thirty. Margaret had placed herself at a convenient distance, from whence she could observe the figures of the crew, their gestures and their faces. She dared not come nearer; for she began to be oppressed with a doleful presentiment that William was not among them. Her apprehension was but too true. Her gaze became / keener and more keen; probability advanced further and further, till it turned itself into a dreadful certainty; Margaret took her last look, and sunk insensible on the bank. Her father, her mother, and a friend who had accidentally joined them at Plymouth, were with her. The old man delivered his daughter into the care of the other two, and charged them to convey her with all practicable speed to the house in which they had resided for the last fortnight. He resolved that he would not himself quit the shore, till by persevering he had obtained all practicable information as to the loss of the ill-fated lover.

At first the unhappy wretches who had just escaped from a watery grave, shook him off with impatience. They were too much disturbed, too much occupied with looking about them, first to the landward, and then to the sea, and then in mourning for the friends, the companions, and the property, that was all, / swallowed up in the wreck, to be capable of listening to the importunity of a stranger. Borradale was schooled by the rebuffs he received, and watched for a propitious occasion. He followed them to an inn to which the majority of them retired, and patiently waited till they had called for and taken such refreshments as they pleased. He then fixed on a young man, who drew somewhat apart from the rest, and was otherwise distinguished by an humane and intelligent countenance. Of him he enquired respecting the youth, who had come to Canada only a few months before with colonel Bouverie, and had since embarked on his return on board the Roebuck.

It happened that the person to whom these questions were addressed, was able to give all the information that was sought. He and William, though previously unacquainted with each other, had associated familiarly during the voyage. He said, that William had appeared / to be the happiest creature on board. He told his new friend, that he was coming home to be married, that he had been driven to go abroad by the inexorableness and hard-heartedness of the father of her he adored, whose only fault it was to be too submissive to so ill-conditioned a parent; but now every thing was reconciled, and he was recalled by the invitation of him who had occasioned his exile. His raptures in praise of his mistress were inexhaustible. His delicacy however was so great, that he never once pronounced the name of her family, but had only spoken of her by her Christian name of Margaret.

The voyage had passed in the most auspicious manner, till, on the evening of the third day from their catastrophe, and when they had already entered the chops of the Channel, appearances suddenly changed. A sharp wind arose, and the temperature became exceedingly cold. The clouds thickened; and, before morning, / they were involved in all the horrors of a tempest. The tone of William's mind for the first time became changed, and he was filled with melancholy presentiments. Is it possible, said he to his friend, that, now that I am come home to happier prospects than ever, I should be destined never to reach the land? God knows my heart! I do not grieve so much for myself (I know that I must die some time or other, in adverse circumstances or in prosperous), as I do for my beloved, if it is her fate to lose me and survive. I could almost wish (for her sake, not for my own), that we were embarked in one bottom, and sustained the same fortune. Next to living together, perhaps the most desirable event was that we should have died together.

After having endured all the vehemence of the storm for two days, and it being evident that the ship could not float for many minutes more, the long boat was thrown out. William / was one of the first to rush to the side of the ship where it lay. Life is dear to every one in the moment of extremity; but William had a motive more urgent than any other soul on board; his venture was not merely for his own life, but for the life of one a thousand times dearer to him; nor merely for her life, but for that which only makes life worth the having. He stepped on the edge of the vessel; a rope which no one had observed, at that moment slung violently against him; it destroyed his balance in the very act of quitting the ship, and flung him into the sea. He presently recovered the shock; he swam towards the boat; one of the crew stretched out his hand, and they missed of each other; a wave came up at that instant, and carried him many yards from his point; we saw him no more.

The situation in which Margaret was left by this event was most melancholy. Every obstacle to the wish of her heart had been removed, / and she was even courted to be happy in the way of her own choice; when a cruel destiny had in a moment bereft her of the individual, who alone in her apprehension constituted the life of her life. Her prospects were closed. There was nothing that remained for her but a melancholy and cheerless resignation. It was in some sort an aggravation of her lot, that no one now opposed her; all had been eager to unite in one accordant effort to place her beyond the reach of envy, when the elements of nature put forth their might to take from her that, which man was anxious to bestow upon her.

It was by slow degrees that she was able to raise her head from the couch upon which despair had cast her. When she opened her eyes from the insensibility which had fallen upon her, she could not at first recollect what had happened. The truth at length burst upon her. Her agony vented itself in piercing / shrieks. She invoked the names of her father, her mother, her William. She had seen the boat as it landed the few persons who were saved from the vessel. She had viewed the sinking of the ship; and she had seen no more. But her father and her mother could tell her that of which she was ignorant. Her father doubtless had been earnest in his enquiries. Perhaps William had swum to shore. Perhaps some of the crew had saved their lives on empty casks and fragments of the vessel, and he among the rest. If so, why did he not make his appearance to dispel her fears? Was there no hope? What was the final result of all the enquiries that could be made?

The father and mother sought to elude her earnestness, and clothe what they knew with some degree of uncertainty. But she would not be baffled. She pressed to know by her importunate enquiry the worst. She was no longer under the control of filial deference. / The eagerness with which she sought the truth trampled on all diffidence and half-measures, and made her utterly irresistible. In piteous accents she implored them to hide nothing from her. Had even his body been washed ashore, to give the last certainty to the cruel tidings that overwhelmed her?

From this moment Margaret sunk into a deep dejection. Her situation was however very different from what it had been during her brief residence in Yorkshire. That had been a condition of continual struggle that wore out her frame. She had looked forward to a future, which, in spite of all her efforts, was inexpressibly odious to her. Nature and fortune had a strife which should gain the mastery, and she had been constant in her determination to subdue her repugnance; but the weakness of her frame had given way notwithstanding the heroism of her mind.

Now she had no one to contend with: every / one about her was desirous to do all that was in their power to mitigate her sorrows. No attempt was made to revive the proposals of lord Borradale. Those proposals had afforded the signal for the commencement of her calamity. And, since the series of her woes had terminated in the destruction of her lover, those proposals had grown a thousand times more odious and loathsome to her than ever.

Her father, from the time in which he had seen her on the steep descent of a premature decay tottering over the grave, had totally changed his character. He had now no object so near his heart as the preservation of his child. As the idea of an insurmountable barrier to be set up cutting off for ever her union with William had almost destroyed her, both her parents felt that there was every thing to be apprehended in the result of the fearful casualty to which her lover had fallen a victim. They regarded her as a creature to be / saved with the most watchful care. They viewed her as a delicate flower to be sheltered from the blast, and to whose existence every keener breath of heaven was in the utmost degree perilous. They sought to anticipate all her wishes, and to remove every obstacle from her path, 'lest at any time she should strike her foot against a stone'.[a] They removed her from one watering place to another, trying how far travelling, change of air, and new objects and scenes, might conduce to restore her strength and infuse cheerfulness into her mind.

The efforts of her parents produced a deep effect upon her. She felt how much she owed them; and she would have regarded it as a baseness and a crime, if she had not done every thing in her power to contribute to their gratification, and conduce to the object they desired. It was a memorable contest on both sides, which should make the greatest sacrifice to the other, or most forget themselves in their anxiety / for the benefit, or consideration for the feelings of the other party. As the calamity that had overtaken her was irremediable, her mind sunk into a sort of hopeless tranquillity, by no means calculated so powerfully or so suddenly to undermine the foundations of human life, as the inward contest between a contrariety of feelings under which she had formerly sunk.

An interval of three years had interposed itself between the catastrophe of William, and the period when I first knew her. She had gradually become resigned to her fate; she endured life as that which it became her to sustain; but she carried a barbed arrow fixed in her heart. She took no interest in any thing, save the welfare of her parents. She considered all that they had suffered on her account; and she thought nothing she could do could ever make them amends. Hourly she regretted that her unhappy state should be a burthen to / them. She was anxious to appear cheerful and contented in their eyes. But she could rise to no higher a virtue than patience; and therefore there appeared in her a perpetual struggle between the shew of mildness and equanimity which she assumed, and the withering consciousness of a disappointment and a sorrow never to be forgotten. /

CHAPTER XVII

From the moment I saw her, I was struck as I had never been with any other woman. She had been resplendently beautiful. Her features were not less perfect than those of the mother of Catherine. The colour had indeed deserted

---

[a] Psalm 91: 12 (adapted).

her cheeks; but her complexion was of the most consummate fairness. Her lips imparted the idea of delicacy itself. Her eyes had a mild and languishing effect, which perhaps can never be found in those of a person in perfect health. Her high forehead was as white as alabaster, and was doubly relieved by a profusion of ringlets of dark brown hair. But the main charm of the whole consisted in the mild expression / of a divine resignation. She was like nothing earthly. Human passions seemed extinguished in her; she was among the admired of her sex, but she 'was not of them';[a] you approached her with awe, as if she were descended from the spheres; a figure like hers, if encountered in the days of the fabulous mythology, would undoubtedly have been worshipped as a goddess.

From the moment I beheld her, I was fascinated. I could see no one else; I could look at nothing but her. I had loved before: oh, how dearly loved! but this was a passion of a different sort. She appeared like a fairy vision, like some creature of the elements, compounded of the lily, the violet, and the morning dew, when first the beams of the rising sun exhale sweetness and freshness from the vegetating earth. There was an unreal and an angelic character in her seeming; she looked as if purified and defecated from sublunary grossness, / a modification of the air, that would vanish if you approached it too rudely. The mother of Catherine, however beautiful, was a being of flesh and blood, a woman: so had formerly been the fair Margaret. But grief had attenuated, and resignation had sublimed her. She was piety and filial virtue, and nothing else: all meaner things, all imperfection, all that allies us vulgar mortals to sense and frailty, seemed as if they had long ago forsaken her. She was a sylph.

Was it infatuation that my heart was immediately struck with the spectacle of this melancholy maid? My feelings were doubtless in some degree connected with the frame of convalescence in which I now found myself. The world was renovated before me. I had lately in a manner taken my leave of sublunary things: and now unexpectedly I felt the sensations of health returning upon me, and the world clothing itself in all life-giving colours. Meanwhile, / my limbs not being yet restored to their robustness, my tastes and perceptions had in consequence a delicacy which I had perhaps never before known.

I approached Margaret; she did not repel me. She had not been extensively conversant with the world; and she found in me a being more than ordinarily in unison with herself. I was neither like the cold-hearted, mere virtuoso lord Borradale, nor the frivolous, empty coxcomb, his son. The tones of my voice were characterised with a spirit of music; my manners were soothing, prepossessing and gentle. I talked to her of sentiment; I spoke of the wife I had lost. Though I had been more than fifteen years a widower, my recollections were green, my emotions were fresh. There was a certain kindred between my sorrows and hers. She loved me for the purity of emotions, which were of so

---

[a] Quotation unidentified.

long life, and had stood the test of time; and I loved her, that she listened to / them with so much patience, and such genuine pity.

But the principal cause of the extraordinary influence which Margaret exercised over my mind, consisted in her sorrows. There are various ways according to which female loveliness and excellence attain their empire over man. Sometimes it is splendid, majestic, faultless beauty, that seems to draw after it a crowd of slaves, who would willingly, but cannot, make themselves free. Sometimes it is a species of beauty, soft, gentle and insinuating, that appears to derive its strength from weakness. Sometimes it is grace of motion and an irresistible carriage, that melts the heart into softness, and imparts ideas of voluptuousness, which subdue the whole man into an entire and passive subjection. Sometimes it is sentiment and sympathy; and sometimes wit that plays about the lips, and flashes a transporting gaiety and a thousand subtle meanings from the eyes. / But sadness had to me a power beyond all these. I should have resisted an imperious beauty, that claimed to draw me a captive at her chariot-wheels. I should have refused to be the victim of the attractions of luxury and voluptuousness. I should have disdained to become the conquest of mere softness and frailty. But I found in beauty, modified by the impressions of grief, something that I could not hold out against. Beauty prepares the mind of man to submit; and pity binds him with an invincible cord. Tenderness is the very soul of love; and when I looked upon Margaret, I felt a tenderness for her that no words can describe.

Another circumstance which exercised a magic influence over my mind, was the recollection of what she had passed through. The history of the human mind, and the inventions of genius, can with difficulty furnish an instance of so absorbing a passion. The resignation / of Margaret served only to illustrate the depth of the feeling with which her heart was penetrated. She could conquer her will; she could yield the train of her actions to the guidance of her father. She displayed an energy and strength of resolution of the most extraordinary cast. But she could not draw out the barbed arrow which was fixed in her vitals. She was hastening to the tomb without a murmur; the all-inclosing air was not broken with the voice of her complaint. But she was dying. Having formed her resolve, she quailed not; she stood as firm and motionless as the pillars which are said to sustain the vault of heaven. But the grave would have closed over her; she would have been gathered to the forgotten things of the world. Nothing could erase from her soul the image of her William; there he stood distinct in all his lineaments; he was the pole-star that marshaled the course / of her thoughts; he was the sun from which the light of her mind was singly derived.

Such had been the feelings of Margaret during her residence in the vicinity of the mansion of Borradale, and for as long a time as she believed that William was numbered in the congregation of the living. There is something exceedingly different in the effect produced upon the human mind by the irreversible decrees of fate, and when the gates of death are for ever closed on our conjectures. We submit to the authority and the harsh edicts of our fellow-creatures, but always with a reserve. The casket they present to us is like that of Pandora: it contains an accumulation of the direst calamities; but Hope is at the bottom.[a] We have still a secret hoard laid up in the mind; there is an uneasy thought, like a living worm, gnawing at our vitals, and suggesting, in spite of ourselves, the imagination, / This is not final; all these things may be reversed. Not so, when death has shut up the scene. Hope, the last possession of the wretched, is then departed. And, strange as it may seem, the heart grows more quiet; its pain becomes blunted and dull; and though happiness, it may be, is farther from us than ever, we fold our arms, and become inert and passive as a statue.

Margaret had passed through these two conditions. In the first she wasted away with a gradual decay; and, had not her father changed his measures, and given way in time, she would have died, a spotless monument of filial submission and obedience. Her present condition was not so critical. There was a pious, a religious resignation in it, that ceased to convulse every fibre of her frame. She was struck, as with a lightning from heaven; but it had nothing in it corrosive and putrifying; it rather seemed to preserve every thing in a state / beyond the reach of alteration. One might compare the beautiful figure that presented itself, to the unperishing remains of the mighty dead of Ancient Egypt; but with this difference, that the mummies we behold are shrunk and withered, an assemblage of bones with a covering, the skin being changed into the appearance of parchment, – while the living figure I saw from day to day in the assembly-room at Harrowgate was of unrivalled beauty, infinitely more dazzling and illustrious than any thing that can be discovered in those customary angelic features, which Death has not marked with the impress of his fatal operation.

When I looked therefore on the person of Margaret, I saw all that love, almighty love, could effect on a human being. She was the temple, in which the god had enshrined himself. She presented to my eyes the image, the sovereignty and empire, of this divine passion. This spectacle produced in me a strange / and most perverse conception, the thought, Oh, that I could be so loved, as William had been loved! There was indeed a mighty obstacle to this. Could his image ever be obliterated from her heart? Were not her powers already used up? Was not the elasticity of her soul worn out by her first passion? No matter! I refused to despair. Here was at least the subject, the living creature originally capable of such things as the multitude of her sex are not qualified so much as to understand. Perseverance might do much; and I resolved to persevere. The

---

[a] In Greek mythology Pandora, sent by Zeus as a gift to Prometheus, brought with her a jar which she was forbidden to open, but she disobeyed out of curiosity, releasing from it all the ills that beset humankind, and leaving only hope within.

difficulties indeed were vast. But proportioned to the difficulties, was the glory of the achievement; or what I valued more, the consciousness I should have that I possessed a prize, such as all the earth could not shew in any other creature.

There was something in the demeanour of Margaret that encouraged this idea. Without declaring myself, my manner and my attentions / became such, as fully to shew to every discerning eye how deeply I was smitten with the pale, the enchanting figure that was placed before me. I was happy enough from the first to find some degree of favour in the sight of the disconsolate mourner. She distinguished me from the herd of those who danced attendance at this scene of apparent gaiety. I sat near her; I spoke to her. My speech was mild, and in harmony with her subdued state of mind. As I said before, her air was abstracted; she seemed scarcely to notice the things around her. But she attended to me. I talked to her, not of those frivolous matters which make almost the sole subject of fashionable conversation. I talked of those parts of England, which we had both of us seen. I talked, without being conscious of it, of those poets and those branches of literature, in which she had been initiated by her lover. She listened to me; she answered me. Her remarks were / indicative of the most perfect taste and the deepest feeling; the tones of her voice thrilled through my heart. The subdued, gentle and low key in which she spoke, the sweet distinctness of her articulation, filled me with rapture. I felt sensations I had never before known, a bliss of a strange character, which, because it was new to me, deprived me of self-government, and carried away my whole soul like a torrent.

I was not slow in opening my heart to the father of Margaret. He consulted his wife. They both of them thought, that, if I could win the favour of their daughter, the happiest result might be expected. They determined, that they would in no sort interfere to direct her will. They had had enough of that. But, if she could be drawn off from the fearful abstraction and quietism into which she had fallen, if she could be induced to form new ties, it might be the cause of a happy revolution within her. She was of so ingenuous a disposition, of / a conscience so perfect and sincere, that she would never enter into so sacred an engagement as marriage (particularly when that engagement, as they resolved should be the case, was entirely her own act), without summoning her whole energies to the discharge of its duties. It was the only chance. She would then be transported into a new world. She would have a husband, servants, an establishment, to occupy her attention. She could not live, as now, only with the extinguished and invisible.

For Margaret, she also, for various reasons, felt inclined to listen to the proposition. She began to be ashamed of her obstinacy and self-will. She felt how much she was indebted to her parents for the indulgence they had shewn her. She resolved not to be an incumbrance on them for ever. She dived into their hearts, and, notwithstanding the entire silence they preserved, saw what it

93

was they earnestly desired. / She had been, as it were, an evil genius to her father, the means of cutting off his hopes, disappointing his ambition, and driving him back upon the low estate which had embittered the best years of his life. She thought her submission to the speechless wish which he had formed in this instance, would prove the best expiation she could make for that scene, in which she had so unwillingly been the cause of his griefs.

Beside this, she also began to believe that she ought to consider, that she did not come into the world for herself alone. She had faculties and endowments. She was capable of imparting good and happiness to others. She was the member of a society, a body corporate more or less limited, of human beings. She had the power of doing good to others, and of exhibiting a praise-worthy example. She resolved, that her humble name should be remembered for a certain worthiness, and that it should / not be forgotten by every one that Margaret had existed.

When she began, as I have said, to feel inclined to the proposition I had submitted to her parents, her conversations with me at the same time began to assume a new character. She was still 'of ladies most deject and wretched',[a] her heart deeply scarred and trenched with the trials she had passed through, and the sorrows she sustained. But her manner towards me was most fascinating and exquisite. When she saw me, she roused herself. The treatment she exercised towards me, was wholly unlike that she gave to the insects that buzzed around her, unlike that which she gave to her friends. It resembled the demeanour which was to be observed in her to her earthly parents: and yet it was distinct from that. She tasked herself to give me pleasure. She treated me as a person already standing in some relation to her, in consideration of the / relation in which it was probable I might hereafter be placed.

This sort of shadowy, undemonstrative observance had a power that no other mode of conduct could equal. It was like the modulation of the speech of a ghost, who, we are told, even when he reveals the secrets of a world unknown, or lays bare the foulness of the most monstrous crimes, still speaks in a tone, articulate and no more, in words which, while they shake the inmost fibre of our souls, have neither accent nor emphasis, but impress us with the weight of the thing communicated, unclothed with the labour and artifices of speech. It is even thus, if I may farther illustrate my meaning, that action, the gestures of the body, the impatient stamping of the foot, are merely the excrescences and disease of eloquence. They mark that the speaker is not at home, nor fully imbued and penetrated, with his subject. Otherwise he would not indulge in these / ambitious ornaments of discourse, shewing that he is labouring to reach, is working himself up to, the idea and the feeling he would communicate. The highest eloquence is concentred. In it the voice is deeply, not superficially

---

[a] *Hamlet*, III. i. 164.

affected, the eye may speak, the muscles of the visage may be convulsed, but the limbs are still. The action of the body, in the estimate of true taste, interrupts the path of a thought, which should proceed straight from the soul of the speaker to the soul of the hearer, to which purpose this restlessness is mere absurdity, and impertinently disturbs the conception, which otherwise would be drunk in with one long draught by him who listens.

I am afraid of not making myself fully understood. My illustrations are inappropriate, but are such as I am able to light upon. Be that as it will, it was thus that Margaret spoke. She was a statue; and by contagion I was turned into a statue. We spoke, not in whispers / for the clear tone of the voice was not disguised, but was uttered in that key, pure, though subdued, which reached the ear of no one but the person for whom it was intended.

Margaret seemed to undergo a metamorphosis and a miracle. The deeply-trenched wound she had received was not healed. Her colour was not restored to her; she was not gay – oh, how far was the sensation of gaiety from the soul of the mourner! But she was all observance, tenderness, and mild devotion. She seemed to be awake to me alone, to see nothing but me. She then only became a living thing, when I approached. The cloud, in which the memory of her William wrapped her, and which hid her beauties and graces from all other eyes, fell off, and was dissipated. Still she was an imagination only, and a memory. Her body was a corpse, if we can figure to ourselves a corpse, void of every thing offending and repulsive, but which on the contrary / was more beautiful, more ravishing, more celestial, than any living mortal could ever be. For the soul that informed this body, was all delicacy, all sensitiveness, tremb-lingly alive.

To be the object of the tenderness and attention of so divine a creature, a creature altogether unlike any thing I had ever seen or could figure to myself, was a trance, a removal to the heaven of heavens. I know not how it was: I had loved Emilia, as much, I thought, as woman could be loved. But my present passion was not like what has been described as

A home-felt delight,
A sober certainty of waking bliss.[a]

Oh, no! It was 'the song of Circe and the Sirens; it took the prisoned soul, and lapped it in Elysium; it lulled my sense in pleasing slumbers, and in sweet madness robbed me of myself'.[b]

What I felt on this occasion can be likened to nothing but a transmigration, a being born / again. I was, as Solomon says, even as 'a serpent upon a rock',[c] the skin of whose figure has, by length of time and the rudeness of the elements,

---

[a] Milton, *Masque*, ll. 262–3.
[b] cf. *Masque*, ll. 253–61 (freely adapted, with omissions).
[c] Prov. 30: 19.

become knotty and gnarled, with a thousand wrinkles, and pursed into fur-
rows, loose and unfitted to the frame within, but who, by continual friction and
rubbing himself against substances the most capable of resistance, at length
detaches and lays aside the deformity which incumbered him, and comes forth
glossy and sparkling, and moves free as air and with the lightning's speed. Just
as we might suppose such a serpent, unweeting[a] of his former self, and rushing
into the joys of a new existence, even such was I.

I lived in the glance and the motions of my new mistress. I turned as she
turned, 'true as the needle to the pole'.[b] Wherever I met her, I saw nothing else.
Her motions, which were gentle, and gliding, and made no noise, ravished me.
The very air seemed to yield / before her, and to suffer neither removal nor
violence, so little did she resemble the creatures of this common earth. Her
voice, which was all soul,

> ... came o'er my ear like the sweet sound,
> That breathes upon a bank of violets,
> Stealing, and giving odour.[c]

When she opened her lips, I dared not so much as breathe. 'Silence was took,
ere it was ware'.[d] There was a melody in her speech, ten thousand times the
more fascinating, because it had a coyness, as if afraid to be heard, a divine
sweetness and beauty, and a measured pace, that enabled the hearer to savour it
all, without missing its slightest and most evanescent graces.

In a word, never was man so entirely and irretrievably caught, as I was
caught. There were no obstacles in our path, and we married. Before this event
took place, Margaret a thousand times called on me to consider what I / was
doing. She was a being, she said, over whom the Angel of Despair had poured
his influences, and who never could be worthy of me. I liked her, she could
perceive, – I loved her, if that were the name by which I chose to call what I
experienced: and this was all well, so long as the situation retained its novelty.
But it was impossible, I could continue to be satisfied. I would find in no long
time that I had taken the shadow only, where I had expected the reality of a
wife. Her affections were blasted; her heart in the grave. What was there left,
that could be entitled to my acceptance?

At the same time that Margaret stated this, she assured me of her resolution,
as far as that could be effected, to conform herself entirely to the state upon
which she entered. She would not juggle with her vows. Conscious as she
should be, that her best services were 'stale, flat and unprofitable'.[e] and that
even at last she could poorly and worthlessly discharge / the duties of that

---

[a] Unknowing.
[b] From the popular song by Barton Booth (1681–1733).
[c] *Twelfth Night*, I. i. 5–7.
[d] cf. *Masque*, ll. 557–8.
[e] *Hamlet*, I. ii. 133.

equality and partnership into which I proposed to admit her, she would watch herself unintermittedly, make her life a school, and each evening a shrift.[a] But it imported not, she said: all that she could do would fall far short of what might reasonably be required by me of a wife; and I should questionless repent of the rashness of my proceeding.

I on my part protested, that the frame of my spirit was such as could never experience a change. I felt that within, which had made me a new creature, and would last as long as sense and reason should be continued to me. I was devoted to her, and had no life but in her life, no pleasure but in rendering her incessant attentions, no satisfaction but in her approval. /

---

[a] A confession.

97

DELORAINE.

BY

WILLIAM GODWIN,

AUTHOR OF " CALEB WILLIAMS," " ST. LEON," &c.

Why that bosom gored?
Why dimly gleams the visionary sword?

POPE.

IN THREE VOLUMES.

VOL. II.

LONDON:

RICHARD BENTLEY, NEW BURLINGTON STREET:

SUCCESSOR TO HENRY COLBURN.

1833.

CHAPTER I

Thus then I entered upon a new scheme and order of existence. I had been married before. I had wedded an angelic creature, whose heart had been exposed to no vexations, whose affections were new. All was reciprocal and in unison between us; we had no secrets from each other. What one thought, the other thought; what one desired, the other desired. We were never happy but in each other's society. The live-long day appeared but too / short for our intercourse, our communications, and our love.

In my second marriage I experienced not less satisfaction and transport. But it was of another kind. It has been said, There is no true love but between equals; and Margaret and I were not equals. We were each full of observance to the other: but upon how different a principle it proceeded! She was the receiver; I the received. She was in a great degree passive, attentive to my lightest wishes, desirous of even anticipating my contentment. Her thoughts waited on my thoughts. But I was full of impulse, fervour, restlessness. I looked to her as the divinity I adored. Nothing I did in relation to her satisfied me. Nothing was good enough to be worthy of her excellence.

Margaret was pale, frail, scarcely qualified to encounter the difficulties and hardships attendant on the commerce of her species. I / looked upon her as an inestimable jewel, inclosed in a purse of tiffany,[a] almost of gossamer. I was anxious to defend her against the rudeness of the breeze that scarcely stirred the leaves of the poplar.

It were nothing indeed, if she had been characterised merely by tenderness and softness. But I remarked, within the bewitchingness of this outward shew, the nicest discernment and the most unspotted integrity. Her life, especially for many months past, for years, ever since lord Borradale had presented himself at the cottage of the Severn, had been a life of sacrifice. Her first purpose had been to consecrate herself, her soul, and all her vital powers, to the obedience of her father. As long as she was capable of perserverance and going on to the goal she had chosen, she quailed not, nor allowed her devotion to swerve. And now, after the melancholy catastrophe of / her lover, her first thought was how she could best console her parents.

Her father had resigned his ruling passion,[b] the cherished weakness of his

---

[a] Sheer gauzy fabric.
[b] The concept of the ruling passion was first developed by Pope in *An Essay on Man* (1733), ii. 138ff.

nature, that he might bring back his daughter to life, to health, to contentment. She had subscribed to this his generous act of self-denial. How could she do otherwise? She began to feel, as he had felt, that her existence was suspended upon the issue. She could not, she grieved that she could not, control the powers of nature. It might be an exalted act on her part to die, rather than seem, even in thought, to disobey the authors of her existence. But this would not gratify her father. He desired to behold her the daughter-in-law of lord Borradale. He could not endure so much as to imagine, that, instead of seeing her a bride, he should see her a corpse, and himself close upon her the portals of the tomb. At last therefore both father / and daughter had agreed that she should be united to the lover of her choice. Thus, in perfect accord with her duty, and with the cordial assent of her parents, she had had the prospect of entire happiness with (as she believed it) the worthiest, the tenderest, the most affectionate, the best of human beings.

But heaven had ordered it otherwise!

Should she then, thus tried, thus bereaved by the almighty Author of the universe, give way to despair? No. She would still apply herself to discharge the duties that were left her. Her father should not see her the victim of irretrievable sorrow. She would shew herself worthy of the parent, who for her sake had made so generous a sacrifice. He had done his part, all that could be required of the most affectionate and exemplary father; and she would do hers. He should see, that she was not like the poppy of the field, its head surcharged / with dew, its stalk broken, and that is no more able to lift itself, no more to be numbered with the flowers of the earth. What could not be restored, should be forgotten by her; or, if not forgotten, should not have the power to prevent her from filling her due place in society, or presenting herself in the eye of the almighty Creator, as one who, if she had received certain talents, had not failed to apply them to such purposes as her opportunities allowed her.

When therefore I looked at Margaret, I found in her nothing but what was pleasant, delightful, adorable to the eye, while all within was simplicity and wisdom, entire integrity, and consummate virtue. When I saw her, I saw the most transcendant, and at the same time the most delicate thing, that ever met the eye of man, or that imagination ever framed. I thought of her as of a pearl beyond all price. When I met her at the breakfast-table, clad in / all the simplicity of her morning attire, my heart rejoiced within me. When I saw her amidst the parterres of her garden, she was the fairest flower, or rather she was as the orb of day, from which all of them derived their colour, their health, and their sweetness. When I returned to her from a short absence, what were the transports with which I beheld her! In absence she was my dream; I turned a thousand times to view the curling smoke as it rose from the residence in which she dwelt. Or, if every token of its existence were rendered by distance undiscernible, still I knew the direction in which it lay, and my heart beat and trembled, even as the magnet trembles towards the pole.

In every thing I studied her pleasure, and never ceased to enquire within myself what could tend to her gratification. Her health was precarious; her frame was delicate; and still I thought what food, what exercise, what / reading, what topics of conversation, what amusements, what scene of residence, the atmosphere of what part of England, or of Europe, would be most congenial and sanitary to her. I watched her eye, her lips, the indications of peace or uneasiness, of content or discontent, that were to be found in her countenance. When she spoke, how I hung on the tones of her voice! That little organ is capable, I had almost said, of millions of modulations. The catalogue, digested by my penetration and vigilance, did not certainly comprehend them all; but it was of considerable extent. If her eye brightened, how was I penetrated with joy! The clouds and sunshine of the human countenance, and these are infinitely more numerous and variable than those of an April day, I could read them all. When a thought or a feeling was yet but half-conceived, and lay unmatured and in embryo, I caught it, I discerned it, I encountered it, as / the case might be, with cordial welcome, or with opportune prevention.

Margaret was to me what a favourite toy or plaything is to an affectionate child. She was like the little bird, that the child thinks she can never enough caress, or testify her fondness for. She was like the fetiche[a] of an Arabian devotee, a relic in which a portion of the divinity is supposed to take up its residence, and which is as an amulet, that, as long as it is retained, fails not to 'keep far off each thing'[b] of calamity or evil. I considered the house as blest that contained her, and every thing upon which she smiled as deriving from that smile a character of inviolableness. It was impossible then that I should not be superlatively happy; for did I not possess her? and, as often as I pleased, could I not satisfy myself with beholding her figure and her countenance? I was ready to exclaim with the queen of Sheba in holy writ, 'Happy are thy men, and happy / are these thy servants, which stand continually before thee!'[c]

Indeed Margaret never appeared to greater advantage, than as surrounded by the establishment, at the head of which I had placed her. She was most scrupulous and indefatigable in the discharge of her duties as a matron, a patroness, a regulator, a directress of all that fell under her superintendence; for duty was the sanctuary at which she worshipped. Nothing could exceed the delicacy, the neatness, the elegance of every service and arrangement that passed under her inspection. And, as I have already said, all that approached her were happy. Her rules were so perfect and so simple, that to wait upon and to follow them was felt like perfect freedom. She spoke to all with such considerateness and kindness, that each individual was delighted with the very sound of her voice. 'When the ear heard her, it blessed her; and when the eye /

---

[a] Fetish.
[b] Milton, *Masque*, l. 455.
[c] 1 Kings 10: 8.

saw her, it gave witness to her'.[a] There was a benignity in her smile, which no imagination could paint to itself but that of him who had viewed it. And she did not confine herself to the imparting pleasure by the kindness of her looks. She studied the contentment, the ultimate advantage, the very desires of all that approached her. No one came near her without being the better for it.

The discharge of her duty in Margaret carried its own reward along with it. Occupied as she was in providing for the happiness of others, it was not in the nature of things that she could altogether fail in sharing what she dispensed. Hers was an active life. For every hour and every minute of the day she had something to do, to think of, to premeditate, or to observe. Not that she was always in action; her life was far removed from restlessness, hurry and perturbation. But that the goodness of her disposition was for ever overflowing upon / others. She constantly meditated upon order, arrangement, improvement, improvement of herself, and of all that came within the sphere of her influence. And, being engaged in this train of doing what her judgement approved, she daily drew nearer to the state of forgetting that she had ever been unfortunate. The image of her William, that was impressed upon her heart of hearts, perpetually grew fainter; it presented itself less frequently than it had done, and not with the same degree of agony.

It was even thus that I experienced weeks, nay months of perfect fruition, so that not a day passed over my head, that I did not congratulate myself upon the inestimable prize that I had drawn in the lottery of life. I was a creature altogether different from any thing I had felt in myself for the last fifteen years. They had had their pleasures. But these pleasures had been few and thinly dispersed over / the current of my days. They were the fertile Oases, the little islands of verdure, scattered over an immense Libyan desert. But now I never woke in the morning without the consciousness of my good fortune. I never lay down at night but in serenity and satisfaction. My sun always shone; my firmament was always cerulean; my garden was enamelled with each colour of the bow of heaven;

And with fresh flowerets hill and valley smiled.[b] /

---

[a] Job 29: 11 (adapted).
[b] *Paradise Lost*, VI. 784.

CHAPTER II

This had a pause. I felt a vacuity; and I knew not why. It was not that I stood in need of still further novelty, or that I wanted a more various succession of gratifications to fill up the craving of my soul. It was that no one of my pleasures, when I analysed it, when I savoured and dwelt upon it deliberately, was complete. It was by slow degrees that I detected this.

I had Margaret, as the partner of my board, as the person who superintended my establishment. I could see her when I pleased. I could sit by her side for hours together, and always found her obliging. She listened to me / apparently with an unwearied attention. She would do whatever I desired; she would sing, or play, or ride, or walk, and to a certain degree be merry or sad, as I gave the signal for the one or the other. Why was not I contented? What could I reasonably desire, that was not within my reach?

It was that the soul was not there. All that Margaret did, was in the spirit of discharging a duty. Her hand was stretched out to me; she was ever ready, at the slightest intimation, to call up all her powers to perform my bidding; but her heart did not beat towards me. From moment to moment she still relapsed, subsided, into herself. I was perhaps too subtle in continually devising my own uneasiness and discontent. If at any moment I looked at her, when she did not expect to be observed, I could see that her mind was absent, that her thoughts were engaged in something remote, and which had nothing to do with her husband. She had / a secret store, a hidden treasure, that no one was to look upon but herself. When she was alone, the casket that contained this treasure, did not wait for her to apply the key, to display to her admiring eyes its reserved beauty; it had a sympathetic virtue, and opened before her unbidden. When she was in society, this hidden idea was never long absent from her thoughts. I most sacredly believe that she did not encourage this wandering of the mind, this departure from what she regarded as her recorded duty. No; she strove against it; and, though it rose a thousand times, she each time wrestled with, and defeated it. But it had an energy that could never be extinguished; the tenacious invader, though wounded in the most vital places, and apparently killed, yet returned afresh to the attack, and shewed a vigour never to be diminished.

Margaret therefore was present with me in appearance, but absent in reality. She was in / my apprehension like one of those *simulacra*, those unsubstantial

WORKS OF GODWIN: VOLUME 8

effigies, spoken of by Lucretius, that 'mock our eyes with air', and seem to be with us, when the actual persons are far absent, and are wholly unconscious of where their representatives are, and what they may appear to be doing.[a] She was like the Hercules we read of in the Odyssey, a mere empty shade, seemingly vexed in Tartarus, when personally he was in heaven, the partaker of endless felicities.[b]

I compared the life that I now spent with Margaret, with that which I had passed with my first wife, the faultless and all-perfect Emilia. That was emphatically an union of two souls in one. Our desires always corresponded; we chose the same things; our frankness was unbounded; neither of us had even a thought that was a secret from the other. That was indeed a happiness which left nothing to be desired. /

What was my present situation? When I saw Margaret, I saw a creature than whom imagination could not shape any thing more resplendent and divine, and who, beside this, acquired an additional interest with me, inasmuch as she was the child of misfortune, oppressed with a calamity that never could be removed, and who therefore called forth that peculiar species of tenderness which is the sister of pity, at the bottom of my heart. But, in the most emphatical sense, she was nothing to me. What I thought, was not what she thought; what I felt, was not what she felt. She had her seat of retirement and privacy, where I must never come; to that which passed in her heart of hearts I was to be for ever a stranger. I had her body, all outward duty, honour and observance; her mind was another's.

It is true, I ought to have been prepared for this. No deception had been practised upon / me. Her virgin heart, the first impulses of her guileless youth, had been given to her William. I had consented, I had eagerly desired, to make myself one with this child of disappointment; I had sued to be the guardian of this beautiful fane,[c] even as it thus lay in ruins. What right then had I to complain?

Alas, what availed it me to reason in this manner? To love, and to be wise, is denied, we are told, even to the Gods above. In truth, was ever man in any case reconciled to suffering, by the consideration that he had deserved no better? She was my wife. She had approached with me to the altar, and had taken the vows which had been tendered to her in that character. By every law, human and divine, she was mine. Could I be contented then, to keep this most precious of earthly possessions, this thing so emphatically my own, while a 'corner' of it was retained 'for others' uses?'[d] /

---

[a] Titus Lucretius Carus (98–55 BC), Roman poet and philosopher. The discussion is in his *De reum natura*, a didactic poem expounding the atomist theories of Epicurus; *Antony and Cleopatra*, IV. xii. 6.

[b] cf. Godwin's own account in *The Pantheon* (1814, 4th ed.), 229.

[c] Temple or shrine.

[d] *Othello*, III. i. 272–3 (adapted).

It is true, that the claim of William was elder than mine. She had loved him, before I was a candidate for her affections. She had given me all that it was still in her power to give. She could not therefore be to blame. The laws of nature she could not reverse; that on which the past had set its seal, it is not in the power of omnipotence itself to recal.

This however, after all, was bare reasoning. I felt that I had a wife, who was in the strictest sense not a wife. I felt that I sat in unblamed communion with the first of heaven's creatures, while I was at the same time in truth a stranger to her.

It was worse than this. Oh, I do not half do justice to the agony of my condition! I knew her thought; I knew in general terms the topic upon which her mind was exercised; though I did not know it in all its detail. She was aware that I possessed her secret, that she had a window in her bosom, that her heart was / transparent to me. But, though she knew this, she dared not speak her thought; she would have held it sacrilege to utter so much as a syllable respecting it. I was aware too of her timidity, her terror, the meaning of her silence, the words that were for ever bursting their bounds, and forcing their way to her lips, but were never pronounced; and I ventured not by the slightest indication to betray my consciousness. Was ever constraint like this constraint?

I was therefore full surely a discontented man. I bore about with me a repining spirit. My bud of happiness was withered; and all the remainder of my days consigned to bleak and barren disappointment.

Yet, in spite of all this, I loved the fair one, with whom I had entered into the public contract of everlasting union. Loved! Nay, I doated on her. She was inexpressibly beautiful. The pale languor that hung about her for ever, the whiteness in her cheek, the sickliness / that impressed its stamp upon her countenance, rendered her interesting beyond the power of words to speak. It was not the sickliness we so often see, which conveys to us the idea of disorganisation, an unhealthful and ruined frame. It was as if a member of the host of heaven, fated to exist through everlasting ages, had experienced some heavy and heart-striking disappointment. I could not live without seeing her. It was necessary for me not only to know that she was safe: I besides required for this the 'sensible and true avouch of my own eyes'.[a] Though she did not by her looks convey to the by-stander the notion of one in whom the seeds of death had rooted themselves, yet even her pure and healthful delicacy, so to express myself, awakened in my mind the idea that she might escape me, and be no more. She needed care, and soothing, and encouragement; and who so proper to exercise that care as myself? It is one / of the canons of our nature, that we love a thousand times the more the being who depends on us for its preservation.

Yes: however paradoxical it may seem, I should not have loved the most

---

[a] *Hamlet*, I. i. 57–8.

beautiful creature in female form, with vigorous and unabated health, with a glad and laughing eye, and whose limbs were alert and active as those of a young roe on the mountains, half so well as I loved Margaret. Tenderness is the name for a lover's most exquisite sensation; protection is implied in his most generous and heart-thrilling impulse.

In a word, I felt that she was not a wife. I confessed that I had promised myself a Juno,[a] and had embraced a cloud. Yet from my heart I forgave her. I was bitterly disappointed; but I harboured no resentment. And wherefore should I? She had practised no deception. I grant that I had been deceived; and that I daily felt that deception more acutely. But I / was self-deceived. What I had expected, and what was necessary to my happiness, was in opposition to the course of nature. I might as reasonably have looked that the sun should return in its orbit, and set at the point from which it rose, as that Margaret should forget all the bitterness of her fate, and be given up, heart and soul, to the unfortunate man who was now her husband.

The position upon which I was thus cast, had a singular effect on my temper and frame of mind. I had for fifteen years been a widower. During that time the train of feelings which belong to the intercourse between two persons of opposite sexes vowed to each other, had fallen into disuse with me. I might be said to have grown old in habits of concentration and uncommunicativeness. But I found, when the trial came, that I had not grown old. The spirit of the affections was as much alive in me as ever. The longer the stream had been / interrupted, the more impetuously did it seem to flow, when every obstruction to its course was removed, or rather when a new channel had been opened in which it might freely spread itself. My observance was probably more fervent and intense towards Margaret, than it had ever been to Emilia. Even the period of life I had reached, appeared to have the effect of rendering my devotion more steady and unalterable. I had lost much of the levity and mercurialness of youth, and the train of my purposes and actions became more profound. And, along with this, came the singularity of my situation with my present wife: ever devoted, ever watchful, never satisfied. My anxiety over her grew, even from this cause, that that consummation, that entire union of feelings and desires, that complete pouring out of the soul towards each other, which marriage in its most perfect form proposes to itself, never arrived between us. /

---

[a] In Roman tradition, the queen of the Olympian gods.

CHAPTER III

In this situation, this state of acute and morbid anxiety, the astounding intelligence reached me, that William lived. Six months from my marriage had scarcely elapsed, when I received the information.

As I have already related, he had by a mere accident been flung into the sea, at the very moment that he purposed to leap from the Roebuck into the long-boat, by whose means all those on board were saved, that were supposed to have escaped alive. He had however recovered the shock; he had been seen swimming towards the boat; he was on the point of being taken in, and delivered from a watery / grave; when an immense wave intervened, carried him many yards from the point he had reached; and he was seen no more. Almost at the same instant, from the force of a new sea, the ship made a violent plunge, and went to the bottom. No one doubted that, in this melancholy crisis, the life of the lover of Margaret had been added to the wide destruction that had then been accomplished.

Several years had now elapsed, during which nothing had been heard of this unfortunate youth. He had been seen to be carried away by the roaring and remorseless element; he had failed of his chance of being taken into the boat; the ship itself, before the very eyes of those who had lately been its inmates, was finally and suddenly submerged in the ocean. What chance was there that in so desperate a circumstance he should survive? If he had, would he not speedily have been heard of? If by some providential interposition he had been / picked up at sea, would he not have been landed on his native shore by those who saved him? He came to be married – recalled from a painful exile, by those who had occasioned his banishment, with the purpose to have his most sanguine wishes crowned with success, to be united to the excelling and constant she in whom his very heart was centred, – was it possible that any thing but death could have detained him from her longing arms? Margaret had never a single thought that could obscure that of her William. She saw him perpetually in her dreams: but she saw him as a ghost. She had been in a manner an eye-witness of his tragic fate: it was too real to be doubted: hope itself could not conjure up the conception that he lived. For a time however she remained a faithful widow to her true lord; she would have 'served seven years, and they would have seemed to her but a few days for the love that she bare him';[a] she knew she /

---

[a] Gen. 30: 20 (adapted).

could never be in a pure and genuine sense the wife of another. But she thought she had duties that survived; and she submitted accordingly. When she had waited for years; when fancy had during that period been her meat and her drink, and she took in a manner no other nourishment; when, if she met the eyes of her parents, she saw what they expected of her, though they would not utter their thoughts, – she recollected what she owed them, how much her father had sacrificed of his darling passion, and she resolved that she would once more force her way into the scene of human things, and do what she could to recompense him for his self-denial.

It was under these circumstances that a letter was put into my hands by my valet. It was directed to Margaret by her maiden name. She was from home at the time, on a visit to her parents. It had travelled to different places, and at length reached the scene of my / abode. It was marked on the outside, 'Ship-Letter'.

The sight of this letter struck me like a thunderbolt. It filled me with all wild and appalling impressions. What was I to believe? I had a presentiment, that in some way or other it related to William. Yet what could there be to be communicated? He was dead. The dead indeed in many cases left relatives, left property behind them, and there was information to be given, and questions to be resolved respecting these. But, after so long an interval, this was not a likely solution. It was besides a 'ship-letter'. When the remorseless waves have closed over a man, and taken away the principle of thought and action from his visible frame, it might almost as soon be expected that they would restore to life that which they had destroyed, as that they would render back to us any precise intelligence how he had died; the tomb is silent; and the caverns / of the ocean yield us no account of the hidden things they contain.

The more I dwelt on these circumstances, the more my uneasiness increased. I felt as if my fate, for all the remaining period of my existence, was folded up in the cover of this little letter: – and I felt truly!

On what was I to resolve? Propriety seemed to require that, as the letter was addressed to Margaret, it should be delivered into her hand with the seal unbroken. But what had propriety to do with a case like this? Ordinary rules are made for ordinary occasions. There is doubtless a decorum that ought to be observed in the common intercourses of human beings. But this was not an affair of usual occurrence. This letter might shut up in it more evils and distempers than are said to have been inclosed in the box of Pandora.

In a word I broke open the letter. Its contents came up to my worst apprehensions.

William was an excellent swimmer. By the / strength of the waves he had been carried far out to sea; and he soon found that it would be in vain for him to think of making the shore by his single exertion. He turned towards the ship. He had been enabled to reach it on the side that stooped lowest towards the waves; and for a moment he felt once more that he had somewhat solid on which the sole of his foot was planted. It was but for an instant. But that instant was every thing to him. The thought darted into his mind, that his only remaining chance for life consisted in his fastening himself to a piece of the wreck. A loose plank lay near him; a piece of rope offered itself to his hand. This he coiled round the plank and his own body in a manner so secure, that they could scarcely by any shock be separated again. The ship sunk; but himself and the spar were unconnected with the ship. He floated; and in a short time was able by his exertions to give an impulse to the plank and himself, that carried him away from the / gulph in which the vessel was absorbed. He thus remained on the surface for hours even after all sense had deserted him. In this state he had been taken up, and placed on the deck of an English frigate. By the assiduous efforts of those about him he was in no long time restored to life; but his powers were so much exhausted, that, for a considerable space, he possessed no distinct recollection. He neither knew where he was, nor what were the events that had immediately preceded. All seemed to him like a dream. He looked with wonder upon the persons around him; every one was a stranger. Before he was able to tell a coherent tale, or signify his wishes and desires, the frigate was already far out upon its voyage. From the effects of what he had suffered while floating alone between life and death, or from some other cause, he was seized with a dangerous illness; and his health long remained in a precarious state. The frigate was already not / far from St Helena,[a] when she fell in with two Spanish vessels, and, after an obstinate resistance, was obliged to submit to the enemy. By her captors she was carried into Carthagena,[b] where it was some time before William recovered his strength; nor was it till after multiplied misfortunes, and having passed through a vast variety of adventures, that he had finally landed on the shores of his native country.

The interval of his absence appeared to him as nothing. It was like the story of the sultan, who in apprehension had passed through a period of twenty years, a state of unrivalled good-fortune, and a state of abject slavery, and found in the result that all this had only occupied the time in which he plunged his head in a tub of water, and drew it out again, and saw all his courtiers standing round him just as before.[c] So William had done and suffered much during his expatriation: but, the moment he came in sight of the land in which resided the fair one / he loved, these realities faded into the painting of a dream. He fancied that he should find every thing, just as it had been announced to him in his letters of recal written more than four years ago. He imaged to himself Margaret still standing on the cliffs at Plymouth looking out for his arrival. He knew her too well to apprehend that her heart could be changed. He would as soon have believed that the island of Great Britain had

---

[a] A volcanic island in the SE Atlantic.
[b] Or Cartagena, Mediterranean port in SE Spain.
[c] The tale comes from the 'Story of Chec Cahabeddin', in *The Persian and Turkish Tales Compleat* II (2 vols., 1714), pp. 19–30.

been swallowed up by an earthquake, as that Margaret would not wait for his return however long, or, even in case of his death, would not have remained faithful to his memory as long as she existed. He had therefore written to her from on board the ship that brought him to England. He had been prevented from entering the first boat that came alongside, and had delivered his letter to the officer that carried the dispatches, with directions that he should put it in the post the instant he was able to do so. /

The letter overflowed with all the earnest impatience of a lover. The writer alluded to the multiplied disasters that had overtaken him, and spoke most feelingly of the grief the person to whom it was addressed must have suffered on his account. He had been a prisoner of war; he had undergone every kind of privation and indignity; he had wandered among 'deserts and mountains, and in caves and dens of the earth'.[a] But, through all these vicissitudes, the image of Margaret had followed and sustained him; he had seen her angelic and benign countenance, and heard the affectionate tones of her voice, constantly amid the darkness of the night; and this had given him courage to persevere and to live through his bitterest reverses. And now he was returned to reap the reward of all his sufferings, while she would pour the balm of sympathy and love into his wounded breast. /

CHAPTER IV

What a letter was this for me to peruse! It stripped in a moment the rainbow colours in which the world had been clad in my eyes, and exhibited in their stead.

> ... all monstrous, all prodigious things,
> Abominable, unutterable, and worse
> Than fable yet had feigned, or fear conceived.[b]

Of late I had been dissatisfied with my condition, and had complained that I had a wife and no wife, a woman who was mine in all external duty, but whose heart was buried with another in his watery grave. But this was a refinement of the imagination, the uneasiness of a man surrounded with indulgencies, but / who pined for something more. I had attention, observance and tenderness. I had a companion, the ornament of her sex, who devoted all her powers to the

---

[a] cf. Milton, *Paradise Lost*, II, 619–21: 'They passed . . . O're many a Frozen, many a Fierie Alp, / Rocks, Caves, Lakes, Fens, Bogs, Dens . . .'
[b] Milton, *Paradise Lost*, II. 625–7.

making me happy, and to the providing me with every species of gratification. Of living creatures I was the one in whom her thoughts were centred. Her eye followed me in all my movements; she regarded it as her sacred duty to watch my thoughts and anticipate my wishes; and what she did for me was done with such tenderness, so single a heart, and so ingenuous a disposition, that I must have been a brute indeed not to have felt the most ardent gratitude and the sincerest transport.

Yes, I had been happy! I felt myself so; I have acknowledged that I was happy. The corner in my heart that I reserved for discontent, was one of its remotest recesses, into which my thoughts retired, when they had been already saturated with sweets, when they / overflowed with serenity, and when in mere wantonness they sought for a proof that I was mortal, that I had not every thing, and that I could find a flaw, a sensible imperfection, in the otherwise round and polished surface of my joys.

What was I now? There was a being to whom the heart of Margaret was devoted more emphatically than to me. But every one was satisfied that that being had long ago been numbered with the dead. Successive seasons, as we believed, had whitened his bones upon some distant shore. I might as well be jealous of the devotion that exalted religion pays to the virgin Mary, or to the almighty Author of the universe, as of Margaret's love for William. She devoted herself to me above any other inhabitant of the earth; and I ought to be satisfied. I had no rival. The chastest spirit may love ideal beauty and excellence without censure; no one would be so irrational as to be / jealous of the creations of Apelles or Raphael, of the radiance of Helen, or the conjugal affection of Andromache;[a] and he who has quitted the busy scene of living things, is 'but as a picture'.[b]

Henceforth my condition was altogether different. There was a man that she preferred to me and to all the world. In the eye of heaven he was her husband. Nothing but death had divorced them. Love had never been proved by such a variety of tests, as the love of Margaret for William. In its first trial she had resolved to sacrifice all the yearnings of her soul in obedience to her father. She persisted; and her life was on the point of becoming the victim of her duty. She could command external things, her actions and her words. But she could not root the image of him she loved from her heart. There it lay, sapping and wasting away the elements of her existence. When she learned with every evidence of authenticity / that William was dead, her situation was different. She became comparatively resigned: she did not struggle against the decrees of

---

[a] Apelles (4th century BC), Greek painter; Raphael, Raffaello Santi or Sanzio (1483–1520), Italian painter and architect, regarded as one of the greatest artists of the High Renaissance; Helen, in Greek mythology the beautiful daughter of Zeus and Leda; Andromache, in Greek mythology the wife of Hector.

[b] *Macbeth*, II. ii. 51 (adapted).

heaven and the laws of nature. But what a picture did her resignation exhibit? She sat bloodless and patient, the image of despair. It was in vain that with her corporal presence she joined in the song and the dance; it was palpable to all, that her spirit was absent, and that she no longer participated in the concerns, the gaieties, or the more serious affairs, of the world.

But then she knew, or she believed that she knew, he was dead. She bowed herself to the visitations of heaven, and acted accordingly. It was impossible to guess what would be the convulsions and throes of her soul, when she received the fatal tidings which this letter imparted. No imagination could picture the sufferings that were reserved for her. In the case of young Borradale she had bended, not merely / to the wishes, but to the imperious commands of her father. She had signified by letter to her lover what was determined on, before it took place; and this was much. She had sought his consent, and received it. But now –

Her father, after severe efforts, and the thorough conviction of his mind, had given his sanction to her union with William. He had resolved never again to interfere with her own election on the sacred subject of marriage. The youth had been summoned from a distant hemisphere; and nothing but what appeared to be the inexorable decree of fate had separated them.

He had not however perished, as had been supposed. He had gone through a multitude of sufferings, which would naturally give him new merit in the eyes of his mistress. He had risen above a thousand obstacles, and was returned to claim the reward of unmingled happiness. /

Her attachment had been entire, never to be rivaled, never to be extinguished. To hear then that he still lived, would be to her the bitterest reproach. False, fickle, inconstant woman! Why had she not waited for him? Who called on her to give up the man, to whose claims her father had affixed his sanction?

To hear that he was living, what a shock would it inflict on her! I could scarcely conceive her surviving it. It would totally change her situation in the world, and even her identity. She would be compelled to regard herself with detestation. What, when she had been free to act at her discretion, when all compulsion had been carefully withheld, that she should then have deserted this God of her idolatry!

He had been reported to be dead. But it is the first dictate of true love, to cling with unalterable tenacity to the object of its adoration, against hope to believe in hope, and scarcely / to yield to despair, even though the evidence of our senses should be called in to induce us to relax our hold. But to yield to rumour! Even in a vulgar trial for murder, when the individual removed is worthless, and perhaps more than worthless, when no interest is involved but that of general justice and the security of the abstract existence of society in its members, the law has wisely provided, that no one shall be condemned and executed for murder, till it has been shewn that the individual supposed to be murdered is actually dead – no absence, no lapse of years, is admitted as satisfactory – the body must actually be produced – the seizure effected by the great conqueror of the world[a] must be fully ascertained. And was not William entitled to the precaution and scruple, that would be exercised in the case of such an individual? These infallibly would be the reflections of Margaret.

And was she was then a wife? Would she count / herself for such? No, she was a being for whom society has coined no appellation. She was the despised and rejected of the human race. She must fly to the most frightful solitudes, and call upon the mountains and hills to cover her.

William was the youth whom only she had ever loved. As a high point of filial duty, as a refinement upon the obligations of a moral being, she had given her hand to me. But she never loved me, in the sense in which she had loved the companion of her youth. She discharged the bonds into which she had entered towards me in the most exemplary manner. She watched for my interests; she watched for my gratifications. But this was an affair of the head, and not of the heart. She did what she did, because it became her, and because she could not hold herself excusable for the smallest omissions. And the steadiness with which she adhered to all this was inexpressibly lovely / and admirable. But there was certainly nothing approaching to romantic in her attachment to me.

Margaret's therefore was not the common case of the wife of two husbands. That of itself is nearly the most distressful situation in which a human being can be placed. But her entire, her unequalled attachment, as I have said, was to William. He engrossed her whole heart. He was the subject of her dreams; his image intruded, in spite of her firmest resolutions, into all her duties. She was absent in spirit, when she seemed most to be engaged in the affairs of her new condition. When she talked to me, and when she listened to me, she paid a kind of forced attention to whatever was passing. But her heart was not there. She was buried with the imaginary deceased; and it was only a delusive semblance of herself that survived. To know therefore that William lived, would shake her whole frame with the / crash of an earthquake: to think that, while he still lived, she had voluntarily given herself to another, would unseat her reason, would in all probability extinguish in her the principle of life, and instantaneously associate her with the dead. Her agonies would be like those which we might conceive an exalted enthusiast to undergo, upon whom, when engaged in the act of sacrificing to them that are no gods, the true Monarch of heaven should visibly descend in all his brightness. /

---

[a] i.e. Death.

CHAPTER V

I was at the present instant the sole depositary of this awful secret. It was my office to take care that the intelligence should never reach the person most deeply concerned in it. But how was this to be effected? I had intercepted a letter. But how was I to be secure that this letter, especially if it remained unanswered, would not be followed by another? William himself would infallibly set out in search of his beloved. When and from what quarter of the heavens would he come? How was it possible for me to encounter and intercept him? If I desired to write to him, and endeavour, by a representation of the real state of things, to / prevail on him to withhold his intrusion, and suffer my wife to remain in her present state of enviable ignorance, to what place was I to address my letter? He had landed on the coast of Sussex, and the post-mark on the cover of what he had written was 'Brighthelmstone'. But was there any chance that he would remain there long enough, for the expostulation I should address to him to reach him?

He would doubtless hear, before he made his way into the presence of Margaret, that she was already married. What then? What would be his conduct, when he had learned these tidings of despair? The most obvious impulses of the human mind would lead him to seek an interview. No, he would say, I will not consent to be assured of my fate from any lips but her own! He could not avoid – he would not be a true lover, if he could avoid – the desire to stand in her presence, that he / might pour out his soul before her, that he might tell her all his agonies, that he might lay open before her her thoughtless cruelty, that he might – not die in her presence – but that at least he might take of her a solemn farewel, that he might unload his 'bosom of the perilous stuff',[a] which he could not long carry about with him and live. It was a melancholy and a fearful gratification, to take one last look of the being he had loved beyond all the world, to hear from herself the account of what she had suffered, and what had induced her to act in a way that a sibyl or an inspired prophet could never have persuaded him to believe she would pursue, and to receive from her her final adieux. This at any rate was the conduct that I persuaded myself William would adopt.

And from this visit, which I nothing doubted would at least be attempted, I

---

[a] *Macbeth*, V. iii. 44 (adapted).

was bound to guard the unfortunate female who had been / cast on my protection. Whom was I to guard? Was she my wife? No. I had conceived an exalted idea of this species of relationship. I had had an immaculate example of it in the case of Emilia. I had been contented in my second marriage to take up with a very imperfect resemblance of this blessedness. But at least I possessed a being of unrivalled beauty, upon whose conjugal affection no creature on earth had a claim but myself. I had a sensitive mind: I had a jealous temper. Could I bear to live in the perpetual presence of a woman, who by the institutions of society was my own, but who, by a law prior and superior to these institutions, was dedicated to another?

If I could, still I could not root out from my memory the fatal information which this letter had communicated to me. I should sit by her side, and for ever recollect, I possess the secret, which, if known to you, would turn / you into stone. You smile now; you look serene; you half forget the deep scar which is trenched in your breast; you think yourself innocent, and exemplary in the discharge of your duties. But this is not so. All the duties you perform to me, are in reality due to the first lord of your affections. Your life is a perpetual cheat; and I, with the knowledge that it is so, must be contented, must think myself too happy that the deception can still be carried on, must enact day after day, as long as the delusion can be preserved, the part of the loving, the affectionate, the satisfied husband. Surely all the torments of hell cannot equal the eternal repetition of this mummery.

And yet, for the sake of the miserable victim, I must take care to keep her for ever in ignorance. Though he lived in the same world, the same country, nay, the same street, if she knew it not, to her he did not live. I / must therefore be the person, to build up the wall that should hide from her this tremendous secret. I must take care that William did not approach her, that no letter from him reached her, that even the babbling wind did not repeat the tidings. Poor creature! if it did, what would become of her!

I had a confidential servant; and to him I was obliged to make an unreserved communication. He already knew something of the history of Margaret, of her intended marriage with the son of lord Borradale, of the cause of its being broken off, and of the miserable loss at sea of the youth to whom she had previously been engaged. Persons of a certain rank in society imagine that they stand at an immense distance from their inferiors, and that nothing is known of their proceedings but just what they are willing should be known. But this is a great error. The menials by whom we are surrounded, take a pride in acquainting themselves / with our affairs, and regard it as the height of sagacity on their part to penetrate into that which we wish should remain unknown. The servant of one family tells what he observes to the servant of another; and, from mutual communication of their remarks, they strike out a light which illustrates the innermost depths of our concerns. But Thomas, the servant of whom I speak, was excited, not merely from an unhallowed curiosity, but from the strong interest he felt in my welfare, to observe with sagacity, and to treasure up the fruits of his observation. I found that I had little more to communicate to him but this last information, which had just reached me, and which was so wide from all anticipation.

I charged then this faithful fellow to take with all expedition the road to Brighthelmstone, and to hold himself on the alert, if by possibility any thing should occur on his way, that / might afford him a clue on the subject of his commission. Though William had not mentioned the name of the vessel that brought him to England, it would not probably be difficult for Thomas, when on the spot, to make out something respecting it. He might also pick up some knowledge respecting the passengers, and by possibility might learn the route that William pursued. I instructed him in that case to follow in track of him by whom the fatal letter had been written. It had reached me in three days from the date which it bore; and, as I had not suffered the smallest delay to interpose, it might still be conceived that Thomas would not be too late. The newly arrived would find neither Margaret nor her parents at the place from which they had last addressed him. The enquiries which would be required to enable him further to pursue his search, might be supposed to take up some time. If he first lighted upon the parents of / Margaret, they would inform him of what had passed in his absence, and would probably have the power at least to prevent his reaching our abode without some previous notice. I intrusted my servant with a letter I wrote, in case of his lighting on the person he sought, in which I shortly informed him of what had occurred in his absence. I told him, that, his epistle having reached my house in the absence of Margaret, I had used the precaution to open it. I observed, that not the smallest doubt had been entertained by any one, that he had perished at the time when the ship foundered, and that the years which had elapsed since seemed to preclude the possibility of his having survived the catastrophe. Margaret, I added, had long mourned his loss; and it had almost been thought that she would have followed him to his supposed grave. At length, when all conception of his return seemed to have perished, she, though in a state of great sorrow and deep / mental depression, had consented to accept the offer of my hand; while I on my part had made every exertion to soothe her grief, and restore her to some degree of tranquillity. I stated, that I felt perfectly how bitter must be his disappointment, in being thus precluded for ever from the possession of her to whom his affections had been so ardently devoted; but I observed, that the evil was now past all remedy, and that it was therefore the duty of one in his unfortunate situation, to endure his calamity with fortitude and a manly spirit. I adjured him above all things not to destroy the last hope of serenity and quiet in the breast of her whom he so inexpressibly valued. It was absolutely necessary, under the present circumstances, that the fact of his having survived should be carefully hid from her; and I felt confident that he would never adopt the ruinous step of obtruding himself into her presence. /

The success of the expedition of my servant was small. He learned the name of the ship that had brought over William to England; but he learned no more. /

CHAPTER VI

In the mean while, during the journey of Thomas to Brighthelmstone, and for some time after his return, I remained in a state of the most cruel trepidation. No further intelligence reached me. The period of Margaret's visit to her parents terminated; and she returned home. I was agonised during the latter part of her stay with the doubt whether William might not discover the place of her father's present abode, and so by possibility encounter my wife without her having received even the smallest previous notice that he was alive. But what could I do? In two days from the receipt of the letter of fatal tidings / would come the time when it was originally proposed she should return home. Two days – nay, a single hour, – might be pregnant with irremediable mischief.

The time however was short; the period which had elapsed between the date of his letter and the day in which it reached me had probably been enough, if he had made all expedition, and no obstacles had intervened to retard his journey. Meanwhile I flattered myself that nothing had yet occurred of the kind of which I had the most terrible apprehension; and I therefore suffered her visit to proceed to its appointed termination. It will easily be imagined what were my sensations during this terrible suspence.

Margaret returned home; and I met her at the entrance of my abode. I looked in her face, and easily saw that nothing remarkable, nothing fatal, had occurred to her. She encountered me with smiles, smiles which seemed / to say how much she was gratified to meet again in peace, him, whom the law had made the partner of her life. Those smiles cut me, to the heart. I said to myself internally, Poor creature, you smile now, because you are unconscious of what has really occurred. You are tranquil; but yours is the tranquillity of ignorance. The arrow is already in your heart; the poison is in your veins, which will drink up in you the very springs of life.

There was no day in which William might not make his appearance. If he shewed himself at the residence of her father, *he* assuredly would not fail to communicate with me on the subject. But I heard nothing. I knew not what precautions to adopt. I remained perpetually on the alert. Whether at home or abroad, I gave strict charge to the servant whom I had dispatched to Bright-helmstone, to be for ever on the watch, to prevent by every possible means the

119

access of William to my / wife, or the delivery of any suspicious communication, and to put into the hands of the stranger, by the first opportunity, the letter he had carried with him in his journey, and which, failing to meet the person to whom it was addressed, he had brought back again.

But, though I had employed all the precautions in my power, I nevertheless felt that all might be insufficient. Every morning that I rose, every hour that elapsed in the livelong day, an event might happen that would baffle all my foresight. I remained, as much as possible. at home. If I were alone, my mind was filled with gloomy anticipations. I was like a man, launched without a companion in a frail bark, totally unprepared to endure the slightest assault of a storm, who had already lost sight of land, and discovered nothing but a boundless expanse of water on every side, but whose attention was caught by a black cloud just rising in the horizon, which darkened / and enlarged itself from moment to moment, and appeared to make his destruction indubitable.

But it was necessary that I should spend many hours of every day in company with Margaret. Such had been the habit of my married life, both heretofore, and in the present instance; and it would have been suspicious and inhuman in me to break it. Here it was also requisite that I should personate indifference and serenity. I looked in the countenance of Margaret. Sometimes I observed in it short gleams of cheerfulness, self-satisfaction and gaiety. Her mind then became momentarily absorbed in the trifling concerns of the day, in the management of her houshold affairs, perhaps in a wife-like way catering for the gratification of my appetite. At other times an occasional cloud of seriousness and melancholy would come over her. In all these cases it never failed to occur to me, how soon / may that cheerfulness be dashed to the earth, how speedily may that composure and indifference be dissipated, or how shortly that sadness swallowed up in a more tremendous anguish, the agony of intolerable remorse, or the abysses of despair!

I spoke to her of things of small importance, the arrangements of our garden, or the succession of the seasons. I related the anecdotes of the neighbourhood, and the news of the day. I tenderly enquired of her health, recommended precautions for its preservation, or poured out my soul in the words of affection, and all the sympathy of a lover.

I could not however continue in this scene for ever. When I had strained my powers of self-command to the utmost, when my heart-strings seemed ready to crack with the exertion, I would ever and anon burst suddenly away from my companion, hasten to the garden, and, as soon as I was out of sight, endeavour to / recover myself from the tension to which I had been subjected, by a sort of antagonist exertion. My limbs had been bound down, my features composed, my voice compulsively softened to soothing and encouraging accents; and now in revenge I assumed all the violence and contortions of a madman, I stamped with my feet, I spread my arms with wildness and ferocity, and roared like a savage beast, who has just escaped from the toils that controled him. I found ease in these strange ebullitions of an agonising mind. And, when I came in again, having exhausted myself in these paroxysms of anguish, and endeavoured to recompose myself, poor Margaret, suspecting nothing, would remark nothing extraordinary, and thus favoured my resuming the same tones of indifference or gentleness, as if all had been well, and the earth in reality did not shake and tremble under our feet. /

CHAPTER VII

I had no sooner entered into a matrimonial engagement with Margaret, than I settled a handsome annual addition to the revenues of her parents, and prevailed on them to quit their humble residence on the banks of the Severn, and remove to a more commodious abode in the next county to me, and only thirty miles from the mansion of my ancestors. This was the reason why the letter of William, directed to Margaret at the place where he had known her, had been forwarded to me, which would otherwise have been conveyed to her at her father's house, to whom she was at that time on a visit. /

William was not long before he followed his letter in person. He repaired to the well-known roof, and found the cottage in the possession of another family, to whom he was a stranger. He might have enquired out and encountered some of the families who had been the associates of his youth; but he was not in a frame of mind to desire this superfluity. He might have desired to learn from the present inhabitants of the cottage some particulars respecting his mistress; but they could supply him with nothing except merely Borradale's address, which they had taken in charge to communicate to any one that sought it. William was therefore too impatient to find his friends, and once more to bless his longing eyes with the sight of her he loved, not to proceed with all practicable speed to the point towards which his course was directed.

He met Borradale at a small distance from the door of the house, which he had just quitted. / In this short interval the visit of Margaret had terminated, and she was, as I have already said, again under the protection of her husband.

The old man felt a strange sensation at sight of the stranger that approached him. His impression was first that of imperfect recollection. I have seen this man somewhere before.

Mr Borradale, my old friend! said William.

Whom do you seek? who are you? replied the other. Indeed I do not know you. – A fearful, undefinable feeling, a sort of shuddering, not unmixed with horror, came over the old man. – No; you cannot be my once-loved, rustic

121

neighbour. Time and events forbid that. I witnessed the waves of the tempestuous sea close over *his* head, and bury him in its unknown deeps.

I am William. Did you not write to me, and invite me to return? Years have passed since; but they have made no alteration in my sentiments. – Where is Margaret? I am impatient / to see her. Every moment is an age to me. I trust she has not suffered so much as I have suffered. But that is all over now. I am come to the season of peace, the recompense of every toil.

Let me look at you. No, it is not; yes, it is, our kind, warm-hearted neighbour. How you are altered! Trust me, I am delighted to see you again. But how has it happened? So sure as we were that we had lost you for ever! I long to hear all that has befallen you in absence. – The old man said this, because he was desirous to put off the evil hour, and to think of any thing, rather than of the disappointment, the embarrassment, the agony, that would attend this unlooked for event. Men succeed each other in the scene of human life, even as one wave on the shore rolls over and carries away another; the place occupied by each man is speedily filled up; the gap closes; and he, who after a while should return to us from the / dead, would find that he was an intruder, that there was no room for him amidst the relations of life, or in the division of the manifold productions of earth.

Borradale led the late-returned wanderer into the house. He said to his wife, Here is poor William, returned after all his misfortunes, restored from the grave. William saluted her.

He looked round with a wistful gaze, but without finding the thing he sought. He fixed his eyes on the door of the next apartment.

Where is my love? he said. Is she at home? Is she well?

She is very well, replied the mother. No, she is not at home.

The Borradales had a painful duty to perform. They told William that Margaret was not at home, that she had been with them lately, but that she was gone.

The mother then tried to change the discourse. Well, she said, but where have you / been? Why did you stay away so long? Why did not you write? How did you escape the shipwreck in which so many persons saw you perish?

William was too impatient, to suffer himself to be drawn to any other topic than that on which his soul was bent, or to answer these questions.

It is no matter, said he, what has happened to me. Do not let us talk about that. It is Margaret I want to hear of. If she is not here, at least tell me about her. How has she been? How did she support herself? Oh, I am sure, wherever she is, she is as eager once again to see her William, as I am dying to behold her, to embrace her, to hold her in my longing arms, to be assured that I have her in security, that we meet, never, never again to be separated.

Borradale caught William by the arm, with a solemn, a mournful countenance.

The truth must be told, said he. Prepare to / hear. Call up your courage. Margaret can never be yours.

William staggered to a chair. His countenance betokened the wildest emotion. She is dead! said he.

She is not dead. She is married. What could we do? We waited for you month after month, and year after year. I thought she would have sunk beneath her calamity. There was no spirit left in her. Despair was written in all her features. Nothing could rouse her. She is married: but, oh, with how little of the feelings of a bride! When she took the hand of her husband, she thought solely of you. We believed you dead. We urged, we importuned her to engage in some new scene of life, as the only thing that could save her from destruction.

Borradale might have gone on talking as long as he pleased. One word, one little word,. transfixed his hearer – had had the power to / turn him into a block of marble. His faculties were withered; his features were fixed; his senses were gone. It was long before his powers rekindled. It seemed as if this one word had put an end to his being.

Perhaps no human creature, in the endless variety of sublunary events, had ever undergone so severe a trial. William had passed through countless adversities, 'in hunger and thirst, in cold and nakedness', in imprisonment and slavery.[a] One thing sustained him. He saw the countenance of Margaret shining through the bars of his confinement; he saw her by day and by night; he consoled himself amidst the evils that surrounded him by the thought of her afar off; he looked, with a hope never to be defeated, to her, as the goal of his race, and the reward of his labours. The compulsory and still varied distance that was ever interposed between them, the uncertain length of the period that held them apart, had no other / effect, than to make him love her a thousand times the more.

His was no vague hope, no shade of that self-flattery, which makes the lover so often interpret in his own favour a smile of seeming encouragement, a momentary gesture of regard, one of those thrilling, sweet, seductive, undescribable tones of the female voice, with which an adorable, light-hearted beauty has so often been known to lead on her unwary admirer into a fool's paradise. He had been solemnly recalled from a remote part of the globe; every thing had been arranged; the most sacred pledge had been given by the parents and their daughter.

He sank at once, as it seemed, into annihilation. His eyes were fixed. His lips were severed. He gasped for breath. His limbs were unable to support him. He staggered to a seat. He remained incapable of exertion, incapable of thought. /

The old people became frightened. They did every thing they could devise, to soothe and to restore him. For a long time he seemed insensible of their assiduities. At length he awoke as from a trance, and recovered the power of articulate speech.

---

[a] 2 Cor. 11: 27 (adapted).

Where is Margaret? he franticly cried. Tell me where I am to find her! She is mine. All the powers of earth and heaven shall not tear her from me. It is the first of necessities that I should see her. I must pour out my soul before her. I must tell her what she has done, and what she ought to have done. Oh, let me look on that face! I will see how falshood sits on that countenance, and beams from those eyes. Can she be false? Oh, then never thing was true! There is nothing sacred, nothing to be relied on; the earth has no centre; and the broad and all-inclosing firmament is built on a spider's web. No; no lips but her own shall ever persuade me that this is the end of all. I / must learn my fate from the surest of oracles, and from none else.

As he spoke this, he started from his place, and was about to leave the cottage. The mother of Margaret threw herself before him, and grasped his legs. There was no time to be lost. If he escaped them in this frame of mind, the most tragic consequences were to be feared. It was necessary to soothe him, to bring him back to reason, now before he left the spot.

William, said the mother, hear me! I am the mother of Margaret. Do you not trace her lineaments in this face? It was I that nursed and reared her through all the feebleness and perils of infancy. I have always been your friend. I have no purpose but your welfare, and that of my only child. I feel for you from the bottom of my heart. You have indeed been most barbarously treated. We have done wrong. We are without excuse. You ought to have been / waited for. Nothing less than the sight of your dead body, or a minute and authentic account of your death and funeral, could have justified us in the invasion of your rights.

Yet, let me adjure you, my son (such I will still call you), to consider what you do, and not uselessly to destroy the tranquillity of her, whom you have loved above all human creatures. The course of events can never be arrested; that which happened but a week ago can no more be recalled, than the deeds over which a thousand years have passed. Margaret is married. The most sacred rites of religion have devoted her to another. Our affair is not with things we cannot recal, but with the things to come. You have ever been the sweetest, the kindest, the purest of human beings. We have always looked to you for blessings, for bounty, for every thing that is good and compassionate. Bitterness could never flow from so clear and refreshing a / spring: you cannot change your nature. We have always thought of you with affection and sympathy. Your supposed death was the greatest calamity Margaret and I ever experienced. No; those hands, which have ever called down blessings on us, can never cause us to fear, to question what misery they will next inflict.

The spirit of William was stirred within him at this expostulation. Mother, said he, I will do my best. Do not fear me. I will return to you. But I must be alone. I must go round through all my thoughts, must penetrate the chaos within me, and endeavour to find out what I am, and what I shall be.

The mother dared not to interfere further. William left the cottage, and resorted to a neighbouring wood. Alternately, as I learned afterwards, he resolved to sacrifice himself. His case was hopeless. He had no place among the sons of men. Why then should he shew himself, involved as he was in an atmosphere / of pestilence, to wither and poison the well being of others? Presently he felt however, that thus to proceed was beyond his strength. The grief that fermented within him must have vent, must break down its barriers, and make its power be known. Why should he suffer alone? What had he done to deserve that this insupportable weight of despair should be accumulated on him?

By degrees he began to fall into a more orderly arrangement of his thoughts. He would not seek to inflict mischief on others; but he must procure for himself the satisfaction of beholding the turrets of the house that was the dwelling of Margaret, of observing the trees that shaded her, and the walks that were occasionally blessed with her footsteps.

> Heaven is there,
> Where Margaret lives; and every cat, and dog,
> And little mouse, every unworthy thing,
> Lives there in heaven, and may look upon her.[a]

To see even the smoke that ascended in curling / wreaths above her roof, would be a relief to him. To have the chance of beholding the carriage in which she went out to take the air, would be gratification unspeakable. He knew that this was nothing. He must in time master himself, gather up the fragments of the wreck of what he had been, and see to what account they could be turned. But this momentary indulgence would soothe, and so strengthen him. It was unreasonable to expect that the thousand cords that bound him could be snapped at once, that so terrible a disappointment could be conquered in an instant.

In pursuance of this determination he proceeded to the neighbourhood of my dwelling. He did not return to Borradale's; but enquired of a neighbour the name of his son-in-law. That intelligence was speedily obtained. He approached the place of my abode. He took up his residence at the nearest town. The distance was four or five miles. He found a / cottage that was less than two miles from me. There was a wood between, shut in on one side by a clear, murmuring brook, with a little bridge leading to the meadow beyond. From day to day he came to the cottage, and wandered in this wood. He made acquaintance with the old woman of the cottage, and her daughters; he asked a thousand particulars relative to the occupiers of the neighbouring mansion. He fed his discontented spirit with such intelligence as he could collect. He ascended a neighbouring brow, which commanded a view of my house and

---

[a] *Romeo and Juliet*, III. iii. 29–32 (adapted).

grounds. From this point he could discern my gardens and the persons who walked in them. He saw the labourers employed in cultivating them; he saw me, he saw Margaret. He filled his mind with bitterness and despair, with imagining all that had once invited his acceptance, and the cup of beatitude that had been dashed from his lips, till he could no longer endure the conception / of what he was. He then fled from the spot, while the fiend of memory pursued him wherever he went; and he returned the next day, to be made more wretched, and filled top-full of the direst misery.

The Borradales, finding that he did not return to them as he had promised, ruminated anxiously on the question what step he would next proceed to take. They concluded that they could not do less than advertise me of the visit he had paid them, and then leave it for me to judge in what manner I might be able to prevent the mischief that threatened me. This precaution on their part was well intended; but it had no other effect than to heighten my alarm, and increase the weight of my misery. /

CHAPTER VIII

In a rural neighbourhood like that in which I dwelt, the arrival of a solitary stranger such as William did not pass altogether unnoticed. As he wandered about among the fields, the vallies, and the roads, without any discoverable object, various comments were passed on this new phenomenon. A lady, who was on a visit at a few miles distance, who had seen Margaret, and knew something of her history, felt her curiosity excited. She was fortunate enough so far as curiosity was concerned, in one instance to pass near the stranger, so as to make her observations. She saw in him great appearance of dejection, a wild and unsettled air, / and other tokens favourable to her conjecture, that this might be the former lover of Margaret, who was supposed to have been shipwrecked, but respecting whose fate she knew that no particulars had ever been obtained. As William passed her in an opposite direction, she hastened to the cottage, which, as she had been informed, the stranger had frequently chosen as a place to which he resorted, and where he had been known to remain for an hour together. She entered into conversation with the cottagers, asked a multitude of questions respecting the individual who had excited her attention, and learned that one of the principal topics of his conversation was respecting the inmates of the mansion, of whom they were humble dependents. The lady led them in her own train of thinking, and awakened in them recollections which might otherwise have slumbered. They confessed, that the stranger had an extremely dejected and disconsolate air, that / they could not account for his having apparently made this spot the centre of his peregrinations, and that he had very much the manner of a man recently arrived from abroad. Persons, who are afflicted with this disease of curiosity, will often be found to have a sort of intuitive faculty, which, though it will sometimes lead them on in a train of conjectures singularly absurd and in a manner impossible, will nevertheless occasionally, as by a sort of felicity, suggest to them inferences, built on very slight grounds, but which nevertheless turn out to be precisely correspondent to the reality of things.

The lady in question could not divest herself of the persuasion, that the person she had seen was no other than William, the former lover of Margaret, but who was supposed to have been long dead. She said to herself, I am sure it is so: but, with all this confidence in her own penetration, she had a latent feeling of doubt, / and was on thorns till she could arrive at the state of making assurance doubly sure. As has been observed, she had seen Margaret once or twice, and could use that as the pretence for making her a visit. The lady had no malice in her nature. She would have started at the bare thought of inflicting on any one a serious injury. But she believed she would somehow be able to gain new evidence to the truth of the subtle discovery she had made, without the danger of serious mischief. And, at any rate, the noble passion of disinterested investigation that inspired her, the desire to add one proposition more to the glorious aggregate of truth, was to her superior to all other considerations.

She accordingly hastened to put her project in execution. She drove to my house. I knew the carriage, and was aware of the visit; but I knew the frivolity of the lady's character, and conceived that, if Margaret chose to receive her, she could not have a more innocent recreation. / Visitors only occasionally made their appearance at our door; and the lady was admitted.

The conversation began with the topics usual on such occasions. The stranger next changed the subject to the series of tempestuous weather that had prevailed not long ago, and the mischief it had done among the shipping. – Margaret felt uneasy: the subject touched on a string which always awoke painful sensations in her mind.

Her communicative friend however seemed to take no notice of this. She went on: Oh, I heard such a story of a shipwreck yesterday! It is too terrible to think about it. – Margaret writhed under the prelude; but she was in too weak a state of spirits to be able to resist the torrent. The speaker therefore went on to describe the splitting upon a rock, the guns of distress that were fired, the leak, the yawning breach that the violence of the sea had effected, / the agony and despair of the passengers, the ineffectual attempts that were made to approach to their assistance, and the final swallowing up of the vessel in the devouring waves. Three hundred souls perished: only ten were saved by a sort of miracle.

Margaret long endured the tale; for she did not feel in herself the strength to interpose and subdue the volubility of the person who addressed her. When at length the narrator came to a pause, Margaret turned towards her with a solemn and melancholy aspect.

I thought, my dear madam, that you had known something of my unfortunate story. But, as you convince me by your mode of proceeding that you are uninformed, I will for once deviate from the rule I had laid to myself, and touch a little upon the brink of it. I am no coward; but I have been endeavouring for years to accommodate myself to my circumstances. I did not come, without preceding / sufferings and distress, into the connection and the duties that now control me. I had a juvenile attachment, before I knew Deloraine. The partiality I conceived was early and deep; and it was death only that dissolved it. The idol of my youth perished in a scene such as you have described. An inscrutable Providence directs the fortunes of mortals; and it is incumbent on us to submit without murmuring, and to devote ourselves to a just and exemplary conduct in the relations in which we shall ultimately be placed. I have therefore held it for a principle to indulge in no vain repinings, to forget the visions, the joys and the aspirations of my dawn of life, and to banish from my memory what can never be recovered. With much perseverance I have done what I could to heal the wounds that past time inflicted on me: and, if you had been aware of what I have now communicated, I think you would have refrained from a topic so agonising to me. / May I request that you would touch on it no more?

The appeal of Margaret was of the most impressive nature. But there is a class of persons whose souls are essentially non-conductors to the electricity of sentiment, and whose minds seem to be filled with their own train of thinking, convictions and purposes, to the exclusion of every thing else. I know a man incorrigibly deaf, who yet gives himself the air of discussing with and answering you, who professes to know exactly what you must have alleged, goes on replying to your imaginary objections, and will talk of things immeasurably wide of and contrary to the topics of your discourse, without the slightest suspicion of the ludicrous cross-readings he is presenting. Like this man are the persons I speak of. The ear of the mind is as completely blocked up in them, as are his bodily organs. Of this class of persons was the visitor of Margaret. /

But, my dear madam, said she, are you certain that he you were so much attached to is dead? I beg your pardon. I would not be impertinent for the world. But I have heard many stories in my time of miraculous escapes. The body of him you so deeply lamented, I believe, was never found. He was observed under circumstances most perilous and critical; and he has never been heard of since. I conceive that is all.

Margaret was agitated in the most alarming way by the discourse of her unwelcome visitor.

Oh, God, she exclaimed, what would I have given that he had lived! But I saw the vessel swallowed up by the remorseless sea. I saw the persons who escaped in the long-boat: he was not among them. I heard the particulars of the accident by which he was thrown into the sea, and so perished. What days and nights, what months and years of inextinguishable sorrow have I suffered since that hour! / The miracle is that I live. I am astonished at myself. Surely, surely, I must have been made of adamant, and my frame constructed of materials that no grief could destroy. Why am I not in my grave! Why does this throbbing brain continue its functions! Oh, that I were dead at once! Oh, that I had never been born! that the day of my birth had been swallowed up in darkness, that the shadow of death might stain it, and that it might never be numbered among the days of the year! God, my Saviour, why am I thus? What have I done, that I should be singled out for calamity above all the daughters of men?

The train of ideas that her visitor had awakened, the deep wounds that she reopened in the heart of Margaret, had the effect, that every thing that had passed, the various circumstances and events that had occurred, since she witnessed the fatal catastrophe from the brow at Plymouth, were utterly annihilated. / She stood once more on the tragic spot; she saw in the most vivid manner the whole picture, all the particulars and the turmoil of the scene, which had then transfixed her with despair. She sank motionless in her place, overwhelmed and convulsed as in a struggle between life and death.

I beg your pardon, madam, said the other. I thought I ought to tell you, that I have some reason to believe that yesterday I saw the person we were speaking of. But I perceive that you are not in a fit state to listen to me. I will withdraw. I will send your servant to you.

And she left the room.

Margaret was discovered by her attendant in a state of insensibility. She had fainted away with the excess of her emotions. The lady flew down into the hall, having first said a few words respecting the condition in which she had left Margaret. She found her servants in / readiness, and drove off without an instant's delay.

I heard the sound of her chariot-wheels in departing, and observed in her no ordinary tokens of hurry and confusion. The next minute I was summoned to my wife, whom the attendants had conveyed to her chamber, and placed upon the bed. I was exceedingly alarmed at her appearance. She was without colour, and without pulse. She remained as in a swoon for nearly an hour, notwithstanding all the remedies that could be applied. I dispatched my valet in haste to call in medical assistance. He met the physician that usually attended my family on the road, and brought him to my house in a shorter time than could have been expected.

I did not discover what had passed between Margaret and her visitor till a considerable time afterwards. It was very slowly that the afflicted one recovered her recollection. She was like a person in whom a sudden invasion / of disease had paralysed the organs of speech. She spoke not; though it was easy for me to perceive the gradations by which her faculties returned to her. Her eyes were generally fixed on vacancy: but from time to time they wandered restlessly about the apartment, as if in search of something which they never found. It is impossible for the imagination to figure to itself such an expression of despair. It seemed as if rocks and stones would have moved, and hungry tigers been excited to remorse at so mournful a spectacle.

For myself, I was launched into a sea of conjectures, as to what it was that had caused the tokens and indications before me. What was it that this contemptible visitor had done or had said, that produced so utter a revolution in this admirable creature? I was acquainted with a miserable secret, which was scarcely known to any other human being. I had for many days devoted all my energies to the perpetuating / the blessed ignorance, in the continuance of which the life of Margaret was bound up. I anticipated every day the arrival of William, or of a letter from his hand. Was there a possibility that he had chosen this foolish and ridiculous woman to be his ambassador?

I could not believe it. Still the question remained, Did Margaret, or did she not know that which I was so anxious to conceal from her? I gazed on her with undescribable intenseness. With the lynx-eyed fervour of my gaze I sought to penetrate into her soul; I endeavoured in the doubtful regions, the lines and changes of her countenance to read her thoughts. The wife of king George the Second died of a disease she never would reveal.[a] How earnestly I desired to see the soul of Margaret in all its nakedness, and discover the hidden mischief that was corroding her vitals! I could almost have adopted the determination of Mahomet / the Second,[b] who is said to have pierced into the bowels of his pages at the expence of their lives, to discover what was become of some fruit that had disappeared.

But no; it was impossible that Margaret had received the fatal information. The woman, who had just left my house, could not be the confident and the factor of the miserable wretch who had just returned to his native shores. Margaret was tremblingly alive at every pore. A thousand follies and indiscretions, a thousand impertinences and matters of thoughtless discourse from such a woman, might have given to her a shock of a very painful nature. – But yet Margaret had a fund of philosophy and stoicism, and what was better, of good sense. It was difficult to conceive how a mere impertinence could have produced in her so total a revolution.

The question as to what had passed, and whether the thing I feared had been in any / way revealed to her, was of the last importance. If the symptoms I observed had been produced by any impertinence or insult, however unimaginable, the first shock would be the worst of the affair, and the mischief might be expected gradually to die away and disappear. But, if Margaret had actually learned the existence of her former lover, I was convinced that a fatal blow had been struck, from which she would never recover. The more she reflected upon it, the worse it would appear to her. Here was the poor fellow, the sufferer from

---

[a] Queen Caroline (1683–1737) is said to have died of a rupture.
[b] i.e. Mohammed II (1430?–81), sultan of Turkey from 1451.

a thousand calamities, bereaved of that reward, which in his eye would have atoned for every thing, and cast forth, like Cain, a friendless, hopeless wanderer through the world. And she, even she, by her levity, her want of deep thinking, and of a feeling sufficiently intense, was the cause of this.

The next day after that of this shock, whatever it was, which Margaret had sustained, / Thomas, my confidential servant, presented himself before me. He brought me very interesting intelligence. He expressed an opinion that he had found the person whom I had sent him to the coast of Sussex in search of. Thomas had endeavoured with the utmost diligence to discharge the function I had devolved on him. He appeared in a considerable degree to have followed in the steps of the lady, whom curiosity alone had goaded in her enquiries and observations. He had at first lighted on the stranger whom he remarked wandering with disordered steps about the neighbourhood. There was some-thing about his carriage and air, which suggested to Thomas at the second glance, that this person little resembled the untaught and homebred rustics, unacquainted with the manners and cities of men, and that he seemed as if engrossed and swallowed up with some heartfelt grief. Thomas traced him to the cottage, and took an opportunity, when / he was absent, to make some enquiries of the peasants about him. He found from them, that this stranger had been several days in the neighbourhood, that he had three or four times taken an occasion to talk to the cottagers, and that what seemed most to interest him was any particulars he could glean repecting the inmates of the mansion below. Thomas did not like to proceed further without fresh instruc-tions from me. Should he take for granted upon these vague indications that this was the person to whom his commission pointed? Such a letter as I had intrusted him with, was not to be put into any one's hands without the surest grounds. Should he ask the stranger his name? If he were the individual we apprehended, it was not likely that he would give a true answer to a questioner he had never before seen.

In the mean time Margaret, when she had sufficiently recovered her self-possession, recalled / to mind, as well as she was able, the particulars which had passed between her and her unwelcome visitor. The last words of this inquisi-tive lady had been, 'I have reason to think that yesterday I saw the person we were speaking of'. But, when they were uttered, Margaret was in such a state of agitation and disturbance, that she could scarcely be said to have heard them. It was not till after a certain period spent in rumination and uncertainty, that they shaped themselves into a proposition, and seemed to affirm something. Was this really what the lady said? Might not the sense of what was spoken be the pure fruit of Margaret's imagination? Guilt is cunning in devising the means of its own requital. And, if Margaret was guilty, how complicated was her guilt? How tremendous would her punishment be? The bare suspicion that she had heard aright, was almost too terrible for her to sustain, and live. /

131

CHAPTER IX

It happened that, on the very day of the intelligence I had received from Thomas, I was compelled to leave my home upon a business of importance relative to one of my neighbours, that could no way be dispensed with. For weeks before, I had scarcely quitted my dwelling, or been one entire hour out of the sight of my wife. This sort of confinement could not be supported for ever. But I persuaded myself that the crisis that gave birth to it, must be of brief duration. For the sake of every one, of me, his mistress and himself, it was necessary that William should go once more into a state of voluntary banishment. I was willing to / make any sacrifice, as far as money was concerned, to procure him an eligible destiny. This was no more than he was amply entitled to from my hands; and the peace of all the parties concerned imperiously prescribed it. It seemed to be the most desirable mode for accomplishing my purpose, that I should myself have an interview with William, should urge the necessity of his compliance upon him with a power of conviction that no other person could attain to, and answer his objections, and remove his difficulties, if any presented themselves. But this was a matter of exceeding delicacy, and that required the utmost previous consideration and meditation. It was true that I had reason to think he was in my neighbourhood. Yet to encounter him would probably be a question of some difficulty. He would scarcely be to be found at the moment that I wished to see him.

It was with the utmost reluctance that I set / out on my journey. I had a presentiment that something of the most disastrous import would occur in my absence. I felt inclined, instead of going forth on the business that called me, to send an excuse. But of this thought I presently grew ashamed. It had ever been a principle with me, to pursue on all occasions the straight line of my duty, and, yielding to what that required of me, to leave the rest to the disposal of heaven. My mind indeed misgave me; but I 'defied augury'.[a]

I however determined in my way to call at the cottage to which Thomas directed me. The information I obtained there was much the same as that which he had already communicated. The persons to whom I addressed myself informed me, that the stranger had spoken with them again and again, that he had been with them that morning, and that it was probable that in a few days

---

[a] *Hamlet*, V. ii. 232 (adapted).

he would repeat his visit. I said no more. I wrote two or three / lines with a pencil as I sat in my carriage, and requested the good woman, when she saw the person again, to put them into his hand. Their purport was simply to solicit an interview with him on the third day from the present, at two o'clock, at the little bridge across the brook, which has been already mentioned. If this appointment, from being received too late, or from any other cause failed, I begged the individual I addressed, to favour me with a fresh rendezvous on the same spot, and to leave his answer with the person from whom he should receive my billet. I signed my paper with my name. I felt considerably uncertain whether the stranger were actually he whom I had in contemplation, and was for that and other reasons reluctant to open myself further on paper. But, whether I was right, or was mistaken, no great mischief could arise from a simple rendezvous, which, if erroneous, might / easily be confessed to be so, and apologised for accordingly.

Having adopted this precautionary measure, I have proceeded on my journey. Nothing that deserves to be mentioned, occurred in my execution of the business that had called me. When I set out upon my return, I had discharged myself of all other thoughts, and of the petty intricacies of vulgar business, in which I had been compelled to take a part; and my mind was left free to meditate, even to bursting, upon the question that involved my condition and my future existence, together with the welfare of Margaret, the sanity of her intellect, and very probably her approaching destruction.

The sorrows of William were terrible, and hard to be endured: but, in the light in which they presented themselves to my mind, they were as nothing compared with what was to be gone through by Margaret and myself. He / had lost a mistress, that he loved above all the world. This was a misfortune that has been borne by many in all ages of mankind. It is true, that his disappointment had various aggravations. After having gone through a severe ordeal, he had been summoned from the other side of the globe to receive his reward. Since that time he had experienced a multitude of distressful vicissitudes: but there remained, as he most assuredly believed, the crown of his rejoicing, secured to him by the solemn engagement of the being he adored, and her parents. And yet, lo, now, all this crumbled away from his grasp, and had disappointed him! What then? She might have died. This is among the commonest of human occurrences. And he was left in no worse a situation than if she had died. He had the world before him, to settle himself as he pleased. He was bound to nothing, free as the air. He was like our first parents:[a] 'Of all the trees of the garden / ye may freely eat; but of a certain tree ye may not eat':[b] one thing only was interdicted him.

But what was the situation of Margaret? If she knew, or at the moment she

---

[a] i.e. Adam and Eve.
[b] Gen. 2: 16–17 (adapted).

should come to know, of the existence of William, that he had been in her neighbourhood, that from the adjoining knoll he had seen her walking in the garden, that he had observed her attitudes and motions, and counted her steps, she would then deeply feel, that there lived a man who had had a right to her hand, to her attentions, to the very pulses of her soul, beyond all creatures that existed. What had she done? She had married. But her marriage was one of mere convenience and decency. She thought well of me: no more! But could this contract come in competition with the claims, both from qualities, from that tenderness which only one creature in the universe can feel for one, from that entire and perfect union of souls, which had subsisted between her and William? Could / that justify a breach of the most solemn engagements, the violation of a faith, which ought never to have been disregarded, so long as there remained the possibility that William lived? And what was she to me so long as he existed? An adultress:

> .... a false fair one,
> Who plighted to a noble youth her faith,[a]

and then profaned the most sacred solemnities that religion could supply, by giving her hand to another.

This was her situation, so far as William was concerned. But there were bonds into which she had entered with me. Before the altar, in the house of God himself, and under the eye of the Omniscient, she had vowed to be mine, to adhere to me, 'for richer, for poorer, in sickness and health, to love, cherish and obey', till death should finally dissolve the tie between us.[b] And this, while her heart, her whole heart – who can control the pulses of / the heart? – was another's; while she loathed the engagement that bound her, and while the voice, the reproachful voice, of never-sleeping conscience upbraided her for the guilt she had contracted by consenting to that engagement. It was impossible she could have one day of tranquillity and peace, her duties, according to the general code of all civilized nations, drawing her one way, and an obligation, anterior to and of elder birth than these duties, drawing her another. She must wither like a flower, when all moisture has been drawn away from the soil in which it is planted, and that which should nourish it is turned into dust. She must die, even as that flower would die, when a wind carrying pestilence in its wings had passed over it, or the locusts of the south had spread themselves upon its leaves. Nothing could cure the mortal wound she had received. If William were to perish even now, she could never more forget the charge of disloyalty she / had incurred, the baseness of her proceeding in giving away to another, that which, by the first of all laws, the law of the heart, was his, and his alone.

---

[a] Quotation unidentified.
[b] Solemnization of Matrimony, Book of Common Prayer.

Such would be the situation of Margaret, from the instant she should be truly informed on the subject. But what was mine? I could only understand that of William or Margaret by the force of imagination, putting myself, imperfectly as I might, in their place and endeavouring to think their thoughts. But my own spoke to me in a quite different language. It came to me through the voice of an internal monitor which could not deceive me. There the business lay in its true nature; and a crowd of venomed thoughts burst every barrier, and at the tribunal of my immortal spirit gave in their evidence, in terms every word of which scorched up my vitals.

I had consented (fool that I was!) to be the husband of a woman, whose soul I well knew / had once been devoted to another in a degree that had never been surpassed in the records of human kind. I so admired the lovely unfortunate whose charms had taken hold on me, that I could endure to be only the second in her esteem. I was like what is related of Bacchus in the heathen mythology, who, when he saw Ariadne, with her attitude and countenance of despair on the desert shore, instantly became enamoured of her, was induced to forget that she had previously been devoted to a mortal lover, and took her to his heart.[a]

This was bad enough; and I had accordingly suffered many grievous pangs, when I was led to perceive by a thousand indications, that I had only her duty, while,

> Incapable of change, her fondness lay
> Buried with William in his watery grave.[b]

But what was this to the state of my feelings, when I knew that William was actually alive, was in England, was in the vicinity of / the fair one he loved, was wandering about my grounds, and watching for an accidental glimpse of the figure of her for the possession of whom he would willingly have died! Here was a task, the task of prolonging her enviable ignorance, which I could scarcely endure for an instant, which it might be incumbent upon me to endure for months and years, and which I must think myself too happy if with all my vigilance I could maintain in existence for ever. No; I felt that this was a task that exceeded my strength. To suffer was one thing. Tantalus and Tityus and Prometheus may be supposed to have strung up their energies to that.[c] But to be perpetually alive to the giving new arms to the torturer, to fling against his

---

[a] In some Greek mythological accounts, when the Attican hero Theseus deserted Ariadne, daughter of the Cretan King Minos, she married Bacchus, god of wine.

[b] Quotation unidentified.

[c] Three figures of Greek mythology all punished for their misdeeds: Tantalus, father of Pelops, had to stand in water that receded every time he tried to drink it, and under fruit which moved away when he reached for it; Tityus, a gigantic son of Zeus and Gaea, suffered by having a vulture feed on his liver, which grew again as fast as it was devoured, the same punishment that was meted out to Prometheus, the Titan who stole fire from heaven.

own lips the bough loaded with celestial nutriment which he was never to taste, to communicate new powers and ferocity to the vulture that preyed on his vitals, this / exceeded all the fertility of the poets of old in feigning ingenious cruelty.

I first applied my powers to the keeping from Margaret the knowledge of that fatal secret, the bare consciousness of which would perhaps have destroyed her.

My next fear was that this miserable stranger should actually in person present himself before her. To know that he lived, and was not far from her, was misery enough. But it was a very different thing, to see him, to peruse those well-known lineaments, to listen to the sorcery of his accents, to see misery, reproach and despair written in his countenance, to hear his voice upbraiding her faithlessness, and awakening her pity. This it could never be supposed she would be able to sustain.

It was mine then to preserve her from present death, death which might be imagined / to be the result of her knowing that William lived, death which was the result most naturally to be expected, if she saw him again invested in a clothing of flesh and bones, a real man placed before her waking sight. Like Semele, when Jove stood before her in his true and proper form, she must be expected to be blasted and destroyed in an instant.[a]

But there was another thought, which I am compelled to own, was more intolerable to me than the decease of my much-prized, much-cherished con-sort. I could conceive myself as bearing to see her dead at my feet. It would be a desperate trial; it would shirivel up, as it were, the surface and the substance of my heart. But it would leave me, after a time, even as Margaret had found me when I first beheld her. I had been a widower before. Suppose then on the other hand it was reserved for me to see her gazing on the countenance of another with looks of speechless love, following / his departing steps with eyes that ran over with tears, or suppose it should be, with fond emotion pressing his hand, and even surrendering herself to what they would call his chaste embrace – no; to think of that was madness. Death is but death. The truest mourner does but weep and smite his breast over an insensible corpse. But the vision I here speak of is the genuine torment of the damned; and the most envenomed demons in all the intemperance and drunkenness of their cruelty could contrive nothing beyond it.

No; I could never bear to know that she loved another living man better than she loved me. To the dead I could yield an ideal preference. They are sacred; they are thin air, or of a substance more subtle than air; they neither act upon us, nor are acted upon by us. But that Margaret should be in corporal substance with me, while there was another man, equally corporeal, with whom

---

[a] Semele, in Greek mythology, mother of Dionysus by Zeus; Jove, another name for Jupiter, ruler of the Roman gods.

her mind and / soul tabernacled and lived, leaving me only the empty casket, that I should be regarded as the loathsome obstacle to what she most aspired after, that she dwelt with all she hated, and was absent from the good most precious in her estimation, this was a thought that I could not live with for a moment, and yet that incessantly obtruded upon my contemplations.

Now, at leisure, the agonising leisure to which I am occasionally condemned, I relate all this in order and with method. But it was not so at the time when these thoughts first offered themselves to my distempered spirit. Then all was disorder and wildness and confusion. It was the counterpart of what most men have at some time experienced in a state of delirium. Faces, the faces of maniacs, seemed to grin upon me from among the parting clouds, or through the horrors of the woodland glades. Some of them were faces that I / too well remembered, the faces of those who were most loathsome to my thoughts, and intolerable to my recollections; and some of them were faces more deformed and monstrous than earth ever owned. Alternately they scowled at me with demoniac malice, and then changed their fierceness into a laugh less to be endured than the wrath of hyenas and tigers. If there had been method in this, it would have been less terrible. But it was ever wild and even abrupt. These spirits, if spirits I may call them, came upon me uncertainly from the east and the west, sometimes seemed to start up as out of the ground, and at other times to descend and cower over my head. At one moment they appeared glimmering and scarcely visible; and anon they shewed themselves with frightful clearness floating on the air, or just before me in my path. Nothing was quiet and stationary with them for an instant; / and it was this perpetual turmoil and disorder, that gave indescribable keenness to my sensations.

But I will take advantage of the present cessation, Margaret and William being already dead, and I shut up in an unknown and inaccessible corner among the dwellings of men, to analyse somewhat more fully what I felt, and to endeavour to make it intelligible to the reader.

I have been twice married. The first contract I formed of this kind, was surely the most felicitous that ever fell to the lot of mortal man. The union between me and my Emilia was perfect. It occurred in the dawn of my maturity, when I was yet a stranger to misfortune, was almost unacquainted with pain. It was formed in the full vigour of my health and strength; and the arch under which I entered to this triumphant joy, may be said to have been covered with flowers of vivid hue / and of exquisite odour in the utmost exuberance. The hearts of Emilia and myself were set to the same key, tuned to each other. We anticipated each other's desires almost before they were formed. We had no concealments and no reserves. Either party carried a window directly over the region of the heart, so as to make our thoughts transparent; and this entire knowledge, the one of the other, was the consummation of our joy. Surely this was happiness.

Between Margaret and me the case was exceedingly different. I was far from possessing her whole heart, as I had possessed the heart of Emilia. I could

137

therefore scarcely be said to have loved her so much. But I loved her; and that with an overwhelming and devouring sensation. With Emilia I reposed in full security. I loved her, and was satisfied. I was convinced that she was truly mine; and every day I congratulated myself on my lot. But / with Margaret I knew that she was not mine; and, though she conducted herself towards me every hour in a manner the most exemplary, I was fully aware that we were not like

> . . . . . the streams of meeting rivers,
> Whose blended waters are no more distinguished,
> But roll into the sea one common flood.[a]

With Emilia my sense was of full security; but with Margaret I was ever restless, discontented, craving. Yet for this reason I might be said in a very obvious sense to have loved her a thousand times the more. I was like a sportsman in the midst of the darkest waters, the object of whose pursuit is the eel. He is ever apprehensive that the creature will slide from his grasp, and for that reason holds it with a more emphatic pressure. With Emilia I had arrived at unmingled confidence, that 'perfect love which casteth out fear'.[b] But with Margaret I never felt secure; I asked myself from hour to hour, what is it that now / occupies her thoughts? By a strange perverseness I valued her the more, because I was never the freeholder of her heart, never had the executed lease of her affections. It is thus, that the man only who has just recovered from a dangerous fit of sickness, and apprehends a relapse, is fully alive to the joys of health. It is thus that the man against whom a suit has been instituted for all he is worth in the world, or who has received intelligence that the house is on fire in which he has laid up the acquisitions of a whole life of industry, understands the value of riches. Every time I looked at Margaret, I said, Will she be mine to-morrow in the same degree in which I may now boast of the blessedness of our union? The alabaster fairness of her complexion, the mild resignation of her eye, the sweet courtesies and winning blandness of her voice, were never lost upon me, never passed by me unheeded, for this very reason. I was like the miser in Esop, / who went twenty times a day, and dug up and counted the gold, which lay hid in an obscure corner of the adjoining field, fearing that his motions might be marked by the eye of every passing traveller, and his prize might escape him.[c]

When my passion for Emilia took its rise, I was in the full vigour of health; and, when I formed my acquaintance with Margaret, I was just recovered from a very dangerous illness, and was in the middle point as it were between life and death. This cooperated with many other circumstances, to give to my passion

---

[a] Quotation unidentified.
[b] 1 John 4: 18 (adapted).
[c] A story also known as 'The Covetous Man', whose servant one day followed him and stole the hidden gold, leaving the miser nothing more to covet.

for her a diseased tone and a sickly hue. During the whole period of our married life my mind was never robust and steady of nerve, but fluttering and tremblingly alive to every trivial occurrence. Love has sometimes been said to rule with more absolute sway in the female than in the male branch of the human species; and in my adherence to Margaret I was a very / woman. I could not bear that she should be out of my sight. I was like a child, with a new and favourite toy, who, if it is withdrawn from him for a moment, vents his displeasure in piteous sobs and piercing cries, refuses to be comforted, and counts every thing else as worthless in the comparison. I cherished her as a thing of inestimable value; I tendered her as the apple of my eye.

Such being my general feelings as they respected her, it may easily be conceived in what a state of fearful commotion they were at the present crisis. During the whole season of our married life I had never felt myself calm, unmolested and assured; but my condition now may best be compared to the uneasy motion of the waves of the sea that foreruns a coming storm. It was broad daylight in the heavens; but all was night within me. The clouds of the mind appeared to thicken on every side, as if some demon had been compounding the ingredients / of immeasurable evil. I was full of horror and despair. I was impatient for some change in my feelings. It seemed as if the arrival of every thing most tremendous and infernal was to be preferred to the state of apprehension in which I was immured and could not escape. – Such was the history of my journey, and most especially of my return, on this decisive day. /

CHAPTER X

William on his part, as I found afterwards, had visited the cottage on the morning of the day after that on which I commenced my journey, and had received my billet. From thence he set out on his accustomed rounds, and had ascended the brow that overlooked my grounds. He saw the entire extent of the garden, but could no where discover the person whom his eyes so earnestly sought. He went and came again; he hovered about the spot; and it seemed as if he could not tear himself away till he had obtained the gratification on which his mind was bent.

Margaret in the mean while had sustained a / terrible shock from all that had passed between her and the unwelcome person who had obtruded a visit upon her. She had forced the attention of my wife to the contemplation of tempests and shipwrecks, a subject from which any one of common humanity, recollecting

139

the trials that Margaret had suffered, would have carefully abstained. She had started a sort of enquiry whether, after all, the fact of William's death had been established beyond the possibility of its being otherwise. So much was certain: so much Margaret clearly recollected of what passed. What followed after this, was to her apprehension involved in obscurity. The whole of what had preceded had so unsettled the mind of Margaret, throwing all her faculties into a state of confusion and uproar, her eyes were in such a disturbed state of vision, her ears so tingled, her perceptions were so indistinct and tumultuous, that she could not form any clear notion of the manner in which the / visit concluded. She had a dim recollection as if the stranger had said something about having seen her ever-mourned, ever-deplored lover on the day before. But no; this could not be. What motive could she have for saying it? What possibility was there that it could really be? It is true that Margaret had not seen William an inanimate corpse, and had never received an exact and specific account what became of his remains. But she had seen the ship sink that bore him; she had seen and read the countenances of all who escaped; she had heard the particulars of the way in which he perished. Years had passed since that fatal day. If he had been any where among the living, he would long ago have found his way to her. Love conquers all difficulties, surmounts all obstacles, and effects what to any other power would be impossible. Oh, surely, full surely, he was dead! Why should she torment herself with vain and maniac fictions? / The laws of nature never had been, and never could be thus superseded.

Still the concluding words of her visitor rung in her ears. She knew that nothing could be so uncertain, as was then the state of her perceptions. Her disturbed mind was in a condition to present to her the things that were not, and to shape sounds and a sense far as the length of the earth's diameter from the reality. Imagination cannot figure to itself a frame of mind more distracting and intolerable than that of Margaret.

It might have been expected that all this uncertainty and perturbation, this horror of soul and dread of she knew not what, would have reduced her to a bed of sickness. But it was not so. In the present instance she sustained herself marvellously. It was as if some unseen power supported her, that she might meet the last calamity, and drink the cup of her misery to the dregs. At first indeed / she had not been able to leave her couch; and it was only from the kind importunity of a faithful female who attended her, that she was prevailed on to take the smallest portion of nourishment. On the second day she walked across the room. On the third she went out into the garden. On the fourth, which was the day of my return, she went beyond the garden, leaning on her maid, into the grounds adjacent. She had proceeded a very little way, when William in person stood before her.

Thus to have met her was a thing the farthest in the world from his intention. Whether he would ever by the dint of desperation and strong excitement have been driven to such an extremity as that of desiring an interview, can never now be known. He had wandered this day for hours in the vicinity, seeking for nothing but the gratification that he had of late enjoyed more than once, of seeing Margaret, himself unseen, and satisfying his eyes from a / distance, with observing her figure, her motions, all that from the remote situation from which he had then viewed her, could make up her identity. It happened however in the present instance that, having in a manner given up his purpose in despair, and turning this way and that unconsciously, he had unawares approached the garden-wall. When he observed that he had done so, he did not conceive any alarm. Each time that he had seen Margaret, she had been within the inclosure; and, as she had appeared to him in a state of much indisposition and weakness, it had not occurred to him to apprehend the possibility of her proceeding beyond.

It is not easy to imagine any thing more astounding than the encounter of these two. It was however most incredible and terrific to Margaret. On his part William had nothing to learn. He knew of the marriage of his beloved, that she could no longer be any thing to him. He had seen her again and again / within a short time, – though at a considerable distance, yet near enough to enable him to swear to her form and figure against the world. When he found himself close on the outside of the garden-wall, he knew that it was by no means impossible that she was walking on the inside, and that they might be very near to each other, though he believed, that if it were so, their meeting was not in the slightest degree to be apprehended, and that they would neither of them ever know the near point in which they had stood to each other. He had a melancholy satisfaction in this thought. He felt as if to seek for an interview might be a crime. He suspected that he ought presently to withdraw to some distant land, and to take all the care in his power that Margaret should never know that he survived. But he believed that the indulgence which had been thus accidentally thrown in his way, was at least innocent. Margaret might be at only three yards distance / from him. If walls had crevices, as an inclosure of planks usually has, he might have seen her. If he had elevated his voice, and shouted aloud, he might have been heard, perhaps even recognised by her. There may, for aught we know, be a slight, undescribed atmosphere which diffuses itself round every living being, by means of which we may act and react upon each other without contact, like the spheres of attraction and repulsion in natural philosophy. We may term this animal sympathy. It might happen thus, that Margaret should feel the near approach of William with a kind of obscure sensation, a preternatural shudder, without being able to assign to herself any cause of what she felt. Thus might these lovers have approached each other; thus might they in a certain sense have touched; and this might have served, in default of every thing else, for an everlasting farewel. – All these ideas, in / rapid and incoherent march, passed through the mind of William.

But how different was the situation of Margaret! She had for years been

141

convinced that her lover had passed from the scene of mortal existence. She had acted upon this conviction in the most important affair of private life. Very recently the idea and reminiscence of William, which had however scarcely ever for an hour been dormant within her, had been stirred up in her brain with more than ordinary vividness by the discourse of her unwelcome visitor. This kind of awakening is by the superstitious regarded

> As harbinger preceding still the fates,
> And prologue to the omened coming on.[a]

But Margaret was in a very slight degree superstitious. In addition to this she had the strange sounds, which to her memory had scarcely the character of articulations, that / had rung in her ears when she fainted, and just before her visitor had withdrawn. She did not dare give them credence. She believed that their meaning was entirely a forgery of her own disturbed and upbraiding conscience. If they were not, what was she? She now began for the first time to suspect she had done wrong in accepting my proposal of marriage. Till now, particularly inasmuch as that acceptance had been in opposition to the promptings of her heart, and in obedience to the conclusions of her reason, she had taken for granted that it was laudable, heroic and right.

Margaret and William stood, suddenly and unexpectedly, in the presence of each other. William was surprised and confounded. What then was Margaret? She was almost turned into stone. She stood aghast, her eyes fixed, her limbs trembling, unable to advance or retreat. She at length recovered her power of / speech; and, with deep, inward accents, like a voice from the tomb, she said:

What art thou? Oh, do not mock me with the vain semblance of one departed! Spare my weakness! Have mercy on my faculties! Yes, I have seen thee even thus, times without number, in my dreams. But now! but here! –

Dear Margaret! he replied, in a tone of undescribable pity and commiseration.

Oh, that voice! – She said no more; but fell to the ground like one bereft of life and motion.

William was struck with the deepest alarm. He threw himself on the earth beside her. There was a small elevation of turf, no higher than a child's grave, at hand: he raised her, and gently brought her towards it.

After a time she opened her eyes, and looked up, like one that was robbed of recollection, just recovered from a deep sleep. Presently however she turned towards the fatal vision / that had deprived her of sense, and fainted again. This swoon was more durable and alarming than the former. It was with great difficulty, and with the lapse of nearly an hour, that a faint colour returned into her cheeks, and she was able to move and speak.

---

[a] *Hamlet*, I. i. 122–3 (adapted).

By a strange inconsistency, to which the constitution of human nature is liable, when Margaret recovered a second time, she seemed to have forgotten all that had passed in the last preceding period of her existence. She was like the persons whose story has been written, that have slept without intermission for several days, and have been supposed to be dead. In this resuscitation the memory of years has appeared to pass away, and they have come back at once to the thoughts of a remote period of life. Margaret forgot that she had a husband, and turned her eyes with unspeakable sweetness and delight upon the friend of her youth. She stretched out her / arms towards him, seeking his embrace. The very fact of her oblivion of the events of her later years, produced by sympathy a similar effect on him. The whole interval appeared like a dream, and he seemed as just reawaking to his former self. He felt as if there was no longer any thing to separate them, and that pure and unalloyed happiness had descended on them. This sort of transporting delusion continued for many minutes.

At the very moment that the lovers were thus engaged, I approached. I have described my journey home, the deep, the complicated, the agonising reflections that occupied my mind, the species of insanity, the wildness and disorder which reduced me to so pitiable a state. Never was journey like that journey. Blackness and despair, hatred, immortal hate, possessed me. I hated my rival; I hated my wife and her parents: but, most of all, a loathing of myself and of all that constituted / my individuality, pervaded the chambers of my soul. I knew nothing of the successive features of the country through which I passed. It was all of one sombre, deadly hue. It was a blank and dreary scene, that seemed as if it would last for ever.

I had hitherto observed nothing of external objects; and yet, now, by an incredible fatality, when I ought to have been most blind, I saw. I had been for some time swallowed up in my own reflections, and had remained motionless. Suddenly I became like one, whom a deep torpor of the faculties, having run its destined course, has deserted. And yet it was not so, for I forgot nothing. Mechanically however I assumed a different attitude. I looked from my window, and saw that I was approaching my home – Alas, I said, no home to me, for it restores me to all that it would be heaven to me to escape! I discerned the wall that formed / the boundary of my garden. It was at a distance of not more than half a mile.

My attention was arrested. I saw two human figures, a male and a female. They sat on the turf; and it was plain – their attitudes, the disposition of every part of the body, shewed – that affection, a mutual, entire melting of souls, occupied them. The external indications were indeed such, as probably to a common eye would have expressed no such thing. But, in the previously sharpened state of my faculties, every hair almost told a several tale. With the same intuitive clearness I knew in a moment who were the parties. I had never seen William before. But I felt as certain, as I should have done if I had lived

143

with him from the hour of his birth. It was an unerring recongition. My carriage drove on. I approached nearer. There was every thing to confirm, nothing to contradict, my first / impression. The parties were so entirely occupied with each other, that outward objects were undiscerned by them. I stopped my carriage, and leaped out. I flew to the spot. I had, I scarcely knew why, loaded pistols on my person. The whole passed with the rapidity of lightning. William had barely time to rise from his posture, and make two steps towards me, when I lodged a bullet in his heart. He fell instantly, and neither moved nor stirred any more.

The deed I thus perpetrated was of terrific violence. I assumed in my own person the robe and the function of public justice. I interposed not a moment for deliberation and the sifting of evidence. Bitterly, and impelled by a thousand reasons, have I since repented what I did. But at the time I had no doubts. The highest and purest of all laws, as I believed, was with me. I saw my wife and her paramour together. I saw, as distinctly as / man ever saw the celestial orbs, correspondence, a mutual understanding and passion, depicted in their gestures. I believed, though I knew not how it had been contrived, that they had taken advantage of my absence to bring about this encounter. Was this to be forgiven? Did it not call for exemplary punishment? Should I not stamp myself the tamest of cowards, if I did not take instant vengeance?

Margaret witnessed my act with inexpressible horror. It had the effect for the moment of driving away from her all preceding weakness, and substituting in its stead an energy that seemed to exceed human energy. Volumes were comprised in that instant. But a brief moment before, she had forgotten me, her husband; she had received William as if to see him again alive was delight, pure and without alloy. The events of the last preceding years were unrecollected. Now they / crowded back again on her mind like a torrent. She did not merely recollect her husband; he stood before her. That object, the sight of which a moment ago had filled her with more than mortal ecstacy, she saw cut down before her eyes, and stretched lifeless at her feet. It was myself, her husband, that had acted this atrocity.

Monster! she exclaimed, Devil! spirit of all evil! was it for this I married you? delivered myself unreservedly into your hands? Yes, you have justly rewarded my confidence. Life, what art thou? Virtue and honour, empty shadows! My life has been all submission, submission to my father, submission to my husband. But it shall be so no longer. Out of my sight, most odious of created things! I cannot bear it. It is death to me to look at you, to think of you. Oh, William! William! revive! take me to you! I know no other friend. /

And, saying thus, she fell senseless on his corpse. The preternatural energy she had put forth, totally overcame her. I believed she had broken a blood-vessel. /

CHAPTER XI

The deed I had acted, and the objects before me, produced a total revolution of my nature, a revulsion of blood from all the subordinate parts of my frame to the heart. It may seem strange: but the wildness and incoherence of my thoughts, the frantic sallies of mind, which had overwhelmed and tortured me from the instant I had set out on my return home, were gone: all within me was a forced and fearful calmness and composure. This was doubtless the result of the critical situation in which I stood. I was called on to determine and to act. Two human bodies, dead, or apparently dead, lay at my feet. It was incumbent / on me to give directions concerning them, and to consult as to the conduct I was to pursue for myself. Three servants had attended me in my journey. Their distance was not such, as to prevent them from distinctly witnessing what had passed. Comformably to the instinct of human nature on such occasions, they hastened to the spot. Curiosity for ever prompts us to watch narrowly what occurs in a tragic scene, and to exercise our understandings in judging of the merits and demerits of the parties, and remarking the winding up of the whole. Margaret's female attendant was also there. By a fortunate chance Rowland, my steward, had been on horseback in an adjoining field, and now made one of the group. They looked first with wonder on the body of William whom I had killed, and then turned their eyes with silent awe upon me.

I conceived the part that it belonged to me to perform. I directed that the body of the / dead man should be conveyed to the summer-house in the garden, and that Margaret, who was perhaps only in a swoon, should be gently and carefully removed to her bed. Before the parties separated to execute my orders, I said:

My friends, you may perhaps think that I am called upon to afford some explanation of what you see. I do not shrink from doing so. Situations like that in which I stand, level all distinctions of rank. I have done only what it was impossible for me not to do. I am desirous that my conduct should stand out before the world, and be judged by the common feelings of my fellow-creatures. But this is not the time, nor this the place, for me to enter into my defence. What I have done, I have done; and I must answer it to the laws of my country. For the present I must withdraw; but the affair will not end here.

I now hastened into the house, and repaired to my dressing-room. I took from my scrutoire[a] / the cash I happened to have by me. It amounted to some hundred pounds. Part of this I gave to Rowland, but retained the principal portion for myself. I ordered my favourite saddle-horse to be made ready. After having thus consumed about twenty minutes, I prepared to depart.

One of the last things I did was to visit the apartment of my wife. I could discern about her no signs of life. There was a copious effusion of blood. I suspected that she was dead. It was however impossible for me to observe farther. Time pressed upon me: I must be gone. I directed Rowland, at the same moment that I departed, to dispatch one of my footmen for a neighbouring physician. I commissioned him to write to the father of Margaret. I charged him to transmit to me a full account of every thing that passed, and to send his letter, with a small portmanteau that I pointed out to him, and every thing that might be necessary / for my immediate accommodation, to the post-house of the principal town of a neighbouring county. I emphatically urged him to take care that I was not observed or molested, nor for a few brief hours to suffer any outcry to be made in the vicinity, but to conduct every thing with composure and discretion.

My servants of course received my orders with the most entire deference. They felt that it did not belong to them to control me. Beside which, it is certain that I had always so conducted myself, as commanded their deepest sympathy and respect. They looked at me with awe, not unmingled with terror, but did not utter a word, except to answer my questions, and declare their acquiescence in all I prescribed. In the countenances of Rowland and the rest I saw plainly depicted compassion, and those good wishes in my behalf, that human beings never fail to entertain for such persons, as they have seen frequently, and / been accustomed to regard as worthy to be honoured.

I set out alone. I directed my course towards the house of an old acquaintance, a schoolfellow and fellow-collegian of my early years.

My thoughts were saddened in an inconceivable degree. But all was methodical and composed. I would have given worlds to have purchased a happy interval of oblivion and insanity. But I felt as if I should never sleep again. The demon of perspicuity, and clear, diaphanous apprehension was at my elbow. The genius of prophetic anticipation mounted my horse with me, clung close to my person, and would not be shaken off.

How total was the change of my destiny! Within little more than an hour I had become a murderer, that is, a person who has designedly taken away the life of his fellow, an exile, a widowed wanderer upon earth. What were / to me all my lands and possessions, the costliness of my furniture, and the magnificence of my paternal mansion? I should see them no more. I must 'shape my old course in a country new'.[b]

---

[a] i.e. Escritoire, a writing desk.
[b] *King Lear*, I. i. 187 (adapted).

I took a long and a lasting farewel of all false refinements. 'When the mind is free', the senses are 'delicate'.[a] I had been idle, full of supersubtle distinctions, jealous. I had had a wife that honoured me, that smoothed my pillow beneath my head, that hastened ever to supply my wants, and anticipate my wishes. But, forsooth, she did not love me enough; I did not sufficiently reign her bosom's lord. These are luxuries of a mind at ease. Where was I now to pillow my head? What friend would be near to comfort me? No; I was an outcast of the world. The stormy skies would be the only canopy above me; the desert wilderness would be my retiring chamber and my eating-room. /

When I look back on this period, I am astonished that I consented to live, and did not cast this worthless carcase upon the same pile with my wife and the man I had murdered. This is one of the strangest phenomena of our nature. The more our existence ceases to have any thing for which we should desire it, any thing pleasing in retrospect, or hopeful for the future, we often seem to cling to it the more tenaciously. As if we said, I have nothing else; but this I swear I will never resign. Stripped of every thing, loaded with grief and remorse, hunted, as I might expect to be, by my fellow-men, and every moment anticipating an ignominious and accursed death, I desperately resolved that, though every misery should be mine, and the world confederate against me, I would not yield, but keep up the combat to the last.

My journey was melancholy: but my mind was no longer at sea, driven before the winds. / The calamity I had perpetrated was too gigantic and wide of extent, not to make me sober. I would have repented; but for me, like the man we are told of, who climbed over the rails at the top of the Monument of London, and clung to them for a while on the outside, there was no room for repentance. The die was cast, for as long as I existed here, or in the dark, unfathomable future. Nor could I perceive how I could have acted, otherwise than I had acted. My fate drove me on. I had seen that which it was impossible to see, and remain inactive. I thought tenderly of Margaret; for I was thoroughly acquainted with all her exemplary virtues, and was satisfied that never human creature had been so deeply unfortunate. Still she was not, and could no longer continue to be, my wife, my companion, the friend of my bosom.

From these useless retrospects I turned to the contemplation of the future. I knew not / from what quarter it would come; but I did not doubt that, as it happens to all men circumstanced as I was, I should be perseveringly sought for, and every effort would be made to render me responsible to the laws of my country. In the manner of the death of William there was nothing ambiguous. It was clear how he came by his fate; and there was witness in abundance to bring it home to me. In my own eyes I stood justified for the act of destroying

---

[a] *King Lear*, III. iv. 11–12 (adapted).

him. But I knew enough of the laws of my country, to know that that which in my mind was a vindication, would not be so received in an English court of justice as to obtain my acquittal of the crime of murder. The death of Margaret, for I believed she was dead, would not fail, though my hands were clear of the charge of perpetrating it, to operate so as grievously to exasperate a judge and jury against me. The two events were parts of one act, and were accomplished in the same / hour. I should certainly be regarded as a monster of iniquity, hardened in crime. It was therefore incumbent on me so to dispose of myself, as to prevent my falling into the hands of the myrmidons[a] of the law.

The thoughts that occupied my mind, did not cease to fill up my time for the hours I was on horseback. I turned up the avenue which led to my friend's house. I then began to consider, what I was to talk of during my visit, and what I was to assign as the occasion of my coming.

The master of the house was at home, and came out to receive me. His manner was full of cordiality. I spoke slightly and uncertainly as to the cause of my visit, but mentioned the town to which I had resorted on business, and which I had quitted that very morning, and expressed myself so as to make my host understand that, by a circuit, I had contrived to / come from thence to his residence, before I returned home.

It was necessary I should remain for many hours at my friend's house, that I might give time for the communication I expected from my steward. My situation here was painful beyond what it is possible to imagine. I had but one conception, one train of thoughts for ever present to my mind, and of this I must not utter a syllable. My meditations were fixed; I could even feel the muscles of my face collapsing continually into an expression of despair; and I was compelled to counterfeit the gestures of a mind at ease, and urge myself forward to talk of the thousand nothings, which make up the substance of ordinary conversation, particularly at the board of a country squire. From time to time I smiled; but it was a mournful and a wintry smile: I laughed; but it was the hollow and frightful laugh of a / murderer. Towards the conclusion of the evening my efforts were wholly exhausted. This my host seemed willing to attribute to fatigue. Never were hours more intolerably tedious. It seemed as if the motion that gives life to universal nature, were still, and that the day would never have an end. At length I retired to my chamber.

I was however new in murder. When I was left alone during the hours of night, with no external incidents playing on my organs of sense, that was worst. I put out my candle, and threw myself on the bed. I had been greatly exhausted by the occurrences of the day; and I presently fell into a sort of slumber. This was merely a licence, delivering my mind from the laws which govern that of a man awake, and introducing every thing that was most frightful and odious. I

---

[a] Derogatory term for a hireling, or other inferior administrative officer of the law. (See note to *Cloudesley, Collected Novels and Memoirs of William Godwin*, vol. 7, p. 87.

passed in imagination through all the scenes of the preceding day. I saw Margaret and William, my / victims. I bathed my hands, and besmeared my arms in his blood. He seemed to expire in agonies. The moment after, he appeared to revive, and mock the impotence of my revenge. He and Margaret joined to insult, to gibe at, and torment me. These scenes were acted over and over again, I know not how oft. Then succeeded visions of chains, of dungeons and trial. By some strange combination of inconsistency, Margaret and William appeared to be the principal among the witnesses against me, urging my fate, and invoking an ample retribution.

What an end was that of my sainted victim! Through life she had been a sacrifice. Blameless in every relation in which she was successively placed. Deserving every thing, yet obtaining nothing. Exemplary in all her duties, yet successful in none of her efforts. If there was ever creature that merited consideration and forbearance from all, and that 'even the / winds of heaven should not visit her face too roughly', it was she.[a] Yet all the inclemency of the elements beat upon her; all the tyranny of man seemed to select her as the object upon which it was to be remorselessly exercised. Upon her tomb it might worthily be inscribed, 'Here at last reposes the most unoffending, the most meritorious, and the most cruelly treated of her sex, entitled to the tenderest usage, exposed on the most trying and momentous occasions to the harshest and most brutal'. /

CHAPTER XII

Morning at length came; and, without again communicating with my host, I set out. I repaired, with a short interval to refresh myself and my horse, to the market-town, which I had appointed for the communications of my steward. This was the first chapter in that series of terrors and alarms that have never since forsaken me. Till I entered this place, I had believed myself safe. I had had no fears of hostility or violence from my servants. Some hours would therefore have elapsed, before any plan could be concerted for pursuing me, and taking from me my personal liberty. In this respect, however annoyed and tortured / on other accounts, under the roof of my host of the preceding night, I had felt secure.

By the time however of my entering the town at which I had ordered

---

[a] *Hamlet*, I. ii. 141–2 (adapted).

Rowland to address his communications, I began to calculate that it was possible I might encounter some effectual obstacle to my further proceeding. Not more than twenty-four hours indeed had elapsed, since my perpetrating the deed I might be called on to expiate. My servants I knew would take no step that might conduce to my loss of liberty. The physician that I had ordered to be sent for, would perhaps be the first person, who might deem himself called upon by his station in society, to interfere for the forwarding of public justice, and it was yet somewhat early for me to expect annoyance in consequence of any thing he should do. In the mean while there is no mode of calculating what might happen in a case of this sort. Some person, who had no motive to favour or shelter / me, might accidentally come to the knowledge of what had occurred, sooner than the physician. It is true that Rowland alone possessed the clue that should direct any one to the county-town I now entered; and I was morally sure that he would not allow himself to be made, directly or indirectly, my destroyer, by betraying that which was confided to him only. The servant who should bring what I required might be a cause of molestation to me; but he would have as little the time, as the inclination, to be the probable means of my being delivered into custody.

Such was the calculation I was able to form respecting my immediate safety. But it was in vain that I reasoned on the subject. The mere possibility that something fatal might occur, was matter enough for my apprehensions to work upon. I no sooner saw the spires of the county-town in the distance before me, than strange suspicions took hold of my mind. / Ought I to enter the main street, or turn down into any of the bye-roads and avoid it? I however rebuked the suggestion, and said to myself, Though I am guilty, I will not be a coward. Though the beatings of my heart be quick and strong within me, I will conquer them.

I entered the town. Once and twice I saw indications, which to my jealous mind afforded matter of deliberation, and exercised my powers of conjecture. I observed some one eyeing me more curiously than I should have judged natural. A horseman advanced behind me with greater than common speed: but he passed me, and took no notice. I went to the inn I had specified, but was told that nothing had come there to my address. I retired to a chamber.

A few minutes after, a waiter appeared, and informed me that there was a person below, enquiring for me. I could feel that I turned pale as he spoke. I speedily learned however / that it was no other than my own servant, dispatched by Rowland. I ordered that he should be sent to me. He brought the letter and portmanteau that I expected.

I looked at him wistfully. I said, Strange things, John, happened yesterday. You will not for the present see me again at home. I am full of grief. At a proper time however I shall appear, and clear up everything that now shews to my disadvantage. You, John, are not my enemy?

He protested, that no earthly consideration should induce him to do me an injury.

You have not spoken to any one here, or on the road, of what has occurred at home?

He had not. Rowland had recommended it to him to be silent; and, had it been otherwise, he would not have uttered a word, that could have been the occasion of mischief. There was in his look an expression of the deepest interest in my behalf. /

I bade him wait in the inn an hour, and I would speak to him again. I told him that it was of the utmost importance to me, that he should be discreet.

This was to me the first consequence of guilt. I was obliged to humble myself to my own servant. It depended upon him to be my destroyer.

I opened the letter of Rowland. It contained little new, more than the confirmation that Margaret was certainly dead. Nothing material had yet occurred under my own roof. He expected from hour to hour the parents of my wife.

I appeared now to have small room for deliberation. The most natural and the safest course, as I judged, for me to adopt, was to leave my native isle, and endeavour to hide myself in some foreign climate, happy if I should be able to effect this unmolested. As long as I remained in England, and a pursuit, / which I did not doubt would be the case, were set on foot against me, I felt that I should be beset with daily terrors and nightly alarms, and should apprehend each hour that this would be the last hour of my liberty. Till now I had regarded personal freedom, and justly, as a part of my inheritance, of which no man could deprive me; and I made no account of it accordingly. I went this way and that, as I pleased. I staid at home in my own mansion, or went abroad for exercise and amusement, or to visit my neighbours; and no man interfered with me, and said, Why dost thou this? I visited the metropolis, or made a tour in my native isle, unmolested. I looked round from the terrace in my garden, and viewed the park, the meadows, the trees, the streams, and a small lake surrounded with my property, without apprehension. There was a road in the distance, along which I saw carriages of all sorts, public and private, horsemen and pedestrians, passing / this way and that incessantly. What mattered it to me to search into their purposes? In the words of the old song, 'I was myself the king of me'. If the concerns of the persons I saw had any relation to my concerns their import was of aid or of deference. If they thought nothing of me, and were busied only in their own affairs, of this at least I was secure, They purposed me no harm. I 'doffed the world, and bade it pass'.[a]

How different was now my situation! Every man I did not know, I had some reason to suspect for an enemy. If he accosted me, I might with probability apprehend that he had a design against me. If he passed along the road in a direction that did not lead from my house, he might be coming to put me under restraint. I had great cause therefore to watch the gestures and looks of every

---

[a] *Henry IV, Part I*, IV. i. 96–7 (adapted).

one I saw. All the world was in a confederacy against me. Every one would rejoice, such is the law of / civilized communities, at my misfortune. What gave me pain, would afford pleasure to every living being who heard of it. Whoever was called upon to arrest my steps, would eagerly place himself in my path with hostile intent, for they would cry, He is a murderer! When I was brought out to die in the face of the world, they would feel satisfied; and, when I expired, they would utter shouts of approbation.

Nothing, I was well aware, was more precise than the expounding and application of the English law in the case of murder. It is like the application of a cloth-yard in a mercer's shop. In the matter of duelling only is it dispensed with. There the common sense of mankind rises against it; and the judge, however well disposed for the most part to be rigorous, finds himself obliged to relax. In all other instances the life of the individual arraigned, is disposed of in obedience to terms and definitions. / The only question is, Does the deed under consideration come up to the rule? Just as in the shop of the mercer we decide, Does the cloth measure three feet of twelve inches each? The investigation is of malice; in other words, Had the individual accused so much time given, between the sight of the offence that irritated him, and the infliction of the mortal wound, as may logically and metaphysically be interpreted to have afforded room for deliberation? Thus the judge rules it, and the jury obey, and the executive government rarely and with infinite hesitation supersedes the rule. No consideration is had of the character of the parties, or the nature of the provocation. The heart of the judge is dead within him, and so of the rest. The whole is determined, in a way that more resembles the turning of a machine, than the decision of that complicated being called man, endowed with eyes to see, and an understanding to discriminate, and a heart to / feel, and a moral sense to judge according to the eternal law written in the skies. – It is further worthy to be considered, that circumstances tending to aggravate are sure to be taken into the account; not so circumstances tending to extenuate.

As I have already said, I resolved, if possible, to quit the island of Great Britain. What did I leave behind me that was worthy of my regret? I had lost two wives, Emilia and Margaret. I left my mansion, my park, and my woods, the terraces of my garden and its embowering shades, the well known apartments in which I had spent the greater part of my life, their furniture and pictures, and a well chosen library, accumulated year after year principally by the taste and judgement of my father, and by my own. I left an establishment of servants, all faithful, many of them, grown old in my service, and who were to me little less than humble friends. What then? / The property and conveniences to which we are accustomed, are but dead matter; and the life of man, or even his tranquillity, is not indissolubly bound up with these. Our servants we are more in the practice of regarding with condescension, than affection; and, even if we sometimes feel a pang in losing them, the wound is in no long time scarred over and healed. I had not lived to these years in the world, always honoured and thought well of, and not unblessed with the faculties, that should amuse the social hour, supply the suggestions of prudence and wisdom, or shew the ingenuousness of my heart and the tender sympathies of my soul, without having acquired friends, some who ranked with me merely as desirable or valued acquaintance, one or two, of whom I shall have occasion hereafter to speak, with whom I had lived on terms of true confidence and reciprocal communication. But they had never occupied my soul, or engrossed all the / longings of my nature, as Emilia and Margaret had done. To lose them all was a dreary anticipation. I had lost them by one monmentary, decisive act, that could never be repaired.

But there was an individual, whom it was agony to me to think of parting withal, and yet from whom I must be separated; and this was my daughter, my only child. Her name has not lately occurred in this narrative. She remained six years on the continent with Mrs Fielding, the sister of Mrs Fanshaw, and her daughters; and when she returned to England, she found me already engaged in the marriage-state for the second time. During her travels she had contracted sentiments of the deepest affection for the family with which she was domesticated; and all the Fieldings joined in the most earnest intreaties to her and myself, that they might not be separated now that they were returned to their native country. It was at length settled that she should reside for / about three months at a time alternately, with me, and with her young friends.

On her arrival at home, I introduced the two persons I loved best in the world to each other. I have omitted to notice their intercourse in its proper order, because I thought it would come in better here. They immediately conceived an uncommon affection for each other. They were distinguished beauties, but of a different order. Catherine was a stranger to deep and soul-harrowing afflictions. Her cheek was smooth and round; and the first bloom of her complexion had never been impaired. Her eye revelled with flashes of life; and her motions in the ordinary communication of society were quick and animated like an epigram. Yet her soul was penetrated with sensibility; her colour changed with every variety of suggestion and emotion; the tear of sympathy was ever ready in her eye; and her quivering lip plainly told, how fully her heart / was accessible to every benignant and generous impression. Margaret on the contrary, though fraught, particularly at that time, with tenderness and watchful attentions, was obviously a glorious temple in ruins. You could see that she was very far from being the lustrous creature she had been. Never for a moment did a certain expression of disappointment and despair forsake her. For a short time, at brief intervals, her eye became animated, and then relapsed into sorrow. Her cheek was white, though of exquisite fairness; and you seemed to see on it the traces of her tears. It has been said, that human creatures often love one another the more emphatically, because they are cast in different moulds, and are of unlike dispositions. Thus it was with Margaret and Catherine. They conceived at once an ardent attachment. They playfully called

153

mother and daughter, though there was but four years' difference in their ages. But they were more like / sisters. In jest they amused themselves with personating authority and obedience, and contented themselves with feeling the equality of the heart. Margaret had been sobered by calamity, and in this sense was the wiser of the two. She had read more, and therefore was more perfect and consummate in the knowledge of authors, and in literary taste. But in knowledge of the world she was a mere child. They shone alternately, accordingly as one subject or another happened to be the topic of conversation. They had each of them stored up in memory passages of the poets, sublime conception, luxuriant imagery, picturesque description; but Margaret dwelt the most upon passages of love, of tenderness, of sorrow and desolation. In criticism, in exact delineation of the qualities and forte of the several writers, and the hidden excellencies of their different works, she was the superior. But Catherine could talk with the most thorough knowledge, / of countries and their manners, of the world and courts, and the gradations of society, of music as it exists in Italy and Germany, and of the wondrous productions of art in the most favoured quarters of the earth. She was also extensively acquainted with the most beautiful and romantic scenery of the more known countries of the world; and in her animated descriptions the hearer was converted into a spectator, and could scarcely believe that he had not personally witnessed what was so fully set before him.

Here then was a pair of friends, the purest, the most innocent, of the most affectionate tempers, and the soundest discernment, that the world ever saw. From the moment they first beheld, they understood each other. Their attachment was like Jonah's gourd, that 'sprang up in the night', and spread forth its branches, and was as 'a shadow over their heads',[a] to protect them from the fierce beams of the sun, / and the changeful inclemency of the seasons. Yet, ardently as they loved each other in the commencement, the feeling was nevertheless susceptible of increase. The treasures of their information and their sentiments could not have been apprehended by each other in a day; and I have no doubt, that the more protracted and various their intercourse had been, the more cause each would have seen, from day to day, and from year to year, to value, and as it were to adore, the other.

And to this friendship I put an abrupt close! I extinguished one portion of this inimitable pair. God knows my heart! nothing could have been further from my intention than to be the destroyer of Margaret. I would not have hurt a hair of her head. I fully appreciated, nobody understood them better, the whole of her merits. When I was most convinced of her unfaithfulness to the engagements she had formed with me at the altar, even then / I most pitied her. But I was hurried on by an irresistible fate. And, at the moment, and for some time

---

[a] Jon. 4: 6–10 (adapted).

afterwards, I believed I was right. Cruel, terrific was the alternative in which I was placed. But I was convinced that the least thing I was called on to do, was abruptly to remove from the stage of existence the man, who returned from the dead (among whom he ought to have rested for ever) with no other possible result, than to crush the happiness of those who survived, himself the un-happiest of them all. /

CHAPTER XIII

Catherine was at the period of this catastrophe with her friends, the Fieldings, in London. I knew we must part, probably never to meet again. But I could not prevail upon myself to leave England, without one last, solemn farewel. As I have already said, there were but two persons from whom it was death to me to be severed for ever, my wife, and my daughter. I had gazed on the pale countenance of the one, as she lay, as it afterwards proved, dead in her bridal chamber. But my heart was then made hard. My conceptions were reduced into a gloomy, deadly sobriety. I looked on; and I said nothing. /

It was otherwise as respected my daughter. Black as were my prospects, red and hateful as were my hands in my mind's eye. I had no guilt, properly speaking, towards her. When I thought of Catherine, my heart was as tender as a new-born babe.

I came to London, that I might see her. I alighted in a remote part of the metropolis. I sent a coach to fetch her to me, and with the coach a letter.

I could not however take this step without terrible misgivings. The thought of seeing my daughter, opened afresh all the wounds of my heart. I had perpetrated a dreadful deed; and it had been attended with tremendous consequences. I had slain my rival; my wife was dead; and I was cut off for ever from the society, the general community of beings, who partook along with me of the human form.

But in what I had done, and what had followed upon my deed till now, I was exalted, / and taken out of myself. I had in fact been another being, from the hour that William's letter was put into my hands, and still more from the hour that I knew he was in my neighbourhood. I felt as if I were the only being in all this complication, that was worthy to be pitied. My victims in my eyes were offenders, and I the aggrieved party. What had I done to deserve this misery? I had married a beautiful young female, with her own consent, and that of her parents. This was certainly no crime, and did not merit the terrible retribution that had been reserved for me. I thought therefore of Margaret with a torture that I was unable to endure; and I thought of William with abhorrence. These ruminations had filled my soul even to bursting, during the excursion I had made from my home, and on my return. As I approached my own house in returning, I saw that which at once worked up my soul to rage and to madness; and I perpetrated the deed, / which could never be recalled, never obliterated, and which followed me with retribution and vengeance for ever.

From the instant that my revenge had been consummated in the death of my rival, my nature, as I have said, had totally changed. I saw what I had done, and felt that I must stand to the consequences. I was desperate; but I was in a state of inforced calmness and composure. I looked to every thing; I provided for every thing. I girded up the loins of my mind, and felt the condition in which I was placed. I must take care of myself; for there was no one that cared for me. 'My heart was turned to stone; I struck it, and it hurt my hand'.[a]

But, when I thought of Catherine, the case was totally different. The feelings of humanity came back upon me with an overflowing tide. I had resolved to see her, to tell her a tale of griefs inexpressible, – of the death of the / new and valued friend she had acquired – but that was little: – I had to tell her of the part her father had acted.

The soul of Catherine was purity itself. It was a piece of unstained paper, fair and bright as the first beams of the morning sun. She had heard of vice and crime. But they had been to her as the theoretical terms of a science treated of in books. 'They passed by her as the idle wind, which she respected not'.[b] She regretted that such things were, and that the species man, so noble in reason, so glorious in faculties, should be stained with such enormities as are recorded of him.

And now she was to hear all this brought home to her father. She knew much that was good of me; she believed every thing. Such is the constitution of the human mind. Plato says, that if we could see virtue in her proper form, all men would fall down and adore her.[c] / But it is even thus that we do see virtue, particularly in the early part of our lives. We are all anthropomorphites. We clothe the qualities that our understanding bodies out to us, and the pulses of our heart approve, in some human shape, gracious, engaging and reverend; and that shape, to a child honourably and happily born, is the shape of its parent.

I had come to London, principally to see my daughter, to take of her a lasting farewel. My heart was torn in a thousand pieces. If ever a pain was mixed with a pleasure, it was my case in the present instance. I could not go back from the interview upon which I had resolved. I could not prevail on myself to see Catherine no more. She must hear the thing I had acted, if not from me. Was it not then incumbent on me to be the relator? I must look in her face, and

---

[a] *Othello*, IV. i. 191–2 (adapted).
[b] *Julius Caesar*, IV. iii. 68–9 (adapted).
[c] cf. Plato, *Symposium* 210–11, where Beauty is thus regarded.

observe how she received the intelligence. If it could be softened to her, / it was I that ought to mitigate it. If she needed the aid of another to enable her to bear it. I ought to be the ally and the comforter.

The letter I wrote was as follows.

My dearest daughter,

I am in London. Come to me instantly. Come alone. I send a carriage to fetch you. Prepare yourself. Call up your resolution. Unless I mistake, you are capable of arduous things; and I grieve to say you will be tried. Unhappy girl! Unhappy father!

P.D.

Say to the family with which you reside that I have sent for you: but shew no one this letter.

It was not long ere Catherine stood before me. I heard her approaching the apartment in which I sat, with indescribable emotion on my part. I looked at her. Her countenance and her whole figure expressed the commotion / of her soul, a fearful anticipation of she knew not what.

My father! she said. Are you alive? Are you well? What is it you have to communicate? Thank God, I have a father!

You have terrified me greatly. But do not fear me! Do not spare me! I am ready, indeed I am ready, for all you can have to say.

It relieves me to hear you. Catherine! my wife, Margaret, is dead!

Dead! Indeed that is sudden! She was surely an angel. I relied that she would have been my nearest, most valued friend. And your loss must be greater than mine.

But, my father, she added after a moment's pause, I see that you have something else behind. You did not send for me with this precaution, you have not used all these preparations, merely to announce this sad news. Tell me at once! Shew me, I pray you, with what your bosom is labouring. /

Well, I have a dreadful tale. I cannot put it into order. Take it, as I am able to communicate it.

Margaret, before she knew me, had a lover, to whom she was contracted, from whom she was compulsorily separated, who was lost, or supposed to be lost, at sea. She loved this individual with entire, engrossing affection; I only came in in the second place, a substitute, to occupy the ruins of a heart.

This man lived; he returned from a tedious exile; I have known that for some time. Two days ago I caught them together, in my own park. What had passed between them I know not; but I saw them in attitudes that implied much. I perceived that they were occupied with each other in entire affection, and had no thought of any thing but that affection. The eyes of a doting husband see this in a moment. I came upon them. I had pistols. My blood boiled within me. The lover was unarmed; / he had no time to resist. I drew a pistol, and laid him at my feet. He is dead; Margaret is dead. She expired from the bursting of a blood-vessel.

Oh, Catherine, why are you condemned to hear this tale of horrors? I could not consent that you should hear it from another. I have been the unhappy wretch, fated to accomplish all this mischief; and the least penance I could impose on myself was that I should be the person to bring you the news. I am going instantly into exile. I have sent for you to bid you farewel.

Never was a young and innocent creature tried, as my child was tried on this occasion. She had known no sorrow; and the utmost imaginable sorrow came upon her at once. She had never heard of crime; and her father stood before her, red from the perpetration of a murder.

The agitation of Catherine was extreme. / And what heightened all her trials, was that she must in no way betray what she suffered. She was silent: but, notwithstanding all her efforts, she grew as pale as death. Her lips were visibly convulsed. She would have rejected with scorn every story that could have been reported to her of crime and disgrace to her father. And here it was, brought to her by myself, explicitly avowed; 'no loop to hang a doubt on'.[a] no refuge for scepticism or incredulity that remained to her. I had shewn myself the slave of passion, incapable of moderation and restraint, hurried into the last excesses, which are usually committed only by creatures without education, without discipline, and accustomed to listen to no suggestions but those of unlicensed passion.

I proceeded: How you must feel this tragic tale I can easily conceive. But, whatever are *your* feelings, I know how the laws of England will judge of it. I have forfeited my life. If / I am caught, I shall die on the gallows. But I will not allow myself to be apprehended, to be committed to prison, to be consigned to a dungeon, to be subjected to the profane and execrable hands of the executioner. I am not content to die an ignominious death, to be recorded a convicted criminal, to have my name placed in the annals of those, whose deeds are read from age to age with detestation. I cannot endure the thought of this for myself; I cannot endure that your innocent spirit and your blameless life should be coupled with such a story. I will go into exile; you shall never see, never hear of me more. Oh, Catherine, when you think of me, do not, do not, load my memory with execrations!

During the whole of this narrative she uttered not a word. Several times she gasped, and with difficulty drew her breath. Once and again her whole frame seemed to shudder. But she roused herself, and subdued the weakness / of her frame to an emphatic steadiness. When I had done, she said:

Father, you shall not go alone. Wherever you are, I will be your companion.

I looked at her with astonishment. I replied: Catherine, you know not what you are saying. You have not understood me.

---

[a] *Othello*, III. iii. 365–6 (adapted).

Not understood you! Every word you have said is written in inextinguishable characters in my heart.

Catherine, I am degraded, a dishonoured man. I have done that which, if there were no laws to punish, would urge all men to fly from me, as they would from contamination and pestilence. And shall your angelic innocence and purity be associated with it? No; drop a tear of sorrow for my misery; and then forget me for ever! Do not let your days of tranquillity and bliss hereafter, be blasted with one thought of the wretch before you!

Father! rest assured of this, I will follow you through the world. /

My child, recollect yourself! Look upon me! I am like a wretch, whom the lightning of heaven has scarred. Never more shall I know one interval of serenity. I feel that a demon from hell will for ever dog my steps. No indication of a smile will again play upon my lips. I shall become haggard and pale. I shall waste away to a skeleton. Balmy slumber will never more weigh down my eyelids. My temper will become peevish and morose; no efforts to serve me will at any time be acknowledged; but, wretched and intolerable to myself, I shall render every one that approaches me miserable. The tyrant of antiquity, who signalised his cruelty by chaining a living body to a dead one,[a] did not entail upon his victim a more tremendous fate, than would be that of the person who should attend me in my wanderings.

Father, replied Catherine, you do but shew me the more your need of a companion, such as I will be to you. Oh, you do not know with / what art and unwearied skill I will medicine your griefs. My patience shall conquer your moroseness. I will prove so considerate and kind, that I will defy you not to smile upon me. You cannot be without a companion; and no companion will be so suitable for you as I am determined to be found.

How, answered I, can I sufficiently thank you for this unexpected good-will? But I foresee, Catherine, what the tenour of my future life will prove. If you could overcome the petulance of a temper, hating the world, and hating itself, yet my life will be one series of apprehension and terror. Such a deed as mine will not go unpursued. Whether in England, or out of England, the beagles of justice will not fail to be at my heels. By night and by day I shall never be in safety. I must fly from place to place, must conceal myself in a thousand lurking holes, and put on a multitude of disguises. I perpetrated the deed I have narrated / to you by myself; and by myself must I endeavour to elude its consequences.

Father, you mistake. In the situations of which you speak, I can many ways be of service. When you grow tired of the task of perpetual escape, I can supply you with fresh suggestions, and by my animation recruit your wasted spirits. An ally in such a case will often be more collected and perspicacious than a

---

[a] In Virgil's *Aeneid*, Mezentius, a tyrant of Caere in Etruria.

principal. I shall be able at one time to interpose, so as to give you time to withdraw, and at another by my ingenuity and presence of mind to put the pursuers on a false scent, and so to deliver you. When the danger is past, I will be at hand with my congratulations, to restore you again to yourself.

There was a time, my child, when I was entitled to your assistance. The duty of a child to its parent is sacred. But it is so, no longer than the parent conducts himself worthily. Such a delinquency as mine divorces / the engagement, and puts an end to the tie. A guilty soul and deeds of blood can maintain no claim on a virtuous mind. Take then, my Catherine, your own way. Wherever you go, good fame and honour shall pursue you. You shall be loved and be happy. Forget that you had a father, who would prove a clog upon your steps, and the remembrance of whom would overcloud the glories that are reserved for you.

What, my father, replied Catherine, and do you think you shall persuade me to leave you? 'A guilty soul and deeds of blood can maintain no claim on a virtuous mind'.[a] Believe me, this is not so. These are the maxims of selfishness and cowardice. The more the world deserts you, the more will I cling to you. What, because the friend of my soul is unhappy, shall I withdraw myself? Shall I leave you, because you are guilty, – in other words, because you are in trouble? These are indeed admirable and praiseworthy principles! No: the more completely / you are alone, the more certainly will I be at your side. If all the world hiss at and scout you, this will be an additional reason for me to be your comforter. I will be at hand to smooth your pillow, when you most need a friend. I will pour the balm of consolation into your wounds, when the world most combines to destroy you. If you go to prison, I will go with you. If you are arraigned in a court of justice, I will be near you. If you mount the scaffold, I will ascend with you. Shall your last hours be hours of solitude and agony and despair, when I might be at hand to cheer and support you?

How can I do otherwise? You bid me seek tranquillity and peace. Enviable indeed would be my tranquillity, if I deserted a father in his utmost need in pursuit of it! I well 'foresee what stories I should hear within myself, all my life after, of discouragement and reproach',[b] if upon this memorable occasion I omitted the / smallest particle of my adherence and loyalty. Your violence, which you so industriously aggravate, was committed under the utmost provocation, and when the boiling of your blood was hot within you. But the conduct you would urge me to adopt, would be premeditated and measured, of the most dastard and cowardly sort, and such as I could never look back upon without loathing and self-detestation. No, my father; were I mean enough to seek only my own ease, assure yourself, I would look for it in acts the recollection of which might convince me that I had been good and faithful, a

---

[a] Quotation unidentified.
[b] Quotation unidentified.

true daughter to a parent that I never thought of but with adoration. Life upon any other terms would be a burthen too bitter to be sustained.

What could I reply to the eloquence, or, which is much better, to the self-devotion of my Catherine? I yielded. I viewed her with reverence and awe, as I might have regarded a being descended from the spheres, to sustain a / weak and erring mortal. But she would not endure this distance between us. She threw her arms round my neck; she sobbed upon my bosom.

Take me, my father! she said. Mould me at your pleasure! Henceforth I have no destination in life, no office concentrating all the powers of my nature, but that of being devoted to your service and advantage. In this service there is perfect freedom; in this religion there is pure felicity. It is the first question of a well-constituted mind, How can I make myself perfectly useful? How can I employ all my thoughts and energies in substantial good? Every hour of an upright spirit is lost, that is not occupied in acts of kindness. Yet how many hours of every one slide away from him in matters of cold indifference? Hitherto it has been so with me. But now I have an object for which to live, a principle that shall direct my smallest actions. Every morning / that I rise, I shall say, What can I do for my father? How shall I cheer him, prevail upon him to smile and be at peace? Every sound that I hear will be an alarm to me, to excite me to defend and preserve him. And my heart tells me, I shall succeed in this. No power shall conquer or baffle my constancy; and heaven itself will second the fervour of my intentions.

It is not to be told, what an effect this generosity of my daughter produced on my soul. For weeks I had been miserable, – ever since the letter of William was put into my hands announcing to me that he lived. From that instant all had been storm and uproar within me. A multitude of tempestuous winds seemed to hurry my mind in contrary directions. I was like a man who had committed himself to a frail bark, which is every moment about to go to pieces. Hollow and portentous blasts roar on all sides around him; the sails flap, and the cordage splits, and the canvas seems torn into / a thousand pieces. If he sleeps, sleep affords him no intermission. In this imperfect shutting up of the senses, he is still pursued by the sounds, whether it be the reality that continues to haunt him, or that his faithful imagination repeats the terror, when the thing itself can no longer be perceived: he is unvisited with a single instant of cessation. Such was the situation in which I stood. No sunshine appeared to me: every thing was black as Erebus.[a]

At length I resolved to shake off this incubus. I was strongly excited; and I yielded to the excitement. I believed that this was the crisis of my fortune; and it was so. But what change was it that ensued? I was loaded with the imputation of the blackest crime; I, whose character had been hitherto as white as snow,

---

[a] In Greek mythology the god of darkness, son of Chaos and brother of Night.

who had gone to bed every night from the hour of my birth, with the consciousness of innocence and honour, and had risen every mnorning with / hands
unspotted with guilt. I was cut off from human society; I was destined to be
hunted as a beast of prey, and to be looked upon by all men with horror and
execration. I said to myself, The hand of every man is against me. Previously to
the crime I had perpetrated, my mind was all uproar and confusion; subsequently all was gloomy composure and hopelessness. I was alone, unsym-
pathized with and unassisted, left to force my way as I could through the
tangled mazes and the wilderness of the world.

Conceive therefore what it was to me in this situation, to find a friend! It was
like life from the dead. My condition resembled that of Peter in the Acts, to
whom, 'the same night that he slept between two soldiers, being bound to them
with two chains, the angel of the Lord appeared, and a light shone in the
prison, and his fetters fell off from his hands'.[a] That I should have one person
to befriend me, who / truly accorded with me, who loved me with rooted
affection, and in whose heart dwelt every thing that was generous and noble,
was transport to my spirit. I was no longer alone. I had a being to animate and
encourage me in my deepest despondency. When my own spirit and energies
were exhausted, I still had an ally, upon whom I could confidently repose, and
who would watch for me incessantly.

There was something in the love of my daughter, that surpassed every thing
that I had before witnessed in a human creature. Margaret may be said to have
loved me, for, though the first fruit of her affections had been irrevocably
devoted to another, yet she had ever been attentive to my smallest wants, and
had on all occasions anticipated my wishes. The love of Emilia was of another
sort. She had been a perfect model of all that a wife could be. Our impulses at
all times harmonised, and the entire cordiality with which we / regarded each
other was never interrupted. But my life with Emilia had been all sunshine; we
were equals in age; and our hopes, our desires and our preferences fully
coincided. With Catherine it was otherwise. It was necessary for her in the
outset to sacrifice her youth, and the propensities inseparable from youth. She
must devote herself to obscurity and mourning, be cut off from the society of
her equals, and excluded from the world. Affection must be indeed sublimed,
before it can arrive at this supremacy. Ours was the alliance of a natural
buoyancy and gaiety with everlasting sadness, of the most animating prospects
with hopeless adversity. Virtue and innocence invited Catherine to the recreations which are best suited to their nature; and she made choice of the alliance
of guilt, because that guilt was her father's. Spotless herself, she voluntarily
took up her abode under the tents of contamination. She chose to dwell in a
scene / of uninterrupted terrors and alarm. Judge, if I did not appreciate her

[a] Acts 12: 6–7.

merit in all this. I earnestly and with fervour dissuaded her from the sacrifice. But, when it was already made, I could not but most ardently admire her disinterestedness, and be in a slight degree reconciled to myself, that I was the individual in whose favour it had been resolved on. /

CHAPTER XIV

The purpose itself being fixed, Catherine returned to her friends, to announce that her father had communicated to her his desire that he might presently be gratified with her society. She apologised to them for the abruptness of removal, but added that the occasion, into the particulars of which she was not at liberty to enter, admitted of no delay. The persons, with whom she had now for some time been in a manner domesticated, could not but observe that something of an extraordinary nature was indicated in her countenance and manner; but they felt too much delicacy to enquire further into what they saw was not / designed to be communicated. They trusted that her removal would not be of long continuance, and warmly expressed the delight it would give them to have again the happiness of her society.

It afforded me exquisite pleasure to have my daughter now for my companion. It took from me in a considerable degree the dreadful feeling of forlornness, to which I had for several days been a prey. The obscure hotel in which I received her, assumed in some sort the character of a home. I changed my name. Hastening to a coffee-house in a busy and trading street, I dispatched one of the porters for any letters that might be lying for me at my banker's. I next repaired to my family-solicitor, to tell him that I had immediate occasion to go abroad, that my absence would probably be short, but that it might prove otherwise, and to direct him to prepare a letter of attorney, authorising him in my absence / to receive my income and call in my rents, so that, wherever I might be, I should be able by my single signature, without specifying the place of my residence, to obtain from him supplies, as I might have occasion. I returned therefore to my man of business the next monrning, that I might execute this instrument.

At the same time a letter reached me from Rowland, acquainting me with the further particulars that had occurred at my family-mansion of Deloraine. The father and mother of Margaret were overwhelmed with the dreadful intelligence communicated to them by my steward. They had for many days feared they knew not what. William, who, after his return in a manner from the dead, had once presented himself before them, and had learned the intelligence which blasted all his hopes, had quitted their cottage abruptly, promising to return. But he had never returned. They saw him no more. They had apprehended / every thing from the steps which his desperation might suggest to him. He had indeed in an extraordinary degree moderated his proceedings, and controled his passions. He had committed no outrage, but conducted himself with that temperance and forbearance which so well accorded with every trait of his character. But the results had not been the less fatal. The utmost violence on his part could not have led to a more tragical conclusion.

The father and mother of Margaret had always loved her, with as much devotion as parents could entertain for a child. Such had been their feeling towards her from earliest infancy. But their affection had been exceedingly increased by every thing she had done since she arrived at years of maturity. No one perhaps had ever carried the sentiment of filial submission to so great an extent. She gave up her first love to the requisition of her father. She finally engaged herself to me in marriage, / not because her parents demanded it of her, but because she saw that, without prescribing it, it was the thing in the world most correspondent to their wishes. And how had this exemplary and self-denying conduct been ultimately rewarded! They had further been deeply impressed with the spectacle of all she had suffered. Her health had ultimately sunk under the violence she had done herself, in conforming to the dictates of her father's unhallowed ambition. When at length that father had given way rather than see his daughter made the victim to her sense of filial duty, and she was encouraged to follow the dictates of her earliest love, the concession had ultimately been made abortive, and she had seen her promised consort shipwrecked before her eyes. The consequence of this calamity had been long years of depression and ill health which brought her to the brink of the grave. Had ever a blameless human / being undergone such a series of uninterrupted misfortune?

Her parents were broken down to the earth, by the fatal intelligence which was now communicated to them. They were not allowed however to yield to the supineness of grief. I was rendered an exile from the dwelling of my fathers by the violent deed I had perpetrated. They were therefore imperiously called upon to proceed without delay to the house of mourning, where the mortal remains of their daughter for the present lay. Rowland received them with the utmost attention and deference, and told them that it was my express order to him, that all was to be done in every point in the affair as they directed. This was the only alleviation that I could afford them; but this very concession tasked the unfortunate old man to more exertion of mind, and the issuing a greater number of precise directions, than was almost / in any way compatible with the depression and distraction of his feelings.

It was with the utmost repugnance that the parents of Margaret entered the house of a man, who by his sanguinary conduct had, to say the least of it, brought their darling child to a premature grave. It was incumbent on Borradale to determine the spot in which the remains of his daughter should finally be deposited. On the one hand he regarded me as virtually her murderer. At the same time in another point of view he felt satisfied that her demeanour as a wife had been free from any particle of blame; and he therefore judged it due to her honour, that she should be interred in the vault appropriated to the family into which she had married.

Rowland concluded his letter, so far as regarded the Borradales, with informing me, that the father of Margaret, having first attended his wife to within a short distance of / their home, joined the melancholy procession which conveyed the body of his daughter to the vault where it was finally reposited, and appeared convulsed with agony when he gazed for the last time on her coffin.

That I may have no occasion to revert again to this part of my narrative, I will add here what I did not learn till some time afterwards. I had placed the father and mother of Margaret in a commodious habitation at a distance of thirty miles from the spot where I and their daughter resided. But the recommendation which this dwelling originally had, that it was conveniently situated for the purpose of reciprocal visits, was now converted into a spring of galling recollections. Beside that, they felt a repugnance to the occupying a house, which had been of my selecting, and for which it was understood that I undertook they should pay no rent. They looked upon the marriage of their daughter as unhallowed, and preferred / the submitting to a series of privations, rather than have any thing appertaining to them, that should remind them of this fatal connection, or should retain the semblance of an obligation to a man, who had been in so many ways, and lastly by an act of the most deplorable violence, the cause of precipitating the destruction of a child, who had been dearer to them than all the world beside. They therefore returned to the scene of their former abode on the banks of the Severn. Not indeed to the same house, for that was in the occupation of another; but to a house at the further extremity of the same village. Here, obscurely and disconsolately, they dragged out the short series of their remaining days. The mother felt perhaps most deeply for the disastrous fate of her child; and she went first. The father followed a short time after. They could not bear to hear the history of their daughter alluded to; and they could never for a moment forget it. The name of / Deloraine was to the last most distasteful to them. It was thus that, by one act of guilty violence, I accomplished the destruction of all who were in any degree connected with it.

The act by which I destroyed a man so singularly excellent and amiable, at the very period of his return to his native soil in anticipation of the most enviable felicity, was in itself sufficiently atrocious. How bitter then were my sensations, when I saw this one unconsidered violence overwhelming in its consequences all those whom I was most bound to cherish and defend from every mischief, the wife to whom I had vowed myself at the altar, and both the parents from whom she derived her existence! Why did I for a moment outlive the perpetration of this portentous evil? That will fully appear in the sequel.

Before the intelligence of the entire consummation of this mischief reached me, I was already far engaged in a struggle for life, / against, as it appeared to me, a world in arms to destroy me: and the more arduous, even the more hopeless, was the struggle, the less could I entertain the thought of giving in, and throwing myself, manacled and defenceless, into the hands of my inveterate foes. No: the very nature of the contest forbade me: as long as I had one resource left, miserable beyond all names of misery as I was, I resolved, like Macbeth, to 'try it to the last',[a] and persevere in the contention, till famine should be the sole conqueror of Deloraine. /

CHAPTER XV

But there was another topic touched upon in Rowland's letter, which closely affected the future fortunes of my life. It will be recollected that I had ordered the body of William to be deposited in the summer-house in my garden. I had given no further direction in that matter. Rowland had therefore felt considerably perplexed how he was to act. Here was the dead body of a person, who had apparently come to a violent end, and that by my hand. It was unavoidable, that some inquisition should be made into this, and that a question should be raised to be decided on by the legal authorities of my country. Rowland / saw that the event of this man being killed had in some way a close relation to his mistress. But I had declined giving any explanation; and he could learn nothing from any other quarter. The person was that of a total stranger. With my last words I had recommended to him to take care that I was not observed or molested in my departure, that for a few hours he should not suffer any outcry to be made in the vicinity, and that he should conduct every thing with composure and discretion. He therefore resolved to take no step till the arrival of the physician I had ordered to be sent for; and he communicated to the other servants the plan he had fixed in this respect.

The physician had no sooner examined the corpse of the unfortunate Margaret, and pronounced that life was for ever extinguished within her, than he began to question the steward respecting his knowledge of the particulars / which had probably led to the event of Margaret's decease. Rowland on his part was not less anxious to state as fully as he was able all that he knew on the subject. He said that he had seen me in the earlier part of the present day, when

---

[a] *Macbeth*, V. viii. 32 (adapted).

I had returned home from transacting a business which had carried me for two nights and a day to the town of ——, but, that, after remaining at home for scarcely more than a few minutes, I had again quitted my house, leaving him in the greatest uncertainty as to the time at which I was to be expected back. It was therefore in the highest degree important to him to obtain the advice of some person of weight in public estimation, as to what it was proper for him to do.

Rowland then related to the physician, that, as he rode out as usual to examine the grounds, and give directions to the labourers, he had seen my carriage quit the public road, and enter the park. He had therefore turned his / horse, and advanced towards the mansion, thinking it not improbable that I might have some orders to give him. He had not proceeded many yards, when he saw his mistress, accompanied by a young man, a total stranger, of very interesting appearance, seated on the turf near the garden-wall. The same object, at the same moment, seemed to have gained my attention. My carriage stopped; I leaped out, and flew most rapidly to the spot. His mistress and the stranger were too deeply engaged with each other to observe this. I was almost upon them, when the stranger rose, and made a few steps towards me. I had already a loaded pistol in my hand, and, swifter than thought, presented it to the stranger, and laid him dead at my feet. All this was scarcely the work of a minute. Rowland added, that his mistress seemed to be worked up to a preternatural horror at what she saw, / that she exclaimed against me as a monster, called the person I had slain her dear, her best-beloved William, and, after a few frantic expressions of a similar sort, fell suddenly to the ground, and spoke no more. He proceeded to relate, that, after having addressed a few words to himself and the servants who had attended the carriage, in which I palliated the violence I had committed, but added that this was not the time for explanation and defence, I hastened into the house, and ordered my favourite saddle-horse to be prepared. I remained at home scarcely more than twenty minutes; and my last directions were, that the dead body of the person I had slain should be removed, and brought into the summer-house in the garden, and that Dr Allen should with all speed be sent for, to see whether any thing could be done for his mistress. The message which Rowland had accordingly dispatched was a / written one, importing that his mistress lay in a very precarious state, and that it was feared she had broken a blood-vessel.

Dr Allen was much affected by this narrative, and was in great perplexity how to proceed. He desired to be taken to the summer-house. The person of the deceased was as much a stranger to him, as it had been to Rowland. The doctor was wholly unacquainted with Margaret's previous history, and knew her only as my wife. He recommended that Rowland should by all means charge the servants to abstain from spreading the particulars of what had passed, and added that he would himself drive to the house of Mr Bartram, a magistrate who lived within the distance of a few miles, relate to him the leading circumstances, and request his professional interference, which appeared to be loudly called for on so extraordinary an occasion. In the course of a few hours Mr Bartram and the / doctor came together, that they might more fully search into the affair.

They were already employed in visiting the bodies of the unfortunate individuals whom I had left for dead when I departed, and eliciting from the servants who had witnessed the tragic event such information as they were able to afford, when news was brought them of the arrival of a gentleman, a stranger, who desired to see them immediately, to speak with them on the subject which was employing their attention. He was admitted. /

CHAPTER XVI

The person who now presented himself, proved to be the especial friend of my rival. He had come with William to England, and had conceived, as was the case with all who had an opportunity of knowing the deceased, the strongest partiality and affection for him. William, as has already been related, had been carried a prisoner into Carthagena. As the Spaniards had at that time been influenced by the greatest jealousy of the English, who were said to have invaded the territories, and illicitly intruded themselves upon the commerce of their dominions in that part of the world, every / Englishman who arrived there was regarded with dislike, and was often treated with contumaciousness and barbarity. William had been exposed to the effects of this state of things. Though he was only an ordinary prisoner of war, he was carried up the country, and subjected to a sort of slavery, just as if he had been a partaker of the contraband trade. He at length escaped, and had travelled in various disguises, and through a thousand hardships, till he reached the French settlement of Cayenne.[a] Here, as every where, he found a friend. The colony of Cayenne was in a condition that had little to recommend it. William was therefore advised and assisted to remove himself to St Domingo.[b] The persons by whom this step had been recommended to him, took care at the same time to furnish him with introductions to some of the most considerable settlers in this opulent and flourishing / island. These introductions were of course from Frenchmen of consideration in Cayenne, to their countrymen in St Domingo.

The individuals to whom William's letters were addressed, contended with

---

[a] Capital of modern French Guiana, S. America.
[b] Island in the Caribbean Sea now divided between Haiti and the Dominican Republic.

each other in the kindness and hospitality with which they entertained him. He had learned to read the French language with ease in the course of his education; and his travels since had enabled him to converse in it with the veraciousness and candour that distinguish the worthiest of his own country, and the fluency of a native. On the third or fourth day however after his arrival, he met in a party a young Englishman, being no other than the person just mentioned, named Travers, between whom and himself there immediately sprung up the warmest sentiments of friendship.

Travers first saw the light in the island of Jamaica, and was of that descrip-tion of persons commonly known by the name of Creoles.[a] His / father had been a leading member of council in the island; and for a series of years his opinions had almost directed the resolves of the assembly, and the policy of the planters. His ascendancy however was not unenvied; and his suggestions did not always remain unopposed. A new governor from England united himself to the projects of his adversaries, and turned the scale of policy in the island against the sentiments avowed by the elder Travers. He had distinguished himself by plans, calculated to meliorate the condition of the black cultivators of the soil, to imbue them with self-respect, and to hold out to them an ultimate prospect of independence, in proportion as any of them might be found to deserve it. His projects were not inconsistent with the true interests of the proprietors; but they were incompatible with the mean thoughts and sordid jealousy that governed their determinations. /

Travers found that he was every day declining in influence; and his cherished schemes were thwarted in the most vexatious manner. He had flattered himself that he had made a safe and assured beginning to a better state of things, and that he should leave behind him the grateful recollection that he had laid the first stone of an edifice, which would grow stronger and more worthy of admiration, when he himself should have ceased to exist. But now the whole face of things was reversed. The progress which he had slowly and indefatig-ably accomplished, was destined to a rapid destruction. Every sun that rose upon the island, witnessed the revival of some evil, and the strengthening of inveterate prejudices. Nor was this the worst. The planters, who had been galled by the advance of the generous projects of Travers, now resolved to wreak their enmity on the old man. Every day they propagated scandal and lies against him. They / petitioned the government at home to concur in his exile from the colony, as a dangerous and pernicious member of society. The poor negroes were the worse treated on his account. Their oppressors augmented the severity and inhumanity of their discipline, for the purpose of signalising their triumph, and by way of vengeance against the virtuous man who had interfered in their favour. Intelligence of incarcerations and death was

---

[a] Native-born individuals of mixed white and black parentage.

169

perpetually brought to his ears; and it was continually asserted that all these mischiefs were to be laid to his charge. The very negroes were incited to vent their griefs in hostility to him. Those who smarted from the lash, and those whose fathers and wives had been brought to an untimely end by the cruelty of their owners, were taught to regard their calamity as the fruit of his weak and romantic support of their cause. They muttered curses against him, and sometimes broke out into open revilings and insult. They / annoyed him with looks of bitter and deadly revenge; and all these things, which would have been severely repressed by the masters in any other case, were secretly encouraged by them in this. They pulled down his fences, and trampled his crops under their feet.

The old man felt the injustice of this treatment more with the temper of a disappointed lover, than with the unalterable steadiness of a philosopher. He resolved for ever to quit the scene of his galling disappointments. He sold off his property in the island. His enemies, though delighted with the thought of his removal, yet entered into a conspiracy to thwart him in this point also. They seemed to shrink from the idea of buying what he was desirous to sell. They expressed themselves as if their pure hands would be contaminated by the bare touch of any thing that had belonged to the sacrilegious reformer. When he left the island of Jamaica for that of St Domingo, he found / the amount of his fortune, the bequest of his ancestors, and the produce of his own superintendence and industry, reduced by more than one half.

Change of place is in a very imperfect degree the remedy of care and vexation. The elder Travers was kindly received by the planters of St Domingo, several of whom appeared to entertain views as to the negroes very similar to his own. But the arrow that he carried with him rankled in his side. He was a true lover of his species; and he could not endure with patience the miscarriage of his efforts. To encounter contumely from the very quarter from which he had merited only love, was too bitter. The insults and malignant triumph of his enemies, were never forgotten by him. To be made an exile, and robbed of half his fortune, on the very soil where he was rather entitled to statues and triumphal arches of gratitude, deprived him of sleep, and wasted his constitution / and strength. In no long time he fell a martyr to the disappointment he had suffered.

The old man, being dead, left his son the sole representative of his name, and inheritor of his property, in that part of the world. The younger Travers had most of the qualities which are said to distinguish the descendants of European parents, born in a tropical climate. He was of the class of 'souls made of fire, and children of the sun'.[a] He had been sent over to the mother-country for education. He was bred at Eton; and his volatility, his lively qualities, and his

---

[a] Edward Young, *The Revenge* (1721), V. ii. 273.

affectionate nature had procured him a certain number of attached friends in that scene. His vivacity was inexhaustible; his large and black eyes flashed as with heaven's own lightning; and his courage was proof against every peril. Yet with all this he was a great and an early thinker, and capable of the most invincible perseverance. He was moody; now communicative and gay, / the life of every party of pleasure, and seeming to have no thought of his soul that was not imparted to every bystander; and anon, busied in inscrutable meditation, –

> ... as patient as the female dove,
> When that her golden couplets are disclosed,
> His silence would sit drooping.[a]

He was sometimes the mere rattle of his form, a shallow stream, such as we occasionally see intersecting the green-wood meadow, imaging every surrounding object, and perpetuating none; while at other times he had fits of study which nothing could divert, as if he would penetrate into all the mysteries of nature, and all the embarrassing involutions of the profoundest reach of human thought.

His father loved him with an intense affection, and could not bear the length of separation which his education properly demanded. He recalled him abruptly to his side in Jamaica. Here at an early age the young Travers / felt himself exempted from all control. His father knew no pleasure so great as that of abetting his vagaries. Many of them were attended with danger; but the old man preferred taking his chance of the injuries the boy might bring upon himself by his caprices, or even the possibility of his untimely destruction, to the ungrateful task of imposing on him the bridle of parental authority. He could not bear that those eyes the sparkles of which were so enchanting, should be dulled with disappointment, or those lips whose smiles were so bewitching, should be robbed for a moment of their flexibility and grace. On the other hand, the young man, though self-willed and incapable of voluntary constraint, loved his father with exemplary affection, and regarded him as the model of all honour and virtue. He did things strange and extraordinary, sometimes annoying; but there was no malice in his levities, which oftener obtained for him friends than enemies. /

The youth however entered deeply into a feeling similar to that of his father, respecting the unpopularity and ill treatment which were heaped upon the elder Travers, in return for his disinterested exertions in the cause of humanity. This circumstance produced strong emotions in his inexperienced bosom. Though, as I have said, his conduct on a majority of occasions appeared light-hearted and thoughtless, he was, amidst all his extravagances, susceptible of deep impression, profound meditation, and inflexible purpose. He ruminated

---

[a] *Hamlet*, V. i. 308–10 (adapted).

on the injustice that a large portion of mankind was capable of perpetrating, and his heart sickened at the conviction. 'Strong was his love; unbounded his resentment'.[a] Thus his character became mingled, by turns bland and beneficent as an angel, and then again darkened with a covered fury and aversion that might better beseem a demon.

Another circumstance had contributed to add / force to the particular tone of his character. An opulent proprietor of his native island, whose plantation nearly adjoined to that of his father, had a daughter, distinguished for the exquisiteness of her beauty, the grace of her form and moving, and the ingenuous sweetness of her disposition. Travers had loved her while yet a child; and, when he returned, after having spent his school-boy years in Great Britain, he beheld her with increased preference and affection. But it was during this period of his absence, that the factious opposition to his father had attained to a portentous height. Young Travers could only meet his favourite fair one with difficulty and by stealth. The father of the lady was numbered among the most inveterate foes of the elder Travers, and therefore took the utmost pains to thwart the growing attachment. Fearful that he might fail of his purpose by other means, he abruptly removed his daughter, upon pretence of a visit to Barbadoes / to a relation he had in that island, and contrived that a proposal of marriage should be the fruit of this visit. The daughter returned to Jamaica; and the suitor favoured by her father, followed her. Travers, agonised by the prospect of losing the mistress of his heart, sought an interview with the planter, and by every inducement he could suggest, supplied by the vehemence of his passion, and the strength of their mutual attachment, endeavoured to prevail upon him to change his resolution. But the greater was the importunity of the youth, the more inflexible did the father of the lady appear. Travers humbled himself almost to prostration; at the same time that the other party only the more insulted over him, and taunted him with the disapprobation and estrangement with which his parent was looked upon by every respectable man in the island. In fine, the fair one of whom he had been passionately enamoured, was wedded to / his rival, and lost to himself for ever. This disappointment, coming about the same time with the expulsion of his father from the scenes which from his birth had been familiar to him, his subsequent misfortunes, and at length his death through what is called a broken heart, soured the temper of the youth, and increased in him the gloom and saturnineness of disposition, with which he had been originally but slightly imbued. His gaiety had not left him for ever; but it occurred by fits only, and was then marked with a sort of alarming and portentous excess, and followed by a relapse,

---

[a] Quotation unidentified.

As if he mocked himself, and scorned his spirit,
That could be moved to smile at any thing.[a]

Meanwhile the first want of his heart was to love; and, when this want was emphatically gratified, he would become a mere child, and overflow with a tenderness and earnestness that could with difficulty find a parallel.

Such was the individual between whom and / William a singular and exemplary friendship sprung up, immediately upon their meeting at Cape François, the principal town of the French division of the island of St Domingo. The similarity of disposition that existed between them speedily blew up their mutual partiality to a flame. They were both of them young men of warm hearts and a kind and benevolent temper. They were naturally of a gay and sanguine cast of mind, full of energy and hope. But both of them had suffered much from the malice of fortune; Travers at the time of their first encounter the most of the two. Deprived by a cruel concurrence of circumstances, of the father he worshipped, and crossed in the object of his love, he seemed to have given up for ever the expectation of a pleasing and acceptable mode of existence. Still his affectionate nature survived these adversities, and taught him to seize with avidity an object upon which he might centre the aspirations of his spirit. /

Travers and William seemed to understand each other at the first encounter. They were the only persons of English birth at the party which brought them together. But, more than this circumstance, the fire that characterised the glance of Travers, and the overflowing love and goodness of heart so conspicuous in the countenance of William, made them feel as if they had been acquainted for ages. They exchanged looks while they sat apart at the social board, which spoke volumes. An incidental remark from one or the other, was listened to with earnestness, and seemed to make the heart of the hearer bound in his bosom. As soon as the forms of the festive board admitted it, they drew together, and retired into an obscure recess, where each of them poured out his congratulations that he had been so happy as to meet a brother, of the same stock, and speaking the same language, in so remote a part of the world, but, more than all, whose / feelings harmonized, and who as by intuition entered into each other's modes of apprehending and judging.

William had the most to tell. Travers could only relate that he had been born in the neighbour island, that he had been sent to England for education and had returned, and that through subsequent crosses and misfortunes he had been obliged to quit the island of his birth, and had recently lost his father. But William had just passed through a series of unprecedented vicissitudes. He had been a captive first, and then in a manner a slave. He had made his escape, and had experienced innumerable 'accidents by flood and field'.[b] In his arduous

---

[a] *Julius Caesar*, I. ii. 205–6.
[b] *Othello*, I. iii. 135.

march he seemed to have subsisted only by miracle. He had encountered continual dangers, in the inhospitable desert, from hungry beasts, and lawless savages.

When the two friends spoke of love, which they did not fail soon to do, this topic increased / their mutual sympathy. The scene had closed upon Travers: his mistress was married to another. William was not aware of any such circumstance in his case. But he had been twice violently separated from the idol of his heart: once he had been sent to Canada, and formally bid to despair; and then, when recalled with every promise of approaching felicity, had been shipwrecked in sight of land, in sight of his mistress, and unaccountably given over to a series of remorseless disasters, which had pursued him for successive years.

Neither of the two had ever met with an individual of his own sex, with whom his ideas so thoroughly accorded. They were like twins, whom some strange event had separated, and cast on opposite sides of the globe, and who, when they met, then for the first time felt a kind of repose and entire content-ment, as if half of himself had been torn away from each, and was now restored, so that he became perfect, / equal to any encounter, and armed against every assault of nature or fortune. Travers was the one best provided with worldly means to effect whatever he purposed. Travers was the first to swear eternal friendship. He unburthened his mind, and related to his new associate all the particulars of the strange malice that had pursued the author of his being, who had first been defamed and partially impoverished, and had at last died, a martyr to his too much virtue. The recollection of this, together with the wound he had himself received in the tenderest point, filled young Travers top-full with ill will and bitterest gall, and prepared him in a just and generous cause, to pursue the man of evil, or whom he should judge such, to an irremissible extremity. He was called upon by the last injunctions of his father to pass over to Europe, and there to communicate with the remaining branch of his family, the elder branch, that had staid at home to cultivate their original / demesnes, while he, of a junior stock, had crossed the Atlantic, to seek 'fresh woods and pastures new'.[a]

Travers and William soon became inseparable in their pursuits and amuse-ments. They read the same books, and talked of the same authors. They found a surprising coincidence in their tastes. The same page that had enchanted the one, charmed the other. When it happened otherwise, when the one named an author with approbation with which the other was unacquainted, or quoted a passage of deep reflection or exquisite grace which the mind of the other by some accident had never rested upon, it was like the opening of a new vein of some precious metal. It was valued for itself, and valued for the sake of the

---

[a] Milton, *Lycidas*, l. 193.

hand that guided the steps of the needless wanderer. It was the same with the beauties of nature and art. They rode and walked together. In fishing or hunting, in botanic research, and in their occasional visits / to the select societies of St Domingo, they were inseparable. In one point only they differed. William was impatient to return home, for there his dearest treasure was garnered, and there he anticipated the fruition of entire felicity. To Travers, who had no such anticipation, all quarters of the globe were equal, except as he desired nothing so much as to attend upon the wishes and fancies of his newly acquired friend.

While they were waiting for a vessel, which was shortly to convey them from Cape François to Havre, they in one instance joined a party of young men, who had engaged to pass over from the bay to the neighbouring island of Tortue, distant about two leagues, the object which engaged them being a hunt of the wild bulls with which the lesser island abounds. The sport was plentiful, and the party in a high state of exhilaration. In the midst of a scene of social gaiety, it is almost impossible that the most / gloomy and dejected character should not for the moment forget his sorrows. Travers no longer thought of his exile and his mistress; and even William just then lost sight of the image of his Margaret.

In the evening they returned home by the same boat which had carried them out. The youngest of the party, a mere boy of ten or twelve years of age, who had gone with the rest rather as a spectator than a hunter, by some accident fell overboard. Travers, who saw the fall, with the lightning activity and decision so characteristic of a Creole, leaped immediately into the sea to his rescue. By this time the whole party became anxious spectators of the scene. Travers presently caught hold of the youth, and by his strength and skill became almost certain of saving him. But just at the moment an enormous shark, the universal terror of these seas, appeared in sight. One of the peculiarities of this animal, which mainly / contributes to the consternation with which he is regarded, is the astonishing rapidity with which he cuts the waves. It remained certain that Travers at least, who appeared particularly aimed at by the shark, would perish. William perhaps was not so skilful a swimmer as his friend; but the warm regard which had in a manner sprung up in a day between him and Travers, penetrated him with energy and resolution. He caught at a drawn sword, which, in the earnestness of excited feeling, was held by one of the company; and wresting it from its holder, plunged with it into the sea. Whether or no he was so expert a swimmer as a Creole, might be disputed; but he was no mean proficient in the art. The affection he felt for his newly acquired friend, the most earnest that had animated him towards any one he had seen since his shipwreck at Plymouth, augmented his powers, and guided his hand. He dived below the body of the creature that was now / almost on the point of accomplishing its fell purpose, and in an instant inflicted a mortal wound. The waves were stained with the blood of the shark; the animal writhed in agony, and then presently turned on its back, and was still. The friends, and the boy whose heedlessness had produced this terrible scene, were all saved. The mutual attachment of both the saver and the saved, was by this adventure made stronger than ever. /

CHAPTER XVII

It was not long after this incident, that Travers and William embarked together for Havre. William, who had at length arrived within a short distance of his natal shore, was animated with the most impatient desire to stand once more within the presence of Margaret, and to accomplish that union which had been so disastrously interrupted. Travers on the other hand, who had come to Europe merely in compliance with the injunction of his father to renew the intercourse with the elder branch of his family, felt no unwillingness to defer for a short time the completing of that purpose. The friends therefore, who had lately been inseparable, / now agreed to cross the English Channel by the earliest conveyance.

William as I have said, made it his business to forward a letter to Margaret, by the first boat that came alongside as they approached the English shore. He did not wait for an answer, but proceeded with all expedition in personal search of his beloved. As he approached her residence, or any place in which he imagined that she resided, he conceived it to be due to the sacredness of their relation, that he should approach alone. This was the reason why Travers was not a witness to his visit to her father. William desired his friend to wait his return at a village at no great distance.

The change which Travers observed in him when they met again, was truly alarming. Hitherto he had seen nothing in his associate but an eager desire to bless his eye with the sight of her from whom he had been so calamitously / separated, and an anticipation of unspeakable joy. But now, when this time they met, William appeared more like a bloodless, unlaid ghost, than the presence of a living man. They had parted for scarcely more than an hour; and in that short absence the lover had become so altered, as to be scarcely recognisable for the same individual. His gaiety, the exuberant life which had pervaded every limb and articulation of his frame, was gone for ever; and in its place had succeeded indications and an expression of despair that Travers could not witness without terror.

The West Indian was in a field adjoining to the village inn, when he perceived William approaching. He ran towards him. William could scarcely sustain himself. He fell on the neck of his friend in speechless agony. At length, Travers, he cried, it is all at an end with me! Why have I outlived the disasters of years? Why did not I perish by shipwreck? / Why was I not so happy as to die in slavery among the Spanish colonists of America? What evil genius urged me to cross the deserts, to summon up an unshrinking courage, to encounter hunger and privations of every sort, to contend with infuriated beasts of prey, and the contriving and subtle malice of the savage, man? I have been reserved for that which is incomparably more dreadful. For God's sake, restore to me the worst and bitterest of these calamities, restore to me the blessed ignorance, with which, if it had endured to my latest breath, I might have smiled upon the king of terrors, and said, Still am I the beloved, the favoured and happy darling of my Margaret, never thought of by her without smiles of consolation!

By degrees William recovered strength and composure to detail his misfortune to his friend. Travers would fain have disbelieved it. He said, Surely there must be some mistake! When he could no longer have the gratification to / doubt, he felt almost as deeply as William, that his calamity, with all its aggravations, was perhaps without a parallel. The bystander, where there is an entire attachment, is in some repects more to be pitied than the principal. The principal in a manner glories in the excess of his woe; he drinks to the dregs the cup of unutterable anguish; he says, I stand alone; I am a spectacle for men and angels. His mind is confounded, his wits unsettled with the depth of his suffering; he is mad. But the bystander sees it all, and makes no mistake. He is in the eclipse of a gloomy sobriety; all with him is orderly and perspicuous; he has no majestic part to play; he sees that his friend is beyond the reach of consolation; and he is cast down to the dust with the sense of his own impotence. Such was the condition of Travers.

William regarded it as the last indulgence of which he was susceptible, to repair to the / dwelling in which Margaret resided. To look upon the roof that covered her, and the window by which she occasionally passed, would still be a gratification. He might chance to gain a distant view of her figure, himself unseen. Travers could not oppose a proposition, apparently so harmless, He said to himself, I will suffer my friend to take his full swing in the natural indulgence of his sorrows; he will be the better for it. It is in vain to endeavour to stem the ocean in the omnipotence of its rage. By and by it will have spent itself. A calm naturally succeeds to the violence of the tempest. Lassitude and a sort of calamitous repose are the inevitable sequence of preternatural exertions. It will then be time to try what I can do. Little, alas! very little will be in my power. But so glorious a creature, a man so formed to scatter incessant blessings on all around him, must not be lost. – Travers therefore encouraged William in his fantastic / enterprise, and only conditioned with him, that he should in all cases be a spectator, never an actor, in his meditated expedition.

The friends took up a temporary abode at a town four or five miles distant from the residence of Margaret. Here William insisted that Travers should

177

remain and proceed no further. I go, he said, as Petrarch made a pilgrimage to the grave of his Laura.[a] for the luxury of weeping with the tomb of my beloved before me. The ancient and venerable mansion of Deloraine is her mausoleum. On such an occasion my sorrows are sacred. No living thing, who can read my feelings, and interpret my gestures, must approach. I must be surrounded with solitude, even as if the mausoleum stood by itself on a desolate island. There must be nothing to restrain the overflowing of my agonies. They shall be spent, – Travers, I swear to you, they shall be spent, – on myself alone. To the conceptions of ordinary mortals / Margaret still lives, and is mixed with the affairs of human beings. But to me, she is like Merlin, the prophet, shut up by an omnipotent charm in a tomb of her own constructing, where she must remain, alive and conscious, but without power of escape, till the final close of earthly things shall arrive.[b]

Travers conformed himself to the desires of his friend. Every day William set out on his pilgrimage to the dwelling of his beloved; and every night he returned, overlaboured and spiritless, less living than dead, to the care and anxious watchfulness of Travers. His friend began to be alarmed in conjecturing where all this would end. He endeavoured to expostulate and draw William away, and to say, This is enough! But still the predestined youth persisted.

At length the day arrived, when William returned no more. Travers became greatly alarmed. Hitherto his friend had never failed / to show himself nightly at the town, though often in the most pitiable state. Travers well knew the direction in which William had proceeded. The unhappy youth had wandered in many an irregular maze, and had worn the sod in a manner bare with his incessant perambulations. But there was one point that was sure to be the centre of his circuits. Of this Travers was fully aware; and he set out, with impressions of the deepest anxiety, to ascertain what was become of his friend.

With no great difficulty he discovered the cottage, where William had been in the habit of calling and engaging in casual intercourse with its inhabitants. Travers entered their apartment, and solicitously enquired after any intelligence they could give him of his friend. The old woman and her daughters said, they had never been able to make out the character of their visitor. He had always been most particularly inquisitive concerning the family / at the mansion-house, yet had never shewn himself at their doors. They saw that he was a person that had been a good deal in foreign countries. He was something like a sailor, yet had very much the manners of a gentleman. They sometimes fancied that he might have been a former lover of the lady at the great house,

---

[a] Francesco Petrarca (1304–74), Italian lyric poet, whose collected odes and sonnets were almost all inspired by his love for Laura de Noves, the death of whom he lamented in *Canzoniere*.

[b] In Arthurian legend, Merlin was a magician and counsellor to King Arthur. When he revealed his secret craft to Vivien, the Lady of the Lake, she entangled him in thornbush, where he lies until Eternity.

and had come home, and found the person married, whom he had counted upon making his wife. But he had never dropped a word to them that looked that way. Two or three times persons had called at their cottage, and enquired with some earnestness respecting their accidental guest. One was a lady, not the lady from the great house, but another who lived several miles further from them. More lately, a servant belonging to the squire had come on the same errand. But, only four days ago, I had myself driven to the cottage, and left a billet for the stranger, written with a pencil, which, the day after, he had received / from them. What were the contents of the billet they knew not; but the stranger pursued his course as before, hovering round the great house, which he appeared to regard with much attention from the brook, and from the hill which afforded him a wider prospect. Thus he had employed himself that day and the next. Each day he had spent a few minutes at their cottage. On the third they had seen him for the last time. He had gone forward as before in the direction of my residence.

This intelligence added considerably to the uneasiness of Travers. It was on the evening of the third day, that Willian first failed of returning to the neighbouring town. The fourth was dedicated by his friend to the endeavouring to ascertain the cause of his absence. The cottagers had seen him, as nearly as Travers could discover, in less than two hours from the time when he had left his lodgings. As the Creole appeared anxious to obtain the fullest information / they could afford, the old woman proceeded to the wicket before her door, and pointed out to him the path which led to the brook with a bridge, and the knoll that commanded a view of my house and gardens.

Aided by this direction Travers set forward. After a short time he ascended the brow, and looked down upon the house and gardens which he had never before seen. There was a footway that led along under the garden wall. In this foot-way he observed a peasant, who paused in his walk, and seemed to be looking carefully at some object which had caught his attention. Travers hailed him, and hastened to the spot where he stood.

What is it, my good man, said he, that you are looking for?

Nothing, replied the peasant: but I felt surprised to see the grass on this spot stained with blood. Some accident has happened, perhaps to one of the sheep. /

Travers observed, and thought the blood on the grass more than such a cause would account for. The peasant passed on. Travers did not attempt to detain him. Upon a narrower inspection he discovered that the spots of blood, though inconsiderable after the first effusion, went on, and at length stopped at a small door leading into my garden.

He wanted no further hint than this, to induce him to push forward, and hasten to the principal entrance of the house. At the door he encountered the carriage of Dr Allen. He asked of the attendants whether this was the house of Mr Deloraine, and was told that it was. He immediately entered the hall, and was doubtful for a moment how he should proceed. A servant presently came down the great stair-case. Travers addressed him, and asked for his master. Mr Deloraine was from home. When was he expected? The servant could not tell. He had left the house yesterday. /

There was something in the general appearance of Travers, that seemed to call for more than ordinary attention and respect; and on the present occasion his mind was excited, and the fire in his eye was unusually striking. The footman felt that he could not shake him off, or quit him abruptly.

There was a carriage, Travers observed, at the door, which seemed to be the carriage of a physician: was any one ill?

The physician was sent for to his mistress. But the footman was afraid it was too late. He feared that his lady was dead.

Dead! and the master left home yesterday! This struck Travers. Had she been long ill?

She had been ill some time. But her death was sudden.

Had she been out lately? Travers began to suspect that Margaret and his friend might have met each other by accident.

She walked a little way only yesterday. /

Walked yesterday! and dead to-day! This was much. – Travers paced the hall with impatient strides. He could scarcely contain himself. He directed the footman to signify to the doctor that a stranger requested immediate admission. It was granted. Travers found Dr Allen and the magistrate together. /

CHAPTER XVIII

Travers apologised for his intrusion; at the same time that he trusted his motive would sufficiently explain his abruptness. He had come in attendance on a dear friend to the neighbourhood of this place. They had for several days taken up their residence at the town four or five miles off. Though they were separated during the day-time, they met and slept every night at the chief inn in that town. Last night for the first time his friend had failed to return; and he had set out in search of him. He had traced him to a cottage not far distant; and the people there had directed him to Deloraine Park, as a spot he had almost / daily haunted. Travers climbed a knoll that commanded the whole prospect, and had been led by accident to a spot outside the garden-wall, where he saw a considerable stain of blood. He traced this blood to a small door leading into the garden, and there it stopped.

You must excuse me, gentlemen, he said, if you should consider this as an insufficient apology for my intrusion. My friend, whose name and history I could detail to you, if this were the proper place, had irresistible motives that impelled him to haunt the house of Deloraine. Yesterday he was seen near this spot. To-day I approach the garden, and beneath the wall I discover a considerable effusion of blood. I could not resist the impulse to enquire further. I find that the lady of the house expired suddenly yesterday, and that Deloraine left his home shortly after. One question I must be allowed to ask; and, if that question is fairly and satisfactorily answered, I shall cease to / give you any further trouble. Is there at this moment only one dead body in the house, or are there two? Can you give me no light respecting the sudden and suspicious disappearance of my friend?

Dr Allen acknowledged that there was another dead body, that of a stranger to himself and every one in the house, who appeared to have met a violent death from the discharge of a pistol. Steps had already been taken to summon the coroner of the district, that he might pronounce officially upon so unfortunate an event; and they every moment expected his arrival. The doctor added, that the other gentleman Travers found with him was a neighbouring magistrate, whom Dr Allen had requested to favour them with his countenance and advice on the occasion.

Travers demanded that he should instantly be admitted to see the body of the stranger. His worst fears were realised. In the garb / and features he instantly recognised his unfortunate friend. For a short time he was absorbed in grief. Here then ended the history of the unhappy William! He turned to the by-standers. He said, This is indeed the man I came to seek. Every thing relating to the catastrophe is mysterious. It must be searched to the bottom. I cannot leave the spot till the matter has been fully investigated.

Dr Allen and the magistrate immediately admitted the right of Travers to be present on the occasion. After having remained as long in the summer-house as was necessary, they suggested the propriety of quitting the apartment, and locking the door. Travers, with the consent of the other two, took from the pocket of the deceased certain papers, which he cursorily exhibited, and which established beyond a doubt the identity of his friend. Dr Allen then locked the door, and gave the key to the magistrate. Travers refused again to / enter the house, and employed his time in walking up and down the garden in every direction. It sufficiently appeared in the sequel that his thoughts were engaged in vowing that no stone should be left unturned to arrive at the whole truth repecting so deplorable a catastrophe, and that whoever it was that had been the means of depriving William of life should be pursued with unremitting diligence, till the vengeance of law in its fullest extent had been executed upon him.

The coroner in no long time arrived. As soon as he came, Travers was invited with the rest to attend him. A jury was impanneled to sit upon the bodies. Mr Bartram, the magistrate, consented to be the foreman. It was suggested as a matter of propriety, that as few of the jury as might be should be chosen from among my tenants. The coroner issued his precepts; and the inquest was appointed for the following morning. /

It was soon found that my servants could give little information; and the coroner readily assented to hear from Travers whatever he thought proper to relate of the history of the deceased. Travers accordingly stated, that he had first known William about twelve months since in the island of St Domingo, and that all he could relate that bore on the present enquiry he had learned from the lips of his friend. But they had been on terms of unreserved intimacy; and he had often heard him speak of the affection which had susbsisted between himself and Margaret Borradale. He had returned to England, after three years of compulsory absence, to claim the hand of his betrothed; and Travers had accompanied him in his expedition. A few weeks ago he had learned with inexpressible horror that Margaret Borradale no longer existed, but that, believing him dead, she had become the wife of Deloraine. It was now about a week that the two friends had / taken up their abode at the neighbouring town, from whence William had set out daily upon a pilgrimage to gain a sight of the house where his beloved resided. He constantly assured Travers, that he would on no account intrude into the presence of Mrs Deloraine, but that he could not for the present refuse himself the indulgence of looking at her habitation, and, as it might chance, seeing her in her carriage at a distance, himself unseen. The day before yesterday Travers had spoken to him for the last time, and, missing him in the evening, had set out with the dawn of the next day in search of him. He felt that he knew much of his motions and his haunts; and accordingly, from that circumstance, and favoured by accident, he speedily traced him to the spot on which he expired. Travers added, that the servants of Deloraine, if they would speak the truth, could give the best account of his last and closing scene. He advised, that the inhabitants / of the cottage should be summoned, who were the last persons to whom William had spoken. He concluded with solemnly asserting, that the deceased was a person of the most unspotted manners and unimpeachable character, and that, whatever causes had led to this deplorable catastrophe, it was impossible that he should have been in the smallest degree in fault.

The remaining circumstances were supplied by my own servants. They admitted that the stranger had fallen by my hand. There was no opporunity however for a charge of previous malice, as having produced the catastrophe. Every thing passed on the instant, I having leaped from my carriage with a pistol in my hand, and advanced with eagerness to the fatal spot; not a word had been spoken on either side. On another point the servants delivered themselves with delicacy and reserve, being at once anxious to palliate my violence, and not / to cast any unbecoming imputation on their unfortunate mistress. They admitted, that Margaret and the stranger had been discovered in a familiar and confidential attitude sitting on the turf; and they affirmed their persuasion, that it was this spectacle that worked me to extremity. They were required to state precisely what they saw; and the result was that they observed nothing in any way licentious or indecent, but that the inference was a strong expression of kindness and entire good understanding between the parties. They were farther called upon to speak as to any previous knowledge they might have had of the person of the deceased. To this they answered with the utmost clearness. Up to the day, and to the very instant of the catastrophe, they had never seen him. They were of course wholly ignorant of any previous intercourse between the stranger and their mistress. He had never visited at the house; and Margaret, for a considerable / time past, had scarcely been from home. The cottagers had little to add to the evidence already given. They had seen the deceased almost daily for several days past under their roof. He had been from the first most particular in his enquiries respecting the family at the great house, and his walks, when he went from them in the day-time, had always been in that direction.

Such was the sum of the evidence laid before the coroner's inquest on the following morning. The task devolved on that gentleman to comment on the testimony adduced. He said, there could be no doubt that the deceased fell by my hand, that I was armed, and the person I had killed was weaponless, had discovered no intention of assailing, and had had no space for resisting me. These were the principal constituents of what the law denominates the crime of murder. The only farther cirumstance for the consideration of the jury, was / whether there had been sufficient time interposed to afford room for what our jurisprudence regarded as malice aforethought, or whether my act had been so suddenly perpetrated, as to exclude what was technically styled malice. The law was wisely jealous on this head; and the slightest interval between the provocation and the consequent act, giving opportunity for deliberation, was always construed as inferring malice. The life of man was the most sacred of all possessions; it must not be trifled withal; and instinct itself had wisely hedged in the thought of destroying it with indescribable shrinking and horror. As to the cause that prompted my violence, the provocation had been discovered by me as I sat in my carriage; I had opened the door, had leaped out, and had run a certain distance; this interval undoubtedly constituted such an assignable portion of time as the law prescribed to a malicious killing. Jealousy was certainly one of those impulses / which the law regarded with special allowance. There might be many circumstances of mitigation in my favour; and he hoped I should be able to establish a case which would clear me from the capital charge. There was enough however in what had now been sworn to, to make it imperative on them to pronounce a verdict of wilful murder against me, and to send me to a jury of my country. This verdict was accordingly found and recorded; and the coroner in conclusion issued his warrant for my apprehension. The case of Margaret was next considered; and she was pronounced to have died by 'the visitation of God'.[a] /

---

[a] Frequently used expression for cause of a death in reports of coroners in 18th and 19th centuries.

CHAPTER XIX

Travers listened to the whole of this proceeding with intense interest; his countenance and his gestures discovered in a variety of ways the perturbation of his mind, though he endeavoured by all the means in his power to control them. He regarded William, from every thing he had known of him, as of all men the most worthy to be loved, and the most unfortunate. He resolved that a lasting tomb should be erected to his memory, and that, as among the ancient Greeks, the blood of a human sacrifice should be spilled upon it. He considered himself as the being upon whom the care of fulfilling this to the minutest letter / was devolved. William had left no kindred, and, through his long absence from his country, had perhaps scarcely a friend in Great Britain. I had doubtless taken advantage of this circumstance, and had flattered myself (so Travers painted it to his thoughts), that I could remove an unwelcome intruder upon my enjoyments and my peace, and that no man would regard it. But it should be seen here, even as we read it in the Scriptures, that God should shew himself 'able even from the stones of the earth to raise up' an avenger.[a] Himself, from a distant quarter of the globe and another hemisphere, had been brought to the very spot for this special purpose, to teach me that the life of a man ten thousand times worthier than myself, should not be sacrificed with impunity to my causeless jealousy, and my fear even of the shadow of a rival. He had known all William's unspeakable excellencies; he had studied them from day to day without ever / coming to an end of them, could read in that record and combination of high qualities for ever and for ever. William had delivered him from the jaws of the sea-monster, when in the act to devour him; and the life he had saved should now in this extremity be wholly consecrated to shew the sense Travers entertained of the benefit he had received. He would hunt me to the earth's utmost verge:

> He would dwindle, peak and pine;
> Sleep should, neither night nor day,
> Hang upon his pent-house lid:[b]

he would penetrate into every hiding place that could conceal me; 'no place, though e'er so holy, should protect me: no shape that artful fear e'er formed

---

[a] cf. Matt. 3: 9 'able of these stones to raise up children unto Abraham'.
[b] *Macbeth*, I. iii. 19–23 (adapted).

should shield me':[a] but I should suffer to the utmost letter the vengeance that the law has reserved for the most unspeakable of crimes.

Travers obtained by his importunity a duplicate of the warrant for my apprehension. He / said there was reason to fear that I might be upon the point of quitting England. The ordinary officers for executing such a warrant might be indifferently qualified, and would scarcely be prevailed on to make exertions beyond a certain point, or to pass to foreign countries to inforce it. He desired nothing but justice; if the law pronounced me guiltless of the crime of murder, he should be contented. But he was resolved I should be placed under the judgment of that law. If I had passed to other countries, he would not on that account cease to pursue me. If he possessed a duplicate of the warrant, that would be a document, authentically designating me and my offence; and the proper officers in foreign countries might be induced to back it, and to assist in my apprehension, and in the delivering me up. There could be no impropriety in granting his request; and, if it were refused, it would be too plain that, while they pretended a zeal for / justice, they were disposed to stir as little a way as they could, and were inclined to shelter the opulent, and, as they might call it, the honourable offender, against the cause of the friendless.

The last desire expressed by Travers was that the body of his friend should be surrendered to his care. This was readily conceded to him. He sought out the village-churchyard where the father and mother of William had been interred upon the banks of the Severn. The funeral was with all privacy; there was none but Travers to mourn. The churchyard was obscure, humble and unpretending. A few yew-trees were scattered here and there. Three of them grew near the grave of William and his parents, as if shadowing out the modest and virtuous three that there lay buried. The paths that led to the churchyard were few; the place was solitary, and the approaches little frequented. /

Travers had waited on the simple solemnity of the interment. After it was over, and he had the scene entirely to himself, he returned by the light of the starry heavens to take a last leave of his friend. He said, Thou hast fallen untimely, like a tender and delicate flower withered by the nipping blast. Thou wert born to be loved; and yet I see no one but myself who approaches to mourn thee. A short banishment of three years has sufficed to disperse the companions of thy youth, to send them to distant abodes, or to engross their thoughts with newer undertakings and pursuits. She whom thou prizedst above every competitor, by a strange fate forgot thee first, and then perished by the same blow that brought thee to the tomb. Rigorous and unparalleled has been thy destiny. Accepted first, to be afterwards rejected. Early sacrificed by her whom thou hadst chosen, to an exaggerated sentiment of filial obedience; and again recalled. / A victim to shipwreck and the contention of the elements, and

---

[a] Quotation unidentified.

then driven far away by a concurrence of events, for three years thou con-
tendedst with miraculous perseverance against them all, and finally camedst off
conqueror. Did ever man, under the bitterest and most aggravated disappointment, conduct himself with such marvellous temperance and self-denying
virtue as thou hast done? But all thy moderation has proved vain. The wretch,
who first robbed thee of a treasure beyond all price in thy judgment, of thy
heart of hearts, has now, driven by a gust of passion, prompted by a senseless
jealousy that spurned all deliberation and enquiry, finally deprived thee of life.

But dearly shall he rue his unconsidered precipitation! I will sacrifice all
other thoughts to the desire of vengeance. Not a hasty retribution! The slow
and tormenting process of law, which takes no account of any human feelings,
but delights in the sternness of its / march and the unaltered steadiness of its
pace, and causes its victim with slow respirations to drain off the last drop from
its cup of woe, shall be reserved for the offender. The longer shall be the
pursuit, the more bitter shall be its sensations. At every escape he shall feel that
the last retribution is but suspended, that the chase is but begun, that the dogs
of scent are ever at his heels to baffle his swiftness, and the beagles of the law to
embarrass him in his doublings.

Thus strange was the result of my unhallowed violence. Whatever I had yet
to suffer was the result of the deep sympathy that had grown up between
Travers and William. They were persons of so affectionate a temper, as has
almost never been equalled. Yet by a concurrence of events, or by the original
construction of their minds, William was of unalterable gentleness and tenderness of disposition, that would scarcely crush the bruised reed, or be / roused
to fury and hatred by any injustice; while Travers, setting out in appearance
from the same point, would convert all his kindness of nature into gall, and
proceed in a remorseless career of vengeance, from which, as it seemed, no
expostulation would turn him, and which no lapse of time would diminish or
remit.

Before he finally set out on the expedition he prescribed to himself, Travers
directed that a mural monument of choice marble should be placed in a
conspicuous situation against the wall of the village-church, near the spot
where the remains of his friend were interred, with an inscription signifying,
that he whose bones were deposited in the place beneath, had fallen a victim to
the sentiment of an inviolable love, that he had preserved this passion undiminished through three years of wandering and distress, and that finally he was
welcomed to his native land by an act of the most unparalleled violence. It went
on to say, that the mistress of his dearest / affections died on the same day that
marked him for the tomb, and that, though their ashes had not been mingled in
their final receptacle, yet her devotion to his love had remained undiminished,
and her agony for his unmerited fate had been the cause that she died in the
same hour, and on the very spot where he had been slain.

I have in this place related a number of particulars that I did not come to the full knowledge of till a considerable time afterwards; because they were necessary to the exact delineation of the position in which I now stood; and I was willing the reader should clearly understand the perils that environed me, even at the time that I was lulled into comparative security.

It is also right that I should apologise for having recorded the visit of the parents of Margaret and their unhappy fate out of the exact order of time. They did not arrive at the house / which contained the body of their child, till the inquest of the coroner had been completed.

The necessary consequence of my exile was that the house in which I had been born, and where I had spent so many years of my existence, immediately became uninhabited. Rowland took possession of the lodge at the park-gate, and held it for his duty to visit the mansion for the most part on every day of his life. But the house remained without a tenant for a number of years. The garden exhibited obvious tokens of neglect; and thorns and thistles sprung up in it abundantly. The peasants intuitively shrank away from the spot which retained, or was believed by their affrighted sense to retain, marks of the blood of the murdered, and made many a devious circuit to avoid it; while the apartment in which Margaret had been laid out and coffined, and still more the summer-house in the garden, got the reputation of being haunted; and the lovers who had / perished thus untimely, were seen to trouble the walks within, and the path on the outside of the wall. Lights were said occasionally to glimmer from the windows, and fearful noises to be heard. A female figure appeared to pass from apartment to apartment, and to ascend and descend the great staircase. The longer the house continued untenanted by the living dwellers on the earth, the more was it regarded by the ignorant and superstitious rustics as appropriated to the use of the supernatural and unearthly. These were circumstances that added not a little to the odium in which my name was held by the meaner class of my tenants, who, while I lived among them, had ever found me a kind and indulgent landlord, and had poured down blessings on my name. /

187

DELORAINE.

BY

WILLIAM GODWIN,

AUTHOR OF "CALEB WILLIAMS," "ST. LEON," &c.

Why that bosom gored?
Why dimly gleams the visionary sword?

POPE.

IN THREE VOLUMES.

VOL. III.

LONDON:

RICHARD BENTLEY, NEW BURLINGTON STREET:

SUCCESSOR TO HENRY COLBURN.

1833.

CHAPTER I

Having made the necessary arrangements with my solicitor, and received the latest intelligence from my steward, and my beloved daughter having insisted upon being my companion in exile, and obtained my half-reluctant, half-joyful consent, I suffered no delay to interpose that might increase the difficulty and danger of the voyage upon which I had resolved. I had employed a portion of my time during the last two days in enquiring out a / vessel by which we might most speedily pass over to Holland, and had fortunately met with one that was to sail early on the morning of the day after that in which Catherine had conclusively joined me, on board which we could be immediately accommodated.

I was very far at that time from being fully aware of all the dangers that beset me. I believed I had slain a man, friendless and obscure, just arrived from a three years' exile and wandering in various parts of the globe, without connections in England, or any one that would feel a more than ordinary anxiety to avenge his death, – though assuredly none of those considerations had had the smallest weight with me at the moment that I perpetrated his destruction.

I had slain, as I believed, the friendless; and, lo! full soon, though not immediately, I found, that I had conjured up an enemy, the most deadly, with intellect and wit to conduct / his purpose, and means abundantly to feed his undertaking, – a man, that promised never to relax in his design, and the tide of whose passion was unlikely at any time to 'feel retiring ebb'.[a]

But, before I was aware of this circumstance, I was at no loss for arguments to convince me of the perilous situation in which I stood. I knew the unconquerable horror with which man in society contemplates him who wilfully sheds the blood of his fellow. The turf under the wall of my own domain was widely stained with human gore; I had left behind me the body of one pierced with a deadly wound; he was weaponless; the eyes of several bore witness that I had been his destroyer. I knew therefore that in the course of things I should be sought for; I had abundant reasons forbidding me to stand the ordeal of a public trial; I was indifferent in my choice as to what region of the many-peopled earth I should fix on for / my future abode; I had but one tie that was left me, uniting me with my species, my exemplary and admirable daughter. I

---

[a] *Othello*, III. iii. 456 (adapted).

believed, as I have said, that there would be some pursuit set on foot against me, that a warrant would scarcely fail to be issued for the apprehension of my person. But I conceived, that the search that should be made for me would be temporary, that the noise occasioned by the act I had committed would soon blow over, that I and my crime would to a great degree perish from the memories of men, and that, if I could escape from the first ardour of enquiry, I might afterwards safely sit down in obscurity in some foreign land. I had gained a main step, if I succeeded to transport myself to some province or kingdom on the continent of Europe.

It was with a deep feeling of sadness and awe that I embarked, and that I conducted my daughter, on board the vessel which was to sever us from our native country. I had been / by birth one of the privileged members of the commonwealth of England, a man succeeding to an ample landed estate, which descended to me from a long line of ancestors, which classed me among the prime gentry of my country, ranked me as the associate, and I may say the equal of its nobles, and surrounded me with a body of tenantry, who looked up to me with mingled honour and affection, as to their patron and protector, the individual who was to watch for their safety, to assist them in their emergencies with indulgence and counsel, to overlook their errors, and in certain prescribed and important cases to command their services. Of all these advantages I now saw myself stripped. It is true that, as long as I retained my personal liberty, I should perhaps be able to draw the pecuniary produce of my estate, and spend it at the bidding of my discretion in foreign climates. This was surely but a narrow and formal part, the mere husk, of the advantages / to which I was born; and all the rest was gone. My only child, my daughter, was destined to succeed me in this, and, if she married, would by such union convey it to her husband; but she, with unheard-of generosity and self-devotion, had, for a long and indeterminate period at least, surrendered these benefits, and made herself the partner of my pilgrimage and my dishonour.

We descended the Tower Stairs, and placed ourselves in a wherry, that was to convey us on board the slight vessel with the master of which I had agreed for our passage.[a] We went alone; for it was essential in my circumstances to cut off, as completely as I could, any thing that should connect me with those with whom I formerly had intercourse, or afford a clue to discover my intended concealment. The morning was clouded and gloomy, and sufficiently responsive to the tone of my mind.

The vessel contained eight or ten passengers, / beside ourselves, the captain, the steward, and four common sailors. I was no sooner on board, than I cast a stealthy glance round on my fellow-passengers, and then crept into a corner,

---

[a] Tower Stairs, steps leading down to the river Thames near Tower Bridge; wherry, light rowing boat.

and concealed myself as much as possible from observation. I could not perceive that the ship contained one human creature that I had ever seen before; and I congratulated myself accordingly. We passed Greenwich, Gravesend and the Nore.[a] At Gravesend we took in one additional passenger.

Among the persons on board I early observed one who eyed me intently. It was my cue to pay as little attention as possible to those with whom I sailed. I however watched my opportunity to steal a glance at him unperceived; but I by no means recognised any features with which I had been previously acquainted. The man was clad in garments that appeared to have seen considerable service; and, though / of a common and ordinary figure, he had something of the air of a decayed gentleman. By and by he walked up to the part of the ship where I had placed myself, and looked over the side of the vessel, as if watching the rippling of the waves. I did not like the nearness of the position he had chosen, and was preparing to change my retreat for one that should free me from this annoyance. He suddenly addressed me.

I beg your pardon, said he. I have been trying to recollect where I had formerly the pleasure of seeing you. If I am not mistaken, your name is Deloraine; and I had once occasion to apply to you at the court of the elector of Saxony, where you were the resident. My name is Stevenson; I was engaged in a commercial affair in which I had need of the representative of the king of England to see that I obtained my just rights; and I have / ever felt that I was greatly indebted to you for the promptness and firmness of your interference.

I recollect, replied I, something of the matter; but I did not call to mind your person. In the case you mention I did nothing but my duty, and should have done the same for any British subject.

I do not wonder, he rejoined, at your not recollecting me. I am but an ordinary man; and misfortunes since have greatly altered my appearance. But you, sir, are of another order of persons; and there is something in your cast of countenance, which, when once observed, can scarcely afterwards pass from the mind.

I answered, carelessly as might be thought, but with a deep, though suppressed sigh, It may be so.

You then, replied the stranger, appeared with splendour and a considerable train, as became your appointment. I hope, added he, / looking round, and observing to himself that I did not seem to have a single attendant, I hope you have not, like me, been unfortunate.

I shrunk from the impertinence of my companion, and answered with haughtiness, I can scarcely pretend to the honour of your acquaintance.

All this was but 'bald, unjointed chat';[b] yet on many accounts it affected me

---

[a] Gravesend, river port in NW Kent on the Thames; the Nore, sandbank in the Thames estuary, SE England, once a famous anchorage.

[b] *Henry IV, Part I*, I. iii. 65.

deeply. It was extremely mortifying to me that I should be thus recognised, after a lapse of years, by a man who had seen me only once. The idle remark of so vulgar a person, that there was something in my cast of countenance, which, when once observed, could scarcely afterwards pass from the mind, was peculiarly distressing to me. I had wished to withdraw myself, without leaving a clue to discover in what quarter I had disposed of my person. In going abroad, I had desired that it should rather be supposed that I was hidden in some / obscure part of the metropolis, or in some deep and impenetrable rural retreat in my own country. It was my interest to throw the persons, who I had no doubt would be employed in searching for me, on a false scent. And here, at the first step, I encountered an individual, who recollected my person, called me by name, and knew that I had withdrawn myself from England and crossed the sea between Harwich and Holland. My secret in this regard was in the keeping of one who had no inducement to respect it. He did not at present know that I was escaping from the retribution of a crime I had committed. But how long would he remain in ignorance of this particular? It was in the ordinary course of things that a reward would be published for my apprehension. This man was as likely as any one else to hear the intelligence, and might be tempted to seek the proffered advantage. If not, the proposal of such a reward / would not fail to make my situation and my crime a subject of conversation; and what reason had I to expect that the man would treat me with any extraordinary forbearance? Every one is delighted with the possession of a secret; and mere vanity would prompt him to tell what he could, or at least to indulge in 'ambiguous givings out', and to say, 'Well, I know what I know; and if I list to speak' –[a]

The adventure which thus occurred was of evil augury, and led me to reflect perseveringly on the means I might be able to employ on any critical emergency, to conceal my identity with my former self. Man, in the strictest sense, is nothing but a principle of thought, which no material force can arrest or imprison, which bids defiance to all limits of space and time, and speeds its course in a single instant 'from Indus to the Pole'.[b] I had always reflected with scorn upon the power of other men to control and enslave me. Yet, by / means of this vile incumbrance of our mortal body, we may be brought down from our loftiest flights, subjected to every kind of indignity and disgrace, laid open to the observation of the senses of other men, and exposed to their pursuit and their tyranny.

It appeared to me, that there are four circumstances principally, by which the person of any man may be identified, features, figure, carriage and voice; to which may be added as inferior particulars, the colour of the skin and complexion, and the characteristics by which the hair of one man differs from the

---

[a] *Hamlet*, I. v. 178 (adapted).
[b] Pope, 'Eloisa to Abelard' (1717), l. 58.

hair of another. These circumstances, sometimes one more prominently, and sometimes another, have the effect in perhaps all cases, that a diligent observer may recognise and select the man whom he has had due opportunity to observe, among all the millions of his fellow-men. The man therefore who can counterfeit and disguise these sufficiently, though he cannot / put off the vestments of flesh, may yet escape from the resentment and ill will which may be harboured against him. He may go forward unblenched, and, like Æneas[a] in the streets of Carthage, may pass through the midst of the people, and pursue his way. I did not therefore despair that I might yet insure my safety. I had read the histories of men who, by a careful attention to these considerations, had succeeded to elude the bitterest persecution. I had often had occasion to observe in myself a flexibility of organs, of the lines of the countenance, and of limbs, that promised to do wonders for me in this respect. And I resolved, having already committed the precipitate act, which cut me off from the society of my fellow-creatures, and exposed me to their malice, and that act being irretrievable, that I would not play booty in my own cause, but would carry on the contest to the furthest extremity. /

CHAPTER II

It is time that my narrative should revert to Travers. He, as I have said, had formed an unalterable resolution, that he would sacrifice all other thoughts to the purpose of vengeance against me, and that the grave of him whom he deemed the worthiest, the most excellent, and the most injured of men, should 'have a living monument'.[b] But he was thoroughly aware that mere determination, without deep contrivance, and the accumulation of adequate means, was nothing. He had succeeded thus far by his exertions, that a coroner's inquest should pronounce a verdict of wilful murder against me, that a warrant should be issued / for my apprehension, and that a duplicate of this warrant should be placed in his hands. The warrant was of course consigned by the coroner to the proper officers for the purpose of its being executed. These officers used the customary diligence, and, after the lapse of a few days, returned an answer to their superior that I was not to be found in the county.

---

[a] Aeneas, in Greek mythology a Trojan prince who was driven on to the N. African coast while travelling from Sicily to Italy. He was kindly received by Dido, Queen of Carthage, who wished to marry him, but the gods ordered him to leave Carthage.
[b] *Hamlet*, V. i. 319.

And here, but for the intervention of Travers, the question would perhaps have rested. The coroner indeed transmitted a memorandum of the business to the principal police-office of the metropolis; and a proclamation containing my name, a description of my person, and an account of the crime with which I was charged, was issued in the established forms. But Travers immediately set out for London; and, through his instigation, a fresh proclamation was ordered by the secretary of state, with a reward of five hundred pounds to the person or persons who should produce me in custody. / Even this did not satisfy him. It was not enough, that he should excite the cupidity or sharpen the sagaciousness of others. He resolved not to trust to accident, or to spare any thing of his own diligence: he determined to be himself the soul of every exertion that should be made to bring me to justice. I might be concealed in England; I might have found means to pass over to the continent. Meanwhile he foresaw a difficulty by which he would immediately be met in the search he proposed to engage in, he being entirely unacquainted with my person.

Fortune, without any effort on his part, supplied to him this deficiency. My paternal mansion, as I have said, in consequence of my disappearance was presently shut up, and my establishment dismissed. Before that proceeding was completed, my servants of course anticipated that such a measure would be adopted. I had ever proved myself an indulgent and / liberal master; and therefore the feeling of the majority of my domestics was that of pity for my disaster, and a sincere wish that I might escape the troublesome, if not tragical, consequences to which my precipitation had laid me open.

There was one however in the list of my domestics, whose sentiments materially differed from those entertained by the rest. At the period of my marriage, Margaret had brought with her a servant, by name Ambrose, who had previously attended upon her for a considerable portion of time. He had waited on her at Harrowgate, at the time I first became acquainted with her. He had been on terms of the most unreserved communication with the maid who had been in her employment for years before; and from this maid he learned the original cause of his mistress's ill state of health, and the history of the unfortunate William. Among various speculations that / had occurred between these two servants, Ambrose had started the notion, that they had no absolute demonstration, no complete proof, that William was dead; though the ship-wreck which had passed under the eyes of the family, combined with the circumstance that nothing had been heard of him for years after, reduced it almost to a certainty. This talk never went farther than between the two servants. The maid was not disposed to entertain the same scepticism on the subject, as the man. And they both of them agreed, that it would be highly improper to suffer a whisper of this unlicensed talk to reach the ears of their superiors.

Ambrose however, who was of an uncommonly delicate turn of mind for his class in society, had always regarded with invincible repugnance the idea of his

196

mistress's marriage with another, and had therefore constantly viewed me during the period of my courtship / with sentiments of disapprobation, if not of aversion. If William were really dead, as in all likelihood he was, yet Ambrose thought it a sort of profanation that Margaret should unite herself in wedlock with any one else. He called to mind every thing that he had heard of her history. Her first love had been William, the companion of her childish years. They had opened their hearts to each other; their affections had been undivided; and she had owed many and important obligations to the friend of her youth. Her heart had never swerved from him; she had been overpersuaded by her parents to consent to a union with the son of lord Borradale; and now it was by the suggestion of others, and not the prompting of her own mind, that she had become my wife.

It is a part of the great process of human events, that we grow reconciled, and our minds gradually accommodate themselves, to whatever is irrevocable. Though the marriage of his / mistress had by no means been approved by Ambrose in the first instance, yet time gradually undermined his repugnance. Our establishment was creditable and splendid; we were visited by all our opulent neighbours; and no one uttered a whisper to our disadvantage. We lived in apparent order and harmony; Margaret proved to me the model of a tender and affectionate wife; and Ambrose by degrees became a loyal member of our establishment, contemplating me, scarcely less than his mistress, with sentiments of true adherence and willing subjection.

The speculations however that had previously revolved in his mind, and the tardy and gradual way in which he had reconciled himself to the existing state of things, prepared him to regard the horrible catastrophe that occurred, with very different feelings from those of the other spectators. The commencing loyalty that he had felt for my service disappeared in a moment. / The toleration with which he had considered me was only founded on my commendable demeanour towards his mistress, and the unvarying attention she had always manifested for my welfare and peace. Margaret was to this young man the being in all the world that he honoured most. He felt towards her all the deference and devotion of a lover, without approaching in any degree to the ideas which grow out of equality. In his own person and thoughts he imaged out her sentiments. She was his model of perfection; and he copied her as nearly as possible, in all that she expressed, and all that she did. She for ever studied for my happiness, and sedulously employed herself in discharging the offices of an exemplary wife. He therefore, in proportion to his station, imitated her in this; treated me as the head of the establishment, because she so treated me; and exercised a genuine zeal in performing my commands, because such was the rule of her conduct. /

But my last act reversed his whole system of thinking in a moment. He discovered in that fatal scene, as if by an instantaneous ray of divine inspiration, who was the unfortunate person, whom I had laid at my feet; he recollected at

197

once all William's misfortunes, and the cruel destiny that unremittingly pursued him. Ambrose observed, with the closest attention, and with the deepest horror, the effect that this catastrophe had produced upon his mistress. He refused to distinguish at whose breast I had presented my pistol, and in whose heart I had lodged the fatal bullet. He pronounced me, directly, without intervention and qualification, the murderer of his mistress. From that instant he became transported out of himself. He was wrapt up in thought and the contemplation of a thousand purposes. He had the gestures and demeanour of a maniac. Of this I had indeed scarcely obtained a glimpse. From the instant that I had / perpetrated the destruction of William, my thoughts were necessarily turned to the withdrawing myself as speedily as might be, from the scene of my precipitate deed. But the attention of the rest of the servants was drawn in a considerable degree to Ambrose's singular demonstrations and behaviour. He however spoke little, and shewed no signs of any determined system of action.

Meanwhile, when Travers made his appearance, and still more as the coroner's inquest proceeded, the situation of Ambrose became essentially changed. He appeared however little more than a silent, but a deeply anxious spectator, during the transaction. Towards the close, and as Travers was engaged in soliciting a duplicate of the warrant for my apprehension, and in expressing his resolution that the warrant should be executed in its strictest letter, and that he would, if necessary, pass to foreign countries in pursuit of me, Ambrose drew near / to the stranger. When Travers had obtained all that he desired from the coroner, and was on the point of quitting the house, this young man requested that he would favour him with a private hearing of a few moments, before he departed.

Having obtained this, he poured out his whole soul to the stranger, and said, that he perceived they were both engaged, though from different incitements, and with unequal means of gratifying their wishes, in the pursuit of the same object. His attachment, the attachment of a servant, but not on that account the less fervent and unalterable, was to the unhappy lady who lay dead in the chamber above stairs; that of Travers to the unfortunate youth whose body was for the present deposited within the walls of the summer-house. He had for years been a faithful servant to his lady, both before her marriage and since, and should esteem his strength and his life gloriously spent in accomplishing / vengeance against her destroyer. He could imagine no act, so inhuman, so atrocious, and of such complicated barbarity, as that by which I had destroyed in a single moment these constant, most innocent, and most unhappy lovers. We are then, proceeded Ambrose, you and I, engaged in one and the same pursuit. I intreat you to pardon me, for thus presuming to couple myself with a person of your figure and appearance. But I feel a no less fervent passion than you do, for accomplishing our common object, the bringing this criminal to justice. And my mind whispers that I can be of use to you. You have never beheld the person whose punishment you eagerly desire. This, particularly in

foreign countries, and where you cannot suddenly gain an accession of information, will be a material disadvantage to you. I on the contrary have lived for a
considerable period under the same roof with the murderer, can single him out
among a thousand, and recognise / his person, as far off as I can see him. I
intreat you then, sir, to accept of my offer, and take me into your service, at
least as far as this special purpose is concerned.

Travers of course consented to the overture of Ambrose with no less promptness than the other made it. While the creolian was engaged in superintending
the interment of William, the youth whom he had thus taken into his service,
employed himself in the few preparations that were necessary for his departure.
He then proceeded immediately for London, and joined Travers at the hotel
where he was directed to wait on him.

Here then were two men of different habits and stations of life, each acting
from a several impulse, that entered into a common league to accomplish one
object: Travers from the love he bore to the saviour of his life, whom at the same
time he regarded as the most amiable and injured of men; and Ambrose from the
horror / he conceived at the destruction of his mistress, and his devoted
admiration of her excellencies, living and dead. Travers was new to Europe; his
attention was not distracted by a variety of contending claims upon his powers of
activity; and he vowed that he would contemplate this purpose alone, till the end
he had in view should be completed. He was not to seek for the revenue and the
means, that should enable him to pursue his object to its consummation. It would
have been difficult for him perhaps, from the aristocracy of his education, to have
stooped to all the obscure and devious paths in which it might be necessary to
travel for the accomplishment of that which he undertook. The haughtiness of
his nature, or the generosity of his spirit, would have stood in his way. He could
not have moulded himself into a thousand shapes, have proposed all the artful
questions, and crept through all the devious passages and windings that should
interpose themselves. / But in Ambrose he had a coadjutor, that would amply
supply the requisites in which Travers was deficient. Travers had a stubborn
sense of honour, that would often counteract his wishes, and engender an
intestine battle, materially injurious to the pursuit of his end. But Ambrose was
single-minded; the map of his purposes was without a wrinkle. The course of his
education had taught him no unecessary scruples. He thought only of the object
he had in view, and saw nothing else. He was no sooner satisfied that that was
becoming and pure, than he heartily approved of all the means that led to it. He
was of the mind of the poet: 'Entire affection scorneth nicer hands'.[a] Nay; he
took a sort of pride in all indispensible humiliation. The more crooked was the
road he chose, the more he became convinced of the rectitude and soundness of
the principle that impelled him.

---

[a] cf. Edmund Spenser, *The Faerie Queene* (1590–6), I. viii. 40: 'Entire affection hateth nicer
hands'.

A more formidable combination can scarcely / be imagined, than that between the two parties thus united for my destruction. They consulted at every step as to the manner in which their purpose was to be effected: the lofty mind and comprehensive views of Travers shaped the outline of their undertaking; while that of Ambrose, more microscopic, and accustomed to the minutiæ of detail, traced the minuter links and the subtler interweavings of incident with incident, respecting which the other might have failed. The former constructed the workshop of their purpose, and furnished it with all the requisite tools and materials, while the latter was prepared with admirable dexterity to turn his hand to every thing, and to execute like a skilful workman what the other conceived in its general form. Both had the grand requisites of a zeal and perseverance that no obstacles had the power to abate.

Ambrose first recollected the circumstance of the letter and portmanteau, which were / forwarded by Rowland to the principal town of the neighbouring county a few hours after my departure. Ambrose was not then suspected of harbouring any malicious intention towards me; it was taken for granted that all my servants were loyal; and it was therefore not difficult for him, who had already conceived a secret hostility against me, and had his eyes and ears open to every thing, to become acquainted with this commission, and to have two minutes' conversation with my own valet, before he set out on his errand.

Ambrose's first commission therefore, after the league that had been struck up between him and Travers, was to proceed without delay to the town and the inn, where I had appointed the rendezvous with my valet. Here he gained but little intelligence, more than that the rendezvous had actually taken place, and that, when I left the town, it was by the outlet that was distinguished as pointing towards London. /

Moved by this information, Travers and Ambrose immediately set out for the metropolis. Here Travers employed himself in procuring such additional authority as might best abet him in the business of causing me to be apprehended and taken into custody, whether I should be found in England or abroad. Ambrose knew the name and residence of my town-solicitor; and it was therefore his province to watch about this man's door, it being morally certain, if I were in town, that I would not fail to make my appearance there. I had already been once with my solicitor, before Ambrose entered upon his function; the second time he saw me coming from the house. This circumstance afforded him the greatest satisfaction. He had no doubt that, having once come, I should come again. It was in the order of things, that I should shew myself the first time to give my directions, and again to see them fully executed. He was correct in his / calculation; but his error lay in mistaking my second visit for my first. He procured the proper officers from the police, and undertook to be their guide. But he was baffled in his expectation; I came there no more. He waited day after day, but was obliged to exchange his hope in this particular for despair.

One of the sciences which Ambrose had particularly cultivated, was that of what is technically called horse-flesh. He was versed in the various qualifications of roadsters, hunters and running-horses. In an interval of leisure he had therefore mechanically wandered towards one of those repositories of horses for sale, which are to be found in the skirts of the metropolis. He entered it. Here an object which immediately caught his attention was the saddle-horse that had brought me to town. Ambrose would have known it against a thousand. He engaged in a short parley with the groom that superintended the scene. /

I am sure, said Ambrose vaguely, I have seen that horse before.

It is like you may, answered the groom. It has lately come up upwards of a hundred miles from one of the midland counties.

How come it to be for sale? It is a remarkably fine horse.

I have a notion that the owner is going abroad. But I do not well know why I think so.

As they spoke the horse turned his neck, and neighed; a token that he recognised in Ambrose an old acquaintance. When I and Margaret rode out together, Ambrose had many times been with us, attending his mistress, The horse, being now removed to a new scene, felt a human pleasure in recognising an acquaintance.

Aha, said the groom, that horse and you, my lad, have known one another before.

Ambrose advanced towards the horse, and patted his neck. The man and the quadruped / gave each other the *bon jour*, after the mode of salutation known and established in such cases.

Ambrose of course related to Travers what had occurred to him; and, putting together this encounter and that at the solicitor's, they inferred, though perhaps without any sufficient reason, that I had determined to go abroad. Ambrose therefore made a point of frequenting the wharfs and places from which passengers and goods were usually embarked. One day, in the grey of the morning, he caught the glimpse of a figure that reminded him of Catherine. He presently became assured that he was not deceived; for the lady, glancing him at the same time, had instantly endeavoured to shroud herself from observation in her veil. She suddenly turned the corner of a street, and Ambrose lost sight of her. He would have been glad to have dogged her to her residence; but he was anxious to avoid any step that might engender alarm. /

CHAPTER III

Unaware of these circumstances, for Catherine did not even mention to me her momentary encounter with a person that looked like Ambrose, we embarked. We had scarcely passed the Foreland,[a] before a heavy gale overtook us from the south-east, and kept us for two days, not without some danger, beating about in the waves of the North Sea, with the apprehension that we might be obliged to come to anchor in some port of the English coast. This incident was in itself no way of material importance; but, in the frame of mind in which I found myself, and the perilous condition in which I stood, circumstances which at any other time / would have appeared slight, made a strong impression upon me. I regarded this obstruction to my passage as ominous, and became apprehensive that, after the like fashion, every attempt I should make to escape from the tragical consequences of my rash proceeding, would be rendered ineffectual and abortive. Both Catherine and myself had been too much accustomed to the motion of the sea, to be much inconvenienced by that particular.

At length we arrived safely in the road of Dunkirk.[b] I had already determined to fix my abode in the first instance in or near the city of Bruges.[c] It was a place sufficiently remote from the port at which we landed, and was not greatly frequented either by merchants or travellers. In former times it had boasted of seventy thousand inhabitants, and had repeatedly had the honour of being made the residence of the court of the duke of Burgundy. It still retained many striking vestiges of its former / magnificence; but it now also exhibited no less the tokens of desolation, and its population scarcely exceeded the half of what it had formerly known.

In the neighbourhood of Bruges they count up to the number of thirty-seven villages, all of them agreeably situated, with a healthful air and a fertile soil, and pleasantly diversified with little plantations and gardens. Amidst these rural hamlets and retreats I thought I might reasonably hope to hide my head in safety. I assumed a different name, and proposed to pass my days in unnoticed obscurity.

Nor was it the least among my sufferings, that my daughter, the amiable, the accomplished, the sole representative of her sainted mother, the unblemished

---

[a] Headland in SE England on the Kent coast.
[b] Port in N France.
[c] Bruges, city in NW Belgium, capital of West Flanders province.

Emilia, suffered with me. She would in every case have been injured enough. My name would have adhered to her; and, however resplendent she might be in beauty, however unequalled in virtues, she would still, / in the midst of the loftiest society, be styled the offspring of a murderer.

But she chose a fate more horrible than this. She would not separate herself from the lot of her father. Because I was an exile, she determined to go into exile with me. She resolved never to divide herself from my nightly alarms, from the horrors that for ever beset me. She would not be persuaded not to regard it as her first of duties, to devote herself to my support and consolation. Thus she would never become a wife or a mother. She could never have a friend, unless she chose to embrace the mockery of friendship in the person of a man blasted for ever from the world. All the high hopes she had been entitled but just before to entertain, as the heiress of a plentiful fortune, as endowed with the amplest treasures of intellect, and enriched with the purest and most generous moral endowments, a creature that all the earth might fall down and adore, were irretrievably / extinguished. – Such was our situation at the best. It was with this miserable fragment of accommodation, that we had escaped from the shipwreck of the animating hopes and the enviable elevation, which, but for my folly, my unbridled and ungovernable passions, constituted the inheritance of both father and daughter.

Having advanced thus far, I deemed myself safe from the peril of any immediate pursuit. I had withdrawn, obscurely and unattended, from my native country, and embarked at the remotest quarter of its metropolis. I surely believed that I had cut off every clue, that might enable any one to ascertain that I had quitted the island of my birth. I had crossed to Dunkirk under a feigned name. I had then proceeded fifteen leagues by no frequented route to Bruges, and had there set myself down in an old and decayed city, of little resort either for merchants or travellers. Here / I proposed to reside, at least for a breathing time, if not for a more protracted season. I saw no reason why I should not prolong my stay for an indefinite period. If misfortune did not pursue me with unmitigable fury, I might at my pleasure either spend the remainder of my miserable life in this neighbourhood, or, having recruited my strength and tranquillity in this sequestered nook, cast about under its protection, as to what more eligible and inviting spot I might ultimately choose in which to set up my tabernacle.

Lodging therefore within the city at first, Catherine and I amused ourselves, or, I should rather say, I sought a momentary oblivion to my cares and the wretchedness of my condition, by wandering among the beautiful suburbs and hamlets with which the city is surrounded. All of them plainly spoke the contentment of their inhabitants; there was an air of cheerfulness, neatness and salubrity in all. Every thing was / upon a diminutive scale; a slight paling, a few fruit-trees, and a profusion of flowers, clothed in all the colours of the rainbow, and by the healthfulness of their appearance manifesting the careful tendance of the hand that cultivated them, were found on whatever side you turned your eye. A few rows of elms adorned the scene; and the soil was watered from the different canals with which the industry of man has enriched these provinces. Most of the cottages were humble, and expressed the simple equality of their inhabitants. Here and there, but thinly scattered, were dwellings of loftier pretension. But I know not why, these by no means displayed an equal charm. There was a sullenness and a loneliness about them, that plainly told you the owners thought themselves exiles from their proper sphere. They manifested a supercilious negligence, that strangely contrasted with the rest of the population. You could not help believing, that / the dwellers in these houses were straitened in their means of expenditure, and were aiming at a mock grandeur which they were unable fully to sustain. With these exceptions, which were easily overlooked among the general graciousness of the scene, the whole country wore the appearance of a beautiful lake, so tranquil and level was its surface; with this difference, that while water, however soothing to the sense of sight, presents you with the idea of bareness and waste, the wide champaign[a] of the Netherlands was on all hands decorated with fertility, and every where shewed unequivocal tokens of cultivation and care.

The majority of these cottages were tenanted. Many of them descended from father to son; and the occupant who was born in them, would have deemed it little less than sacrilege so much as to have dreamed of removing to another abode. A few were announced by a placard, a little removed in the front of the / house, as being to be let. One day in our rambles, Catherine was struck with one of these, as being particularly inviting to her fancy. It fell back from the line of the rest; and a stranger might pass and repass repeatedly without being aware of its existence. Two or three large beech-trees interposed before it, and rendered it nearly invisible but to the most curious eye. These trees had the effect of darkening the apartments in the front of the house, while those which lay behind, and had nothing that intercepted the clear light of day, were by contrast peculiarly cheerful and gay. The windows on this side commanded a view of the open country, displaying an exuberant fertility of soil and elaborateness of tillage, while, as there were no dwellings in that direction but distant ones, the whole had an air of uninterrupted security and repose. There were trees also on this side, but more distant. There was a pond beneath these trees, the favourite / haunt of the ducks from a neighbouring farm. There were on the same side haystacks, and a few outhouses appropriated to the uses of agriculture; but these could scarcely be said to disturb the general tranquillity of the scene.

Without delay we took possession of this village-tenement. The furniture required was easily supplied from the neighbouring city; and I did not judge it

[a] Expanse of level open country.

inconsistent with my plan of obscurity, 'forgetting all, by all forgotten',[a] to hire two Flemish servants, one male, another female, for our domestic uses. Both Catherine and myself had already resided abroad; and therefore we found little difficulty in such communication with these individuals and our humbler neighbours, as might be required for the ordinary purposes of life.

Catherine easily and without a murmur adapted herself to this low situation, so different from any thing to which she had been accustomed. / She regarded the motive which had brought her here, as shedding a mild and consolatory beam on all she did and all she saw. She was here, attending on her father in his adversity, endeavouring to supply his wants and anticipate his wishes, smiling on his sorrows, with a smile, not cold, and in mockery, but of truest sympathy. She made a point of appearing at all times cheerful and serene, that I might not imagine that she was unhappy, or be reminded of the strange change that had overtaken me. Doubtless she was not without her fears, that, humble as our situation was, we might not be permitted to remain in it without interruption, that vengeance might pursue me, and that by some unlooked for accident our retreat might be betrayed to those who were most willing to hurt us. Guilt can scarcely ever be secure. But whatever were her thoughts in this respect, she kept them sacredly in the chamber of her own bosom. Outwardly she / was all encouragement. She seemed to wish and to expect to remain here for ever.

She had spent a large portion of her life in a state of separation from me; and she endeavoured to call to mind a variety of such characters and adventures as might prove most amusing to me. There was an innocence in her manner of narration, that gave a double zest to all she spoke. Malice and guile seemed to lose their most venomous features, when she was their historian. They drew a peculiar hue from the goodness of her heart. Sometimes you would scarcely suppose that she apprehended the baseness, the selfishness and deceit, that every where abound among mankind; but even then, when you thought she was most their dupe, a peculiar motion of her brow or her lip, a dropping of the eye, or an unexpected inflection of voice, so unobtrusive that it would have wholly escaped the notice of a superficial observer, proved to me at once that her penetration / was rapid and unerring, that she saw through the elaborateness of disguise, and viewed every thing in its true colours. Her narratives had all the charm, which is constantly found to attend upon an enlightened and quicksighted simplicity. Character was painted in them by a few unambitious and natural touches. Incidents seemed to fall exactly into their proper places, and were spoken of neither with disappointing brevity nor tedious circumlocution. There was not a word either too little or too much. A rapt attention waited on her speech. The melodious tones of her voice gratified the sense; while at the same time the spirit and variety of her delineations never suffered the thoughts

---

[a] cf. Pope, 'Eloisa to Abelard', l. 208: 'the world forgetting, by the world forgot'.

of the listener to weary or to wander. Even I, who had a thousand thorns within my breast to prick and sting me, was composed in mute regard, and occasionally forgot my sorrows. In my turn I undertook to amuse my daughter with an account / of scenes she had not seen, or with adventures (such as did not touch upon the acutest recollections of my soul) that were personal to myself. In addition to this, Catherine was an accomplished singer, and played divinely on her instrument, so that, when the evil spirit was upon me, it repeatedly happened that, like the shepherd in the Jewish history, she called forth the talent with which she was endowed, and the 'evil spirit departed from me'.[a] I procured myself books of history, of wit, of imagination, and thus for a certain period beguiled my sorrows, and added wings to the slow foot of time.

Nothing could be more soothing and cheerful than the scenery with which I was surrounded. It was the pleasantest season of the year, when the heats of the summer were in a great degree abated, and the sun shone almost every day with a mild radiance. The crops were gathered in, and the vintage approached; / the farmer was prosperous; the peasantry were satisfied with their labours; and every one agreed to devote himself alternately to repose, to hilarity and amusement. But I, alas, found in myself the complete contrast of the objects around me. Everyone was cheerful; but I was sad. The sun shone to the senses of the rest; but over me there hung a thick and pestilential cloud. The sun did not comfort me; and the stars shone for me in vain. The curse of God was upon me; and the fiends of memory and apprehension haunted me for ever.

I rarely went into the city, and had scarcely formed any connections. I called however sometimes at a bookseller's shop in the High Street; and I dropped in, though rarely, at the house of a Frenchman, with whom I had made acquaintance at Paris, but who for the last two or three years had resided at Bruges. The Frenchman was almost the only person, who could be called a visitor, that had entered / our village abode. He was a man who had devoted himself to the study of the classics, and was distinguished by a pure and elevated taste in the works of art. He was particularly fond of statuary; and his saloon, his study, and his stair-case were plentifully ornamented with choice copies of the remains of antiquity in this kind. Like myself, he had no surviving kindred, but one fair daughter, the 'immediate jewel of his soul'.[b] This girl came to our cottage first with her father, and then more than once without him. She had imbibed much of his tastes, and had a passion for drawing. Bits of landscape she executed with no common skill; and some of her delineations from her father's statues were admirable. She had lived much with an aunt at Paris, a woman of manners not less frank, than they were elegant and graceful. But the Frenchman had been involved in an affair of state-intrigue; and, the cabal into which he had entered being detected / before it was mature, it had been

[a] 1 Sam. 16: 23 (adapted).
[b] *Othello*, III. iii. 156.

necessary for him to engage in a sort of compromise with the ruling powers. They allowed him to retire into the Netherlands, and to retain undisturbed the rents of his property, with the understanding that he should never again set foot in the kingdom of France without a special licence being granted him for that purpose; the consequence of his violating this understanding being declared to be the forfeiture of his estates, and his being subjected to a rigorous proceeding in the criminal courts for the state-offence in which he was considered as being involved. He therefore passed his life in great privacy, and even changed his name.

The degree of resemblance between his fortune and mine, drew us into terms of considerable intimacy. I however was silent as to the real occasion that had compelled me to leave my country, and gave him to understand that, like him, I had been engaged in my own / country in an affair of a political nature, which had imposed on me the necessity of retiring into a temporary place of concealment. I had not however, like him, been fortunate enough to enter into a compromise with my own government, and was therefore in imminent danger of pursuit and apprehension. I carefully suppressed the real cause of my exile. Though M. Morlaix, that was the name by which my friend called himself, had become obnoxious to the government of his country, it did not follow that he would feel himself easy in the society of a murderer. Nor could I think in any case of making a voluntary disclosure of the opprobrium and disgrace that hung upon my name.

Thus we were drawn together by the apparent similarity of our circumstances. We were each under a cloud; we each bore a false name, and were each of us banished from our native country. These particulars prevailed on me for once to break through that thick veil / of solitude and sequestration to which I had thought all my following days and nights had been devoted. We made a sort of confident of each other: M. Morlaix speaking to me ingenuously, and in the fulness of his heart: and I in return imposing on him with a false sincerity, while I carefully concealed the ever living worm that gnawed at my vitals. The very idea that I was throughout a deceiver, and that, if my friend ever came to know the truth, he would fling me from him like a serpent, nay, would perhaps himself be forward to deliver me into the hands of my inveterate enemies, poisoned all the pleasures I should otherwise have had in our communications, and rendered me perpetually uneasy, full of self-reproach and abasement. Such are the consequences of guilt!

The daughter of my friend (if it is not sacrilege so to apply the name) had cheerfully resigned all her former connections, and followed / her father into a land of strangers. There was therefore a considerable similitude between her situation and that of Catherine; and it seemed likely that, if circumstances had concurred with their inclinations, an intimate society and friendship would have sprung up between them. But both of them, and most especially my Catherine, upon whom the sacrifice was most urgent, regarded filial duty and

207

affection as paramount to all other ties. She indeed never forgot for a moment the disastrous situation that had generated our banishment. She considered herself, in whatever place we might take up our temporary abode, as by indefeasible necessity a bird of passage merely. She did not expect to find rest for the sole of her foot. Her perpetual destiny was to eat her meat in fear, with her 'loins girded, and her staff in her hand'.[a] ready to change the place of her abiding at an instant's warning; and / thinking herself too happy, if, by unremitted vigilance, and a spirit of sacrifice that disdained to repine, she might be fortunate enough to preserve her father's liberty and forfeited life. /

CHAPTER IV

We had dwelt but a few weeks in our present place of abode, when it happened one day that I took occasion to visit the bookseller's shop I have mentioned, and amused myself for half-an-hour with turning over the pages of some new publications. There was a room behind the shop, separated from it only by a window and a curtain, which was considered as the privileged resort of the gentlemen of the town and neighbourhood, and removed them from the ordinary customers, footmen and maid-servants, who came for their incidental purchases, and into which it was not the practice for strangers to make their way, unless introduced. / It was in this room that I took my seat. Among other things my evil genius prompted me to lay my hand upon a file of English newspapers. I was alone; and I thought I might indulge myself in the sad luxury of thus visiting in fancy my native country, upon the soil of which I might perhaps never again set my foot. I cast my eye upon the record of marriages and deaths, the persons most of them unknown to me, but some whose names were familiar, and some of them who ranked among my personal acquaintance.

In one of these papers my eye caught, at an instant's glance by an unavoidable cooperation of the exterior and interior sense, my own name. It was most painful. I would have withdrawn my observation, and perused other articles in the sheet; but I could not. The paragraph which had thus fixed my attention was in the nature of an advertisement. It / contained my Christian and surname, the name of my country-seat, and of the county in which it was placed. It specified my stature, my complexion and my features. It stated that a warrant had been issued by the coroner of the county against me, upon a charge of

---

[a] Exod. 12: 11 (adapted).

wilful murder upon the body of William ——. It spoke of me as having fled from justice, and removed to a place of concealment. It mentioned that I was probably somewhere about the metropolis, but added that I was supposed to have meditated an escape to the continent; and concluded with the offer of a reward of five hundred pounds upon my being lodged in the jail of my native county, or being produced and properly identified at any of the police-offices of the city of London, the attestation of the magistrate of such office to his Majesty's secretary of state, being the proper authority for the payment of the reward to the person or persons by whom I should be delivered into custody. /

Though all this was matter of course, was drawn up in the ordinary forms, and might have been anticipated by me almost word for word as I found it, yet such is the nature of the human mind, that a stronger and almost a new effect is produced upon us, when it comes to be subjected to our sense. It lost its vagueness, the misty and obscure form it previously bore, and thrilled through the marrow in my bones. It was like the writing upon the wall, inscribed there by visible 'fingers of a man's hand', which when Belshazzar saw, 'the joints of his loins were loosed, and his knees smote one against the other'.[a]

The paragraph I beheld struck at my liberty and my life. Till the hour of the rash act I had committed, I had been a recognised and authentic member of the aristocracy of my country, protected by its laws in all my immunities and privileges, and honoured by my fellow-citizens. 'When the young men saw me', / they drew back with reverence, 'and the aged arose', and saluted me.[b] Now I was proclaimed as a loathsome and rejected member of the community, and a price was fixed on my head. If I continued to exist, it was only that the arm of public justice was too short to reach me; and I must be indebted for life to the rapidity of my motions, or the subtlety of my contrivances. My head was devoted, a victim to the demands of criminal law; and the code of civilization could not be satisfied without my extirpation. On my grave might with truth be inscribed, Here lies the body of a murderer! Men of reflection and sobriety would shrink from the spot; and the superstitious would expect to encounter my ghost in the shades of night, placing before their eyes the figure of one whom the earth could not hide, but who was condemned for ever to frequent the scene of his misdeeds.

Such were the reflections that haunted my / thoughts, as the paper lay before me that gave birth to them. My soul was in tumults. Alternately the ideas I have above expressed passed in sad and dreary order before me; and alternately they shaped themselves into a wild and terrific dance of death, till I no longer knew either where I was, or what I was. At length my thoughts fell into somewhat of a slower march; and I saw again the things that were before me and beside me.

I was no sooner recovered from this state of delirious confusion and agony,

---

[a] Dan. 5: 5–6 (adapted).
[b] Job 29: 8 (adapted).

than I observed a person, who seemed to be newly arrived, and whom I had never seen before, engaged in discourse with the master of the shop. He distinctly pronounced the name Deloraine. I was by this time sufficiently master of myself to be aware, that this was not the name by which I was known in Bruges, and that it was not probable that, thus pronounced in the ear of the bookseller, it should / have in his mind the smallest connection with my person. The coincidence however was alarming and distressing to me: it had a few moments before been presented to my eye; it was now presented to my ear. What a thing is guilt! How is it with the soul of man, when every trifle shakes it? – I collected every sense I had in the sense of hearing, and was anxious that not a word that was uttered should escape me.

I soon found that the discourse of the stranger related to the affair which was the topic of the paragraph I had read. He told the bookseller that murder had been committed in England, and that the perpetrator had escaped by sea. He said, that he had come thus far for the purpose of causing me to be delivered up to justice, that he had followed me to Dunkirk, and that, after having sought for me to no purpose in various directions, to the south and the east, he was credibly informed / that I had been seen at Bruges. He took out his pocket-book, and drew from it a placard, printed on a large sheet of paper, the contents of which were doubtless the same, as that of the advertisement that had occasioned me so much confusion. The bookseller and the stranger fixed their eyes together on this paper; the bookseller being within-side the counter, and the stranger without. Their heads were almost in contact. The finger of the stranger pointed to one particular and another; and the man of business sometimes shook his head, and sometimes nodded.

There was I alone in the inner room, while all this was going on. A transparent window, with a slight curtain protecting me, was all that divided me from the men who had thus my fate in their hands. I was dumb; I moved neither hand nor foot; I scarcely dared so much as breathe. I expected every moment when the shopkeeper would throw open the / door behind which I was placed, and say, There is your man! He did not stir from the position in which he was placed. He still pored on the words of the placard. At length he raised his head, and fixed his eyes on the stranger.

I think, said he, I can give you some light in this affair. – These few words were succeeded by a momentary pause.

A man was in my shop yesterday, whose person precisely answers to the description in that paper. His appearance was very singular; I could not keep my eyes off from him. I said to myself, That man has certainly done something he ought not to have done. He was exceedingly flurried; and his looks were ghastly. He burst into my shop all at once, and yet seemed scarcely to know what he came for. He took up one or two books from my counter; at the same time looking around and behind with great uneasiness. At length he said, I am /

going to Osnabruck;[a] have you anything in the nature of a Guide, that may be of use to me? I handed him a volume from my shelves. He turned it over in a very hurried manner, asked me the price of it, paid for it, and, without saying a word more, passed into the street. I was so impressed with his appearance, that I directed one of my boys to follow him at a distance, and see where he went to. He lodged him at the Blue Lion. This was only yesterday evening: and he is therefore still there, or intelligence may probably be gained there of his further proceedings.

The change which thus took place, when things seemed to be at the worst, was an inexpressible relief to me. My situation had been like that of a man with a night-mare, who feels that he has the weight of a gigantic and preternatural monster cowering on his breast, becoming heavier every moment, threatening / utterly to extinguish the pulmonary action without which life cannot subsist. I had no power over a single articulation of my frame.

I had however no sooner found this relief, and the bookseller finished the detail of his conjectures, than the street-door opened; and who should enter to the two already in the shop, but Ambrose, the personal and trusted attendant upon my unfortunate wife? He was not in mourning: for, alas! these details, which are inseparable from every other establishment in my rank of life, could have no place under the disaster into which I had fallen. My houshold was scattered; and every one of its members had been suddenly driven to seek new resources for the means of their subsistence. He was not in livery; but he advanced with the tokens of submission and deference which characterise a servant, towards the stranger, who proved to be Travers, the sworn brother and avenger of my unfortunate victim. Seeing / him, Travers turned to the master of the shop, expressed himself greatly indebted to him for the information he had supplied, and he and Ambrose passed into the street together.

What then was the just inference from the new discovery which had thus been thrust upon me? Travers in his conversation with the bookseller had avowed that he had passed from England to Dunkirk, and from Dunkirk to Bruges, for the express purpose of causing me to be apprehended and deli- vered up to justice. I knew nothing of Travers; I had not so much as heard the name of the man who had but now been separated from me by a slight partition. But I could observe that he was a gentleman, a man of manners and education. He was not of the usual cast of the hired retainers of executive justice. He had plainly engaged in the affair from higher motives. He had devoted himself to the pursuit from generous sentiments, from pure friendship for the unfortunate / deceased, and a determination that his destroyer should be visited with an ample revenge. It was obvious that he was not destitute of the means which should enable him to carry on his purpose to the end. By what

---

[a] City in NW Germany.

inconceivable subtlety and diligence had he proceeded in his object so far unerringly, and traced me to the city where I reasonably hoped I could conceal myself for ever? A man of cool blood in my situation, despairing of success, would have abandoned all further contention, would have no longer disquieted himself in vain, but have said to his enemy, Here I am; act your pleasure upon me; dispose of me as may seem good in your sight.

Such was the sober judgment I might have made of my position, when I saw Travers only, and heard the discourse he addressed to the bookseller. In reality I had expected every moment when the master of the house would have thrown open the door on the other side / of which I was placed, and have said to him, There is the person you seek!

I escaped that danger. But how had I escaped? Travers had brought with him a person, who had long been in the habit of seeing me every day and at all hours, and had doubtless retained him in his service, and brought him with him in his inquisition, on account of that very qualification. Till then I had thought, If I can once escape from the apartment in which I am inclosed, if the bookseller does not recognise me by the description laid before him, and deliver me up to my pursuer, I am safe. I was like a bird, by nature free as air, and whose inheritance is the skies, – open the narrow cage in which he is confined, and he spreads his wings, and rejoices in his freedom, and darts into the trackless void, and possesses an unblemished and impregnable security. Even so I, like the bird, beat my wings against the wires of my cage, and was / impatient to get beyond the narrow bound in which I had been shut up.

In the mean time, supposing the door that divided me from my pursuer had been thrown open, I should still not have been destitute of hope. The trades-man and the stranger would have been placed before me; they would have examined my features; they would have compared them with the description contained in the placard they had read. What then? All likes are not the same. Fighting, as I should have been called on to fight, for my personal liberty, and against the threat that hung over me of an ignominious death, I felt full surely that I should have been able to maintain my ground with intrepidity. Nothing more would be necessary than that I should tell my story with constancy and firmness. Who is it that has the audacity to say that my name is Deloraine? I know nothing of the man; I am a stranger to his history; and will you dare to / deprive me of liberty, that I may be made to answer for his crimes? Away with so groundless a pretence! Stand off; and do not think to restrain and shackle me with your absurd conjectures and accusations!

But how different was my condition, when I clearly saw that the servant of my late wife was in the employment of my pursuer! He would have identified me at once. It was no longer a question of the nook that contained me, and my escape from which I anticipated with inconceivable joy. The little room behind the bookseller's shop I had regarded as my prison, and I had pined with inexpressible eagerness to be enlarged from it. Now, on the contrary, I might almost regard it as my sanctuary. The moment I should get out into the street, I should be exposed to the hazard of my enemy. I could not turn a corner, that might not place him expressly in my way. If I were at one end of a street, and he at the other, he would / in all likelihood recognise me, so familiar to his sight were the outline of my person, the dependency of my limbs, and the carriage to which I was accustomed. I must call upon darkness to cover me, and clouds and thick darkness to enable me to pass along unperceived. /

CHAPTER V

I had however small time for deliberation. Ambrose and the stranger had passed out into the street together. As they had not exchanged so much as a word in the shop, it was unavoidable to believe that their first moments would be occupied with the information that Travers had received from the bookseller. They would then in all probability proceed to the Blue Lion, which the bookseller had pointed out as the present abiding of Deloraine. I knew in which direction that object would lead them. The Frenchman I have mentioned, fortunately resided in a different quarter of the town. I had no time for hesitation. There was a back-door / which led from the bookseller's counting-house into one of the lanes of the city. This door, though not often, was sometimes used by persons who resorted thither, as I had done, to read the newspapers and look over the new publications, to whom it afforded a shorter cut to their respective habitations than by passing into the street. I opened this door and withdrew. The circumstance probably would not be adverted to as singular. And, if it were, my situation did not allow a liberty of choice. I proceeded with all expedition to the residence of my friend, the only person who could render me the assistance I needed in my present emergency.

I found M. Morlaix at home and alone. I assumed an air of as much tranquillity and composure as I could put into my countenance. The character I had to personate was exceedingly different from that which truly belonged to me. In political enterprises, however hazardous / and daring, a man necessarily acts in cooperation with others, and for some public purpose; and the conception of the end he has in view, and the approbation and common sentiment of the honourable men with whom he had united himself, sustain him. I had no such support, and drew my only incitement to persevere from that desperate love of life, which is found in almost all cases to increase, in proportion to the seeming hopelessness of the circumstances that beset us.

Presently however I began to consider the subject in a very different light, in a light by no means so disheartening and so withering. I was not alone in the world. There sat beside me the illustrious, the unparalleled Catherine. She had every excellence that could dignify a woman, every perfection that could add lustre to human nature. She had youth; she had beauty; she had a penetrating understanding, and a susceptible heart. She was gifted with / the most exquisite taste; and the treasures of knowledge and intellect were her own. She was the abstract of all that is admirable in woman. Yet this being, thus endowed, gave herself up for me. She voluntarily shut herself out from that world which she was so eminently qualified to adorn. She stripped herself of the glories of her character, and submitted to be my obscure and fireside companion. She shunned the applauses of those who would naturally have been her associates. She watched my slightest emotions, and unweariedly sought to smooth the pillow under my anxious and aching head. She searched out every thing that could amuse and enliven me. She cheated the sad hours of my solitude. To light up one smile on my lips, to elicit one spark from my dim and despairing eye, seemed to her the all-sufficient reward of a thousand labours.

What most of all impressed me, was that I seemed of such vast consequence to this angelic / creature. Poor and despicable as I was in myself, I derived an unquestionable value from her. I regarded myself with inexpressible self-abasement; I was nothing, and less than nothing in my own opinion, a vile and loathsome weed, incumbering the earth, and infecting the air with contagion: but I thought of Catherine, and became in a sort endeared to myself. She seemed to live only in me; there was the appearance as if she would perish without me, that the existence of this resplendent being was indissolubly connected with my frail existence. Oh, then I became of consequence in my own eyes! I was eager to preserve myself from destruction, since so lovely a being seemed to depend upon me, even as the most glorious and delicate flower of the garden draws the continuity of its being from the unsightly root. I saw myself in her. I had a motive for taking care of myself, and preserving me from harm, since the most excellent being I ever knew, the / most purely dis-interested, was only to be preserved, by means of my being preserved.

I therefore entered with earnest heart into the measures which the crisis I was placed in demanded from me. I told my friend that I had but that moment discovered that there were persons in Bruges who were in pursuit of me, and who, as I firmly believed, were armed with full powers to apprehend me, backed by the authority of those who exercised the supreme government of the Austrian Netherlands. I added, that I had myself actually beheld, without being discovered, one of the individuals dispatched from England for this purpose, who was perfectly acquainted with my person and features. It was therefore of importance to me, that I should quit Bruges and its neighbourhood without the smallest delay, and, if possible, leave no vestige behind by means of which the new place of my retreat should be traced. /

My friend saw the earnestness and excitement under which I spoke, and, without requiring any fuller elucidation of my mystery, entered with an entire good will upon the performance of what I required of him. He undertook to provide a couple of horses, such as in England are known by the name of galloways, for the immediate escape of myself and Catherine. In the mean time I dispatched a note to her, informing her of the necessity of our decampment, and desiring her to have every thing prepared. The night was no sooner set in. than I ventured alone into the streets, and, finding no tokens of any one observing me, hastened with all expedition to our village. The horses were fully in readiness; and Catherine was waiting in her travelling dress.

Oh, my child, said I, as soon as I saw her, how bitter a potion is this which I administer to you! We are no sooner sat down in a little apparent quiet, than we are instantly obliged to / quit our abode. My doom is perpetual wandering and apprehension, eternal concealment and ever-new alarm, which can never be terminated otherwise than by the actual occurrence of the worst that we fear. Repent, while there is yet time! Sever your young and healthful frame from my withered and accursed stock! Return to your friends in England, and be, as you are so well qualified to be, the ornament and pride of every circle in which you move!

My father! replied the heroic girl, do not think you shall ever change my determined purpose. Fear me not! I have made up my mind to every thing that can happen; and nothing can shake my firmness, or discompose the settled temper of my spirit. I count every thing that I can do as a glory, and shall think myself hallowed and consecrated by every service I can render you, and every the least mitigation I can afford you in your trials. The greater are your difficulties and distress, the / more resistless is my obligation never to separate myself from you.

How I adored the heroic partner of my toils! She turned her back upon the retirement in which we had fixed ourselves, and cast herself once more a stranger and a wanderer upon the world without a sigh. An unknown and a celestial energy seemed to sustain her. I spoke a few words to our servants at parting. I said that perhaps we should be absent for some days. If the time proved of longer duration, I referred them to M. Morlaix for explanation and orders. /

CHAPTER VI

Catherine and myself speedily gained the high road. It was now deep night, and as dark as we could desire. Our view in the first instance was to attain the city of Ghent;[a] and the road thither was so obvious that we could scarcely miss it. Though the distance between Ghent and Bruges were only thirty miles, yet such a removal, in the first instance, was of inconceivable importance to me. It would set a palpable distance between me and my pursuers; and, till that was done, I felt, as Homer expresses it, their breath sensibly blowing in my neck behind me. I seized the opportunity of our commencing journey, to give Catherine / in few words the leading particulars of that which had occasioned me so much terror and alarm.

We then proceeded for some time in silence and at a round pace. Catherine had been a traveller, and was an excellent horsewoman. We had the road to ourselves; and, having now advanced for an hour uninterrupted, I began to feel within me a comparative tranquillity. Of a sudden, Hush! said Catherine; surely I hear behind us the steps of a horse advancing in the same direction. I thought so too. By degrees the thing became more perceptible; and it was plain the stranger gained upon us. My soul was for the moment bound up in the sense of hearing; and I could perceive that the unknown person was alone. This took off from the feeling of terror and alarm I might otherwise have entertained. I judged at once that it was most improbable that the persons I had seen at the bookseller's shop should be in the / least concerned with this, or could so instantaneously have discovered the route I had taken, and be already in my track.

The stranger was extremely well mounted; and he gained upon us every instant. He was speedily by my side. It is well, said I: as he has advanced upon us so rapidly, no doubt he will pass us as quickly, and be presently out of sight. In this however I was disappointed: the horseman had no sooner come up with us, than he checked his pace, and manifested a seeming purpose to install himself our companion. I was exceedingly disturbed at this. Though I had decided that he had no connection with my dreaded pursuers, yet my critical situation, and the ever-alive worm of conscience did not fail to inspire me with uneasiness, and lead me to question whether my first decision had not been too

---

[a] City and port in NW Belgium, capital of East Flanders province.

hasty. I carefully surveyed the stranger; but he was enveloped in a cloak, even to his very head, so that I could gain no / satisfaction. I intuitively felt a disinclination to speak to him, as if the very sound of my voice might in some way become a source of injury. The scene therefore for a time proceeded in silence. I endeavoured in every way I could to shake off the unwelcome intruder. I checked the pace of my horse to a walk; and presently after urged him into a gallop. Catherine understood me, kept a quick eye upon me, and did as I did. But unfortunately so did the stranger. Determined in my purpose, I caused my horse to stand still; so did Catherine; so did the stranger.

Provoked beyond measure by the obstinacy of the intruder, I felt the necessity of breaking silence. I said to him in French, at the same time disguising the tone of my voice, Sir, have I the honour of your acquaintance? If not, I give you good night.

All men know all men, replied the stranger. And for your good night I would thank you, / save that you are giving that which you have not to bestow.

The words thus uttered sounded incoherent enough. I congratulated myself however that the voice in which they were spoken was entirely new to me. Meanwhile this circumstance did not alter my determined purpose; and I proceeded:

I do not well understand your observations; nor do they seem intended to be understood. All that I have to say therefore is, that it is not my custom to ride with strangers in a public road; and I beg that you will choose your pace, that I may be at liberty to choose mine.

Pace! cried the stranger: I do not know what to say to that. Some men drive; and others are driven. The wisest, of whom I am one, do something between both. You perhaps are for Ghent; now I am going to Osnabruck.

The word Osnabruck immediately struck me, though for some moments I could not tell why. / At length I recollected it as the destination of the false Deloraine, who, fortunately for me, had been substituted for the true in the booksellers's shop.

If I had my own will, continued the stranger, I should now be fast asleep in bed at the Blue Lion at Bruges. But impertinent intruders have forbidden this; and I am accordingly now at midnight at a stand-still on the public road.

Those fellows, he pursued, with their pretence of talking English thought to deceive me; but I was up to them. I got off from my quarters unseen; and here I am, mounted upon my faithful steed, when I please, goes at a rate, that no one yet has been able to overtake.

These observations were truly alarming to me. From them I concluded that Travers and Ambrose had in some way missed of the man, of whom they had gone in pursuit. His destination however was notorious. As he had / proclaimed it at the bookseller's shop, so probably had he at the Blue Lion; and, if I did not take care, the scent of the false Deloraine might serve to guide my enemies in the track of the true. I determined however to make one more effort by mild means to shake off the intruder. I said:

If your arrival at Osnabruck is so important, consider, there are many roads that lead to it. Is it advisable then that you should pursue so public a way as that of Ghent?

Oh, excuse me, sir, said the stranger. I have many reasons for choosing these public highways: chiefly, that it enables me to pick up followers; for a king without subjects is but a shadowy monarch. I know my own greatness; but there are those who would gladly clip my wings. They once tried it, by shutting me up in a house with bars to the windows, and spikes to the walls; but I gave them the slip. And now, to say the truth, / that I have found companions, I care not if they overtake us. My pursuers are but two: and we two are a match for those two all the world over. Not to mention the lady, whose presence is to me the assured harbinger of victory.

As he spoke, the stranger threw back the cape of his cloak, which had hitherto concealed his face; and I took a survey of his person. He rode bareheaded; and I could trace, in the wildness of his gestures, and the disturbed expression of his figure, a confirmation of what I already suspected – that he was a poor, deranged creature, recently escaped from his keepers.

I had tried temporising methods with him in vain. It was of the last importance to me to be rid of him. Exclusively of the circumstance, that his presence might be a guide to my pursuers, and prove a shackle to my proceedings in a case of emergency, I also regarded / him as a spy upon my movements, and as sufficiently reasonable amidst all his incoherence, to be able to give dangerous information respecting my motions. I therefore determined upon a last step to free me from his presence. The thought of the peril to which I was exposed had already urged me to put my horse to his swiftest pace, to which the man had corresponded as before. Without checking my progress, I rode up close to his side, and said to him in an emphatical manner:

Harkye, sir, I have no more time for trifling! – I know you for an escaped lunatic; and it is therefore my duty to seize you, and convey you to a place of safety. – And, saying this, I stretched out my hand, as if intending to arrest him.

This proceeding of mine had the desired effect. The maniac suddenly drew his steed several yards apart from me, and then, – after having indulged in a portentous and fearful / laugh, and exclaiming, I am not mad enough however to be seized by you – urged his horse to the top of his speed, and was presently far a-head of us on the road to Ghent. /

CHAPTER VII

I must frankly confess myself at this distance unable to recollect in order of time and place the endless persecutions I have been fated to undergo. No day could I call my own; no hour have I been free from the direst alarm. The watches of the night have been full of terror to me. All day I have watched, not perhaps with the sense of seeing, for that would have been too perilous to me, but with the sense of hearing, for the approach of the foe, for those stealthy steps which I supposed ever at hand to surprise me. If at any time weary nature within me sought for repose, if my senses were steeped in a short oblivion, / this was far from being a refreshment to me. My visions were wild, incoherent, tormenting, beyond the power of words, to describe; my soul was tumultuously hurried along in restless ecstasy; I felt that every thing which presented itself to my inner sense was inconsistent, contradictory, impossible, yet, impossible, as it was, I was compelled to believe it. My dreams were endless; I wandered among rocks and deserts with failing and wearied steps; yet the actual time consumed by these dreams was but as a moment: I started and woke with ever-fresh alarm, as if of some terrific certainty. My blood was fevered; my brain was maddened; my hours were full of delirious imaginations, which again were sobered and reduced to compulsory steadiness by the near apprehension of some fatal violence. The only mitigation I experienced to these tortures was in the presence and soothing care of my daughter, when I could have her near me, which was not always. /

How then is it possible that, amidst all this disorder of my brain, this frenzy of the soul, I can recollect things in the order of time and place? I cannot. Only here and there by some strange accident I call to mind a memorable scene, which trenched too deep a gash in my spirit ever to be forgotten. These scenes are insulated. I cannot form an image of what went before or what followed. They start up like those rare spots which are found by travellers in the deserts, breaking by brief intervals the gloomy and cheerless monotony of the rest of the journey.

One of these was when, after having undergone various alarms during the day, sufficiently groundless perhaps, but which in the diseased state of my feelings carried with them the force of irrefragable truth, we arrived within sight of a solitary mansion. We were unattended and on foot. The mansion was on the shores of the Rhine. It was built on the crag / of a rock, sheltered on one side by a high wood, and on the other bordered by ravines, which led by an

219

irregular and devious course to the very banks of the river. Between the two, and in the front of the house, ran a narrow road, uneven and rugged in its surface, but sufficient for the occasions of the tenants of the mansion. The road, though of small breadth, and shut in for the most part by the nearly impracticable asperities of the soil, had not however, on the one side or the other any precise limits, but had occasional openings, affording an opprtunity to the traveller to penetrate, if he so pleased, into the less obvious parts of the scenery, and to withdraw himself from the observation of the plodding and ordinary wayfarer. Into the entrance of a sort of cavern, which was among the diversities of the scene, Catherine and I, after some hours of disconsolate wandering, withdrew ourselves to consult upon what was next to be done. We / found a sort of natural bench, which seemed to court us to a few minutes' repose.

We had each of us cast a wistful look upon the mansion which was at hand. There was no other refuge near; and night was shutting in fast upon us. We seemed therefore impelled to seek the shelter of this roof. In solitary situations hospitality to a certain extent is the inevitable duty and lot of the inhabitants; and they are ordinarily prepared to yield it. Suspicion and cautiousness however were entailed upon us; and it appeared more advisable to feel our way in the first instance, than to plunge at once into what might be not unattended with peril. Catherine was young: she had a light and innocent heart, and nothing to restrain her exertions. She accordingly offered, and I did not contradict her affectionate suggestion, to go first, and undertake to sound the disposition, and observe upon the character, of the tenant of the mansion. /

She proceeded accordingly. I, but at a safe distance, and with a fluttering heart, watched her steps. She found that the principal occupier of the mansion was a woman; and Catherine was immediately admitted to her presence. Her appearance was prepossessing; her manner was polished and humane. She was about forty years of age. Though Catherine accosted her first in French, she was both surprised and delighted to find her English. Catherine had been much of a traveller: but English blood still flowed in her veins; and the earliest habits of her life yet savoured of her native country. It may be that the habits of a Frenchman, a German, or a Spaniard are not less congenial to our general nature: but to a native of this island they unavoidably appear in some degree artificial; and we feel ourselves more confidential and assured, when we impart our communications to one of ourselves. Catherine told a simple tale, of herself and her father, wanderers / at a distance from their country, being benighted in this solitary place. The appearance of my daughter told the rest. The mistress of the mansion saw in her a young person of superior character and refined sentiments. Her beauty, her complexion, the elegance of her manners, her speech true to nature and to feeling, interested the heart of the lady, and instilled an undoubting persuasion that she could do nothing but right in yielding to the petition of such a suitor, which she did in the most gracious and encouraging manner. Catherine sought me with her report; and we were speedily installed in a private room, with a cheerful fire blazing on the hearth, and all other accommodations that could conduce to the refreshment of a weary traveller. The manner of our hostess put us at our ease; and we relished with especial zest the sweets of a comfortable roof in a remote and sequestered part of the world, after the toil and uncertainties / of the preceding days. Our hostess sat down with us, and tried to amuse us. She was sparing of questions, as she was too well bred to be guilty of impertinence. We spoke of London and its societies, in a manner that implied that we were familiar with the best circles. We spoke of various cities and courts of Europe. We talked of the various masterpieces of Italian art, of poetry, and of some of the greatest and most striking events of modern history. On all these subjects our hostess expressed herself well, with true taste and genuine feeling of all that is best and most worthy of approbation. Each party gained on the other; and we presently felt, not as if we had met this evening for the first time in our lives, but rather as if accustomed to one another's habits, and familiar with our respective modes of thinking and speaking. Our hostess was clearly a woman of great refinement and much sensibility. My character and habits were / fixed by a course of long prosperity and the consciousness of being well received wherever I went. A cloud indeed had for many weeks come over me, and had so far made me but the wreck of what I had been. But this was new to me, and had not yet become a part of my nature. Whenever the immediate sense of my adversity was for a short time beguiled, my spirits mechanically rose, and I became in a degree all that I had been in my best days. And Catherine, the enchanting Catherine, had always, in the simplicity of her manner, the sweetness of her tones, and the grace of all she said and did, every thing that was irresistible, and that won at least all who were capable of appreciating her, to feel towards her the emotions of a true friendship, that, once begun, could never be dissolved.

While we were thus engaged, and every thing passed in a manner the most congenial to frankness and security, the alarm reached us of some / new arrival and encroachment upon our endeared solitude. I know who it is, said our hostess; but he shall not disturb us, It is my cousin, who was here yesterday, and promised I should see him again to-day. Poor fellow! he is engaged in an ugly enterprise, but which is hallowed, and rendered glorious in his eyes, by the demands of friendship and justice. He is a native of the West Indies, made up of all the fiery elements, which are the inheritance of men born beneath a tropical sun. – But I will tell you more of him, when I have gone and received him, and placed him in the apartment I have destined for him.

Saying this, she withdrew, and left us full of amazement at the few and imperfect hints she had uttered. My God! cried I, Catherine, it is Travers, that our hostess has left us to receive! My conscience tells me so: it can be no other. Thinking that I had reached a place of security, I have rushed into the lion's / mouth. There can be no escape for me now. The very solitude and remoteness of this mansion render it my prison. It will be impossible for us to withdraw

221

ourselves unseen; and, if without notice and leave-taking we attempt it, this will only serve to fix upon us a confession that I am the party which this man has come so far, and taken such a world of pains to secure.

No, replied Catherine; we must do nothing, and must wait the event. The phrases that our hostess has dropped are alarming; but they are in the utmost degree vague, and may mean a thousand other things as well as that which we fear. It is a guilty conscience, that supplies us with interpretation, and points the arrow against us. At all events our surest chance is in neutrality. If it be Travers, and we remain quiet, we may yet get off unsuspected; we may have entered the very den of the destroyer, and nevertheless withdraw ourselves unhurt. /

While we spoke thus, our hostess returned. This youth, said she, is in pursuit of a murderer. The man who has fallen by the hand of a lawless assassin was the most innocent and virtuous of mortals, and had saved my kinsman's life. They had but just come over together from the West Indies to England. Travers, that is the name of my cousin, stung to frenzy by the cruel and remorseless act which has consigned the brother of his soul to an untimely grave, devotes his life to the sacred cause of vengeance, and vows he will never cease from the pursuit, till he has made the perpetrator a memorable and ignominious victim to the shrine of public justice. He knows, as he tells me, that in ordinary cases the apprehension and bringing to trial those by whom criminal law has been flagrantly violated, is consigned to the inferior ministers of justice, men dedicated to this employment, and who are cut off from the more creditable branches of civilised society. / But, devoted as my cousin is to the cause of friendship, and exasperated at so unparalleled and atrocious a violence, he judges that the motive, and the crisis in which he is placed, level all distinctions of action, and render that which in other cases would be vulgar and dishonourable, in the highest degree glorious. In short he has laid all other pursuits, and protests that he will never desert his enterprise, nor yield attention to meaner and ordinary things, till he has brought this to its full completion. He knows that the offender is in this neighbourhood; and he has been two or three times upon the point of falling in with him, when by the most perverse accidents his pursuit has been eluded, and the guilty person has for the moment escaped. But he is confident of ultimate success, and is rendered only the more sanguine in his search by the experience of past disappointments.

What a hearing was this to me! A thin partition / perhaps, at most only a flight of stairs and a closed door, separated me from the man that thirsted for my blood. It was also clear that the lady, whose hospitality has received me, fully participated in her kinsman's feelings, and would rejoice in his success. I had therefore every reason to conclude, that the event she sincerely wished, she would have no scruple to assist in accomplishing.

Yet I felt at once that timidity and a cautious proceeding would be the farthest in the world from affording me aid. The only mode that remained for my escape must be, in endeavouring to make a friend of the person from whom I had just received a detail of these particulars, and, if possible, interesting her generosity in my favour. A resolute and daring conduct, as so often happens in a great crisis of human affairs, was all I had to trust to. My manner and address suddenly became in the utmost degree solemn and fervent. /

Hear me, madam, I conjure you, said I; and at least do not inconsiderately decide to my disadvantage. My life is in your hands; I willingly place it there; I see that in you which assures me I cannot repent my confidence. I am the very man that Travers is in search of. You have only to open that door; you have only to articulate his name; and my fate is sealed for ever. But I am tired of mummery and tergiversation.[a] To you, madam, whom I feel to be truly generous and worthy of all honour, I will practise no deceit. I put my fate into your hands. I am not a base assassin; I had the strongest reasons for what I did. I could clear myself to your satisfaction. – But I will not dwell on that. It is enough that you are the arbiter of my fortune; for that reason I am confident that you will not deliver me, bound hand and foot, to my enemy.

It will easily be supposed that my daughter did not remain a quiet spectator of this scene. / The suddenness of my determination at first terrified her. But in an instant she saw I was right. She threw herself upon her knees, embracing me; she cast a look resistlessly imploring upon our hostess. The innocence of her countenance, her transcendant beauty, the purity of filial tenderness and devotion which was marked in every feature, made the scene inexpressibly interesting. She spoke not; but her silence was more omnipotent than words.

You reason justly, said our hostess. I am placed in a cruel dilemma. But I will not do that, with which all my life after I should reproach myself as a base and dishonourable action. I give no heed to what you say, that, if you had opportunity, you could clear yourself to my satisfaction. Such is the deceitfulness of the human mind, that there is scarcely a criminal in the world that will not go as far. He always in his own opinion had the strongest reasons for what he did. He always had the / highest palliations and the most urgent motives. I rely on my nephew. I know the purity of his principles. I am satisfied of the disinterestedness of his conduct. What but the clearest conviction, could have brought him here, could have drawn him off from the glorious career which in a thousand kinds he had before him, and engaged him in the ignominious occupation of a blood-hunter? I sympathise with him with my whole soul. I wish him success from the bottom of my heart. He has chosen his part; and I am satisfied he has not chosen it but for the most undeniable reason.

He has chosen his part; and I am also to choose mine. You have come under my roof. You have implored my protection, and have obtained it. You

[a] Ambiguity, equivocation.

223

employed no false pretences, though you did not think proper to speak out the whole truth. I could not perhaps do less under the circumstances than grant you the shelter you demanded. At all events I have / done it; and what I have done cannot be retracted. You have sat by my hearth; you have placed yourself in my power. By what I have done, I have engaged myself, that no injury shall happen to you while you are here, that you shall go forth as free and unharmed as when you entered my gates. To this I am bound by every tie of honour; and my bond shall be redeemed to the minutest letter.

We must therefore consider how this is to be done. You cannot be safer than in this house. You are as in a sanctuary. The last thing Travers would believe is, that I, who honour him beyond any other living creature, would extend a shelter over, and undertake to conceal from him, the individual he has crossed sea and land to find and apprehend. That you should have presented yourself a suppliant at my door, is scarcely less than a miracle; that I should have consented to harbour you, after having known you for what you are, is equally incredible. / If Travers saw you with his eyes, and heard your name pronounced, he would not credit the reality. In these respects therefore you are perfectly safe. I may make him believe whatever I please.

But this condition of things must not last longer than it shall be indispensibly necessary. We must wait for the dead of the night, or rather for an hour before daybreak, to release you. I will send with you a trusty servant as a guide, who will do whatever I please, and who will tell no more than I authorise him to tell. Travers knows not that there are any strangers under my roof, nor shall he know. Your arrival and your departure shall be equally a secret to him. /

CHAPTER VIII

Our hostess recommended to us to take a small boat, and endeavour to make our way up the Rhine. There was sufficient convenience for this purpose at a village about a league from her house; and the multitude of craft of all dimensions continually passing up and down the river promised as much concealment in this way of proceeding, as in any that could be thought of. Our hostess had apparently no farther interest in us, than that we should be safely dismissed from her dwelling, and that no misfortune should overtake us in consequence of our having been for a few hours under her protection. /

We arrived without accident at the village she had specified. The dawn of the day broke upon us as we reached the wharf which was the place of our destination. By good luck we encountered a boatman, who belonged to the other side of the river, but who had landed a passenger late on the preceding evening, and who was waiting for the day before he should return. We engaged him to take us on as far as Mayence.[a] The wharf happened to be wholly deserted at the moment of our arrival; and, as secrecy and expedition were specially our objects, we lost not an instant in embarking and setting out. We could not perceive that a single eye witnessed our departure; and thus we seemed cut off from any immediate pursuit. We had only a single waterman; and, but that the wind favoured us, should have had small chance of making our way against the rapid stream of the river, whose force was presently increased by the narrowness of its dimensions, / and the high mountains which shut it in on either side.

This feature however did not occur in the commencement of our expedition. The surface of the river was adorned with a number of vessels of different sizes pursuing their various destinations, either up or down the stream, or across it from one side to the other. I had sufficient reason to believe that Travers was safely housed beneath the roof of our late hostess. I nevertheless anxiously watched every bark of similar dimension to our own, with the fear that it might be freighted with my so much dreaded enemy. Though from haste and alarm I was for the present slenderly provided with the accommodations of a traveller, I had not failed to bring with me a small telescope, the use of which was calculated in some degree to diminish my fears, by rendering the objects which approached me more distinct, and thus delivering me from an apprehension, / which would else have been vague and in a manner universal. As the day advanced, the chance of my being successfully pursued increased. Boats with a slight difference in their construction are often found to make their way with a very different degree of rapidity; and, whenever I saw a skiff with a sail proceeding up the stream, my terror for the moment was increased, and I shuddered through every fibre of my frame. My alarms however for the present were nugatory; and I suffered only from the fear of what might happen.

By and by the wind which had favoured us sunk to a dead calm; and at the same time the bed of the river narrowed, and the rapidity of the stream greatly increased. Our boatman, who was a powerful man, was for some time engaged in making vigorous efforts to contend with the force of the river. All at once however he changed his plan, and without saying a / word, turned the head of his bark, and made for shore. I asked him what he was about.

Why, master, said he, do not you see that with all my strength I am not able to gain upon the stream, but am rather carried backwards towards the place from which we came? I must put into this cove, and wait till a fresh breeze springs up favourable to our voyage. Or you may make signal for the public passage-boat, which will be here ere long, and which will be able to contend with the power of the river, though I am not.

---

[a] French name for Mainz, port in Western Germany.

225

This was disastrous intelligence to me. I was anxious to outstrip the enemy that might be in pursuit of me; and here I was compelled to stand still, as if for the very purpose that he should be able to overtake me. The remedy too that our boatman suggested, was in cruel discord with my views. I wished that all my movements should be secret, and that there / should be no eye to remark any thing particular in me, and observe the indications of what passed in my mind. And he recommended a public passage-boat, where I should be embarked with perhaps thirty or forty persons, many of whom it was likely would have nothing better to do, than to observe the peculiarities of a stranger, and who, by their garrulity which meant nothing, might involve me in the most tragical consequences.

As we approached the shore, I cast my eyes intently round, and with the help of my glass endeavoured to ascertain the face of the country. The shore was rocky and wild, with scarcely any vestiges that could betoken human cultivation and industry. The pinnacles of the rocks were savage and romantic; and here and there a fir or a pine, which seemed rooted among the acclivities by accident, bent its head this way and that, the sport of the elements. On one of the highest points I observed what / seemed to be almost the ruin of an old castle; and I could not but wonder how human caprice should ever have fixed on so unapproachable a situation. It suddenly came into my head, that a situation like this would be peculiarly favourable to my designs; and I thought that if, on enquiry, circumstances appeared to render the scheme practicable, I would here at once take up my abode, in a place scarcely less inaccessible than a desolate island in the South Sea. I enquired of my conductor, whether he could give me any information respecting this castle.

Why, sir, said he, I know very little about it. I only know that it is deserted of its lord, who has two or three eligible residences in a more convenient and inviting part of the country. This castle he abandons to an old *concierge*, who lives in it rent-free, one of the conditions of the tenure to the lord being, that its walls shall remain standing, and that the place shall continue a human habitation. Ruined / as it appears, it is of no small extent, and its apartments and staircases constitute, as I am told, a very labyrinth.

And what distance, I pray, may there be from the creek into which you are about to thrust your boat, to the gate of this castle?

The distance to the flight of a bird is almost as nothing; but among the windings of the rock it is little less than two miles; and desperate hard road it is.

And you can get no further up the river till a fresh breeze shall spring up?

Certainly not. The force of the stream is too great for one man unaided to have any chance to contend with it.

Very well. We shall undoubtedly be near, and shall not fail to observe any change in the weather. If it occurs soon, we shall probably join you, and proceed. If not, I will pay you now what is reasonable for the distance we have come. /

Upon these terms we parted with our waterman, and addressed our steps, though with great and unavoidable deviations, towards the castle above us. The path was often extremely narrow, and was interrupted by huge fragments of the rock and other obstacles. At length we reached a sort of platform or tableland, where we were glad to take a few minutes repose.

While we were seated, a stranger approached us. He was hard-favoured, and had that about him which bore marks of no trivial degree of labour and exertion. He appeared to be about fifty years of age. His hair was black, rough, and in considerable quantity. He was of a dark complexion: and his eyebrows were thick and bushy. His eyes expressed a strange mixture of audacity and cunning. He wore a jerkin of leather; and his lower garments were of the coarsest texture: yet altogether he had not the air of a common labourer, but on the / contrary the appearance of a certain authority, and as if he were oftener in the practice of commanding than of being commanded. I immediately conjec-tured that he was the *concierge* that our waterman had told me of.

He accosted us. May I ask, said he, what you do here? It is a rough road you have come, and few persons frequent it.

We are strangers, I replied; and our curiosity was excited by the wild and romantic appearance of the castle above us. You, sir, are probably one of its inhabitants.

I am. I am not the proprietor, as you may guess. But, deserted of its proprietor, I may in some sort call myself the master.

It seems to be of considerable dimensions. Having thus far conquered the difficulty of the approach, may we be allowed to gratify our curiosity by surveying the building, as far as that may be done without disturbing its inmates?

For that matter it has at present few inmates. / Only myself and my daughter and an old maid-servant. The hinds[a] from the neighbouring hamlet and cop-pices are in the habit of bringing us what we want. I say neighbouring hamlet; but it is not less than a league distant, in the plain below. As to the building, it is, as you may suppose, waste and wild, having no other fixed inhabitant than myself. There are however some of the better apartments that are sufficiently tenantable; and there is plenty of the old furniture. But I have nothing particu-lar to engage me just now; and you are welcome to see what is to be seen.

Saying this, he led the way; and we found the rest of our course less steep and laborious than that which we had already passed. We came to what had been a moat; over which there existed the remains of a bridge. There was a flight of steps that led to the building. We knocked at the gate; and an old woman, the maid-servant our guide had spoken of, / with a thousand wrinkles, the marks of solitude, discontentment and care, admitted us. She knew her master's knock.

---

[a] Farm servants.

The first apartment we entered was a spacious hall, which seemed destined to no particular use, except as leading to the apartments beyond. It was hung round with the antlers of deer, a few fishing-nets, and two or three fowling-pieces. The walls were in many places discoloured and mouldy, and the plaster every here and there peeling away, and tumbling in heaps of rubbish upon the floor below, which no one had been at the pains to remove. At each side of the hall, to the right and left, there was a door, apparently leading to some rooms of humbler use. At the further end of the hall there was another flight of steps which seemed to conduct to the interior and more select part of the building.

These rooms to the right and left, said our guide, are what I occupy for myself. They / are perfectly plain and without ornament. But they are sufficient for my use; and, as being nearest to the outer gate, lie most handy and convenient to me. They have also closets and cellars and vaults in abundance, which I do not suffer to lie altogether unemployed.

We mounted the flight of steps at the further end. Our guide had taken the precaution to bring with him a huge bunch of keys, which hung within the door of his own apartment. With some difficulty and exertion he turned the lock, and threw open the folding-doors which led to the reserved part of the building. What seemed to be a suite of rooms now lay directly before us, and at either extremity to the right and left was a lofty flight of stairs.

This house, said our guide, was built partly for shew, but still more for defence and security. It was constructed in the time of the civil wars of Germany between the Catholics and the Protestants, when every castle almost was / possessed by a claimant of a different religion, and the parties were in the utmost degree exasperated against each other. The castle therefore was formed on the plan, that, even if an enemy forced the gates, and poured with a lawless crew into the interior, the persons most sought and principally persecuted, might still be safe from the lynx-eyed vigilance and hatred of those who pursued them. There are secret stair-cases, the entrance to which scarcely any eye could detect, and places of concealment hollowed in the pillars of the edifice, where every thing appears as solid as if it were hewn out of the rock. Tradition asserts that persons by this means have been hidden here for days, and even for weeks together. The whole castle indeed is a labyrinth in which you would find nothing less than the clue of Ariadne necessary, to guide you through its windings.[a]

We entered the suite of rooms. In each room, as our guide pointed out to us, beside / the door of entrance and exit, there were smaller doors, for the most part concealed behind the tapestry, which led to the secret parts of the building. The rooms themselves were in better repair than I expected, and bore marks of having been inhabited at no very remote period. There was plenty of

---

[a] Ariadne, in Greek mythology daughter of Minos and Pasiphae, gave Theseus the thread with which he found his way out of the Minotaur's labyrinth.

old portraits, frowning in pride and lofty disdain, that hung against the walls; and, as our conductor had apprised us, there was no want of that cumbrous furniture, to which the nobility and gentry of a century or two ago had willingly accommodated themselves.

I was enchanted with all I saw. Here, thought I, is a place in which I might be concealed for ever, and from whence I might defy the malice of the most keen-sighted adversary. This castle is built on a spot so remote from public view, so difficult of acccess, and in its aspect so like an uninhabited ruin, that I might probably remain here for years, without any / persons approaching the place, except the obscure individuals who visit it with a view to the ordinary conveniences of its inhabitants. Even if it were entered by my most fearful adversary, nothing could be more easy than to baffle his search, and with the most ordinary precautions send him away no wiser than he came. Here I might enjoy my coveted obscurity, and enter myself a votary in the cave of oblivion. Every night I might lay myself down on my pillow without alarm, and every morning might awake to a day of sereneness and tranquillity. I might almost forget that I had an enemy, and that by one rash act I had cut myself off from the protection and alliance of political society. Oh, with how little might plain, unsophisticated man be contented! In my past life I have been for ever engaged in false refinements, for ever inventing some new subtlety, without the accession of which all my past pleasures appeared to me worthless and / nugatory. Now my happiness shall consist in the simple recollection, I am safe! This shall be a balsam to me every night, and a source of joyful recollection every morning. The consciousness of life itself, to a mind properly constituted, is a pleasure. And have I not besides the society of the person I most value in the world? Has she not devoted herself for me, and shall not this give me a value in my own eyes? Her innocence shall be an assurance to me that I am innocent, at least that I have still that within me which is worthy of an innocent attachment. From the beams of her eyes I will drink in satisfaction and peace. Have I not the means of subsistence? Are not my limbs active and free? Does not the same sun shine upon me as upon the rest of the world? Happiness is comparative. And, when I am disposed to repine, I will recollect all that I have now for months endured, and compare it with my present inviolable security. /

CHAPTER IX

But I was reckoning too fast upon my supposed advantages. They rested entirely on the arbitrary will of the man, who served us as a guide, and who seemed anxious to make us acquainted with all the resources and recommendations of his place of residence. How was I sure that he would be willing to enter into my views? He had the appearance of a sturdy, independent rustic; and such persons will often be found as great sticklers for their rights, as many of those who may seem to have much more valuable immunities to defend. He was a plain man, and likely enough to be contented with slender indulgences and luxuries. As I saw him, he / was master of every thing around him, and had no one to control him. But, if he were disposed to enter into my views, from a master he would be converted in some sort into a servant. I should occupy the choicest apartments of the castle; and it would become his duty to attend to my wants. The question therefore to be tried was, Would he prefer a simple, but sufficient mode of living, in which no man could say to him, 'Do this; comply with my wants and caprices', and he was master of every thing he saw: or, was he a man accessible to pecuniary temptations, and who, for the sake of them, and the supposed advantages they would procure, would surrender much of the liberty he at present enjoyed? – I might however bring this matter to an immediate issue.

I see, my friend, said I, that you have many more apartments in this castle, than you have yourself occasion for. You in fact only occupy the vestibule, and leave the main part of the / edifice unused. May one, without fear of offence, ask you whether you would have any objection for an adequate consideration to yield to another the use of those apartments which at present are left unprofitable and idle?

I understand you, sir, said the *concierge*. You are enamoured of the solitude of my residence, and the many and unsuspected modes of concealment it affords.

I was struck with this reply. It seemed as if the stranger, all rustic and unpolished though he was, had the power of reading my thoughts.

That however, he continued, is nothing to me. I have something else to do, than to pry into other people's affairs. Provided the man with whom I deal is just to me, I do not enquire how he acts towards others, or into his past life. My scheme of morals is perfectly simple. It is all from man to man. What have I to do with mankind, with a mere abstraction, the creature of the fancy? I act justly towards every creature / with whom I enter into any engagement. Previously to such engagement, we are both in a state of nature; and it is lawful for either to take such advantages as fall in his way. In our original state we are each of us for ourselves, uncontroled and at liberty. But, when I have entered into a voluntary contract with any one, it is my principle to be just to the minutest letter.

Thus much I have said, that you may understand my character at once, may know for what I give myself out, and in what points you may place a perfect dependence on me.

The fact is, that the lord of the castle allows me to live here rent-free, and is besides contented that I should make any advantage I can of the edifice, provided any one takes a fancy to reside in it. It is but a queer and uncouth sort of home, attended with many disadvantages, and where a man cannot be provided of even the necessaries of life without some forecast and / some labour. I am cut off from the rest of the world, have no social relaxations, and spend the evening of every day in cheerlss solitude. But I do not much matter that. I have my thoughts to myself, and have no enjoyment of the noisy and riotous scenes in which so many other men place their delight. The lord of the castle is however aware that every man is not so solitary and savage as I am, and is therefore willing that I should take every fair advantage of my situation, find my account in it, and be the better reconciled to its inconveniences.

You may perceive that these apartments have not long been uninhabited. I rented them to a M. Brissac, a person in all likelihood in circumstances similar to your own. Worked up to desperation and fury, he had killed his elder brother, who by law had engrossed the paternal estate, and in addition to that had won the heart of the lady with whom M. Brissac was in love. These were in the eyes of the younger brother / satisfactory reasons why he should assassinate his elder; but they were not likely to be judged so by the laws of the country. M. Brissac fled. He came from the circle of Saxony to this place. He had heard of my castle, and judged that it would afford him the means of security. Our views coincided; and we speedily came to an agreement. Though he had fled hastily, he brought with him a sum of money sufficient for his subsistence for many weeks. He disbursed to me punctually; and I kept his secret, and supplied to him all he wanted. This was our contract. If his supplies had lasted longer, I should have continued faithful to him. But his hoard went on diminishing; and he did not seem to consider what a difference that made in his situation. He appeared to expect that I should go on the same, when the means of remuneration were at an end. Once and again indeed he told me that he looked for some recruit to his purse. But I perceived that that / was all a delusion. How could he be supplied, when he did not dare to discover his residence to a human creature? At length he fell into a state of total inactivity. You will allow that it was then time for me to look about me. There was a reward of a thousand ducats offered for his apprehension. If he had continued to pay me as at first, no power on earth should have induced me to break my bargain. But here was the criminal a gratuitous burthen upon me. If I had thrust him out on the world, he would have been helpless, and some stranger would have reaped the proffered reward. No; I knew better than that. I soothed him, and supplied him as long as was necessary with the utmost attention, just as I had done in the outset of our engagement. But I wrote to the proper parties in Saxony, offering, if I were secured of the ducats, to deliver him into their hands. They came upon him; they took him, when he was least aware that such a thing was in the / wind; and, about this time last month, he paid the penalty of his offence.

Thus, sir, I pass myself upon you for neither better nor worse than I am. My principles are sober and practical. And, in my opinion at least, such a man is much more to be depended on, than the men of high flights and romantic soaring, who tickle your ears and their own with swelling words, but who never talk any thing definite and to be understood. If you make a bargain with me, I will fulfil it on my part most scrupulously. But I give you fair warning that my execution of our contract will depend upon yours, and that, when our mutual advantage ceases, our agreement is at an end.

I was not ill pleased with the plain and, as I thought, sincere speaking of M. Jerome, the *concierge*. I did not entirely deceive myself in his character. I saw how exceedingly different he was from the persons with whom I had / hitherto associated, the friends of my choice. I saw how diametrically opposite his principles were to those I had hitherto cherished. There was nothing elevated in any of his notions. Every thing in his system of thinking had reference to himself; and he regarded nothing with approbation in the sentiments or conduct of other men, but in so far as he was or might be the better for it. Vice upon a general scale did not awaken his displeasure, nor virtue his complacency. But, strange as it may seem, this very circumstance contributed to my confidence in him. As he had no sense of general excellence, he had no motive to dress himself in false colours. All that he said of himself therefore that conduced to my purpose, I implicitly believed. He was a downright, 'bold-faced villain': there was 'no falshood in him; he looked just what he was':[a] or, at least, such was my interpretation of his character.

Beside this, I certainly felt small pleasure in / being classed by him with M. Brissac, the fratricide, a man who, by Jerome's account, perpetrated a horrible crime from the most vulgar motives, and had not shrunk from the basest assassination upon his nearest alliance, so soon as his worst passions were thoroughly roused and in activity. He had in consequence, and worthily, suffered the last penalty of the law in the face of his countrymen; and his very remains were devoted to perpetual execration. I assuredly looked upon my offence in a very different light. The provocation I had received was of the deepest and most inexpiable sort. There was no mixture of depravity and

---

[a] Quotation unidentified.

vileness in what I had done; and, however the vocabulary of undistinguishing law might call my act and that of M. Brissac by the same name, I was fully convinced that a sound and discriminating judgment would place an eternal distance between them.

I felt in the mean time but too bitterly the / effects of the situation in which I was placed. I had forfeited all title to delicacy and refinement. No good, no honourable, no untarnished man would look upon me. I had cut myself off from my species; and my name was turned into an opprobrium. I must accommodate myself to my degraded situation. None but persons dishonoured like myself could be fit for my purposes. The narrow morality of M. Jerome seemed to me peculiarly adapted to the urgency of my situation. He had no fastidious purity, that should lead him to shrink from a man who had done that which should compel him to hide from his fellows; if the ministers of criminal law were on the alert for his apprehension, that was by no means a signal to M. Jerome to desert and abandon him to his fate. – Add to this, I was by no means in the condition of his late lodger, who, when he fled, had brought away with him only a certain sum, which was speedily exhausted. My revenues / were secure; and I had made such arrangements before I left England, as freed me from all apprehension of my supplies being cut off.

I therefore without delay came to an understanding with M. Jerome, giving him to see the advantage he proposed to himself, an ample compensation for his trouble, and yet not upon a scale which should shew me improvident, and reckless in the disposal of my substance.

In the mean while the feelings of Catherine were very different from mine. She was restless and uneasy in the presence of M. Jerome. She was all apprehension, and foreboded she knew not what of tragical and destructive. The simplicity of her nature furnished her with an index that revolted from the depravity of his. She felt a repulsion, – that they had nothing in common, that they were formed of dissimilar and contrary elements. The transparency and sensitiveness of her nature were at war with the hardness and brutality of his. The 'pure and / eloquent blood that spoke in her cheeks',[a] and told every thing she thought, and at the instant the thought occurred, was in diametrical hostility with the impenetrable darkness and obscurity of his. Every articulation in her frame was warm and alive; but his muscles were rigid and insensible like the limbs of one already dead. She felt for every thing that lived; but he felt only for himself. She had principles, which it was more than death for her to violate, something that did not depend upon an anticipation of consequences, that was original and primary in her, and which, though heaven itself were to tumble into ruins, she must still cling to. But with him nothing was sacred and inviolable; he brought every thing to the test of calculation, and chose it or

---

[a] John Donne, *The Second Anniversary* (1612), l. 244.

refused it by the rule of what was to follow for his own advantage or disadvantage.

She trusted at once to the unerring suggestions of her spirit, while I entangled myself / in the webs of a sophistry, which, though I felt it to be infirm and unsatisfactory, was powerful enough to delude me, and lead me a thousand miles astray from the sound and right-onward course.

I and my daughter therefore had a certain degree of animated contention, relative to my purpose of taking up my abode in the castle, and under protection of the *concierge*. She urged her objections with some warmth; for my safety and the end of all my precautions were at stake. But, having urged them again and again, she then felt it her duty to acquiesce and be silent. The affair was most truly mine; I had lived longer in the world, and ought to be a better judge than she of the character and motives of mankind; I was her parent, to whom she had been accustomed to look up for light and direction, when she had as yet neither observation nor experience to guide her; and now, that she was in many respects on a par with me, / the religion of deference, and the comparative fewness of her years rendered it impossible for her pertinaciously to contend with me. In spite of herself however, she still retained a certain portion, shall I say of her suspicions, or of her convictions? She watched M. Jerome furtively; and she lay awake at nights stringing together her own conclusions, and thinking, if those conclusions were true, what he might still do so to put an end to our poor remains of security for ever.

The connection I had formed with M. Morlaix was particularly fortunate for me, as furnishing a medium for my obtaining supplies from England. He knew me by my real name. I had so arranged with my solicitor, that, wherever I might be, I should be able by my single signature, without specifying the place of my residence, to obtain from him supplies, as I might have occasion. M. Morlaix was not like me placed in a situation of peril, or / that demanded particular caution. All that was required of him by his government, was that he should on no account set his foot on the territories of France. I transmitted to him therefore from time to time draughts upon my solicitor in London. He had the kindness, sometimes with less trouble, and sometimes with more, to cause these bills to be regularly presented. Travers in one instance traced my connection with M. Morlaix; but it happened by some extraordinary good fortune, that this clue did not appear in his eye of any special promise; and he therefore did not for the present continue to pursue it. Jerome I was obliged to trust, to obtain my remittances from my friend at Bruges; my feigned name served as a passport between these two. I took care to make it worth while to Jerome, to take the two or three journeys to Bruges that were necessary during my residence at the castle. And, as I have already said, Jerome's morality / was of a peculiar cast. Though entirely selfish in his proceedings, he was in his own construction perfectly an honest man. He omitted no legitimate occasion of feathering his nest; he by no means based his conduct upon any principles of high honour; but he 'held it for very stuff of the conscience'[a] to be faithful to his engagements; he would not, at least such was his present proceeding, purloin a single farthing of that with which he was trusted, though 'only the midnight moon and silent stars had seen it'.[b]

Alas, to how many perils was I exposed in spite of all my precautions! I intrusted both M. Morlaix and the *concierge* to a certain extent with my secret. With the vigilance of Travers and the advantages of Ambrose, I might expect every day to have my hiding-place and last refuge discovered, and myself exposed to the utmost malignity of my fate. I knew that my condition in the castle was to / the last degree insecure; and I could not find how to change it for a better. For some time I escaped unhurt: but at length this clue, as will afterwards be seen, led my pursuers to the very place of my retreat. /

CHAPTER X

Meanwhile it was settled for the present between Catherine and myself that we should remain in the castle; and it became a question how we should dispose of our time so as to render its progress most agreeable, or its tediousness least annoying. We were cut off from the world; we had no outdoor amusements; no places of public resort to repair to; no neighbours with whom to maintain an inter-change of visits. We were restricted from even almost all excursions without the walls of the castle; for, with the terrors that hung over me, I never thought our privacy could be sufficiently complete. It was no matter that we / were placed in a remote corner of the world, where strangers sometimes did not approach within ken of us for weeks together. If one stranger approached us, and if many weeks elapsed even without that, yet that one might be the individual whose observation would be most fatal to my peace. And then of what avail might be my multiplied precautions and my endless restrictions? Such were the miserable anticipations of a man like me, who by one lawless act had placed all that he valued at the mercy of others.

If I had been alone, and under these restrictions, I should undoubtedly have felt my time hang insupportably on my hands. My perpetual state of alarm would have made every instant susceptible, and inspired each, as it were, with a separate life, while my want of wholesome occupation, and of pursuits to beguile my time, would cause every separate portion to be felt by me as if it

---

[a] *Othello*, I. ii. 2. (adapted).
[b] Quotation unidentified.

235

would last for / ever. This state of existence would have terminated in madness, or, if not in madness, in a heaviness and a torment that we may doubt whether the infernal regions could cope withal. It was now therefore that I felt what a benefit beyond the power of words to express, my daughter had conferred on me by the voluntary postponement of her happiness to mine, by her surrendering all her objects in life, and all her pride, to the securing my peace, as far as that was in her power.

I spent a few hours of every day by myself, nor was that arrangement without its gratifications, since I knew that this temporary sacrifice of the society of Catherine would have its reward in the inestimable pleasure of her presence and her communications. We found in a neglected corner of the castle a small collection of books, French, Spanish, German and Italian, and even a few of the classics; and these were an incalculable treasure to us. They / had been much neglected, and were in no very creditable condition: but what matter was that to us? We valued them for the stores of knowledge and entertainment they comprised. If they were ragged and dog's-eared, they did not the less present to us inestimable advantages. If they were every here and there maimed and imperfect, we attended, not to what we had lost by this, but to what we still possessed.

To the classical languages my daughter was a stranger, and it was an inestimable entertainment to us, the one to teach and the other to learn the inflections and idioms of these tongues, the one to explain and the other to apprehend the tastes and peculiarities of nations and classes of men long since extinct. We read much together; and, to those who have not tried it, it would be difficult to conceive the new sources of enjoyment that are opened by this mode of proceeding. There is no pleasure that is not damped and checked by / being reaped alone. To the solitary reader his books are indeed a dead letter. To feel that the conceptions and images imparted to the mind from the unliving and unconscious page strike at once on the sensorium of two, enhances the gratification tenfold. The eyes of both parties meet. A smile of approbation, or a glance of censure springs up on either side, and gives new life to their common occupation. We lay down the book; or we point to the page, and say, What means this? or, What ought we to think of it? The very idea, expressed in words, or only by an involuntary gesture, This is excellent; or, Is this altogether as it should be? – makes the proposition, the fact, or the sentiment, leap as it were from the insensible page, and become impregnate with life. When a difficulty presents itself to a solitary reader, he either slurs it over with indolence, or he investigates it with a sullen perseverance, stripped of the true / intellectual charm. But, when two persons bring together the force of their combined intellect, and contribute the stores of their several observation and experience, while even the difference of their humours and temperament sensibly adds to the light collected in the common focus, then the question is pursued honestly and in good faith, and neither party lays aside the weapons of his warfare, till he has achieved a common victory over the difficulty towards which their efforts had been directed.

But, if this is universally the case wherever two ingenuous minds unite in attention to one common theme, how infinitely were the zest and social enjoyment increased between me and my daughter! The sacred relation itself, when all minor circumstances and accompaniments are in harmony with it and swell the current of affection, mixes with every thought, and colours every sentiment. The mind of / Catherine was genuine, was pure, full of sensibility and taste. We were so accustomed to each other, that we did not fail to understand at half a word the sentiment meant to be conveyed. And yet sometimes the arch and pointed remark, the acute perception, and the deep and heart-felt impression would not be shut up in the compass of half a word or a whole one, but would overflow in an eloquent and well turned period, or would ever and anon burst forth with one phrase or sentence accumulated upon another, till the heart was eased, and the whole thought was adequately and powerfully conveyed. Sometimes too with our graver studies and more serious disquisitions we would intermix 'grateful digressions, and solve high dispute'[a] with sportive interruption, and affectionate caresses, such as might best beseem the father and his daughter.

While we were thus occupied I could not fail occasionally to contemplate Catherine with / an enthusiastic and a religious feeling, as the disinterested being who had discarded every thing for me, and who, while she might have been the ornament of drawing-rooms and palaces, uniting the admiration of the elegant and the high-born, was contented to inhabit a dilapidated ruin on a barren rock, having from day to day and from week to week no other society than that of her blasted, dishonoured, and outcast father. Yet she was contented; she did not cast back one repining thought; neither by look nor gesture did she betray the slightest consciousness of the unspeakable sacrifice she had made.

We had therefore no intervals of vacuity or spleen. Here, alone, and cut off from all the world, we found full occupation, and a delightful variety and succession of industry, earnest employment and amusing relaxation. But for the stings of conscience, but for a sense of degradation, and apprehension of the dark and / uncertain future, I could have been satisfied to have forgotten all the agitating, sometimes the delightful, sometimes the brilliant scenes of my past life, and to have been consigned to everlasting oblivion by all whom I had ever known.

We occasionally ventured, though at the same time sensible of the rashness of what we did, to quit the castle by a small and obscure door broken in the wall, and to wander among the rocks. This we did chiefly by night, assisted

---

[a] Milton, *Paradise Lost*, VIII. 55.

perhaps by the light of the moon and the stars. The situation was wild and romantic beyond conception. Every thing human was absent; every thing, except occasionally the bleating of the flocks, the song of the nightingale, the hooting of the owl, or the howling of the wolf. Here and there, particularly by moonlight, some ambitious point caught the brilliant radiance, or perhaps a long glen was illuminated with one breadth of light, while the depths not thus favoured had by contrast / an inconceivable, an impenetrable, and a wide blackness. At intervals we could observe the bright and silvery stream of the Rhine, that image of incessant life and silent solemnity, here and there but rarely interrupted by a skiff or a larger vessel, which did not fail to pursue its industrious course, shrouded as it was by the stillness of midnight.

I felt a strong repugnance to the idea of Catherine setting out on these excursions alone. There was unquestionable hazard in her venturing on the unevennesses and the ruggedness with which the rocks were every where interspersed; in addition to which I apprehended an impropriety in committing a frail and delicate female form, say by midnight, to the possible encounter of brutish hunger, or of lawless and desperate man. But, notwithstanding my precautions, she occasionally hazarded this dangerous achievement. Once or twice she took advantage of my being surprised with sleep in / my usual hours of wakefulness, and with agile steps and observant senses penetrated amidst windings, scarcely practicable to any but one so young and so fervent of pursuit. She had ever in her thoughts all that she feared from the duplicity and falseness of the *concierge*, and meditated how at worst we might escape from the bitterness and activity of his malice. /

CHAPTER XI

We had resided now some weeks in the castle, and had encountered nothing that should give us occasion of terror and alarm. I congratulated myself again and again upon the choice I had made of this obscure retreat, and began in some degree to lose sight of the apprehensions that had dogged me, ever since the fatal moment when I had surprised Margaret and her paramour together, and had taken upon him a sudden and an ample revenge. One morning, when I had hushed myself in security, and least of all anticipated any molestation, the *concierge* returned to the castle, after having been two hours absent upon his ordinary occupations. / He appeared to be in a state of considerable perturbation.

I am come, said he, that I may give you a timely warning. As I stood just now on the peak of one of the neighbouring hills, I saw a boat with five or six persons on board push into the cove below. This creek is scarcely ever entered, unless by such whose object is the castle of which I have the care. I suspect therefore that they are coming hither. I have always been aware, that the object you had in view in becoming my lodger, was concealment. What occasion you have for concealment it is none of my business to enquire. But, believing that this is the thing you desire, I should think that I failed of my part of the engagement between us, if I did not take every reasonable precaution that you should not be surprised against your will. As I told you at first, the castle affords a multitude of hiding-places, where those who chose it might remain in the / utmost security for weeks from the search of the most expert and practised discoverers.

I felt infinitely indebted to the *concierge* for his friendly concern. I cast a glance on Catherine, expressive of my triumph, and reminding her how much more correct I had been in my estimate of Jerome than she was. As the case stood, I felt that we could not do better than trust ourselves to the fidelity of our host. I told him at once that he was right in his conjecture, that conceal-ment was of vital importance to me, and that I judged it by no means improbable, that the persons in the boat he had seen, were come hither for the purpose of my apprehension. I thanked him therefore fervently for his solici-tude and begged that he would point out to me the place of concealment that he conceived would best answer my purpose.

He immediately led me to a thick column sunk in the wall of my customary sitting-room. / He opened a door in this column, which was fitted so exactly that no eye, but of a person previously apprised of the state of the case, could have detected it. With a thin plate of iron, which he had in his pocket, and which he used something in the nature of a chisel, he caused this door to start open. It had hinges of a careful structure, which might be perceived on the inside, but of which there was not the slightest indication without. Within there were three ascending stairs, which led to a small apartment, with a recess to the right and left, something in the nature of an alcove, and a slight table. The room was imperfectly lighted from a loop-hole above, and in each alcove there was a bench, hollow beneath, and with a door so as to answer the purposes of a cupboard, calculated to hold a few necessaries or conveniences. There was a bolt inside the door of the apartment, to secure the persons within from any sudden invasion. We conveyed / a small stock of provisions into this apartment, and prepared in all respects for a blockade. Having taken these steps, we waited in a sort of fearful tranquillity.

Jerome was right in his conjecture. The party that was approaching was led on by Travers. Determined and indefatigable as he was in his pursuit, he had essayed in a thousand ways to discover the place of my retreat. He had made experiment of both sides of the Rhine, but no no purpose. At length he returned to Bruges, where with no small difficulty he fully ascertained that I had taken up my abode for weeks. The description of myself and my daughter, with the accuracy which Ambrose was able to give it, served for a clue of no small efficacy. They discovered the village and even the house where I had taken up my residence. Travers made out, by a perseverance that scarcely any other person would have exerted, that the bookseller's shop / where he had first enquired respecting me, and the house of M. Morlaix, were almost the only dwellings in Bruges that I visited. He laid no great stress however on this circumstance, till one day that by an extraordinary accident he discovered that M. Morlaix had received a courier from London. This circumstance fixed his attention, and excited his suspicions. He knew, that the way for obtaining what he sought, was not to make enquiries of M. Morlaix, but by watching about his house to endeavour to acquire farther intelligence. He had some advantage for this purpose, as he and Ambrose could relieve each other in their task. At length Ambrose, who happened to be at that time on the spot, marked the person of Jerome, whose appearance was sufficiently singular to command his attention. The old man had the air of one entirely separated from the haunts of men, rustic and uncouth, and who seemed as if he had scarcely ever been in / familiar intercourse with his species. He went into the house of M. Morlaix, and in about half an hour came out again. There was that about him which said that he was a stranger, and that he was brought thither by an unusual errand. This happened on the third day after the arrival of the courier from England.

All these were but slight circumstances, but, in the absence of any thing more definite, and bent as these persons were to neglect no clue, they were sufficient to determine them to pursue the object before them to the end. Once and again they lost sight of their man, and lighted on him afresh; they lodged him in a little inn; and, choosing a convenient time when he was otherwise engaged, made some enquiries respecting him. Here they learned that he lived in quality of *concierge* at a ruinous castle twenty miles distant. They became informed of the story of M. Brissac, and received other intelligence, which added to the / apprehended value of the trace upon which they had got. Having obtained sufficient information, and a perfect direction to the castle where Jerome resided, they no longer judged it necessary to pursue him by sight, and avoided every thing that might awaken uneasiness within him. They repaired to the castle, and surveyed it on all sides. They chanced to encounter one of the hinds, who were in the habit of bringing provisions to the castle, and entered into conversation with him. He confirmed to them the story of M. Brissac, and added, that he believed there were new inmates in the castle, since the removal of that unfortunate person, as he found that Jerome required more provisions, and those of a somewhat more costly quality than he could otherwise account for. Putting these things together, and connecting them with Jerome's visit to M. Morlaix, and M. Morlaix's receipt of a courier from England, Travers fully persuaded / himself that he had at length ascertained the place of my retreat. He had accordingly left Ambrose on the watch, while he proceeded to the nearest municipality, to get his warrant backed by the local authorities, and to procure some additional force, that he might cut off from me the hope of resistance or escape. It was these persons whom Jerome had observed entering in a boat the creek below. They landed in the cove, and were presently joined by Ambrose.

They assailed the gate of the castle with loud and thundering knocks. Catherine and I immediately withdrew into our place of concealment; and Jerome opened a wicket in the door, to enquire into the cause of so unusual a disturbance. One of the followers whom Travers had procured, and who was invested with the emblems of authority, exhibited to Jerome the warrant under which he acted, and said that they were come thither in pursuit of a murderer, / threatening, in case of resistance or concealment, all the severities of offended justice.

Jerome perused the warrant attentively. He then said, It is true, there has been here for weeks such a person as you seek. He left this place only yesterday. I have more than once received persons who fled from civil justice. A variety of petty faults, a matter of mere miscalculation, adverse circumstances which no sagacity can foresee, and to which a man may be exposed without any moral delinquency on his part, may render an individual unable to encounter his creditors; and on such a man I have compassion, and am willing to shelter him from the relentless of law. I do not enquire of a person who seeks refuge within these walls what occasion he has for concealment; and, if I did, I should not be foolish enough to expect, in case that which reduced him to the condition of a fugitive was criminal, that he would confess so much to me. / The man specified in that warrant came to me under specious appearances, and I received him accordingly. By and by I felt that I had reason to suspect him of something worse; and I taxed him with my suspicions. He denied the thing stoutly; but there was something equivocal and unsatisfactory in his replies; and I warned him to provide himself with another lodging.

The officer in whose hands Travers had placed the warrant retorted upon Jerome. Friend, he said, you are not always so nice and distinguishing as you give yourself out to be. It is but lately that you harboured an unnatural monster who had murdered his brother. You sheltered him as long as you could make any thing of him; and, when the possibility of that was at an end, you betrayed and sold him to an ignominious execution. All this is upon record; and it is idle for you to suppose that we, whose business it is to inforce / the last awards of retributive justice, should be ignorant of what every one knows.

Well, well, replied Jerome, it do not signify our talking; and, for that matter, what you say only proves the truth of my story. I determined not to give refuge to a real criminal; and therefore, as soon as I found M. Brissac out, I took care to give him up to the due course of law. But it is no odds. Seeing you do not believe me, you may come in and look. I tell you there is no stranger within these walls, and that the man you seek bundled out no longer ago than yesterday.

241

The party then entered. They were diligent in their office. They looked into impossible places. They pulled about the furniture, and rummaged into holes and corners, chests and closets. They left the habitable part of the building, and sought into that which was decidedly in ruins. They clambered over the declivities, and searched among the caverns. / They at length returned to the apartment, in a column of which we were concealed, and where from our hiding-place we could hear every word that was spoken. They had employed successive hours in their inquisition: and Catherine and I remained in a vicissitude sometimes of apparent security, and sometimes of intolerable apprehension from the nearness with which they approached us. It was like the school-boy's game of hide and seek, – with this difference, that we played for every thing dear to us, for liberty, for life, for all those protracted horrors (supposing us to be discovered), which the hearer himself lifts up his hands at, and is astonished that human muscles and articulations can have the force to endure.

They now asked Jerrome for some refreshment. That is a good joke, said he. If you would have taken my word at first, you would have saved yourselves all this labour. And now, that you have given me the most trouble / you could, you ask me to reward you. – He felt however that there was yet something to apprehend; and he believed that the best way of blunting and putting an end to their activity was by complying with their demand.

Travers was greatly chagrined with his disappointment. It was the confidence with which he relied on the result, that had led him to add to his force, that he might make assurance doubly sure. He lingered about the apartments, and by a vigilant application of his senses of seeing and hearing still hoped to baffle and overset the positive assurances of the *concierge*. Catherine and myself perceived the reluctance of our besiegers to break up their blockade, and were pursued with ever fresh alarms. At that moment a bar of no great weight accidentally dropped from my hand, and was heard without. Hark, exclaimed Travers, does that noise proceed from any one of our party? Jerome boldly said, It was / I, who dropped my pruning-knife; and at the same time he stooped, and pretended to take it from the ground. At length we overheard the enemy drawing off his forces, and unwillingly confessing the hopelessness of any farther examination. They rose together; and the coarser individuals of the party trod heavily along the floor with their jack-boots. They went out; and the wicket swung to its place. Jerome almost immediately approached the column, and said, They are gone; but remain close for a time; they may come back. /

CHAPTER XII

Subsequently we held ourselves the more secure for the ordeal we had thus passed. It was like a certificate of health in a city of the plague, or rather like a sign on the door of a house in a town taken by storm, to signify, Let no violence be done here; all within are friends! We therefore passed our days for some time in comparative peace; and we had a degree of reliance on Jerome, for he had been tried, and found faithful. Still Catherine retained her intuition: she could not deny that in this instance he had been found above reproach; but she looked in his face, and read there in characters / that seemed evident and without ambiguity, cunning, treachery and falseness.

It was some weeks after this incident that I lighted, among the rubbish under a staircase, on part of a torn sheet of a Mercury, or a French periodical *brochure*.[a] By what accident I know not, I took it up carelessly, and was going to throw it down again, when my eye suddenly caught the name, Deloraine. This was in probability nothing; the name itself was rather French than English; nor did it seem that it could have any relation to me. I glanced on it with a sort of indifference; but I did not throw it down; I read on.

To my utter astonishment I found that it was of the last interest to me. It purported to be the translation of an English narrative. I myself was the person to whom it specially related; the disaster that drove me from my country a fugitive, was its theme. But the events were so distorted by their pretended historian, and / the whole seemed composed with so diabolical a malignity, that I had a difficulty in supposing that the facts which had actually occurred, could have furnished the materials to so odious a misrepresentation.

It treated of a murder committed, as was affirmed, under circumstances the most aggravated and unparalleled. It described the murderer as a rich man above the middle of human life, who had bought an angelic creature in her teens, of her poor parents. The girl had previously been contracted, with the approbation of her father and mother, to a youth every way suitable to her condition. They were desperately in love. But an ungenerous advantage had been taken of the young man's being engaged in a sea-voyage, where he had been shipwrecked, and had met with many disasters. Part of these had been heard of by the parents, who nevertheless wrote to the young man, urging his

---

[a] Short printed work, stitched together.

speedy return, and assuring / him that they waited only for that, to make him supremely happy according to the forms of the church in his beloved. He arrived in England, with the assurance amounting to certainty, of being united to the mistress of his heart. All his sorrows, years of slavery, a shipwreck from which he had been saved only by miracle, were forgotten in this earnestly desired consummation.

In the mean time, the old Deloraine, with no feelings but for his own selfish gratification, had obtained in marriage this beautiful creature, the sacrifice to his unhallowed desires, and the grasping passion after wealth of her unfeeling father. The unhappy exile, upon his arrival, seeing the hopelessness of his situation, and resolved to immolate the sentiments nearest his heart to the slightest prospect of tranquillity and peace to her he loved, only sought a last interview that he might pour out the feelings of his bosom, and bid adieu to her for ever. This / consolation was denied him: denied by the obduracy of the jealous-pated fool, the husband; denied by the immaculate purity of the victim-wife. The exile however could not prevail on himself to forgo this last allevia-tion. An interview finally took place in all innocence; on the part of the lady, unexpectedly, without her concurrence and consent; on the part of the lover, in the spirit of an everlasting farewel. Meanwhile the tyrant-husband had his spies. He came upon them by surprise at the moment of their virtuous adieux, and, without allowing the unhappy lover an instant to put himself on his guard, or so much as to see his enemy, shot him at once through the heart.

Having executed this murder, the husband proceeded to load his despairing wife with foul language and the most virulent abuse. He charged her as to the last degree shameless and abandoned, swore that she should never again come under his roof, that he would never / allow a shilling for her subsistence, but that she should be turned out on the world to starve. The poor lady, seeing her lover dead at her feet, and weltering in his blood, terrified at the remorseless-ness of her husband, and feeling that she was without support and without hope, – her heart burst in twain, and she instantly expired.

To complete the tragedy, the poor father and mother, who without one feeling of remorse had sold their daughter, and who were now, when he saw all his views of selfish gratification frustrated, abandoned by the wretched miserly husband, at length became alive to the enormity of their proceeding. They could not shew themselves in public without being pursued with hootings and execration; the ghosts of their daughter and her lover were ever before their distempered imaginations; and a short month put an end at one and the same time to their miserable career. /

Of this wide-spreading calamity Deloraine was the only author, and he alone came off with triumph. Had he fallen under the clutches of the law, his fate would have been at once inevitable and unpitied. Every court in the world would have held that he was responsible for four murders. The unhappy and exile youth he had slain in the most dastardly manner like a bravo; the unhappy lady by his brutality and the horrid suggestions of his tongue. The sight of the wretched lover killed in cold blood, with his wound streaming, at his mistress's feet, could not for a moment mollify his flinty heart. He seized the occasion of this miserable scene, of which he was the only perpetrator, to overwhelm the virtuous lady with the most heart-rending reproaches. Nor was he less the murderer of the misguided parents. He tempted them to crime, when they thought of nothing but good; and the consequence was their being hurried untimely to one grave. And yet this / man, the author of the mischief, came off with impunity. He was said to have hid himself in a foreign land, where he secretly revelled in the victorious contemplation of his unpunished crimes. But it was to be hoped that justice would yet overtake him in the midst of his imagined security. There is a God, whose eye is over all, and who in his own good time never fails to reveal the hidden things of darkness to the indignation of an exasperated world. Add to this, there was a person, the friend of the murdered lover, who had devoted himself to avenge the crime; and a reward of twelve thousand livres was offered for the apprehension of the murderer.

What a scroll was this to present itself to the eyes of me, the unhappy fugitive! The first thing that struck me in it, was the inconceivably distorted appearance that was here given to all the facts of the case. I knew that the world would be in arms against me for what / I had done; but, in the midst of all my calamity, I took this consolation to myself, that where the truth was known, and men were left to the exercise of their unadulterated feelings, I should be found less worthy of blame than of pity. And here I was painted as an unparalleled monster, heartless, selfish and sanguinary, totally indifferent to the sufferings of others provided my appetites were gratified, and triumphing in the midst of unheard of atrocities.

Meanwhile there was one thing in the midst of this mass of misrepresentations, that struck me, which might be true, and which had never occurred to me before. I had surprised Margaret and William together. I had seen in them the most unequivocal symptoms of an entire sympathy. I saw the eyes of my wife turned with unspeakable sweetness and delight upon the friend of her youth, her arms stretched out towards him, and seeking his embrace. I saw / him in ecstacy meeting these advances, forgetting all else in the world but the mistress of his soul. My contemplation of the two was but for a moment; but, in the then sharpened state of my faculties, I apprehended every muscle and every gesture; every hair almost told a several tale. Oh, if it had not been thus, could my heart in an instant have been freighted with inexorable vengeance! I read their guilt, their abandonment of all honour and principle, as plainly as if it had been written with sunbeams. This, in looking back on what I had done, was all the consolation that remained to me. I cared not for the world and its constructions. I felt in my heart that I was justified in what I perpetrated, and that I could have done no less. I knew that my act was in appearance black and inhuman, and that the undiscriminating vulgar would cry shame upon me. But

245

my own heart acquitted me. Come what come might, as the / consequence of my action, I might lament the fatal necessity that urged me on; but I never could repent.

This paper, as I have said, first suggested to me a doubt of the all-sufficiency of the evidence upon which I had acted. When I went forth on the little journey which had preceded the tragical catastrophe, I believed that I had every reason to convince me that the survivorship of William was unknown to my wife. I had been absent only one night and a part of two days. Could it be that this short period had been used for the consummation of the most abandoned profligacy? Might, not, after all, their encounter have been purely fortuitous? Every appearance indeed seemed to indicate a criminal understanding. But who could say what symptoms might occur even in the fortuitous encounter of two lovers, when one of them had been believed to be for years dead? And, if they had met in all innocence, if guilt had never entered / their hearts, if, as this paper affirmed, they had both of them resolved to sacrifice every weakness of their natures to the rigid rules of properiety and duty, then what name could adequately designate the iniquity of my deed, the deadly flagrancy of my offence? The very thought that it might be thus, was intolerable to me. It occasioned a total revolution in the system of my being. Hitherto, if I thought of William and Margaret in my dreams, amidst the watches of the night, I thought of them as delinquents. I was persuaded that they were criminal towards me, that they had surrendered every principle of integrity, that the consciousness of their fall from honour confounded them, and that they cowered before the resistless energy of my justice. Now, if I saw them in my dreams, I viewed in the countenance of each a look of unspeakable reproach, in Margaret that said, I have given up for you every thing that is valuable in life, I have repulsed / every whisper of human frailty, and behold my reward! – in William, that reproached me, first for having ravished from him a treasure that he valued more than all the world, and then that with a most dastard and cowardly act I had taken his life. I awoke in agonies. I could not sustain the passive reproachfulness of their looks; I could not sustain the bitterness of my remorse.

I asked myself, What means this paper? and by what accident or contrivance has it thus thrust itself on my notice? These questions remained for ever unanswered. The justice of heaven only must be accountable for the event. It could not have occurred through the instrumentality of Jerome. If he had seen the paper, if he had regarded it with a serious eye, if he had applied its contents to me, – though full surely he could have no cause to regard Deloraine as my name, – he would rather have secreted it from me, and have ruminated upon / its contents in the solitude of his own contemplations. – It was thus that I reasoned.

Though this however appeared to me the just inference from the phenomenon, I did not the less intently observe the motions and gestures of my host, that I might infer from them, if possible, what was silently working in his mind. It was all impenetrable. The brown and leathery texture of his skin, the stern inflexibleness of his eye, the bushy shagginess of his brow, and the invariable steadiness of his spirit, set at defiance every power of conjecture. Meanwhile, if there were any change in his demeanour, it was certainly on the favourable side. No doubt all his behaviour in the recent visit of Travers and his myrmidons was calculated to inspire me with confidence. His conduct throughout had been apparently frank and single-minded. He had given me notice of the approach of my foe; and all that he did was steady, resolute and unflinching. His subsequent / proceeding was marked with a greater cordiality than before. It seemed to say, By this time we understand each other; and you must see that you have reason to rely on my constancy.

After much deliberation I shewed the paper that had fallen into my hands to Catherine. At first I seemed to feel some terror from the cunningness of its insinuations. But I said, No: surely my daughter knows me sufficiently; and I am myself at hand to clear all ambiguities. I was also originally unwilling to add new anguish to all that she already sustained on my account. But I presently saw the fallacy of these reasonings. The more she had sacrificed for my sake, the more unquestionably was she entitled that I should have no reserves with her. Beside that, I relied much upon the sagacity of her penetration. Innocence always has an advantage in that respect. Its eye is more steady, and its infer-ences more sound and dispassionate, / than those of one whose perceptions are disturbed by conscious guilt.

Catherine however was greatly disquieted with the perusal. She could not but be annoyed with the colours here put upon the conduct of her father. She had never regarded the deplorable violence that I had committed from the same point of view that I had regarded it. She had believed in the faultlessness and purity of her mother-in-law. She imputed no unprincipled profligacy to the unhappy stranger. She believed that all the provocation I saw, had been mere misconstruction on my part, an unhappy concurrence of circumstances which had supplied food for suspicion and jealousy, and had so rendered me desper-ate. She had not followed me, and devoted herself for my sake, because she considered me as 'a man more sinned against, than sinning'.[a] On the contrary it was the gross error I had committed, the very enormity and unpardonableness / of my guilt, that had attached her to me, and made her feel that it was impossible for her to desert me in my complicated distress. But she could not bear to see all this set down in black and white. And least of all could she bear to see it maliciously aggravated, the worst construction put upon every thing, and views imputed to me the most foreign to my disposition and character.

And, in addition to all this, the paper gave her fresh uneasiness and

---

[a] *King Lear*, III. i. 59–60.

impatience respecting our situation. She could not conjecture how it had found its way into our remote situation; but neither could she credit that it had not been seen by Jerome. Then the reward for my apprehension that it specified, was the very thing that, judging from the adventure of M. Brissac, was the most precisely calculated to seduce him. All her remaining serenity was dissipated under this apprehension. Day and night was she haunted with ten thousand nameless fears. /

Catherine now pressed me anew to dislodge, and to seek another shelter. But I obstinately resisted her expostulations. I observed that, If I had previously conceived a confidence in Jerome, a confidence fully justified by the event, I was authorised in entertaining a still ampler confidence by what had recently occurred. We had found by actual experiment how felicitously the castle was adapted for secrecy, we had found Travers and all his myrmidons baffled. He had visited the castle, and by the fidelity of Jerome had been sent away, bootless as he came.

We accordingly still continued for one week and another without molestation. We fell into our usual occupations; and I could even perceive that Catherine, though still haunted with qualms and apprehensions, yet from day to day recovered a greater serenity.

In the course of the second week I was seized with an inflammatory distemper, which for two days confined me to my bed. By the / application of proper medicines however I recovered more rapidly than might have been expected. On the third day the weather for several hours had been insufferably hot, which in the afternoon was succeeded by a sober, heavy, perpendicular rain, giving a freshness to every surrounding object, and a remarkably exhilarating sweetness to the air. The evening after the rain was particularly beautiful, and irresistibly invited me to partake of its genial influence. The declivity of the rock caused the rain to run off immediately, so as to enable me to partake of the invigorating qualities of the shower without being exposed to any of its inconveniencies. Catherine however was that evening detained within the castle, about some trivial task which she was uncommonly earnest to finish. For my part I for the moment felt a gratification in being alone. A pleasing languor, the effect of my fever, the fever itself having vanished, hung about me; and I experienced / that freshness of sensation, to which robust health is a stranger, and which comes over one like the inspiration of heaven, after a fit of sickness. /

CHAPTER XIII

I opened the small door broken in the wall which I formerly mentioned, and stepped out upon the rugged and irregular ground which forms the descent of the rock. I viewed the parting splendours of the closing day, already more than half extinct, and which every moment yielded a further step to the ashy tint of evening. A life-giving breeze played upon my cheek and my forehead. Presently the evening-star came, to assert its prerogative as precursor of the host of heaven. At that moment all grief, all sorrow, all remorse and reproach of things past, seemed to pass away from me. I / was like a new-born child, conscious only of internal sensation, swallowed up in the calm abstraction of existence. This did not last more than a quarter of an hour. But it was like a solitary green island, firm and immovable under the foot of the stranger, in the midst of the never-reposing waves of a tumultuous sea. I gave myself up to it; and it seemed an earnest of everlasting existence.

When I woke from this delicious reverie, I found that I was still almost under the walls of the castle. I had perhaps neither moved hand nor foot from its commencement to its close. I had previously proceeded in an oblique direction, and now perceived that I was rather under the northern than the eastern aspect of the castle. I applied myself to regain the door by which I had left its walls. In attempting to accomplish this I made a small circuit of a part of the fortification. It was now almost / totally dark; and every thing was as still as death. The ground I trod was of pulverised earth, and my steps were soundless.

I approached a buttress; and, as I approached, could hear the sound of human voices on the other side. I paused for a moment from an impulse of curiosity, and thinking whether the subject of their talk could possibly have reference to me. They conversed in somewhat of an under-key, as men almost always do when their talk is in the nature of conspiracy, even though there should be not the smallest probability of their being overheard. The buttress however was a convenient screen for me, enabling me to advance almost close to the speakers without the risk of being perceived. The evening was remarkably still; so that scarcely a syllable could be uttered by either, without its being conveyed to my ear.

I would not, said Jerome, have thought of a thing of the sort, if it had not been for that / paper. But I never heard of any thing so cold-blooded and atrocious as this man; and I shall feel that I have done a meritorious act by ridding the earth I tread, of such a villain. There can be no mistake of this being the very man?

249

I am sure of it, replied the other. I came from England for the very purpose of apprehending him. But, if not, there is no harm done. I want Deloraine, and him only. I bear no animosity against any other living mortal. If I find that this is not Deloraine, I will not hurt a hair of his head.

I should be mainly sorry to be wrong. I stand upon my character, and would not but be faithful to the very letter of my engagement, to any thing that deserved the name of a man.

But where is he? He is harboured in this very castle?

I will not tell you where he is. He is not far distant; and I can presently put him into / your hands. But, without my aid and consent, you can never meet with him. He is as safe, as if he were hid in the bottom of the sea. But you are sure the reward is twelve thousand livres? I could not take a farthing less.

You may depend upon it. Give yourself no uneasiness. But lead me to him. Do not trifle time.

Soft you, sir. Where is the cash? I must see it. You must count it out to me. I depend upon no promises. I have nothing to do with paper. Gold, and gold only, can make me stir a step.

You shall have it to-morrow. But in the mean time let us secure his person. I count every minute an age, till I have him in my hands.

Excuse me; but you shall have no performance to-day, to be paid for to-morrow. What do I know of you, Mr Travers, or whatever may be your name? You may be as much to / be relied on as the bank of Amsterdam, or you may be a man of air, to be puffed away with a breath. No, sir; I am not to be had so.

Well then, said Travers. I will go to the nearest free-town. It is but a few miles. I will be with you by ten to-morrow. But in the mean time, if the criminal should escape?

Be under no concern about that. I am an old bird; and not to be caught with chaff.

Farewell then: remember ten.

At ten I am yours. The dial is not so sure to the sun, as I am to be on the spot, and in all readiness.

Saying thus, they parted; and I was left in silence and solitude.

What were my feelings in having overheard this conversation? My blood tingled: every atom and fibre within me had a life of its own. Here I stood on the brink of destruction. All my precautions, all my anxieties were dissolved, like 'a thread of tow,[a] when it touches / the fire'.[b] I felt already as if the iron, which dispassionate and ice-blooded policy has hammered out, had embraced my ancles and my wrists. I did not so properly anticipate, as pass through, my apprehension, my being embarked for England, thrust into a post-chaise between two thief-takers, and delivered up to the jailor, the bars of my

---

[a] Unworked fibre of flax, jute or hemp.
[b] Judg. 16: 9 (adapted).

dungeon, the dock of the session-house, and all the dreadful formalities which are concluded with the scaffold and the gallows. By how rare an accident had I sallied out alone at the small and obscure door of the castle, and approached the buttress at the very moment to hear what I had heard! And, but immediately before, I had rocked myself in the most unsuspecting security, a security which is perhaps always the precursor of the hurricane and the earthquake.

I re-entered the castle by the door by which I had quitted it. Is it not strange? – Here dwelt the Judas,[a] that had sworn to deliver me / up to assured destruction, and I placed myself consciously, and with my eyes open, within his walls. What could I do? I could not fly wholly unprepared and naked. I could not leave my vowed and devoted companion, my daughter, to encounter a host of traitorous foes, in utter ignorance of what was become of her father. What would be her feelings? I could not bear to anticipate them. Least of all could I bear, of deliberate purpose, and by voluntary election, to cast upon her such a consummation of her generous and disinterested labours. Where, if I left her now, was I to find her again? How communicate to her the intelligence which most of all she valued, What was become of her father? her worthless father, the pest of the earth, the blight and the curse of her invaluable existence?

I entered the apartment, where sat Catherine, having just completed the task she had prescribed herself. She looked up, and saw immediately / the tokens of the extraordinary revolution that had passed within me. I said:

Catherine, there is but a step between me and death. Travers was this moment at the castle. Jerome has agreed to give me up. All that you suspected, all that you feared, is realised.

I told her every thing I had heard, that Travers had gone, to be here again at ten in the morning with the promised reward, and doubtless with such a reinforcement as to make my escape impossible. Knowing this, I had returned into the lion's den, and placed myself within his fangs, rather than subject my child to all she would have felt at the disappearance of her father, and not knowing what had become of him.

Catherine was cruelly shocked at the intelligence I brought her. The effect however was somewhat diminished to her by the circumstance of her being always suspicious and / on the alert, anticipating what had now actually happened. Add to which, her sportless soul and her well-balanced mind gave her at all times unspeakably the advantage of me. We felt at once that it was necessary for us to conduct ourselves just in our usual manner, and not to take the slightest step, till Jerome had retired to rest, and we had reason to conclude him already in the arms of sleep. We counted the clock; we watched the minute-hand; and we said, So many hours, and quarters of an hour, and our oppressors will be upon us. We might have retired into our hiding-place, and

---

[a] Judas Iscariot, the betrayer of Jesus Christ. See Matt. 26: 14–16.

have shot the bolt; but Jerome knew every nook and recess of the castle, and all our precautions would have been unavailing.

We had nothing for it but to get out of the chateau by the same passage by which I had just entered it, and which was used by no one but ourselves. It fortunately happened, as I / have already said, that the apartments of the *concierge* were detached, and at a distance from those we occupied. He came to us before he retired to rest, said he was glad to see I was better of my fever, and wished us a good-night. As he shut the door after him, I heard a slight sound, which could scarcely be that of a bolt. I dared not try the door immediately; and the impression was so inconsiderable, that the minute after I had forgotten it.

After a brief pause, we put together a few necessaries, and the little provision of money we had by us. We waited more than an hour and a half till the dead of the night. I then went to the door of our apartment leading into the hall, and was petrified at finding that it was locked on the outside. I now for the first time recollected the brief and uncertain sound that had immediately succeeded Jerome's departure.

Here then, at least as our jailor believed, we / were secured, shut up as in a pen, or like wild beasts in a cage, helpless and without resource, till it should please him to open our place of confinement, and deliver me up at once into the hands of my destroyers.

Meanwhile, after a short interval of amazement and despair, I began to cast about what was to be done. I had still a respite of some hours, of which, in time at least, if not in space, I was absolute master, and during which no one would contravene me, or endeavour to interfere with my movements.

I had had the apprehension of my fate at all times before me, and had provided myself with the little implements that might be necessary to free me from obstacles not exactly to be calculated on. Among them were several of the tools of a carpenter. With these I applied myself to the lock of the door. It was strong, and of considerable dimensions; and the years which had passed since it was placed there, / and the rust it had contracted, rendered its removal an affair of considerable difficulty. After repeated exertions however, and being more than once obliged to pause in my labour, I conquered the obstacle, detached the lock from the wood-work of the door, and having forced it from its horizontal position, no longer found any impediment to my reaching the steps that descended into the hall. The distance interposed between the spot where I had been at work, and the apartment of my jailor was a most fortunate circumstance. With cautious and wary steps we went down into the hall. All was perfectly still. We had hitherto been lucky enough to occasion no alarm.

After a minute's pause we proceeded to the small door broken into the wall, which once passed we should find ourselves beneath the canopy of heaven. I had brought with me a little lamp to direct my steps. I had taken the precaution to close again the passage leading / into my apartment. The outer door was just as I had always found it, secured with two light bolts. They were easily pushed back. We went forth, and found the air of heaven breathing upon us. This was in truth the having carried a great point, and the feeling of the breeze was for the moment the presage and assurance of freedom and a security from harm. /

CHAPTER XIV

It was now that the solitary observations and rambles in which Catherine had occasionally engaged, were brought into use. She had found a path at the bottom of the declivity, little frequented indeed, but which ran round a part of the mountain on level ground, and which it was to be presumed led to some practicable route. Other sheep-tracks there were insufficient numbers, which seemed promising in the beginning, but which speedily lost themselves, and only served to mislead the person who should venture on them. We descended the rock with wary and cautious steps, aware of the point we were desirous to / reach. We came to the path of which we were in search. This presently divided into two, the one continuing along the roots of the mountain, the other diverging into the open country. We pursued the last. Our object being to place our followers, if followers we had, at fault, we adopted in preference the direction which it might seem beforehand the least likely we should have adopted.

By break of day we observed an obscure village at no great distance from us. We were somewhat weary from the length of way we had measured, and were glad to resort to a place which seemed to promise us some refreshment and rest. We purposed to enter the obscurest public house, or *cabaret*,[a] for that purpose. We were no sooner however in the street, if a few mean and scattered cottages might deserve the name, and were passing certain sheds, which the villagers perhaps dignified with the name of a market-house, than / we perceived from ten to twenty persons gathered together in a sort of commotion. A cry was presently raised, 'Stop him! stop him! there is the felon'.

The words struck us both at the same moment. A secret consciousness brings a thing home to the individual, and is no less powerful to oppress and dismay than the voice of a trumpet. I did not doubt that I was pursued, that I was indicated, that I was on the point to be apprehended. I looked round me in the deepest confusion. Despair entered my soul, sharp as the point of a sword. I

---

[a] (Walloon) A drinking house or restaurant where singing and dancing are provided during a meal.

said to myself, Every effort I make is vain: the decree of heaven is gone out against me; and what heaven ordains, it finds its own means of carrying into execution!

Catherine recovered sooner than I did, and immediately exclaimed, I will go and see what occasions this uproar. It may be nothing to us. /

I grasped her arm in a significant manner, and held her back. If this clamour is pointed at me, I cried, every thing is at an end. Meanwhile do not force these persons to attend to us! I felt at once, that, when a cry is raised against any one as an offender, no matter whether it is a murderer, or one whose only crime is the picking a pocket, the whole body of vulgar bystanders are in arms against him, are ready to intercept his flight, and feel like so many sworn constables, whose function is the summary execution of the law.

It turned out that the object of the clamour was a man charged with having stolen a horse. The man was innocent. It happened, as is so often seen in these cases, that a forward and confident fellow, who in his life never knew what it was to doubt of any thing he had taken in his head, saw something in the air, the features, the complexion, or the demeanour of an individual, whose whole life was peaceable, and all / his thoughts inoffensive and blameless, authorising him in his opinion to swear to his identity with a desperate ruffian, whose only mode of subsistence had habitually been the daringly appropriating to himself the chattels of others.

We took some refreshment in the *cabaret* I have mentioned, and then, wandering into certain fields, at a distance from any public road, seated ourselves in an obscure and well-shaded nook, with the design of considering what it would be advisable to do next. We canvassed various projects; but the more maturely they were considered, the less did any of them appear to afford a reasonable ground of hope. Travers was so indefatigable, so resolute in pursuing his purpose in defiance of discouragement, so qualified in point of expenditure to execute whatever his thoughts suggested to him, so subtle in recovering and following up every scent that was afforded him, and, above all, was so deeply imbued with the passion of / thoroughly avenging his unfortunate friend, that never-ending terror seemed to dog my footsteps, with the assurance that, however often I escaped him, I should infallibly be caught at last. Had such a contest any temptation in it, that should lead me to continue it further? Assuredly not. Had it not been for the thought of Catherine, and what she would endure from the disgrace, perhaps the ignominious fate of her father, I would immediately have surrendered myself to my country and its laws, with the possibility that the issue might not prove the worst that my fears suggested; but if it did, that I might at least arrive at an undoubted end, close this feverish state of intolerable existence, and finally lay down my head in the silence and insensibility of the grave. /

CHAPTER XV

For the sake of Catherine there was still one experiment that I was contented to try. And this was how far, by a well concerted enterprise, I could divest myself of the indications of my identity so completely, that I might face my enemies, and appear in the midst of them without danger of being detected. I had heard, and I believed, that such an experiment had been made, and with success. The most striking examples of this that have hitherto been known, have been of persons happily endowed, either in bodily conformation or intellectual temperament, for the purpose, who, in mere wantonness and the pride of what has been / supposed an unique talent, have imposed successfully upon those to whom they have been familiarly known, nay upon their most intimate and sacred connections, satisfying them that they were the strangers they pretended to be. But, if this has been done in sport, and for the mere exhibition of superior skill, sometimes perhaps solely for the amusement and wonder of a convivial party, who were several of them in the secret, why should I suppose that, when life and fame and all that was dear to me were at stake, when the alternative was a dungeon, public conviction before a court of justice, and an ignominious execution, I could not be equally adroit, persevering and successful? I had heard one of the persons most renowned for this sort of experiment say, I would undertake to keep up this disguise for any length of time; I would go though France and Switzerland, not less successful and triumphant at the last stage of my journey than at the first. /

This is certainly a wonderful speculation. The moral government of man in society to a great degree hinges upon the question of identity, in other words, that every man is recognisable by his fellows. The system of the world is such, that, amidst the thousands of millions of human creatures that inhabit this globe of earth, each one is individualised by his features, his figure, his carriage, his voice, and a multitude of almost unassignable particulars, so that he is at once identified by the most superficial observer. There is something in the outline and carriage of every man, by which he does not fail to be singled out and challenged by his acquaintance, as far as he can be seen. The distinctions are subtle, and, as we might at first think, in a manner undefinable, yet are such as to answer every practical purpose. Were it not for this, what would be the moral and civil government of mankind? There may perhaps be persons so firm in rectitude, / that, if no human creature were privy to their offence, if only 'the midnight moon and silent stars had seen

255

it',[a] they yet would not endure the consciousness of their own degradation. But the mass of mankind are not thus constituted. They are held in awe by the opinions and censure of each other. Reputation is the breath of their nostrils, the element by which they respire. The construction that shall be made of their proceedings is the thought that awes them; and even the judgment they shall make of themselves is regulated by the judgment of their neighbours. We are members of a community, and can be scarcely said, any one of us, to have a rational existence independent of our fellows. And, if this is the case in comparatively trifling particulars, and what may be called the minor morals, how much more essential will it be found in those weightier matters by which society is prevented from falling into anarchy and barbarism? / Who can tell how few are those individuals who would be withheld from invading the property of others, infringing their freedom, or breaking into the chamber of their lives, were not the rest of mankind set as it were as a watch upon their actions, and did they not severely retaliate, by legal proceeding or otherwise, upon the aberrations of the transgressor?

Such however is the constitution of things in the globe we inhabit, that the law of the social intercourse of man will in almost all cases proceed with regularity. Few men have the power, and still fewer will believe they have the power, of imposing upon their fellows by the obliteration of their identity. An imposition of this sort implies such a tax upon the impostor, as would require him to suppress all the spontaneous suggestions of his soul, to put off his nature, and to act under a perpetual restraint. A man must be held under the terror of an alternative no less awful than that of life and / death, before he can prevail upon himself for a continuance thus to divest himself of nature, and become the mere creature of art.

It is true that I was placed in a tremendous emergency, and was driven by the most distressful considerations to make an election of the conduct I should hold in my present situation. Yet my mind was essentially reflective, and I could not refrain even under these circumstances from speculating upon the principles of society, and the laws of morality to man. It was necessary for me however to put a speedy end to this digression, and to plunge again into the stream of action in which I had been hurried on, ever since the fatal morning in which I had taken away the life of William, and quitted for ever the mansion in which I first drew the breath of existence. Involved in this stream, I should never be my own master for a moment, could never act from any genuine impulses, or launch into a free and generous course, but must evermore / be driven, compelled to regulate my proceedings by the dark and perplexing anticipation what would be the proceedings of my enemy. Indeed both parties in this unnatural contest are chained down to a perpetual dependency, each

---

[a] Quotation unidentified.

speculating what would be the conduct of the other, the one having for his object to surprise and to capture, and the other to elude and escape.

I resolved however upon a totally new mode of proceeding. For a considerable time it had been my ruling purpose to make the place of my concealment unknown, either by putting it at a distance wholly remote from the point to which suspicion or sagacity should direct my pursuer, or by so covering it from the discovery of the keenest sight, that the pursuer might cross it a thousand times without so much as conceiving that he approached it. This was slavery. It was attended with momentary and incessant terror. The individual who acts on / this design, should be able to creep into indivisible space, or to make himself penetrable, and impalpable to human touch or sight. It would be a very different thing, if I could boldly face my pursuer, and say to him, I am not the person you suppose me to be. The more narrowly you survey me, the more will you be convinced of your error. Or rather, if, preventing the very thought, I could, by first perplexing the senses of the observer, and then carrying him away with an audacious composure and incredible presence of mind, at once impose myself upon him for a stranger whom he had never seen before.

In execution of this plan I deemed it necessary immediately to pass over to England. This I did not doubt I could easily accomplish, as it would necessarily throw out in their calculation those who sought me, who would look for me in any other direction, and never believe that, by voluntarily repairing to the country / where my offence had been committed, I should apparently shorten their labour by taking half their business on myself. The advantages I should purchase in England, when I was once there, are obvious. In the disguises it was my plan to assume, in the transmutation of myself into the person of another, it would be most essential that I should possess a perplexing fluency of speech, the most copious variety of brogue and intonation, and all the subtle shades of difference in the modes of expression used by persons in one profession and walk of life and another.

I had arranged these particulars of my scheme, and had already set out on my journey, using all the precautions of obscurity and circuitous routes which my terrors suggested, when to my utter surprise I encountered, in one of the first towns of Holland I came to, that young man, mentioned in an early part of my narrative, from whose kindness I reaped / such essential benefit in my state of widowhood after the death of my first wife, and when I was slowly recovering from an obstinate typhus fever, which had reduced me to the brink of the grave. I there related that this young man, whose name was Thornton, had been the son of one of my earliest friends. I stated that he accompanied me, in my journey for the reestablishment of my health at that time through several counties of England, and proved the most accommodating companion in the world. He was all gentleness, all vigilance, and of the sweetest temper imaginable. When I was disposed to retire into myself, he took care not to disturb me. When I shewed indications of a frame inclined to communication and amusement, he had a

257

particular adroitness in accommodating himself to my humour. He could talk
of poetry, of history, of scenery, of arts, and the world. His society had done me
a world of good, and I never tired of it. – Such / was the man, whom, as I have
said, I suddenly and without the smallest preparation lighted upon in one of the
small towns of Holland, at no great distance from Nimeguen.[a]

I had just set my foot upon land from an insignificant shallop,[b] and was
hurrying with Catherine into a *cabaret*, when I caught sight of him. I had my hat,
as usual, pulled down over my eyes, and my cloak close muffled about my neck,
that I might the better pass without notice. Thornton however instantly recognised me, and, finding that I was about to pass as if I had not seen him, pulled me
by the cloak. I would have shaken him off, but I could not. I perceived that he
knew me, and therefore, after a moment's hesitation, judged it most prudent to
change a few sentences with him. My recollection of his exceeding humanity and
kindness to me on the occasion I have mentioned, rendered it impossible for me
to treat him with hardness and disdain. And I believed that his temper / would
not allow him to make himself a means of injury to me.

I drew him into the *cabaret*, and, having seen Catherine safely housed,
accompanied him into a private corner of the yard annexed to the inn. I said:

Thornton, I suppose you cannot be unacquainted with my unfortunate
situation. I am an exile and a fugitive. It is as much as my life is worth, to be
known to any one. Why have you been so imprudent as to speak to me? But I
know that I may trust you, and have therefore only to intreat that you will on no
account open your lips respecting me, or intimate to any one that you know
whether I am dead or alive.

My dear Deloraine, answered the young man, how could you imagine that I
would injure you? There is scarcely the person in existence to whom I am so
much attached as yourself. I received you as a legacy from my father, he and /
you having been old friends. From childhood I regarded you as nearer to me
than many relatives. The month that I spent in your sole society in travelling,
when you were just escaped as by miracle from the doors of the grave, gave an
additional sacredness to my sentiments towards you. I gazed on you with
intentness from the first, when the colour of your skin was dark and inky, and
you looked rather as if you had been a corpse newly dug out of a grave, than a
living man. I watched you when the fresh breezes of the spring fanned your
cadaverous lineaments, gradually restored you to the congregation of living
men, and from time to time brought a faint red into your colourless cheeks. I
left you at Harrowgate to a great degree restored; and I visited you repeatedly
afterwards, when you married a second time. It gave me delight to see you, as
you grew as it were young again, and were reinstated, in your primary robustness and contentment. But, oh, / how are you altered now! How much more

[a] Nijmegen, inland shipping centre on the River Waal in E Netherlands.
[b] Light boat used for rowing in shallow water.

fearful and pitiable is your appearance! In your valetudinarian journey you were feeble and languid, with a sort of premature old age; but you were resigned, and displayed no tokens of inward disquietude and contention. Now you are fleshless and emaciated: but that is not the worst. Your countenance is haggard; your eyes are roving and wild; you seem for ever to be looking for something, which, though you do not see, you apprehend; you are always uneasy, haunted with terrors, appearing like one that has done some terrible thing, the recollection of which he cannot endure.

And have I not occasion? replied I. You speak as if you were not aware of the terrible revolution that has overtaken me, casting me down from a station which the mass of my species might envy, and rendering me an object of universal execration and abhorrence.

Thornton expressed himself towards me with / a kindness and unreserved sympathy, which I had experienced in no human creature, from the hour that I took an everlasting leave of the halls of my ancestors. This kindness had the effect of opening my heart, and healing for a moment the wound in my bosom. I had no longer any reserve with the young man, and led him at once to the apartment in which I had left my Catherine.

Here he explained to us the particulars of his present situation. He had come to Holland to reap the succession of a near relation of his mother, a citizen of that country. He had now completed the business on which he came, and was on the point of returning to his native residence in the county of Essex. Won by his friendship and cordiality, I disclosed to him my new project, so far as related to the putting an end for the present, and as I believed for ever, to my wanderings as an exile, and taking my chance of concealing myself, perhaps as effectually, / in England. Thornton did not exactly understand by what process of reasoning I was led to this conclusion; but he regarded my design with a certain complacency, inasmuch as it afforded him a prospect of being further useful to me. He had a small vessel lying at Helvoetsluys[a] in readiness to transport him to Harwich, in which if I would consent to embark, I should be more secure from the inquisition of idle or curious persons, than I could have the hope of being by any other means. I consented to his proposal; and my consent gave him unequivocal pleasure. We planned that he should go on before, to have every thing in readiness, and that Catherine and I should follow obscurely, and with such precautions as unfortunately we were too much under the necessity to practise. Every thing happened as favourably as we could have wished; and we had the advantage to embark without obstacle or accident. /

---

[a] Hellevoetsluis, a port in SW Netherlands near Rotterdam. William Prince of Orange embarked here for his 'invasion' of England at Torbay in 1688.

CHAPTER XVI

We hastened to the paternal residence of Thornton in the hundred of Ten-dring, remote from any public road, but lying in a bird's flight nearly in the middle, a little however to the south, between Harwich and Colchester. It was a low and ancient building, embosomed in trees, so as to be nearly invisible, till you came somewhat abruptly upon an obscure avenue leading immediately to the door of the house. It had battlements, and a dry ditch, which had formerly been a moat. Scarcely any one ever approached this residence, unless persons who had express business with its inhabitants, either tenants to the lord of the / manor, or persons from the nearest town who supplied them with such provi-sions as were not the growth of the soil. Visitors there were few; for the young man had but lately come to the estate; and, almost ever since he succeeded to the property, he had been absent on the continent, in Holland, and elsewhere. The extreme obscurity and solitude of the mansion were inexpressibly soothing to me; and the kindness of the owner was balm to my hurt mind, and a draught of the most salutary nature, bringing at least a temporary oblivion to my woes.

Thornton was incessant in his efforts to reconcile me to myself. He said, Nothing could be more unjust, than to impute any thing criminal to me, or that I should take remorse to myself, for the unfortunate deed I had perpetrated. The man I killed was undoubtedly the object of the first passion of my wife, the only person that had awakened in her the genuine / sentiment of love. How they came into the situation in which I found them, had, he understood, been disputed. It was however undeniable, that they were swallowed up in each other, forgetful of all other considerations, and this not in a corner, but in the open face of heaven. This spectacle presented itself to me on my approach to my own house, after the absence of a day and a night. I could not have been a man, if I had not been transported out of myself at the sight. There was no time for deliberation, not an inch of place given for the exercise of the freedom of will. The act was an irresistible necessity, and flowed from an uncontrolable impulse. There was no alloy of malice or forethought. It had in it no mixture of infirmity or weakness, but merely stamped me a man in the truest and most honourable sense. If such then was the just description of the deed, no unfortunate consequence that followed upon it could alter its / nature. If the same act that took away the life of her paramour, also brought to a premature close the existence of Margaret, if ultimately it hurried to the tomb her unfortunate parents, still the cause remained the same. It is weakness and folly, to judge of an act by its collaterals and consequents. I had been guilty of no atrocity. My mind was spotless. From my youth upward I had been without a fault. My dispositions had been such as to engage every one that knew me to love me. And it was absurd to suppose, that one deed, and that sufficiently justified by circumstances, and in fact unavoidable, should involve me in the bitterness of self-condemnation and hatred, or render me a fit object for the unfavourable verdict and hostility of my fellow-men.

It was thus that Thornton, in the generosity of his soul, and the tenderness and affection of his spirit, sought to appease the deadly shock I had received. And it was so new to me to be / treated with kindness, and sympathy, or with an approbation however qualified, by any one but the dear relative who had devoted herself to my consolation and aid, that it breathed as it were a new life into my dry bones. I walked up and down in the saloon of my friend, and felt myself at home. I cast my eyes on his servants, without seeing one individual who looked askew upon me, who had heard a syllable whispered to my disadvantage, or of whom I could form the imagination that he would betray me. (There was, as will appear hereafter, one exception to this.) I was in a new world. I was as if I had at last come ashore in a remote island in the Pacific Ocean, where every thing talked of calm and repose, where all the inhabitants were innocent, affectionate and confiding, and entertained not a doubt that I was as spotless as themselves. I had left my adversary on the banks of the Rhine, prying narrowly into every corner of the castle of the *concierge*, and remaining, / as I trusted, without a hint that should lead him to suspect that I had crossed the North Sea, or had conceived the audacious and desperate project of voluntarily returning to my native country, the very country whose laws I had so grievously offended. Thus for a few days I felt myself lightened of the oppressive weight, which I had been condemned to carry about with me by day wherever I went, and which lay on my breast during the night watches, rendering my respiration tormenting and laborious.

It was not that I was for a moment deceived by the generous sophistry of Thornton. I knew the condition under which man is permitted to subsist on the face of the earth. I knew that the state of a moral being admits not of an excuse founded on the idea of his being hurried into an act pernicious and destructive, without the power of resistance. This doctrine I was well aware would open the door to endless and profligate abuse. An accountable creature must / learn to be watchful over his steps, to be distrustful of himself, and to be at all times upon his guard as againsat an enemy eager to lead him astray. He must subject his passions to the great law of moral right, and must never relax the reins of his conduct. He must at no time take a specious excuse to himself, or allow himself to varnish over his faults and his follies. It is incredible how much may be effected by a habit of vigilance and distrust; and he who does not practise this habit, must expect to fall into deplorable and unpardonable errors. He who allows himself to talk or to dream of a resistless

261

temptation, by so doing enters at once in the catalogue of living beings for a beast, rather than a man.

It is thus in reality that every one is judged by his fellow-creatures. The offender may seek to delude himself with an effeminate and poor-souled excuse; but it is not so that a just and enlightened by-stander will pronounce upon / him. Atrocious deeds are atrocious, however circumstanced and however qualified. He who, without being absolutely called upon in self-defence, imbrues his hands in blood, is a murderer, and stands responsible for the consequences of his deed, be they never so multiplied and tremendous. He is cut off from the society of his fellow-men, and marked as an object to be shunned, to be hated, to be reserved for exemplary punishment.

And, were it otherwise, what sort of consolation would it be to a being of any spirit, and with one sentiment worthy of a man about him, to say that this individual, being too weak, too void of all firmness and self-government, to be subjected to the general law of his kind, must, like a lunatic, or like an outcast drifted off to sea without compass or rudder, be held excused for a breach of those orders, which foresight and good-sense, in possession of the instruments that a state of civilization would supply, would / have imposed on him? This is the true alternative to which a human creature, who by his form is understood to be endowed with reason, is subjected; and the man who does not feel himself 'punished with a sore distraction',[a] would perhaps rather undergo the ignominious treatment awarded to a felon, than be counted a cipher in the community of men, and excused as a creature destitute of the higher faculties of humanity.

But, beside all general and ordinary considerations, my act was attended with aggravations that it is scarcely in human imagination to parallel. I destroyed, it may be, the two most lovely creatures then subsisting on earth. I did this with my eyes open, or at least with such information, and such perfect knowledge, as left me without the shadow of an excuse. The merits of William had been unfolded to me by lips that could not err. When his name was mentioned, when any chance circumstance / had brought him to the recollection of Margaret, in the course of our intimate familiarity, I could see reflected in her countenance the consciousness of his spotless purity, of that assemblage of virtues and admirable dispositions, which through life had won for him all hearts. In what language was it that Margaret had talked to me of her former lover? With few words. She felt that it would not be graceful in her to enlarge me on such a subject. She felt that it would not become her, being now the wife of another, to let her mind loose to expatiate on his praises. But her words were such, of such significance, delivered with that deep and chastened accent, that spoke volumes. Once, and but once, upon an unexpected and irresistible

---

[a] *Hamlet*, V. ii. 229–30.

occasion, she had broken out, and uttered largely what she felt respecting him, with super-human eloquence. No: I had received such impressions and communications respecting him, that, if my mind had not been hardened in ill, / would have prompted me at once to reject all ambiguous appearances. I had the clue in my hand, that would have led me through the labyrinth, and like the sun have enabled me to penetrate every obscurity. To allow myself to be deceived even for a moment, after such preparation, was the worst of crimes.

Then I had invaded the sanctuary of his life in the presence of Margaret, in that sacred presence which had virtue enough to disarm a fiend. I had had no consideration for her unparalleled wrongs, for the unmerited destiny which had pursued her through life. She had once sacrificed the dearest affection of her heart, that in which her very existence was bound up, upon the altar of filial duty. When at length even her father relented, and agreed to call back her William from the shores of the St Lawrence,[a] he perished, or appeared to perish, in her sight, a victim to the remorseless waves. It was / through the evidence of her deep feeling, her divine and hopeless resignation on that occasion, that she first won my heart. Yet to this being, so resigned, so exemplary, whom no misfortune ever spared, and who so fully and with so irresistible a grace discharged all her duties, – it was in her very presence that I had the barbarity to destroy the individual to whom her heart was consecrated, and by so doing bring upon her at once the most odious of imputations, and the last despair. So circumstanced, the mildest of human creatures broke out into bitter execrations against me, and her 'flawed heart',[b] overwhelmed with an agony too mighty to bear, burst at once. I had seen these two, the loveliest of human beings, whose attractions no mortal could withstand, stretched on the funeral bier, cut off in a moment by this cursed hand. No: never for an instant did I give retrospective entertainment to any palliation of my offence: / never did I regard it but as the most aggravated and atrocious crime that imagination itself could devise.

I did not therefore deceive myself, or suffer my better sense to be bewildered by the sophistries of Thornton. I knew that I had passed a bourne in morality from which there was no return, that I could never again lift up my head in innocence and honour, that I was separated from the pure in heart, and those that had suffered no stigma or foul reproach, by a wall that could never be surmounted. Yet were Thornton's consolations not without their effect. Severe as I was with myself, and inexorable in condemnation, I nevertheless experienced a sensible alleviation from the thought and the sight of a man who excused my errors with a clemency so unlooked for and so fascinating.

My interval of tranquillity was too short to be envied me, scarcely by the bitterest enemy of my crime. A servant of Thornton was sent / by his master to

[a] River in SE Canada.
[b] *King Lear*, V. iii. 198.

Harwich for some necessary affairs, and brought back a tale which involved me again in unspeakable alarm. He had seen in the port to which he was commissioned two strangers, the appearance of whom for some cause attracted his attention. They had come by an ordinary Dutch fishing-smack as passengers; but they did not seem to belong to the class of traders, who usually pass between Holland and the coast of Essex. They enquired particularly respecting a sort of bark, which had left Helvoetsluys in the preceding week, and which he knew by certain tokens to be his master's. They were curious to ascertain what persons it had brought over, and whether the gentleman to whom it appeared to belong was an inhabitant of the county. The manner of these strangers particularly excited the observation of Mr Thornton's servant.

There are individuals, who seem never to be happy but when they are prying into other / persons' affairs. From the slightest indications, from a word dropped at hazard, from gestures, from winks, and nods, and smiles, they make out a connected story, adorned with a vast variety of circumstances. Sometimes they are grossly mistaken; and, though there be considerable acuteness and plausibility in their conjectures, yet, from miscalculation perhaps in one link of the chain, from laying undue stress upon an ambiguous indication, they get a thousand miles wide in their conclusions, and, while they think they are raising an edifice that no storm can shake, are in reality building a house of cards, story above story, which the first puff of an infant's breath lays level with the dust. And sometimes, on the contrary, they are surprisingly right, so that one wonders, working with so flimsy materials, by what kind of felicity they arrive at so sound and veritable conclusions.

One of this kind was Joseph, the servant of / my friend Thornton. He saw that I was a wanderer on the face of the earth, having no settled abode. He saw that there was something eminently unquiet about me, and believed that there was a perilous secret of some sort belonging to me, that would not allow me any room for tranquillity. He remarked the frequent consultations that took place between me and Catherine and his master, and was sure that they signified a great deal. He grew persuaded that I had done somewhat that rendered me dangerously amenable to the criminal law. Having got thus far, it is surprising how from half-words, and whispers that seemed to signify nothing, he proceeded from one thing to another, till he seized upon something very like the truth.

With this dangerous, and almost criminal curiosity, Joseph united a very kind and affectionate spirit. He loved his master with sincere affection, and, loving him, was sure to / extend the same good feelings and interest to every one whom his master particularly regarded. The proneness to curiosity which I have described, would in a malignant mind have betokened a person with whom it was dangerous to come into contact. Such a one having gained possession of a criminal secret, or of what appeared to be such, would never have rested till he had made an injurious use of it. He would have regarded himself as the delegate of heaven to bring down retribution upon crime. But the kindness of Joseph's disposition kept far from him a thought of this sort. On the contrary, the very circumstance of his having by his penetration wormed himself into a dangerous mystery, made him feel as if he were the protector, the guardian angel, of the person to whom it specially imported. His sagacity, by which alone he had arrived at the secret, inspired him with the idea that out of it grew a sort of kindred or relationship / between him and the unhappy party, so that he would as soon have thought of turning against his own flesh and blood, as against this person. On the contrary therefore Joseph held himself bound to do me every kind office, and by all the means in his power to shield me from mischief.

Actuated by these feelings, he had insensibly joined himself to the strangers upon the quay at Harwich. One of the persons toward whom they were directing their enquiries, pointed him out, as he foresaw they would, saying, There is a servant from Tendring House, who can give you the fullest information as to the matters you are speaking of. The strangers questioned him. He told them that there were indeed a gentleman and lady, father and daughter as he believed, who had come over from Helvoetsluys to Harwich with his master. They staid, he added, two days at our house, and then left it, to proceed, as he believed, for London, Mr / Thornton having accommodated them with his own carriage as far as Colchester. The more respectable of the strangers, who appeared to be the master, asked Joseph a number of questions, particularly as to their ages, tending to identify the guests; and Joseph's answers appeared to be so ingenuous, and his communications attended with so little reserve, that he left the strangers apparently satisfied with his intelligence, and disposed to set out on their route, without troubling themselves with farther enquiries.

All this however was uncertain. There could be little doubt that the individual who sustained the principal part in the conversation with Mr Thornton's servant, was Travers himself. He appeared, when Joseph parted with him, to be resolved to set out without delay on the road to London. Joseph loitered near them for a while; but he could not persist far in this, without giving them occasion to suspect / a sinister purpose, nor by consequence without weakening the credit they appeared to yield to his information. Might it not be therefore, that they shewed an inclination to proceed, only that they might the more completely throw him off his guard, and that, when they had got rid of him, they might approach nearer to the house, perhaps actually demand entrance, where Mr Thornton's servant acknowledged the person they were in pursuit of had actually been, and whence they had no information but his, that he had certainly departed?

I was in consequence more astounded and distressed than relieved by Joseph's relation. I derived from it the unwelcome and unlooked-for intelligence that Travers had followed me to England. I was indebted, first to Joseph's curious and inquisitive spirit, and next to his activity in baffling my pursuer, that Travers perhaps at this moment was not at the door of the house to which I had resorted for refuge. / But this might be but a momentary reprieve. From hour to hour I might expect his arrival. Even if he went forward to Colchester, he might receive intelligence there, leading him to suspect the good faith of Joseph's relation, and inducing him to retrace his steps.

There was no appearance however for the present of these dreaded intruders, and every thing remained tranquil. Thornton thanked Joseph for his caution and promptitude in reply, and enjoined him not to mention to any servant in the house what he had observed, or the conduct he had adopted towards the strangers; and the fellow earnestly promised that he would be secret as death. Meanwhile it became necessary for me to bring my visit to Thornton to an abrupt conclusion. And, as it was probable that Travers had taken the direct road to the metropolis by Colchester and Chelmsford, I judged it prudent to follow a / circuitous route by Bedford and St Albans, entering London by its north-eastern extremity, as I supposed him to have entered it directly from the east. /

CHAPTER XVII

My project, as I have said, in coming to London was, whenever it should be necessary, to turn the tables upon my pursuers, and to annoy them, instead of suffering myself to be annoyed by them. It had happened to me, in the mere exuberance of gaiety, when young, several times to have tried the flexibility of the lines of my countenance and of my organs of speech, in the way of imposing for a short time upon my familiar acquaintance, and causing them to mistake me for an entire stranger. I was endowed with considerable powers of mimicry, and could imitate with surprising accuracy the gait and carriage of another, so / that from the first I found myself in nearly all cases successful in these attempts. Having for as long as I thought proper deluded my companions, or even my superiors or my father, in this way, the jest was usually terminated by my abruptly throwing off my disguise; when the scene was wound up with a hearty laugh at the deception, accompanied with various compliments upon the adroitness with which I had kept up the artifice.

This has been merely the amusement of my boyish years. As long as the exuberance and jollity of youth remained, it supplied, and perhaps not ungracefully, an agreeable variety of sportfulness. But it was speedily dismissed, and presently was altogether forgotten. My character in maturer years, as has already sufficiently appeared, was altogether in a different vein. Sensibility was the predominant feature of my manhood, and this gave a more than common seriousnss to the usual train of / my thoughts and my demeanour. It was bitter necessity only that at last brought back to my recollection the freaks, as I may say, of my childhood; and that, which I had never regarded but as 'a ribband in the cap of youth',[a] I now determined to have resort to, and to try the experiment at least, whether it might not be made to afford me 'yeoman's service'.[b]

With the permission, and indeed at the suggestion of Thornton, I brought Joseph with me to the metropolis. His fidelity had been tried, and was above all suspicion; and his qualities, his prying curiosity, and his ingenuity in baffling pursuit, and putting the adversary on a wrong scent, might I conceived be of special service to me. He was not only qualified by his zeal to protect me; he could also, in case of need, carry the war into the enemy's territories. He was besides acquainted with the persons of both my pursuers; and / he had the happy faculty of instantly and infallibly recognising the person of any one whom he had once seen. His accomplishments therefore happily accorded with the project on which I had determined.

Accordingly one of the first commissions in which I employed him when I arrived in London, was to find out the residence and the haunts of Travers. Joseph could not well conjecture, why I should be so desirous of being acquainted with the abode of a man, as to whom it would be the greatest happiness to me, that he should be removed to the farthest extremity of the globe. He however cheerfully entered upon the function I prescribed him.

It was necessary to my safety and peace that my person should not only not be recognised by the two individuals who had vowed themselves to my destruction, but that I should be equally placed beyond the cognisance of the / numerous population of the metropolis. A coroner's inquest had pronounced a verdict of wilful murder against me. A proclamation had been issued offering five hundred pounds for my apprehension: and, in defiance of these dangers, I had now placed myself, as it were, upon the very barrel of gunpowder that was prepared to blow me into the air. Though, from the length of time that had elapsed since the alarm had been given against me, the recollection of my story and my crime had passed away from the memory of the majority, yet it must always be uncertain when and where the exception should occur; and that exception might in an instant effect my utter destruction. Beside which, there is at all times a body of persons in London, whose profession it is to trade in the blood of their fellow-men; and, if it were once whispered that I was within their reach, the whole of this body would be immediately set in motion to discover and to seize me. /

I had therefore no sooner set myself down in the obscurest corner of the metropolis, than it obviously became incumbent upon me to provide the most

---

[a] *Hamlet*, IV. vii. 77 (adapted).
[b] *Hamlet*, V. ii. 36.

impenetrable means of concealment that could be devised. I had of late worn a covering of false hair on my head, of the fashion which the manufacturers of such articles denominate *à la Brutus*.[a] I now threw aside this covering, and cast a copious snow of hair-powder upon the stubble that was to be found under it, thus changing my black crown for a white one of an extraordinary and uncouth appearance. I placed a piece of a tobacco-pipe upon my gum so as to protrude itself like a deformed tooth, while my real teeth were by this contrivance completely concealed. The artificial tooth served beside to give a lisp to my pronunciation. With an extremely fine needleful of red thread I confined the end of my nose, so as to shorten that feature by nearly half an inch, and to give / it the figure that is called snub. I further placed a pad of two inches thick under my coat on each shoulder, which served wholly to change the appearance of my figure. I also buttoned the lapels of my coat up to my chin in a military fashion. By a voluntary act of the muscles I puffed out my cheeks, and opened my eyes to more than their natural dimension. All this may appear exceedingly frivolous and insignificant in the detail: but the effect was, as I instantly proved in the experiment, that my own daughter, who had now lived for months with me alone, did not know me. And, with certain artifices of speech, which I shall presently have occasion to explain, I carried on the deception for half an hour, and could have carried it on as much farther as I pleased.

Joseph was indefatigable in the errand I gave him of finding the abode of Travers, which in no long time he discovered in an hotel towards / the west end of the town. Travers would doubtless have consumed a much greater period in finding me, since I purposely fixed myself in an obscure quarter. He would however probably have encountered me at last, had it not been for the disguise that I now habitually assumed. Once assumed, I daringly exposed myself in places of public resort, secure that those persons who had known me best, would not recognise me under my present figure.

In the course of Joseph's enquiries he had met with some information respecting the elder branch of Travers's family, who were in very opulent circumstances, and constantly resided in England; and, according to his usual mode of proceeding, he put together the particulars he had gleaned, so as to compose from them a little history. When he had first told me of the hotel in which Travers was to be found, he next dropped a word relative to the information / concerning the elder branch of the family which had accidentally fallen in his way. It immediately occurred to me that I might make something of this story, to aid me in the project I had conceived to annoy and perplex my persecutor; and I therefore urged Joseph to detail me all the particulars he had learned, and sent him out again, that he might add such farther knowledge as might be of use to me in the scheme I meditated. This was an employment

---

[a] i.e. With a fringe.

particularly congenial to the constitution of my agent; and he in no long time brought me a volume of minute information that I might have recourse to in the execution of my project as I saw occasion.

Thus furnished with credentials, I boldly sought the presence of him, whom for more than twelve months I had above all the world avoided. The first person I encountered, when I went to enquire for Travers, was Ambrose, now his servant, and who had formerly been / mine. I could see that this young man felt some strange sensations at the extraordinary figure I made, but without the slightest suspicion of who it was that in reality stood before him. The character I assumed was that of an humourist, puffed up with the opulence of his means, who had lived almost wholly in the country, and had therefore little intercourse but with persons entirely dependent upon him, whom he overbore and dictated to as he pleased, and who felt obliged to accommodate themselves to all his unreasonableness and perverseness.

I was presently shewn in to the man I came to seek. I accosted him with an air of self-sufficiency and peremptoriness, and announced myself as the head of the house of Travers in England. I said that therefore, having heard of the arrival of my cousin, I had taken the earliest opportunity to call upon him, and offer him my protection. Travers, who felt all the / impetuousness and independent spirit of a West Indian, and did not understand that he was to be in a state of subordination to any one, was utterly confounded with the nature of my address. He several times attempted to assert his equality; but at every turn I cut him short, and begged that he would consider my great condescension in being willing to patronise him. My manner was that of a person totally unaccustomed to listen to more than three words from any lips but his own, and endowed with the highest degree of self-conceit and absurdity. At length Travers, tired out with my nonsense, civilly desired me to shorten my visit. At this intimation I pretended to take fire, and asked him if he considered who he spoke to, and that I was the senior member of the house from which he sprang. Having evaporated however the first suggestions of my rage, I assumed something of a milder tone, and expressed my forgiveness / of his error in pity to the want of breeding incident to the habits of a West Indian planter. Travers, though extremely provoked, did not fail mean while to be somewhat amused with the apparent singularity of my notions and character, the like of which it had never been his fortune to encounter before.

I left him in a state of mixed sensations. It was no longer doubtful that I had thoroughly succeeded in the deception I had determined to put in practice. But this appeared only a precarious and temporary resource. And it may easily be imagined in what frame of soul, with a mind broken down with sorrows, with my prospects in the world thoroughly blasted, and having the worm of never-dying remorse for ever gnawing within me, I could pursue this mummery of personating a feigned character, and pouring out a stream of nonsense, which might answer very well in a comedy, and where the scene was kept up for

269

amusement / only, but which was little suited to the seriousness of life, and least of all to the temper of a man beaten down by the storms of adversity.

Meanwhile I felt myself compelled to persist. I called upon Travers again, and annoyed him with a no less copious stream of absurdity, the particulars of which it is unnecessary for me to repeat. I met him on another occasion in the street. Coming on him in this manner at a time when I least expected it, I felt at first that twinge which was to be looked for, at the presence of the person in all the world the most able, and the most disposed, to inflict upon me fatal mischief. Speedily however I recovered, and accosted him with the old topics, and in the same inexhaustible vein of supreme self-importance and conde-scending patronage. Travers began to think that he should be for ever haunted with this ineffable impertinence.

Having thus far convinced myself of my / capacity for successful persona-tion, my mind ran on different disguises in which I did not doubt to be equally fortunate. But I felt that this would be too dangerous an experiment. Per-suaded as I was that I could play characters very dissimilar to each other in equal perfection, I yet suspected that a mind, so acute as I understood that of Travers to be, would remark among them all a single vein, a similarity of artifice, that would suggest a suspicion, which, once set a-going, might set fire to a train, and blow all my fine-spun contrivances in the air. This sort of personating a variety of characters, in the full execution of which I felt con-vinced that the chances would be an hundred to one in my favour, might be excellent for sport, and when to be detected or not would be a slight question. But it was far another sort of consideration, where the trick to be played was not an affair of amusement, but for life, and where, so to speak, the performer / exhibited with a halter about his neck, which one false step that he made would tighten round the organ of respiration, and so put an end to his vagaries and his hopes for ever.

If success in the execution of my project could be a source of congratulation, I had now sufficient reason to congratulate myself. I had apparently cut off all clue to my persecutors, by metamorphosing myself into a totally different sort of person from that which I had been. It was as if Deloraine, the husband of Margaret, the assassin of William, the man most criminally responsible for the untimely deaths of his wife's father and mother, were dead and buried. He was no longer a subject of question; he was no where to be found. I retained indeed a consciousness of identity with this person. I knew that I was the true author of these tragedies. But I possessed this consciousness to myself. There was but one other individual in the world that was acquainted with / my secret; and in that individual I could place no less confidence that she would not hurt a hair of my head, than in myself.

I was then, as a superficial observer would say, unequivocally victorious and triumphant. But I did not feel it to be so. At what price was I triumphant? At the price of putting off my nature, and banishing every genuine impulse of my soul. I might think freely indeed (a mighty and expansive privilege!) when I was shut up alone in my closet. I might spread out my arms, use the gestures which my constitution of mind and my habits prompted, and employ the faculty of speech with unstudied phraseology and intonations. There was besides one other person, with whom I might be myself, and move and speak and express my thoughts, even as my own heart prompted me to do. Thus it was in the sequestered seat of my lodging, and with no one but my daughter to witness what I did. In this estimate I do / not count Joseph, because, though I ever found him faithful, and though he was of immense service to me, yet after all, he was only a servant, he had but just now become known to me, and that at first by a sort of accident. I was not familiarised to him; and even had it been otherwise, what sort of unbending of spirit and opening of soul could I hope for or expect with a person of his narrow education, and limited stock of ideas, and whose principal accomplishment lay in cunning, contrivance and subtlety?

The moment I opened my door, all this was at an end. When I presented myself to the view of my fellow-creatures, my situation was no more eligible, than that of a man who should have been bound hand and foot, and in that condition subjected to their examination. I could not move an articulation of my body but in correspondence to a preconcerted system. I was like a puppet, all of whose motions are / regulated by the wires, the string of which is held by the conductor of the shew. No person who has not had experience of the situation in which I was placed, can imagine its insufferable annoyances. The essence of the nature of man lies in the spontaneous obedience of his limbs and his organs to the genuine impulse of his mind. We move as free as air. Our thoughts wander to the farthest corners of the earth; and our language, and our gestures, and the expression of our features, hold an exact correspondence with the march of our thoughts. But to act a part the most in opposition to the true vein of our souls, and for that part never to have an end, is intolerable beyond the power of words to express. To have a watch upon all our motions and upon every expression, and to conform them to an artificial rule, is the worst of slaveries.

To be subject to all this was surely an abundant calamity. And it was rendered the more / bitter by the consideration of the penalty annexed to the smallest failure. If I did not draw the cloak of concealment on all sides close about my person, if the slightest indication betrayed itself that I was not what I pretended to be, it was all over with me. I was like the ass in Æsop's Fables, who disguised himself in the skin of a lion. At first he was triumphant, and terrified all the beasts of the forest into flight. But the moment a suspicion intruded that he was not what he appeared to be, a total reverse of fortune was at hand. If I relaxed my attention for an instant, if any incongruity was found in the part I attempted to play, shame and defeat would be close at my heels. I should be detected and exposed. Multitudes, by means of the proffered reward, were armed against me. I should be dragged to chains and to prison; and

271

the very disguise I had assumed would be used as an argument of my guilt, and would / double the confusion and disgrace that would overwhelm me.

To all this must be added the peculiar circumstances under which a man playing a part must be perceived to stand. It requires a certain gaiety, an elevation of spirits and a determination of mind, to go through a borrowed part. In the sort of character I assumed, a species of swagger was necessary, a boldness that should overbear opposition, an air of triumphant conceit and self-sufficiency. How was all this to be made compatible with my broken heart, my blasted name, my ruined fortunes, my pitiless exile, and my prospect, in case of the slightest miscarriage, of a public execution, pursued with the curses and imprecations of my kind? No; I bore every where about with me a deep and mortal wound. I did justice to all the guilt I had contracted, and hated the memory of myself and my action. It was impossible therefore / that I should long, and still less continuously, personate feelings and habits that were foreign to my own. The malice of the most ingenious tyrant could not invent a punishment so terrible. /

CHAPTER XVIII

Besieged by these reflections, and exhausted with the successive efforts I had made in sustaining my artificial character, I came home one day to my lodging and to Catherine in a state of the most fearful desperation. I had passed through a series of agonies, each one more insupportable than the agony that had gone before; but this last finished the business. I shut the door of our apartment, and turned the key in the lock. I disentangled myself with impatience from the different articles of my disguise. This was quickly effected. I seated myself in my chair, and made Catherine sit in front of me. The poor girl saw that a / more than human thought was working within me; and she trembled. She was accustomed to witness the horrors of my spirit amidst the ceaseless trials that beset me; but, after all she had seen, her soul confessed something more terrible in the present situation.

Catherine, I said, I have come to an unalterable determination. I have gone through enough; I have tried experiments more than enough. I have fled from city to city, and from country to country. I have hid myself in places solitary, almost inaccessible. I have watched by day; sleep by night has fled from my eyes. I have seen in every bush an adversary; every sound has penetrated my soul, as if it were the harbinger of a final conflict. To all things there is a limit. What is the value of life on these conditions? At best existence is but a questionable gift. Many men have found it an insupportable load, even though surrounded apparently with blessings. They / have discovered in it a tedious-ness and a secret agony, when fortune seemed most to smile upon them. And shall I hesitate to throw off the load?

I have borne it for you, my Catherine, when otherwise I would surely long ago have given up the contest, and delivered myself to my enemies. But even generosity and self-denial have their limits; and I can endure the contention no longer. For your sake I have submitted to this last experiment. I have returned to my country; I have endeavoured to turn the tables on my adversaries; I have undertaken to disguise my person, my carriage, my modes of speaking, and my language, with the most consummate art. I have succeeded; and success has been to me the most insupportable misfortune. Oh, how I long for the time when I shall no longer have a part to play, a feigned character to sustain! How I long for the time when hope and fear shall be no more, and I shall / know the worst at once! Despair seems to me the most enviable of blessings. I will hug it to my heart, and be at rest.

I have chosen my part therefore, and have only to intreat that you will give way to me, and not oppose. I will now allow to my adversaries the glory of surprising and capturing me. I will triumph to the last. I will surrender; but, in surrendering, I will shew that I surrender only because I please. I will replace the articles of my disguise for the last time. I will present myself to the proper magistrate; and removing one by one before him these shreds and fripperies of concealment, will shew myself as I am, and tell him who I am.

I could not reconcile myself to the taking this last and decisive step, without fairly apprising you of my intention. I owe you more than ever one human creature owed to another. Your faithful attendance on me through all my calamities, your bearing with my terrors and my / impatience, your surrender of all the charms and allurements that the world held out to tempt you, and becoming the most wretched of fugitives for my sake, constitute an accumula-tion of merits, which, if ever the story could be told to future ages, the world would agree to regard the most incredible of fictions.

I know that the purpose which I now announce will sound terrible in your ears. You will have much to go through. Would to God I could relieve you from the impending distress! But I cannot. I have committed the crime, and must sustain the punishment. It is your miserable fate to be my daughter, and you must submit to it. All I can recommend is, that you should arm yourself with patience.

The determination to which I have come, may seem to bear on you with particular hardship. But, carefully weighed, and compared with any other plan I could adopt, it is the mildest and most beneficent. I take from you an insupportable / burthen. I remove a black and pestilential atmosphere, that suffocates your energies, that poisons your enjoyments, and that will render every day, so long as I live, hopeless and odious to you. You must pass through

a severe trial; but it will be short. You will become self-centred and independent. You will be valued every day for yourself, and I shall be more and more
forgotten. Men will at first remember that you had a dishonourable father; but
that will by sensible degrees pass out of their minds. Your excellence and your
virtues, which will shine the more, the less there is of an antagonist cloud to
obscure them, will engage all men's attention, and put every thing of a contrary
nature into speedy oblivion. Even my fatal error, which had nothing in it of
what is base, sordid, or of deep and engrained malignity, will be in some degree
excused, when I shall have suffered the penalty, and passed off the stage; and
men will drop a tear of pity for the cruelty / of my fate, however they do not fail
to regard me with horror so long as I live.

Of one thing more it is necessary to speak, though I know that to the loftiness
and generosity of your spirit it will be painful to hear. Your father will be blotted
from the roll of living beings: the sooner my name is consigned to everlasting
oblivion the better. I can easily believe that your truly filial spirit will never allow
you entirely to forget me. But, when you shall see me no more, when you shall
know that this heart has ceased to beat, and that this form has become as a clod of
the valley, an insupportable weight will be taken from your bosom. I shall be no
more. But my lands and my income will remain. The inexorable determinations
of the law ordain, that the entire property of a convicted felon shall escheat to the
crown. But there is a recognised and established remedy for that. It is practicable, at any time before conviction, to make over / property in chief to another.
And that shall be seen to. Though your father shall forfeit his life to the laws of his
country, you shall never become a beggar. I will go this instant, and concert with
my solicitor on that point.

I thus disburthened my spirit with an energy and eloquence that would not
be restrained; and Catherine sat with mute astonishment, and listened to me.
But, though she did not interrupt me with an articulate sound, it was plain that
she passed through a series of unspeakable emotions. She clenched her hands,
and strung with semivoluntary energy every fibre of her frame. At one moment
she pressed her lips together with resolution and firmness; and at another they
were convulsed with agony. She fixed her eyes upon me anon with inexpressible wonder; and anon the big tears rolled unheeded over cheeks of more than
mortal paleness. I ended; and she spoke.

Oh, my father, she said , did I ever think it / would come to this? I have
borne for you, as you say, more perhaps than ever daughter bore for a father.
But in all there was hope. I endured, because I looked for a reward. I struggled,
because I anticipated a victory, or at least an escape from peril, imminent and
instant. Uncertainty was the cordial that supported my spirits; and, as long as
there was uncertainty, I obstinately believed in good. It was for a father I
exerted myself; and what would I not have done for such a father? My energies
were more than mortal; I was omnipotent; nothing could subdue my strength;
nothing could extinguish my perseverance.

And now you come to tell me, that all this is over, and that you will voluntarily put a close on the scene in the most tragical manner. Have you the heart to do it?

And with this announcement of your purpose you coldly tell me, that all this will ultimately work for my benefit that, when you have perished, / and so perished, I shall be happy, shall recover my cheerfulness and equanimity, shall become an ornament to society, be hailed with the esteem and cordial good wishes of all, and be placed in a scene of the most enviable prosperity.

I tell you, sir, that I shall never pass the line, which, once passed, is to confer all this happiness. It is very well to talk this. But to see the triumph of your enemies, to see you dragged to prison and to judgment, to count the hours that you shall pass in your lonely cell, to hear that you are brought out before the eyes of multitudes for trial and execution – No; I thank my God, I shall never witness all this; death will have laid his grasp on me long before. I could have exerted myself for you for ever; but passively to behold the worst, of this I am incapable.

Why did I devote myself for you, why did I count all I could do for you as nothing, and regarded / conflict and misery as my supreme felicity, but because I lived in your life? I esteemed you as my only good: to know that you were safe, to hope that all would be well with you, was every thing I asked. We were inseparable; and the deed that separates us will to me at least be mortal. The only thing on which I valued myself, and for which I lived, ever since the moment when I became acquainted with your fatal encounter, was my vigilance and my exertions for safety; and, those concluded, my business in this mortal scene is over; that moment I die. I could live transportedly to know that you had escaped from every danger; but to be convinced that all our efforts are concluded in disappointment, I cannot.

And yet, my father, I do not seek to change your resolution. I do not wish you to do any thing for my sake, if you find the condition under which you live too bitter to be longer / endured. I ask of you one thing, a small thing, and that I feel you will not deny me. Grant me only till this time to-morrow. Suspend the execution of your purpose for so long. Do not ask me what it is I will do. For that time grant me your unlimited confidence. I think I have done enough to merit this concession.

Much as I had witnessed of the excellences of Catherine, I own she astonished me now. I yielded. How could I do otherwise? I, who had endured for so long a time, might well endure for this additional period. It was indeed a critical moment for my daughter. I anticipated that she would not give way to a vulgar and common-place weakness. I believed that she would display a real greatness on the occasion; but in what kind I knew not.

Catherine attired herself gracefully in a garb of sober grey. Her garments were all of one colour, and fell in folds to her feet. Her head-dress was also of grey, and descended nearly to / her eyes. Her appearance was such as that of an order of nuns, of whom that should be the appropriate costume. She dispatched Joseph to procure her a carriage that might have an air of neatness and gentility, and directed him to mount behind it. She took her leave of me with an air of the deepest melancholy, yet at the same time marked with sedateness and inflexible resolution at parting. She pressed me to her bosom, and said, Remember, and expect me with patience! I shall very likely be back in two or three hours: in case of necessity I have demanded twenty-four, and you have granted them. She ordered the carriage to drive through the principal streets towards St James's.

I was astounded at all she did. It was dark and inexplicable, like the prompting of insanity. Yet she proceeded with a style of firmness, and bespeaking clear conception, that awed me. It was as if an impenetrable veil / was spread between me and the approaching future, which I could not, and which I wanted the boldness to endeavour to look through. But, though I felt awed, I was nevertheless destitute of hope: and no sooner had Catherine left me, than I called up in order the steps I had announced my determination to take, and the results to which they might be expected to lead.

I revolved with horror and commiseration all that Catherine had told me – that it was impossible for her to survive the execution of my purpose. I knew that she was not a person to say this lightly, or to utter an empty threat for the mere purpose of deterring me from what I meditated. Yet I entertained a hope that the issue would not be thus tragical. I harboured a faith in the strength and elasticity of youth, to recover from what seemed to be desperate, to clothe itself afresh with the sinews of energy, and to break out, even like the glorious / sun after the blackest tempest and the most tremendous storm.

But, be that as it would, this was a part of my miserable fate, from which there was no escaping. I had intended only the death of William, if I could even be said to have intended that: but what I did, inevitably involved the premature destruction of my wife and of her parents. And it might be, that I should indeed occasion a broken heart to my only off-spring, to the person whom I now singly valued in all the world. What could I do? It did not depend upon myself. If by any effort of mine I could have instantly dispelled the fate that hung over me, would it not have inspired into me the happiness of Gods to do it? But I could not struggle on for ever without hope of an end. I must cut the Gordian knot[a] at once. And even, considering the question only as related to my daughter, would it not be better that she should die at once (if die she / must) in the full prime of her youth, than that she should go on without end, through a series of perpetual privations and ever-new alarms, cut off from all society and comfort, and with no associate but her broken-hearted and guilt-blasted father? /

---

[a] In Greek legend, a complicated knot tied by King Gordius of Phrygia, which Alexander the Great proceeded to cut with a sword.

CHAPTER XIX

I will relate every thing, not in the order in which I learned it, but in that in which it actually passed. Catherine had gone but a few streets, when she stopped the carriage, and told Joseph of her purpose, which was to seek the presence of Travers. She met Ambrose at the door of the hotel, who of course instantly knew her. She directed him without delay to lead her to his master. There was that in her manner, which left him no choice but of implicit obedience. She approached Travers with firmness. He was awed, almost fascinated with her appearance, and felt at once that the beautiful, the almost superhuman figure that / approached him, was come on no trivial errand. She shut the door; and Travers and she were alone.

I am the daughter of Deloraine, she said, of the man to whom you have vowed immortal hatred, and whom for many months you have hunted, with the determination to bring upon him the death of a murderer. You have given yourself up to this single pursuit. You have thought that you had no other business or design in life, till the vengeance for the unmerited fate of your friend had been completely executed.

I have come to you with the full knowledge of this, with the perfect consciousness that you feel your resolution to be as unremovable as the pillars of the creation. Yet I have come with the persuasion that you are a man, accessible to human feelings, the pleas of justice, and that you have bowels of clemency and mercy. It is scarcely a feminine office that I / have undertaken; but, urged by the holiest of earthly duties, and strong in the principles of eternal truth, I have not hesitated. Why I undertook this no sooner, I can scarcely tell. It is only circumstances of irresistible energy, that call up all the springs of the human mind, and cause us to see things apart from the hazy atmosphere which is the ordinary dwelling-place of mortals, and in the transparency that is the prerogative of a divine nature.

What is it my father has done? He married a woman, whom he and every one believed to have been freed by death from all former ties. He entered with her into the most sacred of human bonds, that from which all the other relations of society take their source. He found her poor; he was himself rich. He took her according to God's ordinance, 'to love and to cherish, till death should divide them'.[a] He

---

[a] Solemnization of Matrimony, Betrothal, Book of Common Prayer (re-expressed).

engaged himself to her in conjugal duty; he 'endowed her with his worldly possessions'.[a] / Margaret appeared the most amiable and faultless of women. She amply discharged the offices of her station; she seemed to live only that she might anticipate his desires, and watch for his comfort.

Then came the trial. The grave, so to express myself, opened, and yielded up its dead. No one perhaps was to be blamed in this. William had been seen by several apparently to perish in the tempestuous sea. No one suspected, imagined, that he had survived this catastrophe. If he had, would he not have been heard of? Not days and months only, but year after year had elapsed, and all was deep and unbroken silence.

This however was fallacious: William lived. If death had in it no certainty, if those who perished could rise again, 'with twenty mortal murders on their crowns',[b] what havock would this make in the scene of human life! It is no matter how loved, how valued once, were / those who have ceased to live, – with what deep sorrow, and heart-breaking lamentation, their loss was deplored; it is the condition of human life, that the place that knew them should know them no more. It is the condition of human life, that its connections and affairs, its changes and succession of property, its contracts and engagements, should go on in never interrupted succession. And, if the dead that were once most loved, could repass the boundary that separates them from living, there would no longer be room for them found in the community of mankind.

Well: this event, which in the usual train of human affairs happens to none, happened to my father. From the hour that he received the astounding intelligence that William lived, all happiness, all tranquillity was at an end with him. He was to keep this, once much desired, now baleful and peace-destroying intelligence from his wife, not for his own sake / only, but for hers: for what would she become with this double claim upon her, on the one side consecrated with all the ceremonies that mankind in their care for the general welfare have invented, on the other with the endearments of a first love, and the fondness that no subsequent occurrences and fortunes could obliterate? All happiness and tranquillity were at an end with my father. Every rising and setting sun might bring the news that should baffle his wisest precautions.

After the compulsory absence of a day and a night Deloraine returned to his own habitation. The first spectacle that presented itself to his sight, was William and Margaret seated together on the turf on the outside of the wall of his garden. Here then was an end at once to that secret to which he looked for salvation. But it was worse than this. Their attitudes, the disposition of every part of the body, shewed, that affection, a mutual, entire melting / of souls, occupied them. What had passed in the short interval of Deloraine's absence to account for what he saw, he knew not. What mattered what had passed? What

---

[a] Solemnization of Matrimony, Wedding, Book of Common Prayer (re-expressed).
[b] *Macbeth*, III. iv. 81.

he saw was enough. He leaped from his carriage; he had pistols at hand; he lodged a bullet in the heart of the intruder. This was the extent of his offending. He had meditated no act of violence before; he harboured, he perpetrated no malice after.

I know how the law construes all this. It scorns to take account of previous circumstances, of any of the strings that twine themselves round the human heart. It comes with its scales, and weighs every thing to the partition of a hair. It comes with its measures, and takes account of roods, and yards, and inches of space, and reckons hours, and quarters of an hour, and minutes, and seconds of time. And it finds in the present case the required sum of space and time, and pronounces / a crime of malice prepense,[a] and a verdict of wilful murder. It hurries the actor therefore to an ignominious death. – But I speak to a man, who has not by long poring on precedents and cases purged himself of all sentiments of humanity, to a West Indian, who has quick pulses beating in his heart, a 'soul made of fire, an offspring of the sun'.[b]

I know how hard was the case of William, how infinite his sufferings, how unparalleled his merits. I know the perfect friendship that subsisted between you and him, and the grounds of that friendship. I do not wonder at the sharpness with which you felt his destruction, or at the eagerness with which you pursued its revenge. But William suffers no more. He is happy in this, that he is cut off from the evil to come. He has no consciousness of your revenge; and, if he had, such was the placidness and philanthropy of his nature, he would have no pleasure in it. The dead, William, / Margaret, and her parents, are all dead. 'There is no work, nor device, nor wisdom, nor knowledge in the grave'.[c] Its tenants are unconscious of all that we do, and reap no benefit from any thing we may achieve.

Suffer me then, thou true friend, inspired with so deep a feeling of injuries and benefits, to call off thy attention from them, and to turn it on the persons who live, and who are largely capable of joy and of agony. Deloraine, however unfortunate in the offence he has committed, has not deserved the retribution you seek. He has no felonious qualities. He is neither profligate nor malicious. Though he shed the blood of William, he did not imbrue his hands in guilt. He has contracted no moral defilement. He could not fail to be sufficiently un-happy in the memory of the wide-spreading and tragical consequences of the act into which he was hurried. What necessity was there, that you should hunt him from place to place / and from country to country? Why should you ever have degraded your noble and generous nature by the vilest of all offices, that of a hunter of human blood? Oh, my father, can it be, that without profligacy and without malice, you were destined to disgrace the illustrious line of your

---

[a] Malice premeditated or planned beforehand.
[b] Edward Young, *The Revenge*, Act v. ii.
[c] Eccles. 9: 10.

ancestors by a death that is only due to the vilest of malefactors? Oh, let us not always expend our cares upon the impassive and unconscious dead; but let us learn to feel also for those that live, that live through every line and fibre of their frames, whose sinews may be stretched with agony, whose souls may be torn with tormenting visions, who may count the minutes of nights bitter and sleepless, and suffer things that no words can adequately describe! What are we, that we should studiously engage ourselves in the infliction of misery, and derive a chosen delight from the perpetration of mortal agonies? /

Of myself I will not speak. I at least am innocent. You have not in all your resentment imputed blame to me. Yet I am to have my full share of suffering. I have devoted myself for my father. Could I act otherwise? Should I not have been unworthy the name of a daughter, if I had not resolved to do all in my power to alleviate his calamities? But I have had, and shall have an ample portion in the sufferings you are so earnest to inflict. My youth, my innocence will be no protection to me. And now I have left my father with a protestation that, if he dies, I will not, cannot survive. Worn out with sorrows and persecution, he has this morning come to the resolve, that he will put an end to his griefs, and surrender himself to the law. I have therefore just left him, that I first might try whether you are made of penetrable stuff, and whether the truth, poured from the soul of one who stands on the brink of perdition, will move you. I / and my father abide your answer. Our life or death is suspended on your will.

Travers was melted with the fervent expostulation of Catherine. Could it be otherwise? She stood before him in all the radiance of youth and beauty. Her gestures and her speech displayed the utmost refinement of sense and education. She came instinct with the holiest of causes, that of a father; pleading for his existence, to preserve him from a death, not less unmerited in her conception, than ignominious. Every syllable she uttered was pregnant with truth, with virtue and conviction. There is much also in an enlightened confidence. Catherine felt that she could not be repelled, and that she would succeed. She poured forth with impetuosity the stream of divine eloquence; and it was not in mortal to interrupt her.

Travers saw truth in her own 'shape how lovely'.[a] He saw; and every avenue of his / heart opened to receive it; and benevolence and philanthropy rushed in at once with a resistless tide. Travers had originally been good. Gaiety of heart had been his first characteristic; and that gaiety had spent itself in love, in perpetual acts of kindness, and charitable impulses in favour of every thing that lived. This goodness of his nature had been temporarily suspended. The unmerited misfortunes of his father, and his own disappointment in love, had spread a cloud over the sunshine of his soul, and darkened the atmosphere of

---

[a] *Paradise Lost*, IV. 848.

his thoughts. More recently the shock he had received from the unanticipated destruction of his chosen friend, had soured his temper, and filled him 'top-full of dire'[a] revenge. But the voice of an angel in the shape of my Catherine suddenly restored him. And then he wondered at himself, that he should ever have been transformed into a demon, and have degraded his generous nature / by meditations of injury, and the devoting his days and nights to the unworthy object of hunting a fellow-creature to destruction. From henceforth he became all that was most honourable in a man; and I could record an hundred instances, if that were to the purpose of my story, of his unheard-of beneficence, and his coming like an angel from heaven to scatter blessings around him. His life resembled that of the Roman emperor who counted every day as lost, that was not marked with some good deed, and did not rescue some human creature from misfortune.[b]

I prepared to meet Catherine, when she returned from her short absence, with solemn and mournful anticipations. What was the purpose that she had had in view, was a mystery to me. I yielded, for I could not avoid yielding, to her request for a brief suspension of my design. But I was without hope. After a grave deliberation on the position in which I / stood, I determined to surrender myself. I regarded therefore the scene of my mortal existence as closed. The forms were still to be passed through: my appearance before a magistrate, my examination, my being committed for a due season to prison, my trial. I could well have dispensed with these; and have proceeded at once to the last, degrading, agonising scene, with which a culprit, condemned by the law, terminates his mortal existence.

Meanwhile I was not a little surprised at the speed of the return of Catherine. The steps with which she hastened from the carriage, and ascended the staircase, were not those of a person laden with fatal tidings. She ran; she flew; she threw herself into my arms. She sobbed on my bosom. But her sobs, though they testified the perturbation of her mind, were not those of an overwhelming grief, but spoke of gratulation and joy.

My father, she said, as soon as she recovered / the faculty of articulate speech, you are free. Travers is our friend. I have seen him; and he dismisses all thought of annoying you. Oh, why have not human creatures a confidence in the force of truth and justice? Why do they not believe that there is a power in these, which, addressed to an ingenuous spirit, cannot fail to overcome every obstacle? You are free. No more of uneasiness; no more of frightful apprehension and terror. We shall enjoy each other's society, and communicate our thoughts and our feelings once more, without fear of interruption. One day of peace and security shall succeed to another, till at length, if such is the will of

---

[a] *Othello*, V. ii. 2.

[b] Proud that he never refused anyone an audience, the Emperor Titus suddenly realised one evening he had helped no-one since the previous night and said: 'My friends, I have wasted a day.' (Suetonius, *The Twelve Caesars*, Titus, Ch. 8.)

Heaven, in a venerable age, overshadowed, and cut off from many of the sweetest pleasures of life, unambitious, but resigned, I shall close your eyes, and commit you to the tomb.

At length she related to me all that had passed in the interview upon which she had so / heroically determined. What were my sensations? After all her sacrifices and self-devotion for so long a time, this went infinitely beyond them. I had given life to this glorious being in the course of nature; but she, by boldness of enterprise, and generous energy of execution, had returned the benefit ten thousand fold. We withdrew to obscurity, but to harmony and love, satisfied with each other; Catherine with the consciousness of having stood the hardest trial, and discharged every duty, and I in the daily sight and the intercourse of the most exemplary of daughters.

Meanwhile my story is done. Travers conditioned that I should pass again to the continent. The proclamation of a reward of five hundred pounds was still out against me; and it was in the power of every needy and unprincipled wretch to inforce it, to bring me before the tribunal of the law, and to defeat all that had been effected for me by the heroic / interposition of my daughter. I knew that Thornton purposed to pass over again into Holland, and finally to settle himself on the estate which had descended to him in that country. Catherine and myself presently took our departure, and repaired to his house at Tendring. He was delighted to receive us. He had conceived the deepest interest in me from the time he had attended me for one month in the recovery from my typhus, and by his assiduities had so materially contributed to the restoration of my health. Between him and Catherine there rose a softer passion. He admired in her the invincible filial affection with which she had followed me in all my misfortunes and disgrace; and he adored her for the boldness of undertaking, and the more than human eloquence, with which she had finally subdued and disarmed my seemingly inveterate persecutor. They married. Catherine was the illustrious personage that gave / radiance to the scene of our domestic life; for we all lived together. But Thornton and myself felt no uneasiness at her superiority. We were satisfied that every thing was in its due order, and willingly submitted ourselves to her benignant sway. For myself I felt that my career was ended, and that I had nothing to do but to wait for the angel whose stroke was finally to relieve me from sublunary cares. I had suffered a grievous calamity in my second marriage and its issue. I was in obscurity and in exile; but I was calm, and equally free from the perturbations of both hope and fear. /

CONCLUSION

It remains for me to finish my tale. Catherine, the exemplary Catherine, vainly imagined that in freeing me from the terrors of legal retribution she would restore me to tranquillity. It was no such thing. Conscience is too true a monitor, to suffer her dictates to be baffled. I had done that, I had contracted such a guilt, as all the waters of the ocean could never wash away. In the actual experiment I think I may say, that my being driven from country to country, kept in a state of eternal alarm, and not knowing a moment that I could call my own, was a relief to me. It gave me occupation, and called on me for incessant activity. / Even when I put on the most studied disguise, when I moulded every motion of my body, and every intonation of my voice, to a feigned and unnatural strain, this still gave me something to do, and kept my attention on the stretch. I had now one unvaried holiday for anguish and remorse.

It was a bitter aggravation of my lot, that I had passed so great a portion of my life in innocence. I was like what has been fabled of the ermine, whose fair and snow-white fur is all its joy, and who, if one spot or discolouration comes upon it, pines away and dies. But with me it was not a spot. My hue, which had been fair 'as monumental alabaster',[a] was changed at once into the colour of blackest night. I had not gradually subsided into wickedness. One moment overwhelmed, and blasted me for ever; one instant's guilt had sunk me to the lowest pit of hell. For me there was no retreat nor return on my steps. / I had not meditated the crime I committed; the same instant saw it conceived and executed. But there it stood complete and finished to everlasting ages. William lay before me a corpse, slain by my hand. Margaret was lifeless, the consequence of my act. Of what avail were tears or repentance? Nothing could restore them. Generation after generation of mankind can never in my opinion produce their like, two beings so innocent, so guileless, so irresistibly lovely.

It may be said, that the hand of fate had passed over them, that they were reduced to a condition which no longer admitted of tranquillity and happiness. What mattered that? Small blame fell to the share of any in producing this unfortunate condition. But what right had I to obtrude my unhallowed violence? I should have left them in the hands of that inscrutable Power, which often disposes of things in a manner very wide of our expectations, and / often

---

[a] *Othello*, V. ii. 5.

with lenient hand softens to us its apparently harsh decrees. They could scarcely have failed to be unfortunate. But the calamity that reaches us by no mortal hand, we are usually prepared to sustain with resignation. They might each of them have been useful, if not happy. They might each have been exemplary, – examples of edifying, unmurmuring resignation, examples of industrious benevolence, finding their own peace in the joy and contentment of others. But, if either, if Margaret herself, who might be considered as in some degree to blame, had died, yet most unfortunate would it have been for me, if I with rash hand had not implicated myself in the catastrophe.

By cutting them off as I did, I subjected them, to the extent of my power, to unmerited obloquy. I displayed in the most unequivocal manner my own sense of their guilt. And mankind, who are ever rash and wholesale in their judgments, would likely enough say, He / must have been satisfied. He would never have rushed to so tragical a conclusion without unquestionable grounds. I therefore by one and the same act suddenly cut the thread of their lives, and darkened, to all that knew or that ever heard of them, their spotless and well-earned reputation.

'The tongue', says the apostle, 'is a little member; but it defileth the whole body, setteth on fire the course of nature, and is itself set on fire of hell'.[a] And, if this may be said of the tongue, how much more of the hand? It is our single instrument of direct violence. It commits thefts, and every species of fraud. Every rash act in which we engage, is its especial province. It perpetrates indignities; it wounds; it maims. It commits murders, both upon the animal creation, for alleged necessity and for sport, and upon our fellow-men. It executes the bloody decrees of our criminal law. 'From whence come wars and fightings among us?'[b] / It mows down whole armies, and desolates mighty provinces. All the crimes and atrocities that blot the page of history are perpetrated by this single implement. Surely then it becomes us to set a watch upon its use, and deeply to reflect, before we put forth the magnitude of its power!

As I have said – As long as my mind was on the stretch, ever expecting the destroyer, apprehensive that every door that opened would prove the door of irretrievable fate, listening to every sound and believing it the harbinger of vengeance, my thoughts were beguiled. I had not leisure for the bitterest misery. But, now that my person is secure, and I no longer fear the ministers of human justice, my condition becomes infinitely worse. I have nothing to do, but to ruminate on what I have committed. I may fill my cup of remorse to the brim. I may temper it with a thousand deadly ingredients. And the more I revolve in my secret / soul the deed I have perpetrated, the blacker does it shew itself.

---

[a] James 3: 5–6 (adapted).
[b] James 4: 1 (adapted).

I am burnt up with a continual fever. Sleep has become a stranger to my lids. I loathe every species of refection.[a] If I eat of animal food, I image the flesh of him I have murdered. If I drink, my cup appears mingled with blood. I think of myself as the most atrocious of offenders. I say to myself a thousand times, Never was guilt comparable to mine! – This cannot last long.

I am conscious that I am the worthy object of universal hate. Whoever looks upon me, and knows me for what I am, must turn from me with inexpressible loathing. Like the infatuated victims of superstition, when they see a raven or other bird of ill omen, so do those who meet me, prognosticate a thousand evils impending over them from the encounter. Those only who know me not, can look on me with serenity and indifference. Happy was I / when I could slink along unheeded, and those who saw me felt no occasion to lament over the misfortune that dogged their steps. Happy am I in unviolable solitude No; not happy, inexpressibly miserable; but, when a human creature starts up in my path, then I feel my curse, vast, all-embracing, crumbling and dissolving all the muscles of my frame.

Why then do I pen this history? Who can sympathise with me? Who can endure to peruse the tale? Yes, though I am odious, horrible even to the imagining, and past all redemption, yet the narrative has its atoning features. By some inscrutable ordination, though I am thus worthy of execration, the progress of my destiny has allied me to all that is excellent and illustrious in woman, to Emilia, to Margaret, to Catherine, each perfectly distinct in her qualities, yet jointly and successively exhibiting whatever is most precious, and admirable, and life-giving in human / nature. Let then the reader forget, and abjure all sympathy with me; but let him value my tale for their sakes. No other story ever presented such a constellation of virtues.

The reader may also collect one invaluable moral from my history. My offence, though clothed with every possible aggravation, was but the offence of an instant. In all that went before, and all that followed, I was guiltless. What a momentous deposit therefore, and committed to how frail a custody, is human life! There is scarcely an instant that passes over our heads, that may not have its freight of infamy. How ought we to watch over our thoughts, that we may not so much as imagine any enormity! How exactly regulated and nicely balanced ought to be our meditations, that no provocation may take from us the mastery of ourselves, and hurry us headlong ten thousand fathoms beyond the level of a sound discretion! 'Wherewith shall a man cleanse / his way'[b] in the complicated encounters of our mortal state? By binding constancy and truth 'as a sign upon our hands', and wearing them 'as frontlets between our eyes'.[c]

---

[a] Refreshment with food and drink.
[b] Psalm 119: 9 (adapted).
[c] Deut. 6: 8 (adapted).

I am now arrived at the last page of my scroll. I began it in the Netherlands. I continued it in the solitary and ruinous castle of the Rhine. It has constituted a sort of diversion to my anguish. Retrospect, though nearly allied to all I was then suffering, seemed to be the relief of an all-devouring monotony. I leave it behind me to be disposed of by my successors as they please. I do not forbid them to destroy it. If it never see the light, it will yet have served a temporary purpose to myself. Catherine has a child, a boy, beautiful, lovely, and of seraphic innocence. As long as she or her offspring see the light, these papers must never be divulged. I have changed the names indeed; but the story is too full of particulars, many of them well known, for it to / be possible that it should not be brought home. Yet, if Catherine and her husband so please, let this narrative be preserved! It may surely be kept in perfect security. And, such is the endless vicissitude of human things, a century, or even half a century may pass, and all things connected with my tale may be obliterated; and Deloraine, and the fatal name to which that appellation serves as a veil, may have perished from the memories of men; and this story may no more be a libel, than the records of Haroun Al Raschid,[a] or the fortunes of Ahasuerus, Vashti and Haman.[b] /

---

[a] Haroun Al Raschid (b. 765), Caliph of Baghdad 786–808 and author of the *Arabian Nights.*

[b] Ahasuerus, traditionally the name of the Wandering Jew, appears as a king of ancient Persia in the biblical books of Ezra and Esther, and is generally identified with the Emperor Xerxes (485–465 BC); Haman, influential in the court of Ahasuerus, was provoked by the Jew Mordecai's refusal to bow before him, and obtained permission to execute him and exterminate all the Jews in the kingdom, whereupon Queen Vashti pleaded with the king, secured a reversal of fortune for Mordecai, her former guardian, and Haman was executed upon his own gallows.

For Product Safety Concerns and Information please contact our EU
representative GPSR@taylorandfrancis.com
Taylor & Francis Verlag GmbH, Kaufingerstraße 24, 80331 München, Germany